Nothing Prepared Her for the Kiss That Came to Her Lips . . .

soft and warm, alive, devouring. It was as though she had been until that moment made of stone, elegant marble perhaps, beautifully sculpted, but cold, unfeeling. That kiss seemed to breathe life into her, and she felt drenched in sensation.

He pulled away from her, an as yet unuttered apology on his face. She sensed he wanted to be a gentleman and not take advantage of her, but she felt magnetized by his mouth. As he tried to speak, she stopped him, leaning against him, soaking in sensations with her lips.

Again he broke away. "I shouldn't, I—"

She could only stare at him, eyes wide, mouth open, lips moist from his, her body quivering from her awakening. Then they truly embraced, her face turned up to accept his, her arms around his neck, pulling his head down to hers, her body against his. Never had she kissed like this or known it was possible. Then his hands were in her hair, pulling her head back, her face up to his. "God," he said between swift, tender kisses to her face and throat. "I never thought this would happen to me."

A Lasting Splendor

ELIZABETH BRIGHT

Exclusive Distribution
by
PARADISE PRESS, INC.

Chapter One

Sylvia Hartley chose the most spirited horse in her step-father's stable. Turk, a huge black stallion with white fetlocks and a white star on his forehead, had been purchased for his beauty and speed to sire foals at Downhaven, the country estate of Lord Winford "Winnie" Bevins, the earl of Linfield. Few people rode Turk, for at times the animal could be half-wild. Turk could give a controlled, though spirited, ride if he felt like it. But, sometimes, he simply bolted into a hair-raising tear over the Hampshire countryside, defying any rider to stop him. Lord Winnie often said Turk had a mind of his own.

The stallion was certainly no animal for Sylvia Hartley to ride, and the stableboy, Tom Stone, knew it. If anything happened to Miss Sylvia—or Turk for that matter—his head would roll. He looked around for help from the stablemaster, anyone with more authority. There was no one. All were gone on this Saturday afternoon in September, 1910.

Sylvia also knew she should not ride Turk. But she was feeling out of sorts—depressed, restless, more than a little angry that life had so suddenly turned sour for her. She wanted to do something bold, demanding, even reckless.

"Are you going to saddle Turk or not?" There was more than a hint of imperiousness in her voice.

Tom Stone wavered. He knew he should not saddle Turk for Miss Sylvia, but he also knew his place at Downhaven. Who was he to stand up to his lordship's kin?

"Do as I ask, Tom." Then she realized how dictatorial that sounded and added, reassuringly, "I'll be responsible if anything happens."

"But, Miss Sylvia, I. . . ."

Now she smiled at him, quite brilliantly. "Don't be afraid, Tom. I'm perfectly capable of riding Turk."

It was the smile that did it. Sophisticated males of London had been known to stammer in the presence of Sylvia Hartley. A humble stableboy in the country could not help succumbing to her charm.

Although not yet twenty-one, Sylvia Hartley was already recognized as a P.B., or Professional Beauty. Photographers and portrait painters were flocking to her, and one or two poets, hoping to improve their reputations, were said to be composing sonnets to her beauty. She offered them no shortage of inspiration, for she was one of those women destined to be the cynosure of an era. Even from a distance, she attracted notice, for she was tall, and so slender that it seemed the new fashions with the slim silhouettes and straight skirts were designed expressly for her. Not that her body lacked womanly curves—her high bosom and lovely shoulders were the envy of many a woman less ripely endowed. And her carriage was regal, her posture statuesque.

A closer view confirmed that, like Tennyson's daughter of the gods, Sylvia was "divinely tall, and most divinely fair." Her luxuriant honey-colored hair was long, and she usually wore it braided and curled atop her head according to the current vogue, adding to both her height and queenlike bearing. Her face was almond-shaped and her features arresting: the nose short and delicate, the mouth generous with full, rose-colored lips, the flawless complexion like fresh cream.

But it was her eyes that were truly startling and made her the talk of London society. The poets were hard-pressed to describe them, the painters to depict them. The center portion of her large irises, surrounding the pupils, was a vivid green of a shade seldom found in nature. Perhaps the sea could assume this color, but only on a bright day following a storm. This incandescent hue gave way to a wide, sharply-defined rim of dark green, so nearly black it almost matched the pupils of her eyes. Shielded under naturally dark lashes and brows, Sylvia's eyes were completely compelling, altering constantly as her pupils reacted to light and her emotional state. Not everyone had the composure to look at those eyes and remember what he intended to say. Tom Stone, for one, did not.

Sylvia was not yet fully aware of her effect on males, so she assumed Tom was hesitating over whether or not to saddle Turk. She sought to persuade him. "I know I can ride him, Tom." Again, the dazzling smile. "Can't you trust me?"

To his credit, Tom Stone managed to say, "I trust you, Miss Sylvia, but not that blackguard of a beast." Then he shrugged, turned away uneasily and entered the stable. In a few moments, he dutifully brought out the horse.

Sylvia could see that Turk was eager for a run. How beautiful he was, strong and sleek, fairly bursting with animal energy. She went to him, stroking his forehead, patting his neck, talking softly to him. The animal responded to these ministrations by snorting a little and pawing the ground, as if assenting to her proposal of a ride. "So you want to run, do you?" She laughed. "Then see you behave, my beauty." No, she was not afraid of Turk.

With Tom's assistance, she mounted the horse sidesaddle, holding the reins firmly, talking to Turk, patting his withers, gently prodding him forward out of the stableyard. Tom sighed with relief. Turk hadn't bolted. He was on his best behavior—either that or Miss Sylvia was a better horsewoman than he'd figured.

Sylvia held the horse to a walk until she was well away from the house, then made Turk canter a bit before letting him stretch into a gallop. Instantly, she was thrilled by his power and speed. Never had she ridden so fast. For a moment, she had a twinge of fear, as the first hedgerow came up sharply toward them. Then Turk responded to the reins, slowed and practically flew through the air over the stone and briars. She squealed with delight. Yes, this magnificent animal was what she needed, a restorative for this awful day, this whole miserable week.

Sylvia had awakened this morning with a sense of desolation. For the first time since she had returned from St. Regis Academy several years ago, Meg was not there to awaken her, bringing her breakfast tray, opening the draperies, chattering at her. Nor would Meg ever be there again, for this was the day, the dreaded noon, when Meg Gwynne was to marry Brian Trout.

Officially, Meg was Sylvia's personal maid, but in reality she was much more—her dearest friend, her only intimate confidante. Sylvia's mother had sent her to St. Regis to make friends among girls of the upper classes and the nobility, but she had become close only to one, Kitty Shaw, and had lost contact with Kitty after leaving school, when her friendship with Meg had resumed and grown deeper than ever.

Only this week, after Meg told her she was pregnant by Brian Trout and would be his wife—really only since yesterday, when her mother, Lady Constance, had dismissed Meg, driving her away from Downhaven forever—did Sylvia realize all that Meg meant to her. She was her girlhood, often bringing her the only true happiness she knew. And more, Meg was her touchstone of reality, offering her a sense of her real self amid the bizarre machinations of her mother. By sheer will and a lot of good fortune, Lady Constance had risen from the humblest circumstances to be the Countess Linfield, wife of a leading peer with close ties to the Crown. She wanted no less—indeed, a great deal more—for the daughter she had had by Edgar Hartley, a mere army captain.

Sylvia revered the memory of her father, so handsome and dashing in his uniform. He had gone off to South Africa to fight in the Boer War, returning in 1901 to receive the Victoria Cross, Britain's highest decoration, from King Edward himself. Overnight, he was the toast of Britain, seemingly the one bright spot in an unpopular war which had blighted the reputation of British arms. He became an instant celebrity, and so did his beautiful blonde wife, Constance. She saw to that. But Edgar Hartley insisted on returning to South Africa, where he was killed. Sylvia had wept bitterly for her father. Indeed, she was still shedding tears when her mother, taking advantage of her celebrity status, shocked all England by becoming the second wife of the earl of Linfield.

Sylvia was twelve when she went to live at Downhaven and Lord Winnie's great mansion in London. It had all been so strange, even frightening, and Sylvia had at once been thrust into a maze of governesses and tutors and schools. Sylvia knew she would have been totally miserable had it not been for Meg, who had come to Downhaven at almost the same time, as an orphan. Her parents had succumbed to typhoid fever in Hornby, the Hampshire village nearby to Downhaven. Accepting the orphan to his household staff was an act of charity expected of the lord of the manor.

The two girls were instantly drawn to each other. They were the same age and both felt lost and badgered by grownups in unfamiliar surroundings, Sylvia to be a great lady, Meg to be a servant. But, somehow, they stole time each day to be together, talking, commiserating, often giggling over events. To increase her time with Meg, Sylvia begged and cried until Lady Constance, much against her better judgment, allowed Meg to be given a chance as her daughter's maid.

Over the years, the two young women developed a clever charade. In front of others, Meg was every inch the proper maid, curtsying, calling her Miss Sylvia, showing no undue familiarity. But when the two were alone, it was first names, giggles, cascades of chatter, and the total acceptance only close friends can offer. Meg filled Sylvia's lonely hours. Meg gave her courage.

Of far greater importance, and Sylvia knew it, Meg kept her feet on the ground. Spending generously of his lordship's purse, Lady Constance had set out to make Sylvia a P.B., the talk of London, a young woman certain to make a brilliant marriage. This meant the finest gowns from Paris, lavish parties, dazzling cotillions, immersion in the London season, where she met important people, famous artists and the most eligible bachelors. To be noticed and talked about, constantly courted and flattered, was heady stuff for Sylvia. She feared she might have begun to believe it all and become the vain, spoiled, extravagant person her mother wanted her to be, if it hadn't been for Meg. Each evening, while Meg put away her gown and readied her for bed, Sylvia would relate all that had happened, whom she'd seen and what had been said, mimicking her admirers. Together with Meg, she would laugh—often at herself. And with the laughter came perspective. She was not a great lady. She was just plain Sylvia Hartley, daughter of a soldier, and friend of Meg Gywnne. Meg was so good for her.

But Lady Constance had plans for her daughter, and considered Meg an unwholesome influence, an obstruction.

Thus, Meg's position remained precarious at best. Frequently threatened with dismissal, she had always survived somehow—until yesterday.

For nearly a month, Sylvia had kept the fact of Meg's pregnancy from her mother. But it was a hopeless stratagem. The village, the staff of Downhaven, buzzed with gossip that Meg's hasty marriage to Brian Trout, the village handyman, was forced. Lady Constance confronted both Sylvia and Meg, ordered Meg away from Downhaven immediately, and forbade Sylvia to so much as see her again.

Meg had run off in tears and did not hear Sylvia's spirited defense of her or the terrible row between mother and daughter. Sylvia had always known, although she hadn't fully understood until the last couple of years, exactly how her mother had risen from coal-miner's daughter to Countess Linfield. She was willing, perhaps even eager, to bestow her "favors" on any man whom she thought might be useful to her. It was her faithlessness which drove Edgar Hartley to volunteer for a second, suicidal tour of war duty. Her conquest of Lord Winnie had shocked all England. Even as his wife, she was unfaithful to him, although she was extremely discreet.

In her rage at Meg's dismissal, Sylvia threw all this up to her mother, accusing her of the "vilest hypocrisy" and of living a "monstrously unchaste" life, cuckolding both her father and Lord Winnie. How dare Lady Constance stand in judgment of Meg, particularly when for two years she had been encouraging her own daughter to take a lover?

Lady Constance, her platinum hair superbly coiffed, her perhaps too ample figure elegantly gowned, heard Sylvia out, unruffled. All her daughter said of her was true—and much more. Born Rosie Jones to a Welsh coal-miner, she had used iron will and enormous determination to rise to her present position. She had done—and would continue to do— whatever was necessary to achieve her ambitions for herself and her daughter.

She had begun with only two assets, her face and her body. By some quirk of nature, she had platinum hair among the mostly brunette Welsh. Perhaps this gave her the feeling of being special. By the time she was fourteen. she knew she was going to be beautiful. And she was, with fine, fair skin, deep blue eyes and a stunning, full-breasted figure.

By age sixteen, she had run off to London, using her "favors" to finance life there—a fashionable residence, her gowns, her pretensions to passing as a lady of breeding. She took the name Constance as sounding more refined than Rosie. She practiced by the hour to lose her Welsh accent and learn the round tones of upper-class London. She struggled to improve her manners and conduct. To be a true "lady" was a consuming ambition with her. At eighteen, she met Edgar Hartley, a dashing lieutenant in the Royal Horse Guards. At nineteen she was pregnant by him, then his wife. At first, she was bitter. She knew she could have done better than a junior officer. And she hated Sylvia at first, for damaging her figure, for miring her in domesticity. But when Sylvia's eyes took on their remarkable color, Constance Hartley began to think more highly of her daughter. Sylvia was going to be a great beauty. Surely, something could be made of that one day.

Hartley, disgusted by his shallow, scheming wife, went off to South Africa to escape her. Barely skirting scandal, she bedded her husband's superior officers and anyone of title who might be useful in helping her enter society. Often, she took Sylvia along as a foil. Who would suspect a woman accompanied by her daughter? She would sit the child in a parlor, then go off to the bedroom, saying she had to speak alone with the lord or officer she had staked out as her prey. Sylvia found these long evenings of waiting for her mother tedious, but it was some years before she realized the truth about her mother's activities.

Then, fortune smiled on Constance. Hartley's heroism provided her entry into society. King Edward and Queen Alexandra had even received her at the Palace. Then Hartley's death gave her even greater opportunities. She had been stalking Lord Winnie for some time. He was nearly thirty years older than she—quite unattractive to her, really—but he was an earl and a widower with grown sons. She tantalized him, driving him wild with desire until, at last, he consented to make her a countess. But the terms of the marriage contract were harsh. There would be no title for her daughter or any children she might have by him. She was to receive only a modest inheritance upon his demise. But while he lived, if no breath of scandal tainted her, she could be a countess. He wanted her to be a lavish hostess and elegantly costumed, and was prepared to provide a generous allowance for this purpose. And, yes, he would give her daughter every advantage. The former Rosie Jones felt she had come as far as she could realistically expect.

But not her daughter. Even as they stood angrily facing each other in Sylvia's bedroom, the mother recognized again how exquisite her daughter was. With those eyes, that skin, her remarkable figure, Sylvia could have dukes and princes, topple empires. She would have the wealth of Midas, removing the specter of relative impoverishment from her mother when she became a widow. Most mothers, ambitious for a beautiful daughter, would have encouraged virtue as the path to a successful marriage. Not so Lady Constance. Nothing in her own life had suggested to her that virginity was worth a whit to a woman. She knew well the lusts of men, and she had parlayed those lusts into an earldom. She envisioned her daughter doing nothing less. Indeed, for some time she had been displeased that Sylvia was still chaste. Why, she had had a dozen men by her age.

And now Sylvia was making all this fuss over a mere servant. Lady Constance heard out her daughter, then spoke firmly. "I will continue to do what is best for you, as I always have. One day, you will thank me."

"For what, mother, for what?" Sylvia spat the words.

"For making you the most admired woman in all England, if not the world. With your beauty and the connections I have afforded you through my own marriage, you will make a truly famous match. You will have wealth undreamed of by most women."

"But not by you!"

"Indeed, not by me. You will do as I say, conduct yourself as I wish. I have humored you long enough. Meg was an unsophisticated peasant, not a proper maid at all, an entirely unsuitable influence on you. I have wanted a chance to dismiss her. She provided it herself. She is dismissed, and there is nothing you can do about it, Sylvia."

Daughter stood there glaring at mother, her sea-green eyes stormy with rage. Once again, she felt the bitter frustration of having her mother run her life. Lady Constance selected her clothes, whom she saw, what she did. There was never any escape from her domination. Or was there? "You're right. I cannot keep you from sending Meg away. But you, mother, will not keep *me* away from *her*. I'll see her whenever I wish.

She has asked me to be her maid of honor tomorrow. Don't try to stop me."

Sylvia arrived at St. Mark's, the small country church in Hornby, shortly before eleven. With no family present—Brian Trout was a virtual orphan too—and with the staff at Downhaven afraid to incur Lady Constance's wrath by attending, Meg's was certain to be one of the simplest, hastiest nuptials ever. Nonetheless, Sylvia was determined to do all she could to make Meg's wedding as festive as possible.

She arrived bringing the wedding dress. It was one of her own white gowns, hastily and surreptitiously altered to fit Meg's shorter, more voluptuous figure. As she helped her friend into the gown, there were appropriate squeals at the pleasurable feel of silk and satin—which Meg had never before worn—and of delight that the garment fit reasonably well. Indeed, Meg was beautiful with her dark hair, fine skin and smoky, dark blue eyes. When Sylvia thought of beautiful eyes, it was not her own but Meg's that came to her mind.

"You shouldn't have done all this, Sylvie." Her use of this diminutive was but one of the qualities which so endeared Meg to Sylvia. In fashionable society, Sylvia was welcomed as a P.B., for her market-value alone, and she knew that if she ever lost her looks these so-called friends would lose all interest in her. Even her mother's apparent concern for her was an illusion, a selfish ambition to live vicariously through, and profit from, her beautiful daughter. But Meg—and only Meg—loved her for herself.

"I just wish I could do more—and I can." From her bag she extracted a rhinestone tiara. "We may not have a veil, but at least you'll look like a princess." As she fastened the diadem on Meg's head, the eyes of her former servant were as bright as the jewelry.

"Oh, Sylvie—it's so beautiful."

"And so are you, my darling."

The two friends embraced then, full of unspoken love for each other.

A few friends of the bride and groom came to the wedding. Most were from the village, long-time acquaintances of Meg. There were baskets of flowers pilfered from Downhaven and sent over by Sylvia. All in all, it made a lovely scene, Meg in her fine gown, Sylvia beside her in a simple dress of white Swiss, Brian and his best man nervous and uncomfortable in their best suits. The ceremony was simple, the words familiar. Sylvia did not attempt to listen.

Her first reaction to Meg's news that she was with child had been anger. Meg had betrayed her, forsaken their friendship for the village handyman. Worse, Meg was stupid, throwing away a lifelong position on Lord Linfield's staff for a few moments of pleasure. Oh, Brian Trout was handsome enough, with dark, curly hair, strong, muscular arms and heavy shoulders. But what future did he have? He was said to be clever at fixing motor cars. He had even worked on Lord Winnie's machines—that was his pretext for seeing Meg—but what future was there in motor cars? They were mere playthings of the rich, certain to prove a passing fad.

But Sylvia's disappointment and anger had not lasted long. There was nothing to do but hug Meg and wish her well.

"Then you forgive me, Sylvie?"

"Yes, Meg, yes. I only want your happiness. Are you happy?"

"Oh, yes, Sylvie, yes, a thousand yeses. I love him so!"

Sylvia could see the love in her friend's eyes. One question nagged at her, though. Since they had never had secrets, there was no reason for her not to ask. "Meg, why didn't you wait? You could have married Brian, kept your job. This way. . . ."

Meg looked down at her hands. "I know."

They were sitting on Sylvia's bed, facing each other, knees touching. Sylvia reached out and enveloped her friend's hands with her own. "Meg, I—"

"It just happened, Sylvie." She raised her eyes, blue meeting green. "I don't know how."

"Did he—did he force himself on you?"

"No, no, I wanted him to." With great intensity, she said, "I love him, Sylvie. I wanted him to."

"Wasn't it *awful,* Meg?"

The servant was shocked at the suggestion. "Oh, no, not at all. It was—*wonderful.*"

Now Sylvia was aghast. "What do you mean, wonderful?"

"Oh, Sylvie, he was so gentle, so tender and patient, yet so strong, so manly—and powerful, very powerful."

"You *liked* it?"

"Oh, yes, yes. . . . Something happened . . . inside me. I can't explain it—an eruption, sort of. I felt like I was floating.

I didn't want it to stop. Oh, Sylvie, I didn't know anything like it was possible. I couldn't wait till the next time."

"You did it *again!*"

"Oh, yes, and it got even better. I love him so, Sylvie."

Sylvia Hartley was a virgin, but she was not ignorant of what transpired between men and women in bed. Her mother had seen to that, instructing her in what to expect, how to act, beguile, please. The countess had said it would be exciting, pleasurable, but she made it sound only nasty. It had been an intolerable discussion to Sylvia, so embarrassing she could not even bring herself to tell Meg. Nothing about it sounded enjoyable, or even interesting. Indeed, that single discussion, so forthright between mother and daughter in those days, was a major reason Sylvia resisted her mother's blatant encouragement to take a lover from among the eligible swains who surrounded her. Sylvia could not see herself doing such disgusting things, being naked, letting a man touch her, put things into her. She would not do it, no matter how often her mother urged her. She had too much natural reserve and pride, too strong a sense of herself ever to do it. Oh, if she were married and in love, then, of course, that would be different. But to cold-bloodedly use her body as her mother did was unthinkable. Now, hearing this testimonial from her dearest friend, Sylvia was deeply affected. Surprise came first. "You—you didn't pretend—fake anything? You really *felt* something? It wasn't awful?"

"Oh, no, Sylvie. It was thrilling—to have him see me, think me beautiful, want me, touch me—to feel everything. It was wonderful, Sylvie—so beautiful."

"Didn't it hurt? Wasn't there pain?"

"I hardly noticed. He made me feel—oh, like a woman, a full, complete woman." Sylvia saw the dreamy look in her friend's eyes; then, suddenly, Meg turned serious. "I'm not sorry I did it with Brian, Sylvie. Not one minute am I sorry."

As she stood beside her friend at the altar of the humble church, remembering these words, Sylvia once again felt heat suffuse her body. So close was their friendship, it seemed to her she could almost feel what Meg had. She tried to imagine herself with Brian Trout. She could not. Still, this strange heat lingered within her.

When the wedding was over, Sylvia returned to Down-haven. She felt devastatingly alone. She had a sense of great

11

loss, as though part of herself had been torn away, and she was suddenly afraid, for herself and her future. There would be no one to talk to, no one to laugh at her, tell her she was silly, remind her of who she really was. It was as if all her life—the life that mattered, anyway—she had been part Meg, part Sylvia. Now Meg was gone—forever. And she didn't know the Sylvia part of herself, didn't trust her. Standing in her bedroom, she looked at the girl in the mirror—honey hair, strange green eyes, beautiful, but strangely haughty, aloof. She didn't know that girl, didn't like her. The image in the glass bore a strong resemblance to Lady Constance Bevins, née Rosie Jones.

Although it was a cool day, a hint of rain in the air, Sylvia felt strangely hot and irritable. An unaccustomed impatience came over her, and she felt the walls of the house closing in on her. That's when she decided to get out, go for a ride. Demanding Turk had been an impulse, a symptom of her reckless mood.

Turk's good behavior continued a long time, so long that Sylvia, deep in her reverie, lost track of time or where she was riding. About the time she realized that she was lost, Turk, frightened by a rabbit or fox or quail, bolted, tearing off, through pastures and light woods, at a speed which should have been terrifying to her. Strangely, it wasn't. She had not the strength to control the horse, but she could ride him effortlessly. Indeed, she felt exhilarated, thrilled to a pitch she had never before attained. She even laughed and called out, "Go, Turk, go." She knew he would eventually slow down, worn out by his own exertions. This beautiful animal would not harm her.

It was not that the hedgerow was so high, but that it was untidy. Stones had fallen from the wall, rolled down a slight incline. Turk had the misfortune to land on one with his right foreleg. The cracking sound of his breaking leg, her pitching forward through space, landing hard, pain in her right ankle—all came in quick succession before she blacked out.

Chapter Two

Regaining consciousness, Sylvia's first sensation was of dizziness, then of pain in her leg, finally of something brushing her forehead, her cheek. She tried to open her eyes but everything was blurry, so she closed them again, waiting for the spinning to stop.

When she opened her eyes a second time, she saw the face of a man, fairly young, with dark, wavy hair, large, compassionate brown eyes, sharp nose, thin face, angular jaw. His mouth was slightly open. Words came out. "Good heavens, I've never seen such eyes."

He was bent to one knee, cradling her in his left arm, holding her against his leg and chest and gently brushing her cheek with his fingertips. Then his face came toward her, so close she had to close her eyes and, suddenly, his lips were against hers, soft, tender, sweet, so very sweet . . . and unexpectedly she felt her own lips moving hungrily against his.

It was a most uncharacteristic act for Arthur Wicklow. In his whole life, he had never been so bold with a woman. But, then, he had never before seen a woman as beautiful as this one, and here she was, helpless in his arms—the whole situation was fantastic. She was like a creature from another realm, who might vanish into thin air at any moment. Indeed, Arthur had often dreamed of such a woman, but had scarcely expected ever to meet her in reality. In his dreams, he was always the ardent lover of the unknown beauty, and now, impulsively, he leaned to kiss this apparition as he had so often done before in fantasy. Later, he was to wonder at this most impetuous action.

Arthur was the only child of elderly parents, Benjamin Wicklow, a country squire in the southwestern county of Dorsetshire, and his wife, Eleanor. His mother was nearly fifty when he was born, his father a few years older. As a child, Arthur was shy, withdrawn and rather bookish. These characteristics were reinforced by a painful adolescence as an ugly duckling. He was so tall and skinny as to appear gaunt, all legs and sharp bones, and was too ungainly to be good at sports or physical games. And his most distinguishing features were embarrassing. At Eton and then at Cambridge, his schoolmates called him "Beak" because of his nose, or "Adam" in reference to the projection his larynx made in his throat. These nicknames, other jibes and various practical jokes occasioned considerable suffering for Arthur, and gave him such a negative impression of his looks that he failed to realize that, by his mid-twenties, he was emerging into a rather appealing-looking, though certainly not handsome, young man. The prominent nose and Adam's apple were still there but, balanced by his now more mature general appearance, they contributed, along with an unruly shock of wavy, dark hair and the earnest, slightly melancholy cast of his warm brown eyes, to a disarmingly boyish look that would make him increasingly attractive to women. But Arthur, oblivious of his engaging appearance and unassuming charm, became increasingly absorbed in the world of ideas and the major social movements of the times.

Beginning with his lonely childhood in the country and increasingly through his university days, he had found solace in books. He had a natural inclination toward the humanities, and his professors considered him an excellent, even brilliant student. But the seeds of rebellion were in him. A misfit and social outcast at upper-class schools, it was perhaps inevitable that his political views moved to the left. For a brief time he dabbled with Marxism, but after attending a lecture by Sidney and Beatrice Webb, he threw in his lot with the Fabian socialists, who were determined to bring socialism to Britain by peaceful, democratic gradualism.

After Cambridge, Arthur joined the new Labour party, quickly gaining respect for the sincerity of his social conscience, his knack for articulating the aspirations of working people and the mellifluous baritone voice that rose out of his gargantuan Adam's apple. He rose quickly in the party ranks, and in 1908 was elected to the House of Commons from a relatively safe Labour district in Liverpool. At twenty-nine, he was considered a "comer" in Parliament.

Age had alleviated his awkwardness, and his forays into politics and Parliament had reduced his shyness, but he still remained intense, serious and uncomfortable in social situations. He wore loneliness like sackcloth. It was to him an enemy to be fought without quarter, a disease to be eradicated. A man ought to be satisfied with his own company, particularly when he found little pleasure in the society of others. Thus, he had taken this cottage near Hornby, determined to write some speeches and other papers in preparation for the next session of Parliament—but also to battle loneliness. It was a draw at best, and he was often restless and unhappy.

He had arisen from his desk, extremely dissatisfied with the words he had written, and had paced the floor. He was peering out the window at the approaching storm when he saw a horse race through the woods, leap the hedgerow and fall. A girl was thrown. At once he ran to help her. If he had thought, he might have remembered his shyness with women, the giggling when chaps at school had brought in a girl to seduce him, the prostitute whose purchased favors had brought him little pleasure, the haughty society belles whose interested stares he misinterpreted as mocking. But as he gazed into Sylvia's extraordinary eyes, spellbound by their beauty and heartened by their benevolent expression, he had not thought at all; he had simply acted spontaneously and kissed her. And she had kissed him back! Or had she? Arthur's insecurity about his looks made him wonder if perhaps he had only imagined Sylvia's reciprocity. Probably, he decided, she had been too dazed by her fall to understand what was happening.

She felt him pull away abruptly, heard him speak. "I'm sorry. I came to rescue you, not take advantage of you." He was blushing, a pained expression on his face.

"Who are you?" she asked.

"I live over there. I saw you fall."

It was a nice voice, very deep, musical, reminding her of

the young Verdi baritone who had been the rage of London last season.

"Are you hurt?"

"I—I don't think so."

"Then we'd best hurry. It's about to pour heaps of rain on us. Can you move?"

"I don't know. I think so." But as she tried to move, pain stabbed at her right ankle and she cried out. "My leg! I think it's broken."

He reached to touch it, then looked up at the heavens. The clouds were the color of old pewter. Already, the first heavy drops of rain had begun to fall. "Let me get you to my place, then we'll have a look at your leg." In one motion, he rose to his feet, pulling her to a standing position. "Can you hop or something? It's just over there."

"I'll try." But she couldn't. The first hop shot pain through her whole body. By the second, it was excruciating, and she stopped. She was about to say she couldn't, when he bent and swept her into his arms and began to stride toward a thatched cottage.

At that instant, the heavens opened up and rain pelted down in a deluge. With a half-dozen strides they were wet, and by the time they traversed the hundred yards or so to shelter, both of them were drenched to the skin.

He kicked open the door and carried her into a small, cozy room warmed by a generous fire. He sat her on a couch beside it and immediately bent to her leg. "Let's have a look." But when he tried to pull off her boot, she cried out in pain. "I'm sorry. I'll have to cut it off."

"That's all right."

Slicing open the boot took only a moment, her stocking even less, and he was gently holding her bare ankle, moving it gingerly, asking her if each movement hurt. In a moment, he stood up. "I don't think it's broken—just wrenched." He smiled down at her, a nice, warm smile, like the room. "I think you'll live to ride another day—but not that horse, I'm afraid."

She watched him move across the room to a small desk cluttered with papers and books. He was so tall, and very thin. She caught a glimpse of a sharply-protruding Adam's apple. Such a strange-looking man, not at all handsome, yet there was something about him, a kind of presence and an appealing winsomeness. She saw him open a drawer. When he turned back to her, he had a pistol in his hand.

"What are you going to do?"

"Your horse. His leg is broken. I can't let him suffer out there."

"Turk?"

"If that's your horse's name."

"He was so beautiful, so fast."

"It can't be helped. I've got to finish him off."

"But it's pouring buckets."

He laughed. "I doubt if I can get any wetter than I am." He looked at her sharply then. "But you'd better get out of your wet things before you catch your death." She watched him stride to another room off to her left, returning in a moment with a towel and a woolen robe, maroon in color. His robe. "Here. Put this on." She saw him hesitate. He seemed unsure of himself, uncomfortable. "Do you think you can manage . . . by yourself . . . while I'm gone?"

"Yes, I think so."

Again, he hesitated. She saw color in his face. "I'll knock before I come back in—to see if you're decent." Then he was gone, out the door, into the rain.

It seemed to her he was gone a long time. She sat up on the couch and with minimal difficulty stripped off the saturated riding habit, her other boot and stocking. Her ankle seemed suddenly improved, perhaps because she now knew it was not broken. In a moment, she was standing on her good leg, leaning on the mantel of the fireplace, dressed only in her chemise. She hesitated. This was a man's cottage—his. But she was alone. He had given her a robe to wear, and her chemise was nearly as soaked as her outer clothing. Soon she found herself standing naked under the thatched roof of this stranger's cottage.

Quickly, she picked up the coarse towel to dry her skin. But she felt strange as she dried herself—a common, daily-repeated act. Never had her skin felt more alive, her breasts larger, her nipples more sensitive. Indeed, she felt a flush pervading her whole body. He had kissed her! She had opened her eyes, he had exclaimed over them, then impulsively bent to kiss her, unable to help himself. She smiled. Her first kiss, and so nice! She raised her fingers to her lips. Yes, so very nice. Then he had blushed and apologized. A gentle man, tender. But shy. He blushed easily. He wasn't bad-looking, either. Not classically handsome. But he was tall, which was important to her, and slender, very much a man. Such an Adam's apple. She had never noticed that in a man before.

She bent to pick up the robe he had given her. As her breasts became pendulous, she was more than ever conscious of her nakedness. Imagine! Being naked in a man's room. Wait till she told Meg. Then, with a pang, she realized Meg would not be there when she returned home.

Hurriedly, she donned the robe, cinching it tightly at her waist. The garment was miles too big for her, and she felt suddenly small in it, warm, cuddly, and her skin seemed highly sensitized to the fabric. It was almost as though she could feel every thread.

Holding to the mantel, she looked around. A small cottage, two windows and a door, comfortable, not too cluttered, although there was a mishmash of books and papers at the desk. At the side were a pump, basin, the appurtenances of a simple kitchen. Beyond was the door to the other room he had entered. The bedroom, she supposed. An odd, tingly feeling went through her body at the thought.

She thrust the idea aside, pulling a straight-back chair in front of the fire and spreading her clothes on it to dry. Then she heard his knock.

"Come in."

He entered, his suit hanging heavily on him, water running off it in streams.

"Did you?" she asked him.

"Yes. I'm sorry, I had to."

She realized she hadn't heard the shot. "He was—" Sylvia started to say "Winnie's," her familiar name for her stepfather. For reasons she could not fathom, she checked the impulse. "He was Lord Linfield's prize sire. I fear he will not be too happy with me."

"Is that where you're from? Way over there?"

"Yes."

"Well, you tell him it couldn't be helped. Accidents happen."

"I know."

He stood there, perplexed, ill at ease. Then he looked down at himself. "I'm drenched. Let me change, then I'll look after your ankle." Abruptly, he strode off to the other room.

She busied herself, turning and smoothing her clothes on the chair. They were already steaming from the heat of the fireplace. Several times, she cinched up the belt of his robe. It kept slipping. Again, she thought of Meg. Had it been this way for her? Had she been naked, wearing Brian's robe perhaps, intensely aware of being alone in his room? Had Meg had such an overpowering sense of masculinity? Goodness, what was she thinking? She hadn't—she couldn't—the man was a stranger and she—oh, God, she wasn't like her mother, was she? Always thinking about *that*. No, no, the fall had unsettled her, that was all. The fall, and the rain, and wearing that man's robe . . . and the kiss. Did all men kiss so nicely? Oh, she mustn't think such things! Someday, she'd marry and kiss her husband . . . and do those other things her mother and Meg had talked about. It would be all right then, with her husband. But she must stop thinking about it now, must stop remembering how soft and lovely his lips had felt on hers, how he'd looked at her with those huge, waiflike eyes. . . .

It seemed only moments until he emerged from the bedroom wearing dry trousers, a clean shirt and house slippers. Again, she sensed he was uneasy, yet trying to hide it.

"Now, let's have a look at that ankle of yours."

Dutifully, she sat on the couch, extending her right leg over the cushions. She was exceedingly conscious of the robe, trying to cover her leg to expose as little of her skin as possible. He bent to her, picking up her foot, gently moving it. It was necessary, of course, entirely proper, yet she had such a powerful feeling of intimacy.

"It is definitely not broken. How does it feel?"

"Better, actually."

"Do you think you need a cold compress?"

She looked at him. The touch of his hand on her ankle, foot, calf, cool and smooth, sent sensations coursing through her. "I don't know. I don't think so."

"Maybe if I just bound it?"

He left her then, going to the kitchen area, opening drawers, returning with a piece of cheesecloth. He bent over her, picking up her foot, carefully winding the fabric around her ankle. She watched him, seeing the color rise in his face again. He was embarrassed. "Is that too tight?"

"No. It feels good."

In a moment, he looked at her. "We haven't met, have we? My name is Arthur Wicklow." He seemed hesitant. "I'm a stranger here."

"Where is here? I don't know where I am."

"You're on the far side of Hornby from Lord Linfield's estate. You must have circled the village." Again, hesitation. "I'm from Dorset. I rented this place for the summer—to do some work."

"What sort of work?"

Shyness stabbed at him. He didn't like talking about himself. "Nothing important. I wanted time for myself. I have some writing to do."

"You're a writer?"

He hesitated, seemed flustered. "No . . . oh, sort of. I guess you could say so. Yes, I am writing." Bending to her leg, he finished the winding. "Does that feel better?"

"Yes, thank you."

He paused. "And who are you? Whom do I have as my guest?"

Now it was her turn to hesitate. She had time to think, yet later she would have no awareness of any conscious thought. She never calculated the words which came out of her mouth. "My name is . . . Meg Gwynne. I'm on Lord Linfield's staff." Later, when she tried to understand why she'd said that, she would realize that being there, alone with him in a strange cottage, overwhelmed by the intimacy of the moment, she didn't want to be Sylvia Hartley. She wanted to be someone else—Meg.

He did not believe her. He turned to look at her riding habit drying on the chair. "You weren't dressed as a servant."

She laughed, but it was not as easy as it sounded. "Oh, that. I'm maid to Sylvia Hartley, his lordship's stepdaughter. She gives me her castoffs. We were practically raised together."

His eyebrows went up. "I see. And that explains your accent?"

"My accent?" she faltered. Then she realized—of course, her voice was more refined than Meg's, or any other servant's. "Oh, yes, I've worked on that. Miss Sylvia speaks so ladylike." It was only half a lie, she told herself; Lady Constance had certainly worked to acquire her own upper-class diction, and had subjected her daughter to years of elocution lessons.

He was still skeptical. "And does Miss Sylvia arrange for you to ride his lordship's prize sire?"

She bit her lip. "I wasn't supposed to. I said he will be angry with me."

He relented from his quiz. "If you would like me to explain to him about your accident—"

"No, it will be all right," she said hastily.

There was an awkward pause, until he spoke again.

"Is your ankle better, Meg?"

"Yes. I don't think it's as bad as I originally feared."

"Good." Another awkward pause. Clearly, he was not a man of social graces. "Are you hurt somewhere else? You had a nasty fall."

"I—I don't think so."

"Your head perhaps? Something knocked you out."

She raised her hand to her head, discovering her hair was sopping. She had forgotten to dry it. Then she winced as she touched a place above her left ear. "It seems to be sore there."

"Let me see."

Moments were consumed while she pulled the combs out of her hair and unwound it until it fell halfway down her back. Then he was bending over her, separating her hair, looking at her scalp.

"I see it now. A bit of a bump, I'm afraid. But your hair, the way you wore it, cushioned the impact. You might have had a nasty cut otherwise."

She was so aware of him. His proximity was nearly unbearable. "I guess I'm fortunate."

"Yes."

He stood away from her. She saw the slight flush to his face and wondered if she were blushing too. To fill the awkward-ness, she picked up the towel and began to press the water out of her hair. Suddenly, she knew it was a very feminine thing to do, and when she looked up at him, she saw how intent he was on her actions. "I must look a fright. If you have a brush. . . ."

Again, he went to the bedroom, returning with a man's

hairbrush. As she took it, their fingers touched. It might have been hot coals against her skin. "Thank you." She began to brush her hair, hoping to distract herself.

But her feeling of intimacy only increased. Never in her life had she brushed her hair before a man. She tilted her head to the side, tossed her hair forward, pulled up the ends and began to flail at them with the brush. But the movement only made her conscious of the movement of her breasts beneath the robe.

"Would you like me to help you?"

She brushed a moment longer, then looked up at him. There was only innocence and respect in his eyes. Not that awful lewd look her mother's men friends sometimes gave her. His hand, held out to take the brush, contained no threat. "Thank you. It is hard to reach the ends." She gave him the brush.

"Maybe if you stand here, in front of the fire, it will help to dry it."

She obeyed, rising on her good leg, balancing herself by holding onto the mantel. Then she felt the bite of the brush into her hair—long, steady strokes, hard in their repetition. Her head was pulled backward with each stroke. Imagine, letting a man brush her hair! She felt her whole body was blushing.

"This is a first for me. I've never brushed a woman's hair before." What a lovely voice he had, she thought again. So rich, so reassuring.

"And for me, I assure you."

The brushing continued, at the side, over her back. It felt heavenly. Yet the intimacy was almost intolerable. She sought to break it. "So, you're a writer, Mr. Wicklow?"

"Arthur, please—and no, really I can't say I'm a writer. I'm a member of Parliament, actually—from a district up in Liverpool."

She was impressed. "A member of the House of Commons?"

"Yes."

She turned her head to look at him. "But you're so young."

He smiled, partly in embarrassment, partly in pride. "I'm a most junior member, I assure you."

"What are you doing here, in Hornby?"

"This cottage was available. A friend let me use it. I

wanted to be alone." He stopped the movement of the brush and looked at her. "I really am writing, a speech or two. Lately, I'm working on a monograph to be presented to King George. It deals with the Parliamentary Act."

"I see." And she did. The Parliamentary Act was the immensely controversial measure designed to strip the House of Lords of its veto over acts of Commons.

He laughed, nervously. "If you do, you're ahead of me. A most confusing bit of business, really."

"But you are a man of importance. A monograph for the King."

His embarrassment grew. "Not really. Don't make more of it than it is."

To stop her words, he began to brush her hair more vigorously. Then he spoke. "Such hair you have. It is the color of—of, yes, honey." Again, he gave a nervous laugh. "Meg Gwynne, she of the honey hair." Then he stopped brushing, touched her hair, then her cheek. "And your skin is like cream. Honey and cream, that's you, Meg Gwynne. And your eyes. I've never seen such eyes!"

The passion of his words, added to the heat of the fire, the intimacy of his brushing her hair, disconcerted her. She was aware, for just a moment, of being suspended in time, standing near him, her mouth slightly open, expectant, her eyes fixed on his face. A thought entered her mind. It must have been like this for Meg, a feeling of unbearable intimacy, a craving for more, a sense of surrendering into the hands of another. Then his face was coming down toward her.

Chapter Three

Part of Sylvia's sheen of sophistication was her belief that she knew what happened between a man and a woman. She had heard her mother's dispassionate description, Meg's rapturous one.

But nothing prepared her for the kiss that came to her lips, tender and warm, yet passionate, alive, devouring. It was as though she had been until that moment made of elegant marble, beautifully sculpted, but cold, unfeeling. That kiss seemed to breathe life into her, and she felt drenched in sensation.

He pulled away from her, an unuttered apology on his face. She sensed he wanted to be a gentleman and not take advantage of her, but she felt magnetized by his mouth. As he tried to speak, she stopped him, leaning against him, pressing her full lips to his.

Again, he broke away. "I shouldn't, I—"

She could only stare at him, eyes wide, mouth open, lips moist from his, her body quivering from her awakening. Then they truly embraced, her face turned up to accept his, her arms around his neck, pulling his head down to hers, her body against his, their lips a conduit of ineffable sweetness. Never had she kissed like this or known it was possible: Her body seemed molten and she knew she was shaking. Then his hands were in her hair, pulling her head back, her face up to his. She didn't want it to stop, but it did. "God," he said, between swift, tender kisses to her face and throat. "I never thought this would happen to me."

"Nor I." She sighed.

"I shouldn't. I know I shouldn't . . . but—" He was at her neck, her cheek. "You are too beautiful. I . . . can't . . . resist." And he didn't, submerging her mouth in another long, deep kiss. "Your hair, your skin . . . honey and cream. And your eyes. Open them, so I can see them."

For a moment, they just gazed into each other's eyes. His were so huge, more like an Italian street urchin's than a proper young Englishman's—and a member of Parliament, no less! And the way he looked at her, his eyes cloudy with desire, but reverent too, as though he feared to offend her. Sylvia knew she was what the painters termed a "stunner," and she had seen a look of appreciation in men's eyes many times. But always before there had been something disgusting to her in that look, or something cold, distasteful, as if they were appraising her value in the marketplace, or sizing her up as another Lily Langtry. Arthur's look was different—as if she were not only Mrs. Langtry but the Virgin Mary as well. It wasn't a knowing, jaded look—no, he seemed confused. And his confusion confused her, made her feel all weak and melted inside.

"Oh, Meg, I—you . . . you're so. . . ."

Again, she silenced him with her mouth, unable to bear his words without some physical response. It seemed her lips were being devoured, and when his tongue entered, she felt an overpowering sensation. Her knees buckled and she clung to him to keep from falling, pushing hard against him, head bent back, accepting, wanting . . . oh, God, what was it she wanted? It was as though she were discovering her mouth for the first time, its uses, its hungers. In a moment, he tore his mouth from hers, burying his face in her neck and shoulder. She was aware of the robe falling away, his hands gripping her upper arms, then pressed against her back. Each place he touched came alive beneath his hands, as though discovering its true purpose. She trembled uncontrollably, but she was aware only of the maddening need of her mouth to be filled, as she twisted her head, searching frantically, finally clasping and raising his face to seek out and satisfy her need.

Then he was gone again, standing before her, looking at her. She knew the robe was open, nearly gone from her, and that she was looking at him, lips open, panting, wanting only to end this craving. Then he reached toward her. She felt him fumble with the tie of the robe, knew it was sliding to the floor. She didn't protest. Nothing mattered. It seemed to her she could almost feel his eyes on her, and there was wonder in them, and in his choked voice. "My God, Meg, I never thought I would. . . ." His hands finished the sentence, reaching out, touching her. Tingling sensations sparked through her skin. She had never felt anything like it before.

He came to her from below, touching her hips, her flat stomach, the sides of her waist, so slowly, as though each fraction of an inch were being savored. Again, she felt as if he were creating new life in every place he touched, awakening her, causing her to ache with longing. She knew where his hands were going but it seemed forever until he clasped her breasts from below, a hand on each, moving outward, tenderly, lovingly. She could feel herself shaking, but she couldn't control it. She could only watch his eyes, feel her skin come alive as his fingers narrowed, encircling, until at last it seemed her nipples leaped against his thumbs. He spoke huskily. "There can be no other like you."

He kneeled before her, leaning forward. It seemed to her a moment snatched from eternity until his lips closed over her bud-hard nipple, stretching it inward. The tip elongated under his gentle pressure, shooting waves of warmth and pleasure through her, and she knew a wondrous feeling of beauty and womanliness as she held his head against her bosom, running her fingers through the soft, tangled waves of his hair.

She heard him moan with pleasure and knew it was only an echo of her own moans as he passed his face from one breast to the other. She heard him say, "I never believed this—" and silenced him, plunging her other breast into his open mouth, intensifying the pleasure he brought her, holding his head, pulling him toward her, pushing deeper, filling him with her womanliness, wanting, giving, surrendering to longings she now knew had been pent up in her for years. It was as if she had been reborn—a personal, intimate renaissance. Secrets of sensation were being learned, mysteries of desire revealed, marvels of passion unfolded. She could only hold his head, trembling, feeling her flesh was being shaken from her bones. Then new revelations came to her, as his hands brought new life to her thighs, sculpted the curves of her buttocks, caressed the wet walls of her center, discovered a well of delight, which left her gasping and moaning. She knew what was to happen. Let it come—quickly.

As he had before in the rain, he picked her up, seemingly effortlessly, floating her through the cottage to the bedroom, spreading her atop a quilt. Precious seconds, eons to her, were lost, as he stripped off the clothes he had so recently donned. Then he was leaning over her, his hands again upon her, between her thighs, through and around her womanhood. She felt a terrible tension. She was going to burst from it.

"Please. . . ." The sighed word sounded strange from her mouth.

She saw him spread her legs ever so tenderly and felt the hot ache in her center as he climbed on the bed and lifted himself over her. She heard his words, "Meg, Meg, you're so beautiful. I've never . . ." Suddenly, she was afraid. There was no room for it. It was too big. She closed her eyes, not wanting to see, then changed her mind. She did want to see. She had to know all that was happening to her. He was on his knees between her legs, bent over her, his left arm straight to the bed for support. He was moving toward her. She both saw and felt his manhood, hard and hot, pressing against her, tentatively at first, then with gradually increasing pressure, probing, once, again, a third time. She moved her hips and an exquisite sensation flowed through her. Her softness yielded to his hardness and she was being stretched, enlarged, filled up, wholly filled, but slowly, ever more deeply. It was so new, so delicious, so overmastering, that she closed her eyes against the ecstasy of it and groaned.

"Did I hurt you?"

She opened her eyes again. His slender body was above her, and he was looking down at her from above extended arms. She raised her head and looked down. They were joined at the hips. He had made a passage inside her. She contained part of him within her, had somehow consumed him. And it felt so right, as if she were now complete for the first time in her life, as if all previous experience paled before this final consummation and fulfillment of her being.

"Did I hurt you?"

"Oh, no," she sighed. "It's . . . wonderful." Meg had said

that, too. But how inadequate the word seemed to describe the undescribable.

"You're so glorious, Meg."

Her eyes gazed into his, both glazed with passion.

"I'm the first, aren't I?"

"Yes, yes. I never knew. . . ."

He moved. At first, she thought he was coming out of her and she didn't want that. Impulsively, she tried to follow him with her hips. Then he came back and, because of her movement, it was harder and deeper than before. Tension and pleasure mounted in her, and she gasped her delight. Again he rose, met her rising hips and forced her down, and once more she felt a sharp rise of urgency. A third time. A fourth. She lost count, conscious only of this terrible straining inside her.

When he began his movement, she had believed she knew what was to happen to her. Meg had spoken of an inner eruption. Sylvia knew it had to be so. She was ready to burst with tension, and each time he delved into her, it mounted. Her whole body went rigid, but still she teetered on the edge of explosion. Her fingers gripped his arms as he slid his manhood into her again. She clasped at him, pulling herself upward, her head and shoulders off the bed, unable to withstand the dizzying rapture, crying out, "Oh . . . oh . . . oh . . . please . . ." She didn't know whether she wanted him to stop or go on. She couldn't stand either. Tears poured down her cheeks as quivering sensations spread deeper and deeper inside her.

Meg was wrong. It was not an eruption which came to Sylvia. It was a cataclysm of nature, all at once a volcano, an earthquake, a hurricane, a massive tidal wave flooding over her. Clutching his arms, half-risen from the bed, she shook violently, involuntarily, as her whole body seemed to fall apart. Her head fell back and she heard herself moaning, again and again, as the spasms racked her.

Finally, she fell back against the pillow, a heavenly feeling of peace and relaxation suffusing her. But, he was still driving into her. For a moment, she wanted him to stop, let her enjoy the tiny tingles, the afterglow she felt. And she was so tired. But he didn't stop. Faster and faster, ever more urgently, he thrust into her, and in a moment her strength renewed. It was different this time, faster, more precipitous. She did not teeter on the edge of an explosion which would not come. Her tension simply rose rapidly, then burst within her. Only this time, it was longer, harder, and again she heard herself cry out, her moans harmonizing with his as he emptied his passion inside of her and they rocked together in mutual ecstasy.

Sylvia did not feel him emerge from her, extricating himself from between her legs to lie on his back beside her. She knew only the afterglow of sensation, langorousness, a sense of marvel at herself. That she had done it and had known such euphoria was simply unbelievable to her. She had never dreamed such pleasure was possible.

She felt a compulsion to move toward him, not knowing this too, was part of lovemaking. But as she rolled to her side, felt the crook of his arm form a cradle for her head and slid her bent leg over him, reality intruded, jolting her from her trancelike state. She was aware of nakedness—his, then hers. She looked up at his face, now in profile, the closed eyelids, the beaked nose, the sensuous mouth. Why, he was a stranger! She hardly knew him. Yet. . . .

Quickly, then, she moved away from him, off the bed, and stood looking down at him. A stranger. She had made love to a man she hardly knew. How had it happened? Memories flooded her mind: riding Turk, being thrown, the storm, her nakedness, him brushing her hair, the heat of the fire. It had just happened. She had not wanted it or provoked it, had she?

She was again aware of her nudity and instinctively sought to cover herself. Still disoriented, she looked around for her clothes. They were in the other room, before the fire. His robe. She had been wearing that. It must be in the other room too. She took a step to go for it. She had to get dressed.

"Don't go."

His voice surprised her and she turned to look at him. He still lay on his back, uncovered, but his eyes were open now, fixed on her. Then she knew. She had wanted it to happen. Ever since Meg had told her of Brian, she had wanted it, wanted what Meg had felt, wanted—*Oh, God!* What kind of person was she?

"Please stay. It was so nice, just holding you."

A moment longer, she stared at him, realizing she must in some way deal with him, with this situation. "I've got to get home. The storm must be over." She was covered with shame and confusion, wanted to cry, but she knew she must collect herself, stay calm. She had to go home, think it over, sort out all that had happened.

"I'll take you—in my gig. But stay a moment. I want to talk to you."

She saw him looking at her, her breasts, her thighs. Admiration was still in his eyes, but she found no pleasure in it now. She only wanted to cover herself. "I—I've got to get dressed."

"No, please. You're so beautiful."

She hesitated, looking at him, aware of her nakedness, the chill in the room, the flowering of her nipples. It was all too frightening, and she turned and ran to the other room. Behind her, she heard, "Please. I have to tell you something."

She snatched her chemise from the chair. It was almost dry. Quickly, she began to step into it, aware of fluid trickling down her thigh. She should wash, but she couldn't. She had to get dressed, cover herself.

"Meg, listen to me." His voice was supplicating, vulnerable.

Almost frantic, she slid her arms into the cotton garment, pulled it around her, began tying the strings. She felt better at once, now that she was covered.

"Should I be sorry?" His voice was a mere whisper.

She turned to look at him. He stood in the doorway to the bedroom, still naked. Confused, she averted her eyes. "Get dressed, please—take me home."

"God, Meg, I couldn't bear it if. . . ."

He had called her Meg—she remembered her lie. Should she tell him who she really was? No. No! She didn't want to. This couldn't be Sylvia Hartley—not here, now. She shuddered. The things she had done, crying out with pleasure, thrashing her body about wildly. Sylvia Hartley would never do that.

"God, I shouldn't have. I knew it. I tried to stop but—"

"It's all right. Don't blame yourself. I—I guess . . . I wanted you to. It was . . . as much my fault as—"

"Does it have to be anyone's fault? It was so . . . beautiful. Didn't you enjoy it?"

Suddenly, she had a sense of him. She remembered his

shyness, how easily he blushed, his protests that he shouldn't, his gentleness, the wonder in his eyes. He seemed to need her so. How sensitive he was. How vulnerable he must be. She couldn't hurt him.

Her voice little above a whisper, she said, "I did. You know I did." She felt her neck and face go crimson.

"Are you sorry?"

She hesitated. "I don't know. I'll have to think about that." She picked up the skirt to her riding habit. "I really must go. I'll lose my job."

He turned back into the bedroom. A minute later, she saw him emerge and go outside to harness his gig. By that time, she was fully dressed. As she had donned each piece of the riding habit, it was with the knowledge that she was Sylvia Hartley, not Meg Gwynne. Meg was a child of nature, who could indulge her passions without it seeming wrong, somehow. But not Sylvia Hartley. . . .

Now, as she stood before the fire winding and pinning her hair atop her head her hands were trembling. What had she done? He was a stranger. She didn't know him at all. And yet. . . . What had possessed her? She had given herself—no, she had practically demanded it. In heaven's name, why? Because it had happened to Meg? That was no reason. Her mother would die if she knew. Or maybe she wouldn't—that was worse. Suppose she became pregnant like Meg? Despite the heat of the fire, she shuddered.

He entered. "The gig is ready."

She looked at him, her eyes wide, really seeing him for the first time. She had made love to a stranger. . . . Then she knew it was better this way. She couldn't have done it with someone she knew, someone she'd have to see again. She didn't know this man. She must never see him again.

He was still standing by the door, a pained expression on his face. "Meg, I—I can't bear to take you home . . . feeling this way."

She couldn't bear to wound him. He had done nothing to deserve it. "I—I said I enjoyed it." She bit at her lip. "I wanted you to, Arthur. I . . . I have . . . no regrets." How forlorn that sounded, but what could she say?

He didn't believe her. "But why are you . . . this way?"

She tried to smile. "I'm just worried about getting home. I've been gone a long time."

"Really? Is that all that's bothering you?"

She smiled again, succeeding better this time. Her lie was working. "Yes, that's all."

Suddenly, he was beaming. "Oh, Meg, if I had made you sorry, unhappy, I couldn't. . . ." Then he came to her, put his hands on her shoulders. "It was so wonderful, Meg. I never thought it would happen for me."

"Nor I." Her voice sounded very faint to her; suddenly, nothing seemed real.

He kissed her then, gently, tenderly. "Know what I hate, Meg?"

Yes, Meg. He thought her Meg. She had to keep him from ever knowing who she really was. She was a nonexistent person, who had made love to a total stranger. "What do you hate, Authur?"

"This wasted summer. I've been here all this time and didn't know you. Now that I've found you, I have to leave in a few days."

"Where are you going?"

"Back to London."

She felt a stab of fear. She would be going to London soon too, for the season. She must not meet him there.

He was smiling at her. "But we still have a few days. Can I see you tomorrow?"

She didn't know how to answer. "I don't know."

"Don't they give you Sunday afternoon off?"

She felt trapped. She couldn't think. "Oh, that, yes of course." Immediately, she realized her error.

"Then you can come!"

"I'll try, Arthur. But, sometimes, her ladyship has guests and. . . ."

"But you will try?"

She forced a smile. "Of course, I'll try."

He led her out to the gig and they drove home, mostly in silence. At Downhaven, she had the presence of mind to tell him to leave her off at the servants' entrance. The people in the kitchen were surprised to see her enter that way, carrying one cut riding boot in her hand.

Chapter Four

The Countess Linfield was exasperated with her daughter, running off, disappearing for hours. What on earth had possessed her? There was a whole houseful of last-minute guests, including perhaps the most eligible bachelor in all England, dying to meet her. But Sylvia was not to be found.

Lady Constance figured she had pulled off a considerable coup in getting Lord Charles Pendleton, the duke of Glouston, to come to dinner. Winnie had arranged it practically at the last minute, bringing him out from London in his motor car this very afternoon. Indeed, he had arrived minutes after Sylvia had ridden off on Turk.

Lord Charles wasn't much to look at, Constance knew. And there were rumors he wasn't quite right in the head. But he was a full-fledged duke, a distant cousin to the King. Indeed, he was an heir to the throne, albeit considerably down the line. A marriage between Sylvia and Lord Charles would be breathtaking. Imagine, her daughter a duchess. But where *was* Sylvia? She should be at her most captivating, chatting with Lord Charles at this very moment. It was all the fault of that Meg. Lady Constance had intended to tell Sylvia yesterday of her sudden plans for this evening and what she expected of her. But they'd quarreled over her dismissal of that awful girl, and she'd quite forgotten. Then Sylvia had gone off to the wedding in the morning and she hadn't seen her all day. The stable reported she had gone riding and not returned. All this time?

Lady Constance looked around at her guests. They were in the drawing room, having drinks. She had delayed dinner, hoping for Sylvia's return. No one seemed to notice the delay, but how many excuses could she make? She smiled, said something to Lady Palmerston, who was seated next to her, and pretended to listen. Actually, it was quite a distinguished guest list she had arranged on such short notice. Thank God for that new-fangled telephone, which made it possible to reach people quickly. Besides Lord Charles and the Palmerstons, the Smythe-Caldwells, and Sir Robert Sydney and his wife, she had on the spur of the moment invited Philip Waring. She had had a plan involving Waring for quite some time, and after yesterday's quarrel with Sylvia, she had decided to put it into effect immediately.

Graham, the butler, whispered in her ear. "Miss Sylvia has arrived, milady, and has gone to her room."

Lady Constance arose, excused herself, and rushed upstairs as fast as she could.

All Sylvia wanted was to be alone. She had in mind a luxurious bath, maybe a bite of dinner in her room, curling up in bed to think of him, herself, all that had happened, how she was changed, where all this was leading.

It was not to be. Her mother burst into her room, dressed to the nines in a new white gown of the latest fashion. She often wore white. At age forty, Lady Constance's figure had thickened a good deal. The new, slim fashions were a hardship for her, and she was trussed into a diabolical corset, which cinched in her waist and thrust up her bosom. The décolletage of the gown was shocking even to Sylvia, who was used to her mother's exposure of herself. But apparently Winnie didn't mind.

"Where on *earth* have you *been?*"

Sylvia sighed. "I'm sorry, mother. I was riding and I had an accident."

Lady Constance's impatience was at floodtide. There was not a shred of solicitude in her query. "What do you mean? What *sort* of accident?"

"I was riding Turk. He bolted and threw me."

"He *threw* you?"

"Yes. He was jumping a hedgerow. There were rocks on the other side. He landed on one and broke his foreleg. He had to be destroyed."

"Good heavens, Sylvia. Winnie will have a *fit.*"

"I know, mother, and I'm sorry. But it couldn't be helped."

"You shouldn't have been riding Turk. You know what he means to Winnie."

"I know, mother, but it was an accident."

Lady Constance made a waving motion with her hand, dismissing an annoyance. "All right, Sylvia. I'll speak to Winnie. But do hurry and dress. Our guests are downstairs waiting to see you."

"What guests?" She listened as her mother explained who was downstairs, detailing all the excuses she was forced to make because of her tardiness. She was to hurry and dress. The idea of seeing people tonight appalled Sylvia. "Mother, I can't possibly. Make some excuse for me."

"I'll do no such thing. I want you to dress as quickly as you can and come downstairs."

A long sigh escaped Sylvia. "Mother, I've been thrown by a horse. My ankle is wrenched and hurts a great deal. I have bruises and I don't know what-all."

"I'm sorry, but it can't be helped. The duke of Glouston is the most eligible bachelor in the whole empire and he's positively *panting* to meet you."

"Mother, I was out in the storm, drenched to my skin. I'm a mess. I couldn't possibly."

"Sylvia, I will *not* take no for an answer. Now hurry."

Sylvia was saving a last argument. "Mother, I can't get ready in less than hours. I have no maid. You dismissed Meg, remember?"

Lady Constance was taken aback, but not for long. "I'll send you Agnes. She'll do your hair." Agnes was her ladyship's maid.

Sylvia could resist no longer. "At least let me have a bath."

"All right, but hurry." Lady Constance was already at Sylvia's closet, looking at her gowns. She selected one. "Wear this. The duke will *adore* you in it." She tossed the dress on the bed. "Now I must go to our guests. I'll explain why you're late. And I'll send Agnes to help you." Within seconds, she was gone from the room.

Sylvia signed. Her mother always got her own way, and there was no point in protesting or trying to thwart her.

She began a familiar routine. She stripped off her riding

habit and donned a lightweight robe. Then she entered her bath and began to draw a steaming tub, pouring perfumed oil into it. A porcelain tub with hot and cold running water was a luxury in 1910. Lord Winnie had modernized Downhaven shortly after Sylvia and her mother came to live there—and it had cost a fortune.

While the tub filled, Sylvia went back to her bedroom and sat at her vanity, vigorously brushing her hair. At once she felt a great pang of longing. Meg always brushed her hair, standing behind her, the two of them chattering at each other's image in the mirror. Meg was gone, and the novelty of brushing her own hair made her aware of the loss. But after a moment, she smiled at her reflection. Wait till she told Meg that a man had brushed her hair . . . and all that had happened. Meg wouldn't believe it—nor did she, for that matter. Imagine! No, she wouldn't tell Mèg. She wouldn't tell anyone. It was all too strange, too private and personal. And dangerous. If anyone knew. . . . Her mother would kill her—Lord Winnie too. Making love with a stranger in a thatched cottage. Thank God she would never see him again—or want to. She couldn't face a man—afterwards. What had possessed her? She remembered her reckless mood as she rode off on Turk. She must never allow it to happen again.

Quickly, she wound her hair atop her head, holding it with pins, and returned to the bathroom, turning off the water, removing her robe and stepping into the tub. The water felt glorious, and she sighed with pleasure. But she enjoyed it only a few moments, for she knew Agnes would be there any minute, badgering her to hurry. She didn't want that, so she picked up the sponge and soap and began to wash herself. For the first time since her breasts had begun to form and other signs of her womanhood developed, she was conscious of her own body. She looked down at her breasts, protruding in front of her, just at the waterline, made buoyant now by the liquid. They seemed so large to her. Slowly, she did with her hands what he had done, cupping her breasts from below, sliding her hands out the cones, massaging her nipples, now soft from the heat of the water. Oh, how nice it had felt. And she had excited him. Yes, she had. He had wanted her. Despite herself, she shuddered—and it was not from cold. He wanted her to come tomorrow. Should she go? No! Absolutely not! There must be no more of this—ever. She could make one mistake. But two?

"Miss Sylvia, are you out of the tub? You must hurry."

It was Agnes. There would be no chatter with her—Agnes was a termagent. "Yes, I'm coming."

As quickly as possible, Sylvia finished her bath, unstoppered the drain and stood up. An image flicked through her mind: herself naked in the cottage, her body wet and glistening from rain. But she forced the thought away, stepped out of the tub and reached for a towel. Yet, even as she used it, she was again conscious of her body. Why did she feel this strange heat, as though she were flushed?

She put on her robe and returned to her vanity, where Agnes began to do her hair. Sylvia never could feel comfortable with Agnes. She was of indeterminate age, anywhere from thirty-five to fifty, unmarried, tight-lipped and humorless. Sylvia felt she lived in a state of constant disapproval of the world. But she was a marvelous hairdresser and performed a simple, yet elegant coiffure, braiding Sylvia's hair, then coiling it around and atop her head without a part. Then came a chemise, stockings and the torment of the corset. Sylvia felt she was already as slender as she could be—indeed, far slimmer than most women—but fashion demanded that the waist be as tiny as possible. The corset was a torture, making breathing difficult, even painful, but fashion was a tyrant.

The dictator was couturier Paul Poiret, the rage of Paris. His designs had wrought a revolution in women's fashion. Moreover, he had caused an apparently permanent change in how the female figure was perceived. What he did at the turn of the century was to return to the *Directoire* or Empire gown of Napoleon's day, but in a somewhat altered form. A century before, the empire gown had been the height of femininity, bound high under the bosom and falling in folds to the floor. Poiret's gowns were also tight under the bosom, accentuating it. But rather than falling loosely, his dress was fitted to the waist and hips. The skirt, which was often draped or box-pleated, narrowed to the shoetops, allowing women to take only small, mincing steps. The hobble skirt, it was called.

The effect was to give women a long, slim line—a radical

departure from the hoop skirts and bustles they had worn for almost a century. And it was ultra-feminine, placing a premium on height and slenderness. But the style was difficult to wear. Women cinched themselves into corsets within a breath of their lives, then hobbled off to be admired. Indeed, cartoonists of 1910 had great fun with the fashion. The only way to get around in the hobble skirt, according to the caricaturists, was on roller skates pulled by a large dog.

The previous winter, Sylvia had gone to Paris with her mother to meet Poiret. She was unimpressed with the little Frenchman. He dripped arrogance and disdain, and acted like an emperor—which he was, in women's fashion. He brooked no comment, protest or even question. Sylvia thought him insufferable. He thought her a marvel. She had the perfect figure for his clothes, and as soon as he saw her he knew that dressing her would enable him to capture the British market. She would be a showcase for his talents. He struck a bargain with Lady Constance. He would provide Sylvia with special gowns at cost, but she must agree to wear them, just as made, unaltered in any way, at the most important public functions. Delighted, Lady Constance agreed. And Poiret, armed with Sylvia's measurements and a dress form, began to create his boldest, most innovative fashions for her.

It was one of Poiret's special gowns which her mother had chosen for her to wear. Sylvia had thought it was being saved for the London season. The duke who was downstairs must truly be important for her mother to want her to wear this gown.

It was a shade of green which came close to matching her inner irises—chosen for her by Poiret. The fabric was a soft silk, richly draped so that it had a quasi-Grecian effect. The bodice, so deeply-cut it was virtually nonexistent, had narrow straps to her shoulders and filmy sleeves, which draped over her upper arms in Poiret's celebrated kimono style. Sylvia was used to her mother's insistence she wear extremely décolleté gowns, but this one hardly covered her at all.

Yet, such were the attitudes of the day, it was not the display of her bosom which made the gown so shocking, but the reform Poiret had wrought in the hobble skirt. To enable women to walk in the narrow skirts, he had executed a slit over one leg. The fabric of Sylvia's skirt was simply pulled up and fastened with a bow just below her left knee. This created an elegant drape effect, but also revealed the calf of her leg, adorned in a stocking of matching shade. In an era when no proper woman showed so much as an ankle in public, to show a calf was utterly scandalous. In fact, it was too daring, and the fashion lasted only one season.

In the drawing room, Sylvia went directly to her stepfather. "Lord Winnie, I am terribly sorry about Turk."

He smiled at her. "I'm just glad you weren't hurt, my dear. You weren't, were you?"

"No, I'm fine—just knocked about a bit. But he was such a beautiful animal, Winnie. I feel awful."

"Don't, my dear. We can always find a good horse." Again, he smiled at her. "But a girl as beautiful as you—why, that's irreplaceable. Isn't that right, gentlemen?"

Sylvia heard the words of agreement from the others, both the ladies and the men, but her mind remained on Lord Winnie a moment longer. It had taken her a long time to warm to him, the usurper of her beloved father's place. Winnie could be pompous, cold and arrogant, very conscious of the rights and privileges his rank afforded. And, certainly, he wasn't much to look at. Now nearly seventy, he had a large embonpoint and a florid face, with large jowls below iron-gray hair. Indeed, he had a rather dissipated look, and was plagued with painful attacks of gout. Yet she could have had a far worse stepfather. Mostly he left her alone to do as she wished, seldom interfering as her mother did. He was generous and kind with her, and in recent years had shown her increasing affection, as her beauty and grace became ever more apparent.

Sylvia knew most of the guests, but two required introductions. The first was Lord Charles, the duke of Glouston. She knew of him, of course, as the King's cousin, a powerful peer, incredibly rich, and thoroughly eligible. Indeed, the newspapers and gossips discussed the possibilities of Lord Charles' marriage as though he were the Prince of Wales. Any woman he went out with achieved instant notoriety.

As he rose to greet her, taking her hand while she curtsied, she knew why he remained unmarried well into his thirties. Without the title and wealth, few women would find him appealing. He was nearly a head shorter than she. Even without her heels and hairstyle, the top of his head would come only to her eye-level. His eyes were a pale, lusterless blue, and hidden behind thick glasses with wire frames, giving him a serious, owlish look. His mouth was straight and nearly lipless, and when he opened it to speak, his worst feature became evident.

"H-how d-do you d-d-do, M-Miss H-H-Hartley. I've h-heard s-so m-m-much a-about you."

Stammering was a familial trait. King George's second son, Albert, the duke of York was afflicted. Lord Charles did not always stammer so severely, and he was now painfully embarrassed. But he had not expected Lord Winford's stepdaughter to be so beautiful. When she curtsied and he looked down at her creamy breasts and saw the calf of her leg through the slit in her skirt, he was severely affected, and his speech disability worsened.

Sylvia patiently waited him out, hoping no reaction to his affliction showed on her face. When the last painful word was uttered, she said, "And I have heard much of you, your lordship. I am honored to meet you."

"Y-Your b-beauty is m-most c-c-celebr-brated, M-Miss H-Hartley. M-Meeting you, I-I can s-see wh-why."

The smile he gave her was extremely wan. The poor man was suffering, and she felt a wave of pity for him. "Thank you, your lordship."

Nonetheless, she was grateful to be led away by Winnie to speak to other guests and be introduced to the other person she didn't know. She did, however, know *of* him—every woman in London knew of Philip Waring. He was handsome in a rugged, virile way. He had wavy blond hair of a shade lighter than her own, more of a golden color, and a wide, carefully-trimmed mustache of the same hue. Beneath blond brows were deepset eyes of brilliant blue, a little darker than the sky. His other features harmonized perfectly with his face—a straight nose, a wide lower lip turned out full beneath the mustache, strong, cleft chin, which turned up in an inviting manner.

But it was not his handsomeness which so unsettled Sylvia. He wore the uniform of a captain in the Royal Horse Guards—the same uniform as her father. She stared at him and felt her eyes moisten, unaware of what he or she said in acknowledging the introduction.

Then she heard, "So your horse gave you a tumble, did he, Miss Hartley?"

His smile was brilliant, and she felt herself recovering. "Yes. He was a beautiful, fast horse. We were getting along fine until a rabbit or something frightened him. He bolted. Even then, I rode him. It was quite thrilling, actually. But in jumping a hedgerow, he hit a large rock which had fallen on the other side. He broke his leg, fell, and I was thrown." She gave him a dazzling smile. "I fear you will not want me in the Horse Guards."

His laugh was generous and throaty. "If never being thrown by a horse were a criterion, Miss Hartley, we would have no Horse Guards at all. We say a man is not properly qualified until he's been thrown at least fifty times."

"You exaggerate, I'm sure."

Again, he smiled. "Only a little. But it is not possible to exaggerate your beauty, Miss Hartley. And to know you are such a superb horsewoman makes you all the more . . . interesting."

So this was how he did it, bold, straight on, leaving no doubt of his interest. "I did not feel very superb lying on the ground, I assure you." She laughed.

"What did you do with the horse?"

It was the voice of Winnie, still standing at her side. "Turk? I fear he had to be shot."

"I understand that. But by whom?"

The question flustered her. She didn't want to say by whom. "I—I was near the village. A farmer shot him. He and his wife . . . took me in out of the storm. That's why I was so late."

"What was his name? I'll send someone around to thank him, recover the tack and dispose of the horse."

Desperation welled within her. She tried one more lie. "I—I don't remember—at least, just now I can't think."

"No matter. We'll tend to it tomorrow."

Relieved to be finished with the interrogation, Sylvia turned back to Waring, remembering what she had intended to ask. "I did not mean to stare at you earlier, but my father wore that uniform. Did you know him—Edgar Hartley?"

"To my regret I did not. But I know of him, of course. He is greatly honored throughout the regiment—an inspiration to us all."

She felt her throat choke. Greatly touched, she reached out and touched the back of his hand. "Thank you," she said. "You don't know what it means to me to hear that."

"I mean every word of it, Sylvia."

At dinner, Lord Charles sat on her right, Philip Waring on her left. Conversation with the duke was extremely difficult. She almost hated to ask him a question, so painful was his effort to reply. And she had trouble saying very much that did not require comment from him. Fortunately, Captain Waring came to her rescue, regaling the whole table with stories about the Guards. Then he recounted the latest escapade of Emmeline Pankhurst and the suffragettes. It seemed several "ladies"—he said the word sarcastically—had chained themselves to the door of St. Paul's Cathedral the previous Sunday. The vicar had summoned a saw and had the chains cut. Thereafter, all the worshipers had simply trooped over the protesting women and gone to service inside. Sylvia laughed along with the others. All but Winnie.

"I tell you, the Liberal party is the cause of all this trouble. Women marching around, carrying signs, demanding the vote. Why, they're even breaking windows and destroying property. What is the world coming to? I tell you, it is the fault of the Whigs. Asquith as prime minister is a disaster. Along with David Lloyd-George and that young whipper-snapper Winston Churchill. They'll be the death of the empire."

"But why do you blame the Liberals for this Pankhurst woman and her suffragettes? It's the Labour party that spawned them, after all."

These remarks came from down the table. Sylvia, distracted, didn't pay attention to who spoke.

Winnie's answer was already on his tongue. "The Whigs have passed all these so-called social-welfare laws, health laws, education laws, workmen's compensation laws and I don't know what-all. They want to tax the rich to pay for it. I tell you, it's the ruination of this country. It encourages sloth. Everybody will want a government dole and nobody will want to work."

"But the women and—"

"I'm coming to that. Because of these Liberal measures, everyone has their hand out. They want something for nothing. Discipline breaks down. Tradition gives way. It even infects women—at least it has this Pankhurst woman and her followers. Women have never voted. Nor should they. Pretty soon they'll want to work beside men, run for office, even sit in the House of Lords."

Waring laughed. "And if you're right, Lord Linfield, they'll even want to be in the army." He laughed. "Then the men can stay home, keep house and have the babies."

Laughter swept the table, but Winnie was not amused. "I tell you, all this must stop. The veto of the House of Lords is all that prevents anarchy. And if this bloody Parliamentary Act is passed, if the upper chamber loses its veto, then our country is ruined. We must stop it. Have you spoken to the King, Lord Charles?"

"Yes, h-he is s-s-sensitive to the s-situation."

"Good. I'll be speaking to him, too. We all will. But he is so young and inexperienced. And the Liberals are putting terrible pressure on him. If only King Edward hadn't died. That was a black day in May when he succumbed."

From down the table, Palmerston spoke. "But at least the Liberals are delaying action on the Parliamentary Act until after the King's coronation. That gives us a respite, a chance to defeat the thing."

"Yes, and I intend to use it."

The conversation went on for some time, but Sylvia tuned it out. She was not interested in politics. Besides, Waring was speaking to her, his voice low, intimate. "I cannot imagine how I failed to meet you in London. I promise to do my best to correct that error in the coming season."

She smiled and whispered back, "There is no need for such promises, captain. We have already met."

"True, but we are only beginning."

She looked at him, so handsome, such an intimate look in his eyes, full of confidence he had already made a conquest. Unsmiling, she whispered, "Some beginnings are best not made, captain."

"It is too late, Sylvia. We have already begun. I must see you again, and I will."

His gaze was direct and challenging. To avoid it, she turned away, trying to pick up the dinner conversation again.

Later on, she played the piano a little and sang a couple of songs in her small, clear voice. As soon as she reasonably could, she asked to be excused. Her fall from the horse gave her a perfect excuse for her tiredness, and, indeed, her ankle was hurting her.

As the men stood up to say goodnight, Waring said, "I was hoping you might show me your excellent horsemanship tomorrow, Miss Hartley. Perhaps Lord Charles will join us?"

Sylvia was about to protest when the duke spoke up, "I-I'm afraid I-I'm not m-much of a h-h-horseman. You two g-go on."

His stammering gave her time to think. "Thank you, captain, but after my experience today, I couldn't."

His smile was charming. "Nonsense, I won't hear of it. In the Guards we know it is important, once you have fallen, to get right back on. You must ride tomorrow."

This time Sylvia's protest was lost in the words of her mother. "You two can ride early, then we'll have a late breakfast. A splendid idea."

Sylvia knew protest was now useless.

In her room, Sylvia sensed a trap was closing in on her, but she didn't know what kind. The invitation to the duke, that poor, pathetic man, was understandable. Her mother was always conniving to marry her to a title. But why had she invited Captain Waring? He was an infamous rake and womanizer, constantly involved in scandal. He had not met her before simply because he did not bother to go to cotillions where young women such as herself met prospective beaux. It was well-known that he liked women who were older, experienced and preferably married. Why was he here, so insistent on seeing her again? Suddenly, she felt herself blushing. His intentions were obvious. He did not engage in flirtations. But why her?

She strode across the room to look at herself in the mirror. She had dressed so hurriedly, she had hardly had time to evaluate the effect of her new gown. What she now saw startled her. At once, she understood the effect her gown had on men, why the duke had stammered so, why Waring was being so bold in his attentions.

Sylvia often wore décolleté gowns, although none as extreme as this one. Always before, exposing the tops of her breasts and the deep valley between had merely been a touch of daring; the sexual implications of the display had never occurred to her virginal mind. But now, in the mirror, she saw the explanation for the strange feeling she had had all evening. She now knew—as Waring certainly knew also—the uses of her breasts. They were for much more than mere display. Her gaze lowered to her tiny waist, the flaring hips, the outline of her leg against the green silk. Yes, she now knew the uses of her body. Worse, much worse, she now knew men did too. Would she never be innocent again? No, there was no going back. . . .

When she had changed into a nightgown and was under the covers, she thought of Meg. Oh, how she missed her! If Meg were here, she would tell her all about the evening, about Waring's intimate looks, and insinuations and Meg would find it funny. They would laugh at him together, and it would all become easier. But Meg was not there. She had no one to help her cope with all that was happening to her. Aloud in the darkness, she said softly, "Meg, oh, Meg, should I go to the cottage tomorrow?" Then she answered, "No. Never." She must stop thinking about it.

Chapter Five

Sylvia was awakened early the next morning and forced to dress hurriedly for her ride with Waring.

He offered her no gentle canter. From the moment they left the stable, he put his horse through its paces, repeatedly sailing over fences and hedgerows, maintaining a full gallop for a long time. Sylvia stayed with him, occasionally even pulling ahead. She felt invigorated, thrilled by the wild ride and her success as a horsewoman.

Finally, he reined his animal to a stop and turned to her, smiling, "I salute you, Sylvia. You have passed muster. We accept you into the Royal Horse Guards."

She was quite out of breath, but managed to laugh and say, "I am flattered, captain."

"Not flattery, but truth. You ride extremely well, Sylvia."

She was pleased by his praise, but so out of breath she could only say, "Thank you."

"Shall we walk a bit, give the horses a rest?"

She saw him dismount and come around to assist her down, taking her hand, then her waist. Her feet had hardly touched the ground when he was kissing her, his mouth hard on hers, his mustache tickling under her nose. Her reaction was mostly surprise. Finally, she could pull away. "Please, I'm not—"
She never got to say what she was not, as his mouth came on hers again, more open now, softer, the movements more penetrating. Nor did she have a chance to pull away, for he

held her hard against him, hips, even her thighs. It was a shocking, urgent embrace, stunning her with surprise. For a moment, she surrendered to it, but only a moment, then she began to struggle with him. It took some time to free herself, see his laughing face. She raised her hand to strike him, but he stopped her. "Don't be a child, Sylvia. You know you loved it."

Eyes wide and stormy, chest expanding rapidly for air, she spat words at him. "What do you think I am? I'm not—"

"Oh, but you are." Laughter cascaded out his mouth. "A most beautiful woman who excites me very much." Again, more laughter, before he handed her the reins of her horse. "Come on, we'd best walk these beasts."

She had no choice but to follow him, but her anger and outrage did not evaporate. How different Arthur had been, how tentative, considerate. This Philip Waring seemed to claim her as his due—as if she had nothing to say about the matter. "Captain Waring, I am not—"

"Philip, please."

"I will not call you Philip. I do not want to know you. I thought you were an officer and a gentleman. Captain, you disgrace my father's uniform."

He merely laughed. "You are being silly and childish, Sylvia. I do not like that in my women."

She stopped and stared at him, offended and angry. "*Your* woman. I am *not*, sir, your woman. I am nobody's woman."

His answer was only laughter, as he turned away from her and strode forward with the horse. She stood there a moment, staring after him, falling behind. In a moment, she again resumed walking, but made no effort to catch up. She was fuming, her mind full of insults to hurl at him, but she could not single out any one of them.

Two days ago, she would have been equal to it, could have confidently crushed him with the righteous indignation of outraged virtue. But she was no longer virtuous; she had cast off her armor and felt totally exposed. Still, he had no right. . . . Sylvia felt completely at sea. Her upbringing had not been religious—though nominally a member of the Church of England, her mother viewed services as a social occasion, nothing more, and Sylvia herself had always viewed church-going as a mere formality—nevertheless, the word *sinful* now leaped into her mind and would not be dislodged.

It was not hell and damnation she feared, but the present moment . . . and her immediate future. What had happened with Arthur Wicklow, however bizarre or even sinful, had been precious to her—and right, somehow. Not that she believed in love at first sight, but there had been a sincerity on both sides—an innocence, even—that justified their lovemaking, at least for the moment. But now, faced with the overtures of Captain Waring, she felt herself in a false position. He had none of Arthur's tenderness, or reserve—he frightened her, rather, with his candor—and yet, she felt that because of yesterday, she was helpless before his challenge. Indeed, part of her felt excited by him, wanted to flirt back, wondered what he would be like . . . oh, God, no! She mustn't think such things. She must put him down, return to safety and sanity. Oh, if only Meg were there, to restore her to herself. . . .

In a few minutes, he stopped and waited for her to catch up. There was a broad smile on his face. To her it seemed lewd. Still seething, but in better control of herself, she asked, "Captain, why did you come here?"

His smile broadened and he shook his head. "That is an even sillier question. Haven't you ever looked in a mirror?"

She brushed his words aside as a meaningless compliment. "Do me the honor of answering my question. Why are you at Downhaven?"

"Your mother, Lady Constance, invited me."

"I know that. But why did you come?"

"To see you."

"Hardly, captain. You didn't know me. We'd never met."

"Regrettably, that is so."

Sylvia's anger grew. He was being insufferable, toying with her as if she were a victim—*his* victim. "Will you please at least try to be a gentleman and speak the truth for once. Why are you here?"

His smile faded a little. "You didn't let me finish. I may not have met you, but I had heard of you, of course. Your mother offered me the opportunity to meet you and I took it. And I am not one bit disappointed."

She sighed deeply, her chest rising and falling. "Captain Waring, I am not your sort of woman."

Again, the smile. "Please, let me decide that."

"Your reputation precedes you, captain. Your preference

for married women is well-known. You are said to have made more cuckolds than anyone in the history of the empire."

His laughter swept over her and he rendered an exaggerated bow. "Oh, that it were but half-true."

She went on. "I am not married, captain. And when I am, I assure you I will not be unfaithful to my husband—most especially not with you."

More laughter came from him. "My loss, I assure you."

She was severely tempted to mount her horse and ride away from him, but she persisted. "What do you want from me?"

"To make love to you."

She stared at him contemptuously, then moved to the side of her horse, preparing to mount. He stopped her, removing her foot from the stirrup. When she looked at him, he was serious.

"All right, Sylvia. It is admittedly a bizarre situation. I suppose the novelty of it appealed to me." He seemed suddenly ill at ease. She did nothing to relieve his discomfort. "I have known your mother for some time."

"I'll *bet* you've known her." Her tone was acid.

His laughter confirmed her suspicions. "Lady Constance came to me with a little problem. It seems she has a very beautiful daughter with honey hair, skin like cream, remarkable eyes and a stunning figure." He hesitated.

Sylvia could only purse her lips in an expression of disgust. "Go on."

He resumed his narrative. "It seems Lady Constance has great ambitions for her daughter. Great wealth should come to her, at least a dukedom, even a kingdom. A whole empire might be within reach." Again, he smiled. "And having met you, Sylvia, I do not believe your mother is overreaching. You have the capacity to be a truly remarkable woman."

She said nothing, only glared at him until he resumed.

"Lady Constance feels one thing stands in the way of her daughter's success, her . . ." He smiled, although it seemed forced and awkward. ". . . her, shall we say, inexperience with men."

Sylvia's eyes widened as she stared at him.

"Lady Constance feels her daughter is . . . 'unduly reserved.' She believes that once her daughter has had a suitable experience, she will come to enjoy it and thereafter be more willing, beguiling and thereby attractive to suitors."

"I never!" Sylvia was shocked. That a mother—even one like Lady Constance—would go to a man, one of her own lovers, no less, and scheme with him for the deflowering of her daughter . . . and that a well-bred man could agree to such a plan, even relish his part in it . . . such callousness and degradation were incredible to Sylvia.

He laughed, still self-consciously. "In short, Sylvia, she asked me to seduce you. I was merely amused at the idea at first. But knowing you, I find it a most appealing idea. What do you think?"

"I think you are a cad, sir."

"Undoubtedly, Sylvia." He smiled. "I've been one so long I no longer pay attention to it. In truth, I think your mother's summation of you is correct. You have the capacity to set all England on its collective ear. All you need is to learn the womanly arts. And I am the perfect one to teach you."

If Sylvia had ever been more shocked and angry, she couldn't remember it. "You are, are you?"

"You know my reputation. Your mother is wise in wanting your first time to be with a man who knows what he is doing, how to please a woman. Believe me, Sylvia, lovemaking, while a natural act, is often a learning experience—for women, especially. They must break down their fear and shyness to reach full enjoyment. This is best done with an experienced man. Many a woman has been ruined by a bungling lover."

"You . . . you are . . . *insufferable!"* She turned to mount her horse and again he stopped her, taking her arm.

"Sylvia, listen to me. I would have preferred an ordinary seduction. Your kiss a moment ago tells me it wouldn't be difficult. You are a very responsive woman. But your insistence upon the truth has brought all this out into the open. Perhaps it is better. You will have your eyes open. You will learn faster. Believe me, both of us will enjoy it, and you will be better for it."

Savagely, she twisted her arm away from him and mounted her horse. Looking down at him, she said, her words icy, "I know you are the guest of my mother and Lord Winnie, but I want you to leave Downhaven at once. I pray to God I never lay eyes on you again." She kicked the horse hard and galloped for home, leaving him standing there.

Sylvia was still fuming when she arrived. The others were on the veranda preparing to sit down to breakfast. Sylvia ignored her mother. Right now, she couldn't bear the sight of her. But she spoke to Winnie and even managed to smile at Lord Charles and the Palmerstons, who had also stayed the night. She excused herself to go change.

In her room, she tried to control herself, breathing deeply, forcing her mind to function rationally as she removed her riding clothes and took a quick bath. She scrubbed herself harder than usual—as if she could thus wash away this morning's ordeal. Waring's proposal was the most indecent in the history of indecent proposals. It was an outrage. Did he think her a prostitute? Was he trying to make one of her? And her mother. Sylvia had thought herself incapable of being surprised by anything her mother did, but this. . . . And the conceit of the man, saying how much he could teach her, how good he would be. Why, she should have. . . . Suddenly, she realized that she was most angry at herself. She had handled it all wrong. When she became shocked and angry, that's exactly what he'd expected. He saw it as a challenge. She should have laughed in his face, told him she was—

Self-knowledge came to her almost as a slap in the face. Arthur Wicklow in the cottage, waiting to see her again. Yes, *again*. She was already experienced. She had known a man and wanted more. Was she . . . could she be . . . the sort of woman her mother intended? In dismay, she looked at her nakedness in the water. Was she already the woman Philip Waring wanted to teach her to be?

In something approaching horror, she got out of the tub and quickly dried herself. Agnes was in her bedroom, waiting. "Lady Constance wants you to wear this."

Sylvia glanced at the gown. "All right. Help me into it."

The dress was a summer frock, made of white cotton dotted with green. It had long sleeves and a lacy collar that came high to the throat. The effect would have been demure, except that the garment clung like a second skin to her bosom, waist, hips and thighs. Agnes needed several minutes just to fasten the buttons down the back. Just above the knees was a flounce of white tulle, permitting her to walk with some appearance of normality. A wide picture hat, covered in white lace and tulle, completed the ensemble. It was hardly a morning gown, Sylvia knew. But, then, her mother's choice of attire was seldom conventional.

As she came downstairs to the veranda, Sylvia had hopes of laughing at Waring, showing him up. These were soon dashed. Waring was holding court over breakfast, regaling his host, hostess and other guests with story after story. As Sylvia took her place, she contrived to ignore her mother. When Waring began to lavish praise on her horsemanship, forcing her to speak, she could only glare at him. She saw laughter and mockery in his eyes.

The breakfast was insufferable because of Waring, her mother's ridiculous laughter at his jokes and her repeated efforts to call attention to her daughter. As soon as she could, Sylvia sought escape. "Lord Charles, I'm told you collect first editions?"

"I do, yes."

It was the first time she'd heard him say three words without stuttering. "Lord Winnie has a fine collection. Would you like to see it?" When he nodded that he would, Sylvia asked for and received permission to show him the library.

As she and the duke stood up, Waring spoke. "Miss Hartley, I regret I must leave soon. I have pressing business in London, and there is a train going back in less than an hour. I had best say my goodbyes now, since you are going off."

She turned to look at him. The same mocking laughter was in his eyes. She did not speak.

"I enjoyed meeting you, your singing last night, our ride this morning. I look forward to seeing you again—soon." He emphasized the last word. She merely nodded, she did not feel like being civil to him. "Lord Charles, I know I'll see you soon too."

"Yes, W-Waring. I-I'll look f-forward to it."

Sylvia went off with the duke, showing him the library. He became quite animated, admiring various books, explaining the different editions of Chaucer, Shakespeare and Pepys. Sylvia felt compassion for him. He really knew a great deal about books, but his difficulty in expressing himself was exceedingly painful for him, and for her too.

He turned to her, an open volume in his hands, an

expression of great sorrow on his face. "Forgive m-me, M-Miss H-H-Hartley. M-My sp-speech m-m-makes it d-difficult for m-me—"

She stopped him with her hand on his arm, waiting for him to look at her. In total sincerity she said, "Lord Charles, there is nothing to forgive. What is important is what a man says, not *how* he says it. I have heard many people speak utter nonsense with perfect diction. And you know, one of the greatest men England has ever known, Lord Harry Percy, had a speech impediment. Doesn't Shakespeare tell us that 'speaking thick, which Nature made his blemish, became the accents of the valiant'?" She was glad, now, that she had been required to memorize Lady Percy's monologue for a literature class at St. Regis; the quotation was perfect for the present situation.

He looked at her, greatly touched. The first genuine smile she had seen from him graced his face. "Thank you, Miss Hartley."

"You have great knowledge of books, Lord Charles. You must read a great deal."

"Y-Yes. I don't g-go out m-much, as you c-can im-im-imagine."

She smiled. "I like to read too—although my taste is more to Jane Austen, Thackeray and Dickens. I also like Barrie. Do you read him?"

"Yes."

She led him into a discussion of books and authors as they toured the library. When she found out he had an interest in horticulture and bred roses, she showed him the conservatory and the gardens. She did her best to be friendly without being coquettish, genuinely interested in him and his knowledge, and attentive and patient through his stammer, which improved as he relaxed. But, in truth, her mind was on the time. She had such a sense of Arthur Wicklow sitting in the cottage, waiting for her. No, she would not go. Again and again, she forced her mind back to Lord Charles. She genuinely felt sorry for this sensitive, lonely man.

Games of croquet filled much of the afternoon. Waiting her turn to play, having others to talk to Lord Charles, gave her more time to think about Arthur, the cottage. She did want to go. She knew she did. But she was comforted by the fact that it would soon be too late. This decision, like so many others, was being made for her. But one thought kept nagging at her. After yesterday, was she already the woman of experience her mother wanted her to be? Would she now go from bed to bed like Lady Constance? The thought appalled her.

"Your turn, Sylvia. You should be more attentive."

It was her mother's voice. "I'm sorry." She stroked her ball through the center wicket, but her next shot was off-line.

Winnie was next, playing with his usual enthusiasm. Sylvia moved to the side to await her turn. From across the way, she saw Lord Charles looking at her, intently, soulfully. She had caught him doing it several times, but now she had a sense of what he was seeing: a pretty girl on a green lawn, picture hat, form-fitting dress, bending over to strike a ball with a mallet. No, his smile told her he saw something more. He saw her for what she was, a woman who had gone to bed with a man, a woman of breasts and thighs, a woman of experience. Would all men see her that way now?

Captain Waring certainly had. This morning, she had been unwilling to acknowledge to herself the real reason that she had found his advances so upsetting. It was the feeling that he knew, after all, that she was no longer a virgin. Otherwise, he would not have dared to speak to her like that, to look at her so lewdly, so knowingly. Yes, his eyes had told her that he knew, just as Charles' did now. And Arthur? No, his look had been different. But what did he think of her now? Suddenly, she had to know.

Lord Charles and the Palmerstons did not leave until after tea. They were no more than in the car to be driven to the station when Sylvia wheeled and hurried upstairs to her room. She wanted to run, but it was impossible in her skirt.

In her bedroom, with no maid to help her, she struggled with the myriad buttons down her back, finally tearing loose those she couldn't reach. She got herself out of the constricting corset—such a blessed relief to be rid of it—and donned a straight, gray skirt, a simple white cotton blouse and an unadorned sailor straw. As she was going out her bedroom door, her mother was entering.

"I want to talk to you, Sylvia."

"No." She brushed by her.

"Where are you going at this time of day, Sylvia?"

From the top of the stairs, Sylvia said, not looking back, "It's none of your business, mother."

Chapter Six

It was after seven when Sylvia arrived at the cottage in the woods. Arthur emerged quickly to help her down from the gig. "I'd given up on your coming."

"I'm sorry. There were guests. I couldn't get away." She was determined to lie to him as little as possible.

"I know. They promise you an afternoon off, then take it away. That's the English class-society for you." He put his arm around her shoulders and guided her toward the doorway. "More than anything else, I want to give the working men and women of this country regular hours and decent pay—that and safety on the job. If it means breaking down the infernal class-system, so be it. The whole idea that one person is superior to another at birth is ridiculous, anyway."

She was puzzled to be greeted this way, but said nothing. They entered the cottage and he closed the door. He stood there a moment, smiling down at her, so tall and thin. He wore a shirt and tie, but was coatless, an uncommon informality for the day. Then she couldn't see him any more, for he swept her into his arms. They embraced, but did not kiss. Against her ear, he said, "Meg, oh, Meg, it's so good to see you."

"Yes." But it was a tentative response. The thought came to her that this was the second time she had been embraced this day. "Arthur, I have to talk to you."

He stood back from her, both hands on her shoulders, an

almost beatific smile on his face. "Yes, let's talk. I have so many things to say."

His reply startled her. She found herself smiling back at him and saying, "You first. What do you want to tell me?"

He led her over by the fire, sitting with her on the sofa, although not close to her. He crooked his long leg over the cushion and turned to look at her, still smiling. "Oh, Meg, when I'm with you, I forget all else. I awoke this morning, full of ideas. I didn't even have breakfast before I started to write. Pages and pages I scribbled—and every word was a paean of praise for you. Oh, it wasn't *about* you. It was about politics and government and how the world is changing. But you were my inspiration. I thought constantly of you, of us."

She laughed. "That doesn't sound very possible to me."

"Don't laugh."

She saw hurt rising in his eyes. "Oh, Arthur, I'm not laughing at you. I just don't see how I can inspire anything about politics or government. I know so little about them, and couldn't care less."

His hurt look vanished. "Oh, Meg, don't you see? You're so beautiful. Even in a simple blouse, you're unspeakably lovely. And you're intelligent, able. You can be anything in this world. You can make a great contribution. Yet, our class-society condemns you to being a maid to some simpering snob. Why, you're so far superior to—what's her name? Who are you maid to?"

Sylvia sucked in her breath. "Sylvia Hartley."

"Yes, an insipid, idle creature, no doubt. Yet, because she's the daughter of an earl, she—"

"Stepdaughter."

"All right, stepdaughter. It's all the same. She's giving orders to you, treating you like a servant. It's wrong, Meg, so wrong. This country will never achieve greatness until we make the best possible use of all our citizens. I mean it, Meg. It's a waste for you to be a maid."

His words were impossibly difficult for her. "Arthur, I—"

He laughed. "I'm sorry. I am carrying on. But that's what I'm trying to tell you. You inspired me. I really got to the heart of what I've been trying to write. Oh, Meg, you're so good for me."

He stopped talking and just sat there smiling at her, eyes full of tenderness. Sylvia could not help but smile back. She began to speak, but slowly. "Arthur, I thought of you too, all day—but I fear differently. I'm a woman. I don't know about politics. I—I kept thinking of . . . yesterday . . . what happened. I—"

"Oh, Meg, I thought of that too. I can't stop remembering. You were so wonderful. I never, never thought such happiness would come to me."

"Are you happy?"

"Aren't you?" He seemed surprised.

She bit at her lower lip. "I don't know. That's just it."

"But you enjoyed yesterday. You said you did."

"Of course, I did, Arthur, you know that. But that's what I want to talk to you about. What kind of a woman does it make me?"

"It makes you the most magnificent woman in the world."

The pupils of her eyes widened as she looked at him. "Does it, Arthur? Does it really?"

He reached to clasp her hand, squeezing it. "Oh, yes, Meg. Please don't think otherwise."

She pulled her hand away, back into her lap, looking down, pursing her lips. "Arthur, can I trust you? Can I tell you something, knowing you will never tell a soul?"

"Yes, of course." She heard the sincerity in his voice.

"My mother, Arthur, is not a very nice person. Oh, she can be kind and generous. Many people adore her. But—" She sighed deeply. "For as long as I can remember, my mother has . . . has—" Another sigh. "She calls it granting her favors. She has done it . . . with men." She raised her head to look directly at him. "Arthur, after yesterday, am I that kind of woman?"

He reacted as though she had slapped him. "God, Meg, don't even think it!" He bolted to his feet to stand over her, looking down. "Don't let such an idea enter your head. Why, if I thought I caused you to think such a thing, why . . . why, I'd—"

"But isn't it the same, Arthur? How am I different from her?"

"God, Meg, there's all the difference in the world."

"No, there isn't, Arthur. Let's not fool ourselves. I'd just met you, hardly knew your name. Yet, I went in there with you . . . let you. . . ." She sighed. "And it wasn't just you. I wanted it. I did things. I remember everything I did."

"But, Meg, it was so beautiful. Two people caught in the rain. It just happened. There was nothing sordid or ugly or . . . planned about it. Wasn't it beautiful to you, Meg?"

"Yes." The word was barely audible.

"There you have it. Nothing so beautiful can be wrong."

"I'm sure my mother thinks her affairs are beautiful too."

This reply upset him. He clenched his fists, raising his forearms as though wanting to pound some sense into her. Then he abruptly relaxed and turned away from her, leaning against the mantel of the fireplace. When he spoke, his voice was calm, rational. "You said your mother had many men. You said she calls it granting favors." He turned back to face her. "Why does she do it? What purpose has it for her?"

"I don't know—oh, yes, I do. Mother is ambitious, for herself, for me. I believe she thinks her favors will earn some . . . some kind of advancement."

"What's your mother do?"

He startled her. "Mother? Do?"

"Yes, Meg. Does she work?"

She caught herself just in time. "Yes, she works. She's on Lord . . . Lord Linfield's staff . . . an assistant cook."

"And your father?"

"Father? Oh, he's been dead for years." So many lies. She felt she couldn't breathe.

He lowered his head, shaking it sadly several times. "There you have it. This accursed English caste-system drives people to do anything to improve their lot. Our moral character as a nation is being destroyed by it." He raised his head to look at her. "Your mother, bless her, a poor widow, has been driven into prostitution, Meg." He saw her wince at the word. "Yes, Meg, prostitution, giving her body, if not for cash, for some favor—that's why she uses the word—a little bonus, a better position, an extra day off, some article of clothing, a better room in the mansion, perhaps. But you don't do that, do you?"

The twisting of what she had meant was so confusing to her, she couldn't speak. He answered his own question.

"Of course, you don't. You were a virgin yesterday." Suddenly, he was on his knees before her, gripping her fingers, looking into her eyes. "Meg, let me tell you what happened yesterday. We were two lonely people engulfed in a storm, victims of the forces of nature. We sought shelter here.

And, without intending, without knowing it was happening, two lonely people reached out to each other . . . in love. Yes, Meg, it was love—and need and comforting. There was nothing tawdry about it, nothing premeditated. Any comparison with what your mother does is . . . is *odious*, Meg."

She could only stare at him, a tightness in her throat, his face beginning to swim before her eyes. She could only say, her voice husky, painful, "Thank you, Arthur."

He seemed to leap upward to her mouth, his lips devouring hers. It surprised her, but not nearly as much as her own hungry response. She truly believed she had come only to talk to him, to learn what he thought of her after yesterday. She had sworn to resist any physical contact. But here she was, enjoying the sweetness of his mouth, not wanting it to end when it did.

"Oh, Meg, Meg, if I thought I'd brought you pain . . . if I thought I made you feel anything but beautiful and loving—I wouldn't be able to stand it. I wouldn't." He hesitated, searching her eyes, her face, for confirmation. "Meg, do you know what yesterday meant to me?"

"No, Arthur, and I want so to know. Please, tell me."

It seemed a long time before he answered. "Meg, I know who I am, what I look like. I'm shy, easily embarrassed. I'm ill at ease around most people. Women do not . . . find me . . . attractive. I've never . . . before yesterday—"

"Oh, Arthur. . . ." It seemed to her she couldn't bear his confession.

"To have you here, to see you, to touch you, to have you . . . give yourself to me like you did . . . to know, to feel you . . . doing what you did—oh, Meg, I can't tell you what it meant to me."

She looked at him, eyes swimming. "I wanted you too, Arthur. Truly, I did. You believe that, don't you?"

"Yes."

She reached forward, touching his cheeks. "I think you're attractive, Arthur, very attractive . . . very appealing."

His mouth came to her again, quivering, and they kissed. Her head lay back against the sofa and he bent over her. She felt she was drowning in the passion which fell as a waterfall from his mouth, filling her. In a moment, he pulled her to her feet and they swept each other into urgent arms. She pressed against him, wanting to be even closer. Her surrender was a conscious act. She wanted him. Would it be so wrong to make love with him one more time? Then she would never see him again. Never. . . .

It was not at all like the previous day. Gone was her ignorance and innocence. She knew what was to happen and she wanted it. She was not naked under a mere robe this time. Now there were buttons and laces and time-consuming undergarments. But she liked it, the gradual revealing, much slower, interrupted by kisses, yes, many kisses, and words, of admiration and wonder, and the heady sense of anticipation. Then, with nakedness, came the wondrous caresses, now familiar, the moans and gasps, the filling and refilling of his mouth with her womanhood, the carrying and floating, the total arousal and immersion, the final fulfillment, cataclysmic again. Yet, it was different from before.

Sylvia could not realize it, but her mother's plot and Philip Waring's revelation of it had altered, in subtle yet significant ways, what transpired in that cottage between herself and Arthur Wicklow. What had been natural the first time was now, because of Waring's words, a learning experience, something to be improved upon, an educational process. Sylvia did not consciously think in these terms, but her actions and attitudes were affected, nonetheless. Even in her most ecstatic moments, some little spot in her mind observed and catalogued all that she was doing and all that happened to her. Without consciously willing it, she learned. By moving her hips, pressing against him and revolving them, she could heighten her own pleasure, control what was happening to her. She discovered how to teeter on the edge of the precipice, letting her tension build and build; then, with a mere movement or two, bring the whole world thundering down on her. She loved it, loved the sensations that were coursing through her body, loved knowing that Arthur was feeling the same pleasure and that she was the cause of his ecstasy, loved the endearments he whispered in her ear as they made love. . . . But did she love *him?*

As they lay in each other's arms, spent, she pondered the question. He had said that yesterday they had reached out to each other in love. And though that wasn't quite the same as telling her he loved her, she sensed that he did love her, or thought he did. She knew now that it was love that had beamed at her from his eyes yesterday and again today, and it was that love that made his look different from Captain Waring's and Lord Charles'. Yes, Arthur loved her . . . but did she love him? Would it be the same with any other man—no, surely not—but perhaps it was only his love for her that made it different. Perhaps, she only loved her own sense of power—over him, over her own body. God, what an ugly thought. It made her seem ruthless, unfeeling, like her mother, exactly, except for the absence of the mercenary element. No, it wasn't true. She was not like her mother but like Meg, who had given herself to Brian, and only to Brian. Except that Meg and Brian had been courting for some time, Meg had not surrendered impulsively to a stranger. Sylvia sighed. She didn't know what to make of it; she was totally confused and baffled.

Arthur's voice, languorous and tender, interrupted her reverie. "I wish you didn't have to leave. It seems like you just got here."

"I can stay, Arthur." The words just came out. No thought preceded them.

He raised his head from the pillow to look at her. "You can?"

"Yes." An image of her mother as she had last seen her flitted through her mind. Sylvia knew she didn't want to see her, have a confrontation, not tonight, not after this. Impulsively, she said, "I can spend the night if you like."

"How can you do that?"

Lies came effortlessly. "I've the evening off. I won't be missed."

"But Sylvia Hartley. Won't she want you to . . . ?"

"Hang Sylvia Hartley. She can manage without me." Laughter bubbled within her. Yes, Sylvia Hartley was managing very well. She raised her head from his shoulder. "Do you want me to stay?"

"Oh, God, yes, Meg. It'll be—"

She laughed. "Don't say. I know what it'll be."

"We'll have some dinner. We can—"

She felt him moving to get up. She held him back with her arm and silenced him with her words: "Not yet. This is so nice."

"Yes."

They lay in each other's arms then. It was endless time. forgotten minutes, filled with caresses, endearments, the inexorable arousal of youthful bodies. Her hand, seemingly with a mind of its own, slid over his chest, down the concave surface of his abdomen to his manhood. She began to stroke him, lightly, tenderly. "Does this . . . feel nice?" she asked softly.

"Yes, very." The sound of his voice told her it was so. But her left hand felt inexpert to her, so she sat up and with both hands began to explore him, looking at his body, his face, repeatedly asking if this movement felt good and being rewarded with an affirmative that was more sigh than words. She knew she was pleasuring him and she reveled in that knowledge. But it was not until she felt his hand at her breasts that she realized how aroused she was herself. She shuddered as his fingers found her hardened nipples, and she heard, "God, Meg." She turned toward him sideways, and he too turned to face her, as they aroused each other once again to a point of delicious frenzy. This time he entered her as they faced each other sideways, instead of mounting her from the top, and hugged her against himself, caressing her back, as they made love. She loved feeling herself so fully enveloped, loved the touch of his fingers on her back and buttocks, found her own hands circling his waist, then moving up, down, everywhere. Fulfillment came quickly this time, and amid her moans, she heard him cry out, "Oh, Meg, Meg, Meg." Yes, Meg. She was Meg. How much better to be Meg than Sylvia Hartley.

When she again lay in his arms, he said, "It gets better and better, Meg. I don't know what you do to me, *how* you do it, but . . ."

She laughed. "Call it inspiration. You have yours in writing. I have mine too."

"Do you ever!"

They got up soon after that and dressed. She enjoyed the intimacy of being watched as she put on her chemise—how different than yesterday—and of seeing him step into his trousers and button up the front. It was almost like a disappearing act in a magic show.

When she was nearly dressed, he said, "Know what I like about you, Meg?"

She smiled. "I can't imagine."

"The clothes you wear. You're so natural. None of those iron corsets for you. No fancy gowns. You are above the phony world of fashion. You dress so sensibly. You can breath and walk. Women in those corsets and hobble skirts look so silly. One day, all women will be natural like you."

She smiled, hoping her smile seemed natural.

There was another moment of panic when she realized that, believing her a servant, he might expect her to cook the meal. She had no idea even how to begin. But he didn't. Seemingly effortlessly, he whipped up something—it looked like a stew—and hung it over the fireplace to cook. Then he suggested a walk.

Arms around each other they strolled through the waning twilight, enjoying the soft air, watching the stars emerge in a velvet sky. And they talked—or, rather, mostly he did, telling her expansively of his work and his hopes for the future. The Labour party would one day rule Britain. Ramsey MacDonald would be a splendid prime minister, and it would be Labour, not the Liberals or Conservatives, who ended the social injustice and led Britain to true greatness. She said little, hoping it was enough, for his ideas sounded strange to her.

"The Fabian Society is wholly correct. It is the right course for the country."

"What is a Fabian, Arthur?"

"You mean you don't know?" There was shock in his voice. "The level of education in England is deplorable. That must be improved first, I suppose."

"I've heard of it, Arthur. I just don't understand what it is."

"The Fabian Society is a group of intellectuals founded by George Bernard Shaw, the Irish playwright, and Sidney and Beatrice Webb. They are man and wife. I'm a member. The Fabian Society believes—"

"I'm not dumb, Arthur. I just want to know what a Fabian is. I don't know the word."

He broke out laughing, stopping their pacing and turning to her in the darkness. "There's no such thing as a Fabian. It's not a thing—but a person with certain beliefs. The Fabian Society was named for Fabius Cunctator, a Roman famous for being a delayer and procrastinator, yet he won a war for the Romans by the method of gradualism. You see, Karl Marx advocated revolution as the way for the State to assume control of the means of production. The Fabians believe in gradualism, with the world coming to socialism through lawful, democratic means, slowly, over a period of time, without revolution or violence."

"I see. You explain things very well, Arthur." She snuggled deep into his arms as they headed back to the cottage.

They had wine with their dinner, which, though simple, was as tasty to her as any served at Downhaven. She was famished. And she was happy. They were almost like man and wife. Again, she had the sensation of really being Meg. And, as they sat before the fire, arms around each other, not speaking, but fully contented, she felt Meg, the real Meg, must be doing the same thing at that very moment.

Chapter Seven

She awoke ahead of him the next morning, surprised to be in a strange bed, even more surprised to be sharing it with a man. She lay on her side facing him, so he was the first thing she saw.

Memories of the night flooded over her, making her suddenly conscious of her nakedness under the covers. She had never slept naked before. Shaking her head in bewilderment, she told herself there were lots of things she had never done before. Memories of the night of love swept over her.

Slowly, so as not to awaken him, she rolled onto her back, glad for a chance to think. The ceiling came first into view. A thatched cottage. She had spent the night in a thatched cottage making love with a man she hardly knew. Yes, she hardly knew him. This was only their second meeting.

She turned her head to look at Arthur Wicklow. He really wasn't handsome. His face was too long and narrow, and almost gaunt. No doubt of it, Philip Waring was far handsomer. Nor did she understand this man she had given herself to. His background, his ideas, his very words were strange. And he held to his opinions so intensely. Yes, passionately. Imagine being passionate about an idea!

Yet, he was gentle and tender with her. She felt safe with him. He had not come to her as though she were a conquest—as Waring certainly would have. He was grateful, yes grateful to make love to her. And he was solicitous of her

69

and her well-being. She smiled. He was rather timid, actually. And that had emboldened her, made her want to please him—and herself. And she had. And he loved her. No, not her—the person she had pretended to be.

Suddenly, she knew. Everything was pretend, last night, the afternoon before. She had pretended to be Meg, a servant to her real self. Arthur wasn't in love with her, but with Meg, a pretense. If he knew Sylvia Hartley, he probably wouldn't like her at all. She pursed her lips. He must never know. Come what may, he must never know who she was. He would be terribly hurt, and contemptuous too—she represented everything he detested, wanted to overthrow with his Fabian gradualism. As for herself—well, a thatched cottage in the woods might be all right for a night of pretend, but it wasn't the real world, never could be for her. She was no socialist: she liked the comforts of her privileged existence, liked having horses to ride and pretty dresses to wear and a maid to do her hair and help her dress. How Arthur would loathe her if he knew what she were really like. So it wasn't love, not on either side, they were too different. It had all been a mirage, an illusion. Still, she wanted to preserve the illusion—for him.

But what was going to happen? She couldn't continue to live a lie with him. Then she knew. He was leaving for London soon. So was she. And in London they were unlikely ever to meet. When they parted in Hampshire, she would just allow Meg the maid to disappear—forever. This would have been just a pleasant interlude, a sweet memory for them both. Any hurt he felt at not being able to find Meg would quickly pass. Yes, that was the way to do it.

But what sort of woman did this make her? Was she now like her mother, cruel, always conniving to use people? Would there be other men, and still others, until she became cynical and jaded? She firmed her lips into a line. No, by God, never. She would remain chaste from this day forward until she found the man she could love and marry. Then, as his wife, she would bring to his bed all that she had learned here. Yes, she could do that, and she would. Her mother, Waring, no one would change her resolve—ever.

"Know what, Meg?"

She turned to face him and smiled. "Good morning, sleepyhead."

"I'm falling in love with you."

If she hadn't awakened first and had time to think, the statement would have unnerved her. Now she was able to say, "On our second meeting?"

He smiled. "There are meetings, then there are meetings. I would hardly call ours casual."

"Not hardly." She was laughing as she said it.

"Don't worry, I'm not going to ask if you're falling in love with me."

"I'm glad, Arthur. It's much too soon for me. I can't possibly know what I feel—and I don't want to lie to you."

"I know, I understand. You're so honest about everything. That's why I love you."

She turned on her side to face him, an act which helped her ignore the pang of guilt she felt. "Can't we just enjoy each other, being together—while we can?"

"While we can? What do you mean?"

"I have to get back to Downhaven, Arthur—and soon."

"I forgot. Yes, of course."

"And you're going to London, and—well, things happen."

"Not to me, Meg. I'll never forget you. I'll find a way to see you, so help me God." He paused, seriousness like a scar on his face. "Meg, I want to marry you. Oh, not now, but later, when we can. You can't go through life as a servant. You're too intelligent, too beautiful. You will make a splendid wife for a man in government."

His proposal disturbed her. "Arthur, I—"

"Oh, I know, it's much too soon. You're not nearly ready to think of marriage." He smiled. "I just wanted you to know how I feel, what I'm thinking. All I ask is that you think about it, think about being the wife of a member of Parliament, his hostess—" He laughed. "Maybe the mother of his children."

She remembered Meg. "I hope not already."

"It wouldn't be the end of the world. Then you'd have to marry me. Oh, Meg, I'm just asking you to think about it. Will you?"

"Of course, I will. I already have." It was a way to end a painful discussion. And it was sort of the truth.

Then he pulled her to him and kissed her. She felt his passion, but she could not respond. It was over with him. She knew it was.

"Do we have time?"

"I'm sorry, Arthur. I have to get back."

"Of course. I understand. Will there be trouble?"

"Don't worry. I can usually handle Miss Sylvia."

They arose and dressed. While she tried to do something with her hair, he fixed breakfast. As they were eating, the post came and he read a letter somberly, muttering under his breath.

"What is it, Arthur?"

"I have to be back in London Wednesday, Meg, an important meeting."

"Why look so sad? You were planning to go."

"But not so soon, Meg. I can't leave you now. I must see you again." He looked at her. "I'll have to leave tomorrow. But there's a late train that will get me there in time. That'll leave us tonight and part of tomorrow. Can you get away?"

She pursed her lips. "I—I don't know, Arthur. I—"

"Meg, come tonight. If you lose your job, I'll look after you. You must know that."

"Yes."

"Then come, please, come. Two lonely people deserve one more night."

She sighed. "I can come tonight, Arthur. I can always make some explanation. I won't lose my job." It was all a lie. But what could she do?

"Oh, God, Meg. Won't it be wonderful?"

She smiled. "Yes, it will."

The leaving did not take too long. There were not too many kisses, too many expressions of gratitude and wonder at it all. At her gig, which he brought around, he said, "Please, come tonight."

"I will, darling. Don't worry."

She drove away amid feelings of guilt, appalled at her lies, unable to believe her treachery toward this man who had befriended her and loved her. What was happening to her? Her life, once so orderly, was now a shambles. It had all started with Meg's leaving. Meg. She would stop and see her. Meg always made everything better.

Sylvia was dismayed by Meg's domicile. It was little more than a shack tucked up against a hillside on the north edge of the village. She knew that in the coming winter, the winds would whistle through the cracks in the wood, and the small, pot-bellied stove, which served both for heating and cooking, would be insufficient to keep them warm. The interior was small, hardly larger than a small parlor at Downhaven. On the earthen floor, the furnishings were sparse—a table and two wooden chairs. In the corner was a bed, of straw covered with a sheet. There wasn't much else. Sylvia was shocked that anyone lived this way. And for it to be her dearest friend. . . .

None of this showed in their greeting. Meg virtually leaped into her arms, laughing and crying at the same time. "I knew you'd be the first to visit, I just knew it." Sylvia's eyes were moist too, but she wasn't sure what caused it. "Come in and let me show you. It's not much, I know, but it's home, my home."

Thinking of something suitable to say about the house was a torture. She couldn't say it was grand, or even nice. Cozy seemed inappropriate too. So Sylvia restricted herself to smiles, and took refuge in clichés: "A regular homemaker you are," and "you keep it so clean," and "I can see how happy you are, Mrs. Trout."

"Oh, yes, yes, Sylvie. I'm in heaven."

Sylvia laughed. "And where is your guardian angel?"

Meg let out a whoop. "How could I forget him?" She dashed to the rear door and called, "Brian, come here. We have a visitor, and you'll never guess who."

He entered, bending his head to get through the door. He wore an old shirt and trousers, both badly smeared, and his dark hair was plastered against his forehead. But he was smiling broadly at her. "Miss Sylvia, I knew it was you. I didn't have to guess."

Her returning smile equalled his. "I'm not Miss anything to you, Brian. I'm Sylvia." She glanced happily at Meg. "Or Sylvie—Meg's name for me."

"All right, Miss—I mean Sylvia." He extended his hand. When she hesitated, he saw how black it was, covered with grease, and withdrew it.

Sylvia laughed. "I think maybe we'd better just wave at each other for the moment."

"I'm sorry. Been working on a motor car."

"Yes, Sylvie, Brian's going into business for himself as a motor-car repairman. He has his first job, already."

"Wonderful for you both. I know you'll be a huge success, Brian."

He seemed flustered. "I won't be if I stand here. You excuse me, Miss Sylvia, and I'll go back to work."

He was bolting out the rear door as she called after him, "Sylvia, Brian, just Sylvia."

She and Meg stood there a moment, then reached out spontaneously and clasped each other's hands, smiling, both overcome with happiness at being together. Meg spoke first. "I know he's going to make it. Oh, sure, we don't have much right now, but——"

"You have each other."

"Oh, yes, and it's so wonderful. But Brian is strong and he works hard. Things will get better for us—and soon. I know."

"I know it too, Meg." She said a silent prayer that it would be so.

Their smiles and bright eyes spoke many more words than their lips. Then Meg released her. "How about some tea?"

Sylvia didn't want to take anything from two people as poor as this. "I don't think so, Meg. I just had——"

"Nonsense. You must have some tea."

She couldn't refuse. Besides, Meg was already filling a teapot out of a bucket of water. "Fine. I'd love some." In a moment, the kettle was placed on the stove. It had only a single hot plate.

While Meg continued with preparations for tea, Sylvia made a quick inventory of what these two must need. Everything, certainly. But what could she do that would not damage Meg's pride? Clothes. Without her uniforms, Meg had hardly a thing to wear—while she had closets full. She'd bring some things over tomorrow. And flowers. Not necessary, but they would brighten the place. And, yes, she could snitch some food—tea, flour and such—from the kitchen. There were probably some old sticks of furniture in the attic. Maybe even an old bed. Yes. She had to do all she could to help them. She'd even speak to people in the village about work for Brian.

She suddenly realized Meg was staring at her. "You look different, Sylvie. Something's happened to you. You look—I don't know—happier or something."

Despite herself, Sylvia blushed. "I am—to see you. Actually—" She removed her straw as proof. "I'm a mess. Look at my hair."

"Would you like me to fix it? I can do it while the pot's boiling."

"Oh, would you? I'm lost without you." She sat in a chair. Meg produced a brush and comb and began the ministrations. "Are you feeling all right, Meg?"

"I'm fine. Why do you ask?"

"You are . . . expecting, aren't you? You'd better be, or I'll never forgive you for leaving me."

"Oh, *that*. I'm fine, never felt better."

"You're not sick or anything? You know—"

"I eat like a horse. Never felt better."

"Thank God for that." She was silent a moment, enjoying her friend's familiar hands on her hair. "I miss you, Meg. There's no one to talk to."

"Tell me. What's been happening?"

"Oh, mother's her usual ghastly self. She had a dinner party Saturday. The duke of Glouston, no less."

"Really? What's he like?"

"Pathetic, actually. He's short, wears thick glasses and stammers horribly. Can hardly utter a word—poor man." She rendered an imitation of his speech, provoking gales of laughter from Meg. How like old times it was!

"How awful for you, Sylvie."

"Not really. I felt sorry for him, and I tried to be as nice as I could. He's not what was terrible. Mother invited Philip Waring."

The motions of Meg's hands stopped, and she bent around to look at Sylvia. "Not *the* Philip Waring?"

"No less."

"What's he like?"

Sylvia told her, describing his handsome appearance, self-assured ways, the intimate manner he used with her.

"He doesn't sound so terrible to me."

"You don't know what else happened." She found herself telling about the early morning ride, her mother's plot, Waring's indecent proposition.

Meg came around to stand in front of Sylvia. "I never heard of such a thing."

"Nor I—nor anyone else, I think."

"What did you tell him?"

"I told him he was an insufferable cad and I never wanted to lay eyes on him again."

"Good for you." Meg walked around her and resumed braiding her hair. "I know Lady Constance is your mother, Sylvia, but I can't help it. Such gall she has. Trying to arrange a . . . a lover for you, trying to make you into a . . . a I don't know what. How awful!"

Sylvia heard her out, feeling ready to burst. She knew she was about to tell Meg about Arthur, and she didn't want to. But she knew she would. If she opened her mouth, it would all come out. Her mouth opened.

"It was already too late, Meg. I've had a lover."

"You haven't either. I'd have known about it."

"No, Meg." Then it all came out like an avalanche. "After your wedding, I was so upset, so—I don't know—restless. I went riding on Turk and he threw me. I woke up and this man was holding me. Then the heavens opened up and it poured rain."

"I remember the storm."

"I'd hurt my ankle. He picked me up and carried me to his cottage. I was soaked, so I took off my clothes to dry and put on his robe. One thing led to another. I couldn't help myself. It just happened."

She stopped, waiting for some word from behind her back. But there was only silence.

"Oh, Meg, it was just like you and Brian. It just happened. And it—it was like you said . . . wonderful." She couldn't stand the silence. She turned in her chair and looked back at Meg, who was staring down at her, wide-eyed. "I loved it, Meg. It was wonderful, just like you said."

Meg stared at her a moment longer, then smiled. "I'm glad—if you are. But who is he?"

"Don't ask, Meg. I don't want to say."

"All right, but are you ashamed of him?"

"No, it wasn't like that. I just don't want to say."

"Anyone I know?"

"Meg, please, don't pry. It's better if no one knows. Believe me, it is."

Meg's smile broadened. "Whatever you say, Sylvie. I gather your mother wouldn't approve of him?"

Sylvia laughed. "Not one whit. And am I in trouble when I

get home. I spent the night with him, Meg. I just came from there."

Her former servant was aghast. "You're not serious?"

"I did, Meg—and I loved every second of it."

"Sylvie, you didn't? Are you in love with him?"

"No, I—I don't think so. I can't imagine marrying him, anyway. But he makes me feel—oh, Meg, the things that happened inside me. I can't describe it, but you know, don't you? You said it was like that with you and Brian."

Meg could only stare at her.

"Do you hate me, Meg? Do you think me awful?"

There was a pause, then a smile from Meg. "That, you should know, is impossible."

The hair was finished, the tea served and drunk, all amid intimate chatter and shared confidences. When it was time to leave, and Sylvia had said goodbye to Brian, and Meg had walked her out to the carriage, a hand was placed on her arm and three words spoken, "Be careful, Sylvia." Then three more. "I love you."

"I will, Meg. And I love you too. I'll see you tomorrow."

She didn't. Her mother was waiting for her at Downhaven, furious. "Where have you been?"

"At Meg's."

"Don't lie to me. I sent someone over there last night. Your carriage was not there."

Sylvia saw her mother's rage. Somehow, it made her calm. "I didn't say last night. I just left Meg's."

"Where did you spend the night?"

Sylvia gave a small smile. "I'm sorry, mother. It's none of your business."

"None of my business! You'll not talk to me this way, young lady. Were you with a man?"

"Would it matter if I was? You wanted me to sleep with Captain Waring. Does it matter whom I was with?"

Lady Constance's eyes widened as she sucked air into her substantial chest, filling it. The air came out, bearing these words: "If you were with a man, I demand to know who he was."

"No, mother. I'm not saying."

"I *demand* you tell me this instant."

Her mother's face was red. She looked ready to burst from anger. Sylvia didn't care. "No."

"Undoubtedly some *peasant*. Some boy with dirty hands. Some beggar on the street."

"Think what you wish, mother. I'm not telling you."

"I'll not let you ruin your life. I'll not let you waste yourself, the opportunity I've earned for you on some cheap, little affair."

Sylvia smiled. "There's nothing you can do, mother."

Lady Constance glared at her, then gave her own twisted smile. "But there is, Sylvia. I'm taking you to London, now, this very afternoon."

It was Sylvia's turn to be angry. "You can't. I won't go!"

"Oh, yes, you will! You go where this household goes. I'm having a small bag packed for you. Agnes will bring your other things tomorrow. There is nothing you can do about it."

She was right. Sylvia protested, even begged, barely able to hold back the humiliating tears. But she could not prevail. So rapid was the departure, so closely watched was she by her mother, that she had no time to send gifts to Meg or a note to Arthur Wicklow explaining that she couldn't come. She had intended to do that. . . .

Chapter Eight

Sylvia scrawled a florid letter "S" followed by a dot for her signature, laid down the pen and, picking up the paper, began to blow on it to dry the ink. Another letter to Meg. She had been dutiful in her resolve to write her friend once, sometimes twice a week. This was her fifth letter. She had been in London almost a month.

Writing to Meg was a poor substitute for seeing her, but Sylvia was determined to maintain some contact with her friend. She couldn't bring herself to set down on paper the sort of confidences which were so easily spoken, but at least Meg would know something of her activities. Perhaps she could read between the lines.

She read the words recently penned. "My life in London remains radically different from before." Yes, it was true. Sylvia was not being squired to cotillions and balls by her mother. She was no longer being introduced to society. She had been accepted into it, receiving, at least some of the time, her own invitations separate from Lord Winnie and her mother. She was making her own friends and developing her own activities. Her independence was minimal, but to Sylvia it was a wisp of fresh air in a stagnant existence.

"Mother remains mother. Sometimes we even speak to each other." Sylvia smiled. Meg would read the correct meaning into those words. Sylvia could not forgive her mother for meddling in her life, the nefarious plot with Waring, the precipitous departure for London. Oh, there had been no more angry words. They remained civil and correct with each other in front of Winnie and guests. But Sylvia successfully kept Lady Constance at arm's length. There were no mother-daughter chats. When Lady Constance tried to interfere with her life, Sylvia looked at her witheringly or walked away. Sylvia had finally gained a dash of independence.

Clara, her new maid, had helped. Sylvia glanced at what she'd written. "My new maid, Clara, is a far cry from you, dearest Meg. I am not fond of her and I will never be close to her. But I do need someone to do my hair and such." Sylvia reread the words, uncertain whether they set the right tone. Her first concern was for Meg's feelings. She didn't want her to think anyone had or could ever replace her, which was true. Yet, the words were not quite fair to Clara. She was more valuable than this sounded. But, then, this was not for Clara's eyes. And Meg's feelings were far more important than those of her replacement.

Lady Constance had selected Clara, and Sylvia had acquiesced. Since she was not paying her, she had no choice in the matter. Besides, her feeling was that anyone would do. She needed someone to do her hair and help her dress. There would never be a Meg again.

Clara was in her late thirties, a spinster, scrupulously correct and very taciturn. Idle chatter and happy laughter in the bedroom were things of the past. Clara had been chosen because she had formerly been maid to Sarah Hastings, the actress who had taken her life following a scandal. The new maid was a genius at makeup and hair-styling, far better than Meg, Sylvia reluctantly admitted. From the beginning, Clara had begun to shove her mother aside in terms of what fashions to wear—Clara selected her dresses now, not her mother—what invitations to accept, whom to be seen with. She acted as much like a secretary as a maid. Sylvia recognized this as more interference in her life, but at least Clara was subtle about it, suggesting rather than demanding. Besides, Sylvia derived savage glee from knowing her mother had been shunted aside, at least partially.

In less than a month, Clara had reformed her wardrobe in a striking way, discarding many of the more flamboyant dresses selected by her mother and replacing them with more sophisticated garments. As far as Sylvia was concerned, Lord

Winnie's largesse was being spent more sensibly. And her castoffs gave her things to send to Meg. She was disappointed not to be able to help Meg and Brian more. There had been no chance to send furniture or encourage work for Brian around Hornby. When she thought of her friend living in that shack, she wanted to weep. But several boxes of castoffs had gone to Meg. Many of the garments were ridiculously frivolous, but Sylvia suspected Meg would cut them up and make something useful out of them.

Another line in the letter caught her eye. "I have been living a virtuous life, you'll be glad to know." Sylvia sighed. Yes, she had been virtuous. But wasn't it too late? Poor Arthur. He was so much in her thoughts. How could she have done it? What could have possessed her to give herself to him, then return a second time, lying all the while, telling him she was someone else? Oh, what a monstrous web of deception. And to what purpose? To protect herself? To have the world believe Sylvia Hartley was untouched? No, that thought had never entered her mind. She had lied to make it possible for her to do what she wanted to do and did not have the courage to do as Sylvia Hartley. That knowledge brought her little comfort, however.

Poor Arthur. She knew he had tried to find her. A tall, thin man had come to the servant's entrance at the London house asking for Meg Gwynne. The cook was at her irritable best, and turned him away saying there was no such person here. Apparently, Arthur had learned somewhere that Meg Gwynne was now Meg Trout, for he had gone to her house. Sylvia picked up the one letter she had received from Hornby. "The strangest thing happened the other day, Sylvie. A man came to the door. He was very tall, almost gauntlooking, and he asked for Meg Trout. When I told him I was Meg Trout, he just stared for the longest time, said something about making a terrible mistake and left."

Oh, Arthur. The thought of him searching for a nonexistent person filled her with sorrow and self-loathing. Why didn't she write him a note, telling him what had happened and why? But how could she explain? Dear Arthur, I am really Sylvia Hartley, stepdaughter to an earl. My mother expects me to marry a duke, at least, and I can't possibly have anything to do with you, a mere—Oh, God! How awful! Dear Arthur, I only saw you because I was lonely and upset. We live in different worlds, and neither of us can change. Believe me, it is better this way. Lord, what an impossible situation. She didn't want to hurt him, couldn't. He had done nothing to deserve it. She just wanted to disappear from his life. They must never meet. He must never know. But how was that possible? How could she ever have thought they could both be in London at the same time and he never learn her identity? Her photograph had been in the newspaper a few days ago. She hadn't wanted it, but couldn't prevent it. She was in a group of people and the photograph was not very clear. Perhaps he had not seen it or recognized her. But he must know. He must have asked Meg. Do you know a tall, blonde woman with green eyes? Yes, he must have asked. Meg must have told him. He must hate her. And wasn't it better that way? Wasn't it what she deserved?

These thoughts were an almost daily occurrence. Like an act of penance, she had tried to drive him from her mind. She was determined to forget him, to forget all that had happened. It never worked, and it was working less all the time. She looked for him everywhere, on the street, at every public gathering, unable to relax until she was certain he was not there. She dreamed of him frequently, and even awake, whenever her mind was idle, she discovered her thoughts were of the cottage. Her body seemed infected with him. She was so conscious of it, even inside the elegant clothes she wore. Her skin seemed so sensitive, and at times she felt uncomfortably warm, vaguely irritable and restless. So much for her pleasant interlude and sweet memory; the man was in her blood, and it was impossible to forget him.

"Have you finished your correspondence, miss?"

Sylvia had forgotten that Clara was in the room. The woman was preternaturally quiet. Meg had always made her presence felt. "Yes, I am."

"I believe you are sitting for your portrait at Lord Charles' today. You'd best get dressed."

Lord Charles had become an important part of her new life. She saw him nearly every day. He had taken her out a few times, to the opera, ballet or theater, thus making her a sensation in the newspapers. Frequently, she saw him at his home. Perhaps because of his speech impediment, Lord Charles surrounded himself with people who were very articulate. And because of his own interests and scholarship, these talkers were mostly writers, artists, musicians, frequently young and hopeful of renown. Lord Charles was considered a leading patron of the arts. More than a few men of talent had been accepted as long term, seemingly permanent guests in the duke's home. He had introduced Sylvia to his artist friends, and she had at once become their darling, a sort of mascot. Quick poems were dashed off to her beauty. Joshua Wainwright had insisted on doing her portrait. She went nearly every afternoon for the sitting, enjoying the attention, the witty conversation. And, frequently, she told herself how right this life was for her, how much better, more stimulating than the monotony of a thatched cottage with Arthur Wicklow.

"Yes, Clara. Just let me seal this letter, then I'll be there."

As she sat at her vanity, letting Clara fix her hair and face, Sylvia was once again impressed with the woman's talents. She knew a great many things Meg had not known, and as a result, Sylvia knew, she was far more beautiful. Clara used creams and powders to heighten her skin tone and tiny dabs of colors around her eyes, which seemed to enlarge them and magnify their remarkable color. Her hair, already more lustrous from special shampoos and rinses, was arranged in such intricate braids and rolls that Sylvia knew it attracted almost as much attention, from women at least, as her gowns. Nor was Clara's wizardry restricted to face and hair. From the first, Clara had set her to a regimen of exercises, massages and steaming, perfumed baths, which seemed to tighten and soften her whole body, making her skin glisten with health. Sylvia loved it, but it seemed to her Clara was investing a lot of time and effort for a mere maid.

Clara D'Angelo did not think her investment wasted. She knew potential when she saw it. The mother, the countess, was a fraud, a hussy who had, somehow—quite incredibly really—parlayed a large bosom and consummate connivance into an earldom. She was too overblown, too obvious, too everything. But the daughter, oh, the daughter! If saved from her mother, Sylvia could exceed even the famed Lily Langtry. Such coloring, such remarkable eyes, and the figure, the regal bearing. Sylvia Hartley was a chance of a lifetime for Clara D'Angelo. She could teach her, dress her, control her without her realizing it. In only a month, she had worked wonders. And there was much more to do. She had to get this girl into her own house, away from the vulgar influence and taste of her mother. The old woman was using the daughter. The daughter had to begin to make use of the treasures God had given her. If she did, Sylvia Hartley would make a fortune. Men would fall at her feet to hand her purses and jewels. And Clara D'Angelo, bastard offspring of a viscount's daughter's fling with an itinerant Italian actor, knew just how to make it all happen. Sylvia Hartley was her ticket to wealth—and revenge. Her blood was as blue as any of them, yet she was a servant.

"Will you be seeing Lord Charles today, miss?"

Sylvia glanced at her maid in the mirror. "I imagine. I usually do. Why do you ask?"

"I was just wondering. If I may say so, miss, I think it is an excellent thing you do with his lordship."

"Why do you say that?"

"Most people hear only his stammer and ridicule him behind his back. You show him kindness. I'm sure you bring him much happiness."

"Lord Charles is an intelligent, thoughtful man. He merely has trouble expressing himself. I find him interesting."

"That's what I mean, Miss. You are not blinded by outward appearances."

"Thank you, Clara."

One of the reasons Clara had thrown in her lot with Sylvia was the latter's friendship with the duke of Glouston. Clara did not know exactly how at the moment, but she was certain that in some way the stuttering peer was the ticket to Sylvia's house and independence. And she was handling it right, if for all the wrong reasons. Sylvia felt nothing for the duke, of course, but she was kind to him. Their friendship was purely platonic, and apparently Sylvia was not aware the duke was visibly burning with lust for her. Right now, friendship, attentiveness and warm smiles were just the right touch. If that idiotic Lady Constance had her way, Sylvia would long since have forced her way into his bed, scaring the poor, shy man off and ruining everything. Eventually, it would come to pass, had to, and the duke would lavish a fortune on Sylvia, which was far more valuable than the title her mother coveted. Clara was certain she could get Sylvia to do what was necessary at the proper time. She could step forward, speak to this girl, gain control over her. But not just now. This child was not yet ready. Clara knew she must be patient.

By the time Clara finished her ministrations and Sylvia left Winnie's home in Regent's Park for her sitting, she was a vision. She wore a gown of the latest Poiret style, slit to the knee, white in color. The gown was demurely high to the throat, with long, fitted sleeves, and so snug over her bust and corseted waist it might have been second skin. The skirt was straight, narrowing at her ankles with a discreet train in the back. The fabric of soft, clinging silk was devoid of decoration. There was no design in the weave. Nor was there even a hint of lace or bow, pleat or frill. The only ornamentation was the figure and face of the wearer. As Sylvia entered the carriage and told the footman to go to Lord Charles' home, she wore a wide, white straw decorated with osprey feathers. Her silhouette alone almost caused a collision between drivers of a landau and a hansom cab.

Sylvia was to journey from Lord Winnie's home in Regent's Park along Baker Street to the duke's house in Mayfair. A pleasant, not too lengthy trip. Indeed, it was like a procession—a beautiful girl in a handsome victoria, attracting attention as she passed, until Oxford Street, where all traffic came to a halt. Sylvia spoke to the driver who, with a better view, explained that there seemed to be a disturbance ahead. "I think it's them suffragettes, mum."

Sylvia tried to wait patiently, but everyone was blowing horns on their motor cars, scaring the horses, and standing to try to see what lay ahead, so she also stood up. Coming down Oxford Street was some kind of procession. In a moment, she saw it was a group of women, perhaps fifty or more. Several, she saw, had chained themselves together, dragging the links on the pavement, while others carried placards. She read a few. END OUR BONDAGE. FREE US WITH THE VOTE. WOMEN WITHOUT THE VOTE ARE SLAVES. They seemed to be singing or shouting something, but Sylvia couldn't hear for the noises of horns and the catcalls of motorists, cab drivers and pedestrians.

It was a strange sight to Sylvia to see women marching down the street, but she had no political feeling about it. She just wished the traffic would start moving again. Then, right in front of her, police arrived in black mariahs, perhaps a dozen or twenty men, and motioned the women off the street. The crowd suddenly quieted, and Sylvia heard one of the women shout, "We will not leave till we get the vote!" She waved her arm and all the women immediately sat down in the middle of the intersection of Oxford and Baker. The noise from the vehicles and the now quite sizeable crowd was deafening, as the London bobbies moved into the demonstrators and began to carry the women bodily out of the intersection and into the police wagons.

One face caught Sylvia's attention. It was that of a pretty girl, with brown hair and large brown eyes. She was about her own age and somehow familiar as she sat on the pavement, defiance mingling with fear on her face. Then Sylvia knew. Kitty Shaw. Kitty had been her classmate at school, and her only close friend, as well as the brightest, prettiest, most popular girl at St. Regis Academy. Everyone liked her, although there had been some envy. Daughter of a peer, due to inherit bags of money, she was the girl with everything. What on earth was Kitty Shaw doing there in the street?

A bobby came up to her, tapped her on the shoulder and motioned her to move. Kitty suddenly raised her head, then shook it defiantly. The bobby bent down, grabbed her shoulders and lifted her to her feet. Kitty began to struggle with him, finally succeeding in kicking him in the shin. Then she tried to run. Two other bobbies caught her within a few steps, however. Kitty was now just beside Sylvia's carriage, collared by two policemen, although still struggling and screaming at them to let her go.

Suddenly, she stopped her resistance and stared up at Sylvia. It seemed a moment frozen in time, two school chums gaping at each other, one elegantly-gowned and standing in a fine carriage, the other dressed in simple clothing and restrained by policemen. Then she was led away. But the look in Kitty's eyes stayed with Sylvia all the way to the duke's house. Kitty Shaw, her vivacious friend, the girl with everything, a suffragette? Impossible, yet there it was. And that look in her eyes. What was it? Surprise at seeing her in the carriage. Yes, certainly that. But more. Hatred? No, *loathing*.

Oh, well, she and Kitty hadn't been in touch for years. And despite their friendship, there had always been some competition there—the two prettiest girls at St. Regis. But Sylvia was still dazed as she entered the duke's house. Kitty Shaw, a suffragette? It just couldn't be.

"My dear Sylvia, you look like you've just seen a ghost."

It was the voice of Joshua Wainwright, a pale, slender man wearing a paint-smeared smock. His most distinctive feature was a leonine head, exaggerated by immense lambchop sidewhiskers. She laughed. "I think perhaps I have. I just saw someone I know in a suffrage demonstration."

"You poor thing. That would shock anyone." The words came from the effete Timothy Graves, a would-be writer and fulltime dilettante.

"I knew her at school. She was the most popular girl at St. Regis Academy, the prettiest, brightest, richest. Her father's at least a baronet. And we were fairly close for a while. I never thought I'd see Kitty Shaw sitting in the street and being hauled away by bobbies."

Again, Graves spoke, disdain dripping from his voice. "My dear, when you have lived in London a while longer, you will find that nothing surprises you."

"So Mistress Pankhurst is at it again, is she?"

Sylvia turned to Sir Robert Baldwin, another of the duke's hangers-on. "I don't know if she was there or not, Sir Robert. I've never met her."

"Your advantage, I assure you. But it is most likely she was making her presence felt—either she or one of her equally bizarre daughters."

Graves, again: "I just hope we don't see you out in the street, Sylvia, carrying a sign or scuffling with the police. But, then, if you were wearing such an elegant gown as now, I'm sure I wouldn't mind. You look divine, my dear."

"Thank you, Timothy. Where is Lord Charles?"

Wainright answered. "He had to go to Westminster for some kind of meeting. It seems the lords of the realm are gathering their forces to defend the kingdom against the Visigoths and their Parliamentary Act. Come. Are you ready to sit now?"

She removed her hat, gave an unnecessary pat to her coiffure before a mirror, then took her place. Wainwright was doing a large canvas, a full-length portrait. She stood, turned slightly to her right, her right arm resting on what would be painted as a broken Corinthian column. Her face was turned so both her eyes would be in the painting. She would look every inch a princess. The pose was a simple one, yet Sylvia found it tiring. Wainwright had to admonish her frequently to hold her chin up and keep her head at the right angle.

Many men and a few women, came into the studio, observing the work, saying a few words to Sylvia, talking among themselves. All this was pleasantly distracting to her, and she was amused by the repartee, the literary discussions, the mild arguments over the progress of the work or last night's theater opening, the most recently published novel. Sylvia's compassion for Lord Charles had led her into a fashionable and fascinating world, to which her mother, with all her "favors," could not belong. Sylvia loved being here, being accepted by these people. Some were vain and excessively conceited about extremely modest talents, but they were fun and interesting and they had accepted her as their own.

Traffic in and out of the studio was considerable and, maintaining her pose, Sylvia could not see the entrance. Thus, after close to an hour, she was surprised to see a man in a military uniform standing in her line of vision. He spoke to the artist. "Wainwright, I must say your choice of subjects is admirable."

"Oh, hello, Waring. Good to see you, but don't bother me. The color of those eyes is the devil's own to duplicate."

"Yes, aren't they?" He smiled at Sylvia and bowed slightly. "Good to see you again, Miss Hartley."

Immediately, she broke her pose. "If you don't mind, Joshua, I've had enough for today."

"But, Sylvia, you can't. I'm at a most critical—"

"I'm sorry, but I'm tired." She stode rapidly away from her position, toward her hat. Wainwright came after her, protesting. "I know, Joshua, and I'm sorry. The conditions are not good for me today."

Waring, who had followed a step or two behind the frustrated painter, laughed. "All right, Sylvia, I'll leave. I just wanted to see you again. I didn't dream it would upset you so."

Hat and purse in hand, Sylvia turned to face him, the seagreen band of her eyes storm-tossed. "Captain Waring, I'll ask you not to decide whether or not I'm upset—or decide anything at all about me, for that matter. And I don't care if you leave or stay. *I'm* leaving. Period."

And so she did, a dozen pairs of eyes staring after her.

Chapter Nine

A few days later, Sylvia attended Verdi's opera *Rigoletto* with Lord Charles. As always, her first action was to search the audience for a certain face, sighing finally with relief. He was not there. He probably thought opera was frivolous—no doubt he spent his evenings at Fabian Society meetings. Thereafter, she enjoyed the opera. She loved sitting in the box, knowing heads in the orchestra below were turning to look up at her each time the lights went on. She wore a gown of rich blue satin, offset with contrasting panels of green. She knew the color combination was startling, and that she was one of few women who could wear it to advantage.

What doubts she had, and they were enough to disturb her enjoyment of the music, concerned the man to her left. She had been seen often with Lord Charles, two or three times a week in public, and she went to his home nearly every day for the sitting. Tongues were wagging. She was being paired off with him. Sylvia Hartley was going to be the duchess of Glouston.

Her friendship with the duke had begun as compassion for a man with a speech defect—or, really, a move to get away from her mother and Philip Waring at that breakfast. In the weeks since, nothing had changed much. Oh, she was grateful for Charles' attentions, the places he took her, the people he had introduced her to. But gratitude was a no more potent emotion than compassion, and neither justified marriage. She

A LASTING SPLENDOR

was using the duke. He offered her independence. As long as her mother thought she was ensnaring a duke—any duke would do—she left her alone.

The duchess of Glouston, cousin to King George V. Heady stuff, surely. And, with very little effort on her part—only patience, really—she could have it. Many women, probably most, would leap at the opportunity now sitting at her left.

Sylvia could not, and knew it. She had respect for Charles' intelligence and genuine interest in the arts, and she admired his courage in performing his public duties, painful as they were for him. But these could lead to no more than friendship as far as she was concerned. Marriage to a friend, however dear, would mean living in hell. Arthur Wicklow and the cottage came to her mind, and she shuddered. Could she do that with the duke of Glouston? No, she could not.

"Are you c-cold, Sylvia?"

The voice startled her, but she smiled. "No, I'm fine, thank you."

She turned back to the stage, determined to think no more about marrying Charles. Besides, she was being silly and presumptuous. Sylvia Hartley was a commoner, daughter of an army captain, and cousins to the Crown do not marry commoners. She was safe. But as she forced her mind to listen to the singing, a thought came to her. As stepdaughter of the earl of Linfield, she was probably acceptable.

At the first act intermission, she was surprised by a voice from behind her asking, "May I speak to you a moment, Sylvia?"

She turned and was even more surprised to see Kitty Shaw. There was no resemblance to the angry girl she had encountered on the street. Kitty looked quite elegant, though Sylvia thought both her gown and coiffure out of style by a season or two. "Kitty, so good to see you."

Kitty smiled warmly. "That was you I saw in the carriage the other day, wasn't it?"

"Of course, it was," Sylvia answered. "I must say I was surprised to see you there. Those bobbies were treating you rather roughly."

"Oh, that. They were just doing their jobs—and what we wanted them to do. It was a very successful demonstration."

"Did they arrest you?"

Again, a smile. "Not for very long. We're a nuisance to them just now. It's good to see you, Sylvia. How are you?"

"I'm fine, Kitty." Sylvia tried to put as much warmth into her own smile as Kitty had shown her. After all, she remembered now, it was Kitty who had sought her out and befriended her at St. Regis. Kitty hadn't lacked for friends, herself, but she'd seemed to sense Sylvia's loneliness (how she'd missed Meg during that brief separation!) and had done her best to relieve it. Sylvia had to admit to herself that it had been she, more than Kitty, who had created a sort of rivalry between them, and now she recalled, with a twinge of guilt, her former classmate's generosity and affection, and the letter Kitty had written her after graduation, which she, reunited with Meg, had never answered.

"You look positively breathtaking."

Sylvia laughed lightly. "And look who's speaking to the kettle. You always were the beautiful one at school—and you are now."

Kitty joined the laughter. "Let's not start a contest in compliments." She paused, growing serious. "I'd love to talk to you, Sylvia. May I?"

"Of course."

"Not here. I mean, *really* talk. Could I call at your home?"

Sylvia hesitated. "I gather you want to talk about more than old times?"

"Yes."

Sylvia pursed her lips. "Kitty, I—I don't think. . . . I wouldn't want to take your time."

Kitty's smile was brilliant. "It will be painless, Sylvia, just talk."

Sylvia relented. "All right, why don't you come tomorrow? We'll have tea."

"Thank you, Sylvia. I'll see you then."

Lord Charles turned toward them then, and Sylvia introduced him to Kitty. One would have thought Kitty Shaw had never heard of Emmeline Pankhurst.

The next afternoon, Sylvia greeted Kitty Shaw with apprehension. She simply was not interested in politics. And trying to envision herself sitting in the street to be carried away by the police was impossible. She could not, and would not.

Letting Kitty come at all was a mistake. Little of this showed in her greeting of her old schoolfellow, however. Since it was a blessedly warm fall afternoon for England, their tea was served in the gazebo in the garden. It made a nice scene, two attractive young women ensconced in a lovely setting, laughing, chatting about school days. Most pleasant, and Sylvia became more relaxed as she listened to reports of the activities of various alumnae of St. Regis.

"Do you remember Jane Weathersby—Lady Jane Grey we called her?"

"Oh, yes, certainly. What's she doing?"

"She's one of us."

The sudden shift in the conversation startled Sylvia. "Oh, I see, you mean a suffragette?"

"Yes, although we aren't entirely pleased with the term. We are the Women's Social and Political Union."

Sylvia sighed, knowing the dreaded moment had arrived. "Kitty, I—"

A laugh silenced her. "I know, what you saw on the street the other day appalled you. You can't see yourself, even remotely, doing that. Isn't that about right?"

"Yes."

"I was the same as you, Sylvia." She smiled. "I was horrified. I couldn't imagine Kitty Shaw doing a thing like that. The W.S.P.U., indeed! But I came to it, and so will you."

"No, I couldn't." The mere thought of it repelled her.

"Then don't. You don't have to. Our movement embraces women of all strata of society, all ideas and attitudes. Believe me, we have lively arguments over tactics. Many of our members are thoroughly opposed to militant methods, yet they remain devoted to the cause of women's rights."

Sylvia could only sigh again.

"Believe me, if you don't want to demonstrate, there is plenty of other work to do. We need women to write letters, make speeches, or simply attend meetings. Just being physically present, even if you don't say a word or do a thing, is a big help. When we visit the East End or go to factory towns, we try to have a large group of women present. There is strength in numbers. Our speaker is likely to be listened to if there are women at her side, supporting her. We need you, Sylvia."

A LASTING SPLENDOR

"Why me, Kitty—when there are so many others?"

"It is women like you we need the most. You are the daughter of an earl and—"

"You know I'm not his daughter."

"All right, stepdaughter, but you live with him as though you were his own. You're already a P.B., a celebrity. Why, the newspapers are full of your name. And you are being linked to the duke you introduced me to last night. Attending the opera with the King's cousin, no less. Don't you see, Sylvia? If you join us, a thousand other women will too. If the celebrated Sylvia Hartley believes in suffrage for women, it will become—how else can I say it? It will become fashionable."

"Please, Kitty, I—"

"Sylvia, I sometimes think—in fact, I know, our most effective work is not what you saw me doing the other day. It is necessary, but we are at our best when we persuade. Sylvia, if you could persuade the duke, his friends, the many people you know—heavens, even your stepfather, of the simple justice of our cause, why, you would have done the work of a hundred street parades!"

Sylvia saw the bright eyes of her friend and heard the passion in her voice, but she was not moved. "If, as you say, the . . . the scene I witnessed last week is not effective, why did you do it?"

Kitty answered without hesitation. Obviously, she had practiced her arguments. "Because we must. No one ever just *gives* another person freedom—or power. King John was *forced* to sign the Magna Carta. A bloody civil war was fought to make Parliament supreme over the Crown. English, Scottish, Welsh men took to the streets to win suffrage for the common man." She smiled. "Now, it is the turn of women. Half the adult population of this country is disenfranchised. We will win the vote only if we fight for it. I wish it weren't so, but apparently the vote will come to us only when the streets are filled with women demanding it."

Sylvia sighed. "Is it so *terribly* important—the vote, I mean?"

"Oh, yes, Sylvia." She smiled. "Left to themselves, men have made a botch of things, don't you think? All this poverty, sickness, poor housing, illiteracy. I think women

A LASTING SPLENDOR

understand these things better. We won't begin to solve our social problems until women participate in government."

Sylvia opened her mouth to speak, but got no chance.

"The real reason we need the vote is to improve the conditions of women—our less fortunate sisters. Did you know the average pay of women wage-earners is only seven shillings and sixpence a week?"

Sylvia saw Kitty looking at her and knew she must answer. "No, I didn't."

"Well, that's what it is. There are women who have been driven to prostitution because they cannot earn enough to live decently. I think Emmeline Pankhurst says it best. When she was registrar in Manchester, she was shocked by the number of young girls who came to record illegitimate births. She often discovered the young girl's own father or some near male relative was responsible for the pregnancy, yet nothing was done to him. And if the desperate young mother exposed her baby so it died—or if it died from sheer hunger—the girl was hanged for murder, while the wretch who was the real murderer received no punishment at all. Women's lot will not change until we have the vote."

Another example came to her. "There was a case not too long ago of a woman who ran a brothel specializing in procuring young girls for degenerate men. She was sentenced to three months in prison—while we have had W.S.P.U. members sentenced to a year or more for simply demanding their constitutional right to petition the government. Women have been enslaved all these centuries because—"

"I'm not a slave, Kitty."

"Oh, but you are." Her smile came close to condescension. "Anything you have, any independence or freedom you possess, is a grant from some man. If he is rich and generous like Lord Linfield, you live well and your bondage appears painless. But if your father or husband—your brother, for that matter—is penurious or cruel, if he is drunk or lazy, if he gives you a life filled with babies, poverty and broken health from overwork, you feel your chains, your helplessness. In either event, you can do nothing about it. Women must have the vote. We must begin to be represented in the affairs of this nation. We must assume control of our lives, and our destinies."

Sylvia heard Kitty's voice rising, and she hardly wanted this conversation overheard by her mother or anyone in the household. Her own voice little above a whisper, she asked, "If, as you say, women ought to have the vote, how is parading in the street, being arrested, going to achieve it?"

"It will, Sylvia. There is apparently no other way. We've tried reason and persuasion. But Parliament will not act. Actually, our situation is maddening. If the issue of votes for women went before Commons, it would pass easily. But Prime Minister Asquith, Chancellor of the Exchequer Lloyd-George, Home Secretary Winston Churchill—he lost the election in Manchester two years ago over the bar-maid issue, you know—and other leaders of the Liberal party, will not let Commons vote. They are dead set against us. Lloyd-George calls us 'mewing cats' and Churchill says we are 'hen-peckers' and 'she-males.' Well, 'Madame' Markiewicz showed Churchill, she did. But in reality, it is this handful of willful, stubborn men that we are fighting. And we will fight. We will not surrender, if we must fill every jail cell in this country! If we must starve and be force-fed. If we must fill the streets with protest until the commerce of this nation is brought to a halt—that's what we'll do."

"Has that happened to you, Kitty? Were you a hunger striker?"

"Oh, yes, several times."

But Kitty said it so matter-of-factly, Sylvia thought nothing of it.

"Isn't it insane, Sylvia? The government will come to terms with Irishmen, Ulstermer, militant trade-unionists, but they will not give the vote to women. It's ridiculous!"

Sylvia desperately wanted to end this conversation, but she didn't know how.

"Every group in the country fights to protect its self-interest. Why, even the crusty old House of Lords is doing battle to protect its veto by defeating the Parliamentary Act. Why shouldn't women protect their interests?"

Sylvia tried to distract her by offering and pouring more tea, insisting she have another scone. Kitty accepted and bit into it. This seemed to have a calming effect on her. Smiling, she said, "Actually, I didn't come here to convince you of anything, Sylvia. I hardly expect you to say you'll join us right away. I just wanted to start you thinking. Will you?"

"Of course, but—"

"Don't give any buts now. Just think about it. I'll send you
some reading material. And I'd like to invite you to Clement's Inn, our headquarters, to meet some of our people.
You'll adore Emmeline. Oh, I know, the press makes her out
to be an ogre, a wild-eyed radical, a battle-ax. But she isn't.
She's the sweetest, most feminine and courageous woman I
know. You'll love her. And she'll love you—one of her
daughters is named Sylvia, you know."

Sylvia smiled. "I've often wondered what Mr. Pankhurst
must think of her."

"Oh, her husband died years ago, in ninety-eight, I think.
But if he were alive, he would be with us. He was one of
the early members of the Fabian Society, a socialist, I believe."

Sylvia remembered Arthur's description of the Fabian
Society. "Don't Fabians believe in gradualism, change
through peaceful means within the framework of government? Aren't they against revolution?"

"Yes."

"Then how do you equate throwing rocks, cutting telephone lines and—forgive me—disrupting traffic on Oxford
Street with gradualism? Sounds like revolution to me."

Kitty's smile was deprecating. "We don't want revolution.
We want Parliament to give us the vote. We must force them
to—"

Sylvia silenced her with laughter. "I know, I know. You
told me."

"I do carry on, don't I? I promise to stop—for now." She
stood up. "I must be going. We have a meeting today." She
paused, her eyes on Sylvia. "Whatever happens, whatever
you decide, Sylvia, I've enjoyed seeing you again, talking this
way. I was so pained when you were staring at me the other
day. I hope I'm not so hateful to you now?"

"You're not. You never were." So Kitty hadn't been
looking at her with loathing then, not at all. Moreover, she
had thought Sylvia hated her.

"I'm glad." She hesitated, her smile fading. "If I may I'd
like to ask one thing. If you cannot be for us, try not to be
against us."

Sylvia found herself unable to reply to that. She wanted to
embrace the other woman, but her limbs felt paralyzed.

"And if you have any questions, contact me. If you want to visit—"

"Actually, I do have a question."

"Yes?"

"What does your father think of all this?"

She smiled, a bit wanly. "Father? Why the poor dear has disowned me. Mother too. I'm quite out on my own, now."

Chapter Ten

The letter from Meg came just as Sylvia was leaving for her sitting. She read it in the carriage on the way, smiling often at the news and the sense of Meg the letter conveyed.

The first page was, predictably, a paean of praise for Brian Trout. Her new husband was a very good motor-car mechanic, and he was getting more and more work. Their financial situation was improving. They had bought a used bed, a real, honest-to-goodness bed with a tester and real mattress. Now Brian could get a good night's sleep. And they had found an old chair in a junk shop, got it for practically nothing, and were fixing it up. Brian would have a proper place for his leisure now. Next they hoped to find a garage, at least some kind of old building where Brian could work. They hoped to do this before the cold weather came. Brian couldn't continue to work outside too much longer.

Next came extravagant thank-yous for the clothing Sylvia had sent. Something was being done with every thread of it. She was herself the best-dressed young wife in Hornby, or would be when she got her figure back. Sylvia smiled. Meg had cut up a couple of the dresses, making a maternity gown for herself, even a shirt for Brian. Sylvia's eyes moistened as she read: "From the blue dress you sent, I made several outfits for our son. Brian insists we are to have a boy. Wants to name him Brian, Jr. I haven't told him, but I'm hoping for a girl. I want to name her Sylvia. You'll never guess who after."

There was a bit more from Meg, about her cooking and keeping house, how ecstatically happy she was. Only a sentence near the end disturbed Sylvia. "I'm feeling much better today. My stomach has decided to behave and the swelling in my ankles has gone down. I'm fine." Sylvia reread it, concern gripping her. Meg hadn't been well. A third rereading comforted her. She did say she was better now, fine in fact. A certain amount of discomfort was probably normal when having a baby. Was she going to a doctor? Sylvia was promising to ask her in the next letter as she arrived at Lord Charles' home.

Joshua Wainwright, Timothy Graves, Baldwin and many of the usual crowd were there to greet her, and Sylvia readied herself and quickly assumed her pose. All went well until a stranger entered and whispered in the painter's ear. He sighed, and laid down his brush, looking up at Sylvia. "My dear, I must ask a favor of you."

"Yes?"

"I can't possibly do justice to you or my work if I am being pestered by lovestruck swains. An artist much have *some* peace of mind. He needs concentration. These bloody interruptions must stop."

Sylvia was amused by his display of petulance. "What are you talking about, Joshua? I have done nothing to—"

"Not you, my dear Sylvia. That bloody horse captain, Waring."

She stiffened at the name.

"The young fool is pestering me to *death*, Sylvia. He wants me to speak to you on his behalf. Personally, I couldn't care less. If the idiot has done something to offend you, then he deserves your wrath. But he is pestering *me*. The man is outside just now. As an act of kindness to me, as a contribution to an artists' work, will you please hear the man's bloody apology? He is positively *abject*."

Sylvia was about to refuse when, quite to her surprise, she laughed. The idea of Philip Waring, the arrogant guardsman, being abject, was just too absurd. "I will see him, Joshua," she said, "but only as a favor to you."

"Thank you, Sylvia, a thousand thank-yous." He turned to the stranger who had begun it all. "Tell the blackguard he may come in."

Sylvia resumed her pose and sensed Waring's presence in the room before she saw him. The knowledge he was somewhere off to her left, looking at her, strangely excited her. But she refused to move a muscle.

It was Wainwright's voice she heard. "You wanted to apologize, Waring. Now's your chance. Get at it."

"But I can't apologize to someone who isn't looking at me."

"Then move over there where she can see you, you fool."

In a moment, he stood before her, all blond handsomeness in his uniform. His eyes were bright with admiration as he looked at her. This continued for some moments until, prompted by Wainwright, he finally spoke.

"My dear Miss Hartley, I have come to—"

"Joshua said you were abject. The mere thought of seeing a captain of the Royal Horse Guards abject amused me. I must say, you don't look a bit different."

He smiled. "But I am abject, Sylvia—totally bereft. The thought that my unfortunate remarks of last month so offended you has left me—well, I haven't slept a wink since."

Despite herself, Sylvia had to smile. "I can see that. You do look ghastly, captain."

He bowed formally. "I have no one to blame but myself. I'm serious, Sylvia. Please accept my apologies. I was rude, offensive and boorish. I know I do not deserve it, but I want nothing so much in this world as your friendship and regard."

His sincerity affected her. No more formal words of apology could have been offered. And from the lips of Philip Waring, the lady-killer of London—drawing rooms of the city would be buzzing within the hour. She should accept the apology, she knew. She would demean herself if she did not. Yet, she hesitated.

"In God's name, Sylvia, accept the poor wretch's excuses, so I can get on with my work."

She glanced at the painter, then at Waring. "I do, of course," she said softly.

Her words were greeted by applause and even a cheer or two from others in the room. Out of the hubbub, Sylvia heard the high-pitched voice of Timothy Graves. "Now you must tell us what this scoundrel did to you, Sylvia."

She knew she was blushing slightly from the attention, but

her aplomb did not desert her. "I shall not. An apology has been made and accepted. I no longer remember the incident."

She saw Waring smile and nod his thanks.

During the rest period, he came up to her. "I meant every word I said, Sylvia."

"I believe you, captain. You needn't repeat it." She smiled. "You realize, of course, your public apology is already known to half of London."

"I do." He laughed. "I've been behaving myself lately and the gossips are suffering for news, I'm told. Today should please them."

"It should be interesting to hear what the wagging tongues conclude you did to apologize for."

"Indeed." He grew serious. "I do appreciate your discretion. Knowledge of my . . . my unfortunate . . . proposal would be—well, embarrassing, to say the least."

"And for me too, captain. It shall remain our secret."

There was a moment of awkwardness before Waring spoke. "You look lovely, Sylvia. It does not seem possible, but you are ten times more beautiful than when I saw you in the country."

"Thank you."

He cleared his throat. "I don't suppose there is . . . you could—" He smiled. "May I take you to dinner, the theater perhaps? There is an excellent show at—"

"I'm afraid not, captain. I don't think it wise. I will be your friend—but only in the company of others. Do you understand?"

"Quite. The duke is—"

"Neither Lord Charles nor anyone else has anything to do with it. I just feel we should not be seen alone together."

He smiled. "Very well. I am fortunate to have an invitation to the ball your stepfather is giving this Saturday. I will see you then." He bowed and excused himself, but she found herself staring after him. A strange man. An apology was the last thing she had expected from him.

The Earl and Countess Linfield entertained so frequently, Sylvia rather took it for granted. But she could not help but become aware of the preparations for this latest ball. Lady Constance, quite in a tizzy, drove the staff unmercifully to prepare the house. Additional kitchen help was brought in to prepare food, and deliveries to the mansion in Regent's Park came daily. Sylvia, still estranged from her mother—she had had no apology from her, indeed had never discussed the incident with her—remained as aloof as possible, going about her affairs. Still, she was impressed with all the activity.

Friday evening, her mother came to her room, confronting both her and Clara. "Sylvia, I want you at your very best tomorrow night. This is our most important event of the season. *All* the leading people of society are coming. Winnie and I expect—"

Sylvia sighed as she interrupted her. "What is it you want from me, mother?"

"I want you to be your most beautiful, Sylvia. I expect you to be on your best behavior."

Sylvia was tempted to ask when exactly she wasn't, but she knew such a remark would only start a quarrel. "Yes, mother. Anything else?"

"I expect you to be my co-hostess. That means not giving too much attention to anyone in particular. You will, of course, be in the receiving line. I expect you to be your most charming—to *everyone.*"

"Yes, mother."

The Countess Linfield turned to Clara. "You will have her at her very best. You know the gown she is to wear?"

Clara curtsied. "Yes, mum."

As her mother turned to leave, Sylvia made a face behind her back. Why, oh why, had she been cursed with such a mother?

The following day, Clara obediently acted on her employer's command. She designed an intricate, even exotic coiffure for Sylvia, first washing and brushing her hair till it shone, then braiding and weaving the strands into a novel pattern atop her head. Yet, there was still enough hair to create a fall of curls behind Sylvia's neck. Clara was a genius. No doubt of it.

The gown she wore was certain to be a sensation, and Sylvia hesitated to wear it. For some time, Poiret had had a new vision of how women ought to look. The gown he made for Sylvia and sent by fast ship to London was startling, to put it mildly.

Sylvia viewed her image in the mirror with excitement

mingled with dismay. The gown was of thin, clinging satinet of the shade of green Poiret preferred for her. It had an extremely narrow skirt, with a short train in back and his now-celebrated slit over the left calf. What dismayed Sylvia was the near-total absence of a bodice. The dress was held up by thin straps at her shoulders, to which Poiret had attached flowing, capelike sleeves. There was virtually no back, just a huge V reaching almost to her waist, and practically no front, just a tiny well of satinet into which her breasts, pushed up and together with whalebone, nestled. Her nipples were barely concealed. The effect of the gown, Sylvia saw, was of height, slimness, a sort of flowing femininity because of the sleeves—and near nakedness. She could wear no corset, obviously—itself most shocking. Indeed, she wore no under-garments other than some new, thin, abbreviated pantaloons Poiret had come up with. As she looked at herself, Sylvia was torn between admiration for the loveliness of the gown, the daring, sensuous effect it created and uncertainty about whether she was ready to accept the sensation it would surely cause.

She glanced at Clara's reflection in the mirror. Her eyes were bright with wonder, delight and admiration. Sylvia had never seen such an expression in her eyes. "What do you think, Clara?"

"I think I have never seen such a gown." Her voice was husky with awe. "No one has."

She sighed. "I gather I must wear this?"

"Yes. The countess has promised Monsieur Poiret you will wear whatever he creates for you. He expects you to wear this tonight. I'm told he will have an emissary here to see if you are wearing it."

Sylvia shrugged. There was no point in arguing. The day had not come when she could choose her own clothes. "At least, I won't go unnoticed. Should I wear a necklace?"

"I think not, miss. It will . . . distract. Just earrings, I think."

Clara began to fasten long, pendant earrings of tiny emeralds alternating with diamonds. They were her mother's, but Sylvia often wore them. The task was just finished when there was a careful rap at the door. "Come in," Sylvia said. The door opened and she was surprised to see her stepfather.

It was a rare appearance by him. and she was startled. "Lord Winnie, do come in."

He was staring at her, open-mouthed. Finally he spoke, "My dear Sylvia, I have never . . . !"

"Nor I." She looked at him seriously. "I'm told I have no choice but to wear this."

He continued to gape at her. "My dear, you look utterly lovely."

"I hope so."

"My dear, my dear, I'm so pleased. You make me proud."

"Thank you."

Somewhat imperiously, he motioned for Clara to leave. When the door was closed, he said, "I wanted to have a moment alone with you, my dear."

"Of course. Won't you be seated?"

"No, this will only take a moment. I wanted to appraise you of the importance I place upon this evening." She waited for him to continue, but he seemed just to stand there, staring at her. "My dear, I cannot tell you the pleasure you have brought this old man, having you here, watching you grow up into the stunning creature you are."

She smiled her thanks.

"As you know, Sylvia, our country is in what I believe to be great peril. Sooner or later—sooner, I fear—we will have war with the Kaiser. He seems determined, and we must be prepared. But we will not be if we are divided at home. These bloody Liberals are determined to wreck this country with their social measures, their income taxes. They even want to pay members of Parliament for doing their public duty—if you can imagine such a thing. But their worst treachery is the Parliamentary Act. Those blackguards, Asquith, Lloyd-George and that young Churchill, are determined to emasculate the powers of the House of Lords, take away our historic veto. I am determined to do all in my power to stop it. Do you follow what I'm saying, child?"

Sylvia did not. She was looking at him, seemingly attentive, but she had tuned him out almost at the first syllable. All of this was familiar, and she cared nothing about it. "Yes, I'm listening."

"I am holding this ball tonight at the request of a small committee of Lords. Your friend, the duke of Glouston—and

I am so delighted by your friendship with him—is a member. We hope to gather here tonight the most important people involved in this controversy. Oh, there will be no politics discussed. We have all agreed on that. Not one word about the Parliamentary Act will be mentioned. Our hope is that these men in the House of Commons who are so deadset to pass the measure will come to realize the folly of their ways. We have failed to convince them through argument. Our hope is that at least a few of them, when they see how we live, the type of people we are, will realize that it's sheer treason they want. Does that make sense to you, my dear?"

"I suppose." She was becoming more attentive.

"We really have staked a great deal on this evening. We are hoping they will see that, although we come from different classes of society, all of us have a community of interests. We all want the same thing, the grandeur and safety of our nation. Now is no time to disturb our traditions."

He paused and Sylvia knew she must speak. "I will do all I can to help, Lord Winnie. But I don't know what it is you want from me."

"It's very simple, my dear. As you know, the House of Commons is equally divided between Tories and Whigs. The Liberals rule through a coalition with the Irish nationalists and the Labour members. We are taking steps to undermine the Irish. We have made certain offers which we believe will be effective. None of that conerns you. But the Labour members are something else—radicals all, sent among us by the bloody trade unionists. They would destroy the Lords. Some even want to be rid of the King. Many are Marxists—even Bolsheviks. Horrible, I tell you."

He paused, restraining himself from a harangue. "Our real effort tonight is toward these Labour party members. We must get to them in any way we can. Do you understand?"

"Yes." She sighed. "No, I don't—at least, what is it you are asking from me?"

"Sylvia, you are an attractive young woman—extremely attractive. I have witnessed the effect you have on young men." He laughed. "Indeed, if I were forty years younger and not your stepfather, why, I'd court you myself. I know for a fact Lord Charles is quite smitten by you."

She looked at him levelly, trying not to react, waiting. All this was leading somewhere.

He continued. "I would simply like you to give a bit of extra attention to certain people tonight. Ramsey MacDonald is one. You may know him?"

"No." But, somehow, the name was familiar.

"Well, he's the leader of the Labour party. I would like for you to make a special effort to smile at him, talk to him. You know better than I how you ladies do these things. Will you?"

The idea was a little repugnant to her, but she said, "If you wish."

"I do, Sylvia. I have not asked much of you, my dear. You have been like a daughter to me, a good daughter who has brought me much pleasure. Is it too much for me to ask you to go out of your way to help me tonight?"

She was touched. "Of course not. I'll do all I can. You ask no more than any good hostess should do."

"Exactly. I'm glad you understand. I mentioned that blackguard MacDonald. There are others. I won't burden you with the names now, but when we are in the receiving line—you will be next to me—I'll make a point of using the word *Labour*. If I say so and so is from a Labour constituency, that will be a signal that he is of special interest to me—and thus to you, I trust."

"Yes, I understand."

He hesitated, clearing his throat. "There is one person in particular, Sylvia, a young Labour MP, who seems to have great influence. We hear he is most articulate in stating these ridiculous views of the socialists. A spellbinding orator, I'm told. We figure if we can get him to change his mind, we might defeat this Parliamentary Act. And we feel we have a chance with him; the chap is really a traitor to his class. His father is a member of the gentry down in Dorset. We believe—know, in fact—that blood will prevail in the end. This young whipper-snapper will come to his senses." He smiled. "Particularly, if he meets a most attractive young woman like you. With your beauty . . . in that gown, well, I submit that the poor fellow doesn't stand a chance."

She saw him smiling and tried to force a return smile. It was all so boring to her, these political machinations.

"I think you get my meaning, Sylvia. I would not be averse, not at all, if this young radical were to—to put it bluntly, fall in love with you. Of course, I don't expect you to have anything to do with him—I would quite forbid it, in fact—but you know what I mean. Ladies have a way of charming young men."

Labour MP. Young radical. Dorset. Suddenly, she was apprehensive. No, no, it couldn't be. . . .

"I know this is a great deal I ask, my dear, but I must. I know you will not fail me." He laughed. "Think of it as something you are doing for your country."

Finally, she could speak. "What is his name?"

"Didn't I mention it? His name is Arthur Wicklow. I'll point him out to you."

Chapter Eleven

Sylvia was almost numb with apprehension as she stood in the receiving line. Fortunately, she was required to do little more than smile, extend a hand, curtsy a few times and say a few words of greeting. She roused herself to greater warmth in greeting the duke, Philip Waring, others she knew. And she performed admirably when introduced to the Labour MPs and others Lord Winnie wanted her to charm. Her smile was most dazzling and she concentrated on making eye contact, as well as trying to listen and express a desire to chat with the person a little later. It was enough. Her stepfather was pleased.

But her mind was filled with dread at Arthur's coming. What would he think? What could she say to him? At first, she tried to convince herself that he would be amused. He would realize that she had been pretending to be someone else, her former maid, a clever joke. He would laugh and say she never had fooled him a bit. But in her heart, she knew it wasn't so. Arthur Wicklow was going to be hurt, angry, and she was headed for disaster. This fear led to new hope. She would explain how it happened. Surely, he would understand and forgive her. He was a decent, compassionate man. But he had been taken in, had wanted to marry her. What would he think?

Thus, her period in the reception line ground on remorselessly, her stomach roiling, her nerves rubbed raw. There was one advantage. Her apprehension made her forget, for the most part, the sensation her gown was causing. Women gaped at her, men stopped to ravish her with their eyes and the whole room buzzed with talk about her attire. Ordinarily, she would have been ill at ease, but in her extremis of worry, she was scarcely aware of the effect she was causing. All she could do was glance ahead to see who was next in line.

Mercifully, it ended, and the receiving line was breaking up. Lord Winnie said to her, "I thank you, my dear. You were simply splendid."

"Is that all?"

"Oh, you mean the young man I mentioned? I fear he has not deigned to honor us with his company tonight. Too bad. He missed a most attractive young woman."

She sighed, and that act seemed to expel from her all the tension and worry of the last hour. He hadn't come. Merciful God, he hadn't come! She had escaped. He must know who she really was and be too angry to come. Thank God, she wouldn't have to face him. For the first time, her smile was one of true happiness. "From what you say about him, Lord Winnie, I suspect he wouldn't have noticed me."

He smiled. "Perhaps. These serious chaps often miss the important things in life. Go, my dear, enjoy yourself. You've earned it—although I hope you'll not refuse the attentions of those I pointed out."

"I'll do my best, father." As far as she knew it was the first time she had ever been able to bring herself to call him that. But so great was her relief, the word just came out.

He stared at her a moment, obviously moved. "Thank you for that, my daughter." Then he smiled away his own emotion. "Now, go favor these young men with your charms."

She went first to the duke, who was standing with a group of people. She recognized a couple as members of Commons, one Liberal, another Labour. The duke was obviously politicking. When he saw her, he said, "Are you w-well, Sylvia? You l-look very p-pale."

She smiled. "I'm fine, milord." At the last moment, she remembered not to be too familiar with him in front of others. "I sometimes get a little tense during formalities. So many names to remember."

"I q-quite understand. Re-remind m-me to teach you a f-few t-tricks of the t-trade, so to sp-speak."

She smiled. "I'd indeed be grateful."

She remained there a bit, chatting with the group. She made a special effort to ask a question or two of the Labour MP, a short, burly man, obviously recently removed from a factory or mine and greatly ill at ease. He seemed grateful to be spoken to, but discomfited that it came from a beautiful, scantily-dressed young woman.

In a few minutes, Philip Waring was at her side, bowing, saying, "Will you do me the honour of the next dance, Miss Hartley?"

"Of course." Actually, she was grateful for the opportunity to escape what had become stultifying boredom.

As he led her to the dance floor in the adjoining ballroom, she felt his hand against her back. It was shocking, then she realized he had no other place to put it. She looked up at him and smiled. He was terribly handsome, and as he moved her into the circles of a sedate waltz, she felt his power and magnetism.

"You will have to forgive my hand, Sylvia, but there is—"

"You could have worn gloves."

He laughed. "And miss touching your skin? Not on your life."

She found herself laughing too. "Captain Waring, you are incorrigible."

"I am more than that." His face was suddenly somber. "At the risk of having to make a thousand public apologies to you, I will have my say. I would trade all the women I have known for you this night. You are absolutely captivating, irresistible."

It was not his words alone which were so unsettling, but the seriousness with which he said them. Bristling a little, she replied, "Why, because I am half-naked?"

Still serious, he said, "No, although your charms are obvious. It is the wearing of such a dress which captivates me. I can think of no woman in this city who has the *savoir faire* to be attired as you are. Oh, there are many who would wear such a garment. But, believe me, there is no one who could be so exquisitely, boldly womanly, yet remain demurely genteel at the same time. I salute you, Sylvia."

She stared at him. He was a charmer, a very sauve charmer. Finally, she spoke, her face unsmiling. "I think no apology will be required this time, captain."

He smiled broadly. "Thank the Lord for that—although I would have made it. I meant every word, Sylvia, rehearsed it, in fact, as I watched you. Couldn't take my eyes off you. As one of His Majesty's officers—" He smiled. "If not a gentleman, I appreciate daring and courage and the flair to pull it off. You have my admiration."

She smiled woodenly. "Thank you."

"Any other woman would look brazen, a tart, obvious and—"

"No more, Philip, or I will have you back at the studio."

He laughed. "All right, I surrender. I always go too far."

"Yes, you do."

"But, please, let me take just one more risk."

"If you must." It was so easy to fall into this languid, flirtatious pattern. She felt herself endangered, but somehow could not stop.

His hesitation was only brief. "I wish more than anything else in my life that we were beginning fresh—that that bloody morning at Downhaven had not happened."

She was affected by him, the closeness of the dance, the music, his handsomeness, the power of his words. But she made no reply. *Watch out, Sylvia,* an inner voice seemed to warn her.

The music was ending. Quickly, he said, "Can we . . . start over? Can I see you alone, just the two of us?"

The music ended. The dancers were leaving, a few staring at them. As he returned her to the duke, she said, "Thank you for the dance, captain." She saw amusement and admiration in his eyes. At least, she was not making a fool of herself with him.

It came as a cruel surprise. Over an hour had elapsed. She had quite forgotten her earlier apprehension. Then, her stepfather was at her shoulder, coming up from behind. "Here is someone I want you to meet, Sylvia."

She turned. *He* was there.

"Sylvia, I want you to meet one of our new, young MPs, Arthur Wicklow. I'm told he has a brilliant future in the House."

Both stood, rigid, staring, mouths open.

"Arthur, my beloved daughter, Sylvia Hartley."

She saw the shock in his eyes, then recognition, aware-ness . . . pain.

"What is it with you two? Do you already know each other?"

For a moment longer, they stood there, Sylvia unaware her fingertips had come to her mouth, in a womanly reaction of surprise. Arthur recovered first. He bowed to her, but, oh, so stiffly, his manners returning. "No, I have not had the pleasure of meeting *Miss Hartley.*"

Lord Linfield completely misread the situation, figuring Wicklow was having a normal reaction to Sylvia's beauty and the extraordinary gown she wore. But why was Sylvia staring at him? "Have you lost your tongue, my dear?"

"I'm sorry." She struggled a moment longer for her poise, then said, "How do you do, Mr. Wicklow? I've heard of you, of course."

"And I of you, *Miss Hartley.* The papers are full of your name."

Winnie, suddenly hearty, clasped them both on the shoul-der. "Good, you will have something to chat about. I'll leave you alone to do it."

The silence between them was terrible, a long, lingering ordeal, which she had no words to end. She had expected anger from him, and she could have dealt with that. But she saw something far worse in his eyes, anguish and great pain. He felt hurt—betrayed. Why hadn't she written him, explain-ing? Even the most foolish letter would have spared him this moment. She saw him look downward, his gaze lingering a moment at her bosom—oh, this monstrous dress—and the pain in his eyes augmented.

It was he who broke the silence. His words had a terrible cutting edge. "Do you use the name Meg Gwynne always? Or do you have various pseudonyms?"

She felt the wound. "Oh, Arthur, please, let me explain."

He looked around, measuring the distance to other guests and the chances of being overheard. He seemed to stand more erect, covering himself in his dignity as he spoke in low tones. "There is no need to explain, Miss Hartley. I quite understand. The upper classes find a life of idleness boring. Diversions are necessary. I hope you enjoyed . . . slum-ming."

Again, the edge cut into her. "Oh, God, Arthur, it wasn't that at all."

"I recommend that you lower your voice, Miss Hartley. You may be accustomed to being a public spectacle—" The quick lowering of his gaze added insult to the words. "But I am not."

Her sigh was a desperate one, as she tried to calm herself, to remember the explanation she had rehearsed so often in her mind. It had seemed so easy to her imagination. "I know you're hurt, Arthur, angry—and I don't blame you. But—" Suddenly, the words were not there, making her frantic. "Oh, God, it's so hard to explain."

"I'm sure it is." His sarcasm cut her to the quick.

"Arthur, there really is a Meg Gwynne."

"I know. I met her."

"She is my dearest friend, my former maid."

"How democratic of you, Miss Hartley."

Frantic, unable to think, she was nearly incoherent. "That day . . . Meg got married . . . I was . . . I wanted . . . when I was with you . . . I wanted . . . Meg was on my mind . . . it just came out . . . then I couldn't . . . you thought . . . ." She let her voice trail. The words made no sense, she knew.

His dignity, his exaggerated efforts at good manners, mingled with his hurt to give him a terrible coldness. "Perhaps it is I who should apologize, Miss Hartley—for being so gullible. I had thought you most unmaidlike. Your demeanor, your speech, your apparel did not suggest a servant. When I discovered Meg Gwynne was an entirely different person, I should have suspected—I should have realized you were really Sylvia Hartley, that renowned beauty of which I had read in the papers. Again, my apologies. I should have spared us both this moment."

She could feel her eyes smarting, the tears coming. "Arthur, please, I never intended . . . ."

"I know. I understand. It was impossible for you to be seen with me. Aren't you linked with some duke or other? To take a false name was necessary."

False. The word pierced her heart. She fought the tears, sucking in gulps of air, swallowing to try to remove the blockage in her throat. She couldn't cry, not here, not in front of all these people.

"And I suppose I should thank you. I do. It was a most—"

Through swimming vision she saw the pain in his face. "A most . . . let's say I found it educational. I will never be such a fool again."

He was turning to go. She reached out, touching his arm, stopping him. "Please, don't hate me, Arthur. I can't bear it."

He stared at her a moment. "I don't hate you, Miss Hartley. I—I—" The pain was there and the coolness, but mostly resignation, contempt. "I just feel very sorry for you."

He left her standing there, biting at her lips, struggling against her tears. She stared after him, blinking frequently, as he strode, erect, his shoulders squared back, out of the ballroom, out of the house, out of her life. She felt herself gasping for air, swallowing hard in an effort to hold back sobs which gathered in her throat.

"M-my dear. W-What has h-happened?"

She felt a hand on her arm and slowly turned to face Lord Charles. Through unshed tears, she saw the concern on his face. Then there were others crowding around her, all startled, questioning. It seemed to her she didn't know any of them.

"W-what did that ch-chap d-do to you?"

Still, she stared at them, blinking and swallowing in her struggle for composure. All she wanted was to be away from these people, to run, anything to be gone from this place. But she couldn't. She was Sylvia Hartley, a P.B. She was at an important ball, surrounded by London society. *I just feel very sorry for you.* Oh, Arthur, Arthur!

Someone offered her a handkerchief. She took it, dabbing at her eyes.

"Shall I s-send someone a-after that m-man?"

You may be accustomed to being a spectacle, but I am not. Oh, God.

"No, Charles, it's all right."

"B-but wh-what did he d-do?"

A moment longer, she dabbed at her eyes, then she managed a sort of smile. "He did nothing, Charles. It's all right."

"B-But something u-upset you."

She had to say something. "He brought me unfortunate news. My former maid—w-we were very close—is ill." How easily lies dribbled from her mouth. *Do you always use the name Meg Gwynne? Or do you have other pseudonyms?* He couldn't think her so base!

"I'm so sorry, my dear." The words came from Lady Pamela Leighton, a long time friend of Lord Winnie's.

"Thank you. I was upset. But I'm all right now."

"I do hope so. We all thought something serious had happened."

Sylvia looked at her sharply. An illness to Meg, a mere servant, was not serious. It seemed to Sylvia she was seeing this woman, whom she'd known for years, for the first time. She was, at that moment, hideous to her—old, wrinkled, trussed-up in a corset, trying to look young, dripping in jewels. Meg was worth two of her. Meg was better than any of them—far better than herself. Meg had given herself to a man she loved—and married. She had been sincere, commited. *I quite understand. Diversions are necessary.* "Lady Pamela, she is my dearest friend." *How democratic of you, Miss Hartley.*

"I'm sure she is, dear." It seemed to Sylvia she had never heard such condescension.

"W-Would you like some w-wine?"

She turned to Lord Charles. He was holding a stemmed glass of champagne toward her. Suddenly, she saw him with new eyes too—short, half-blind, stuttering dumbly. Pathetic. Grotesque. "Thank you, Charles." She took the glass, raising it to her lips, sipping, swallowing. All these people were hideous. She was surrounded by ugliness. "Please, all of you, don't fuss over me. Enjoy yourselves." She moved back, away from them. She had to get out of there. The throng around her gave way. She smiled and turned away, as though going to mingle with other guests.

"Heavens, Sylvia. You're making a spectacle of yourself."

It was her mother, beside her, trying to whisper while smiling. But it seemed more a hiss. Sylvia turned to her and saw a woman who was frantic, overbearing and ugly. Her dress was a nightmare. Her breasts, thrust out and pushed up, looked like cow udders.

"Yes, I suppose so, mother."

"What happened?"

"You just said it. I was making a spectacle of myself."

"Well, try to behave. I will talk to you later."

"Oh, I'm sure you will, mother." *To take a false name was necessary. False, false, false! Oh, no, not false. . . .*

For the next few minutes, she tried to mingle with the guests, do her duty by Lord Winnie. But it was impossible. Everything seemed so ugly and futile and stupid to her. The room was too hot and she felt it shrinking around her, suffocating her. She had to get out of here or she'd have a screaming fit. *False. False. No, Arthur, true. . . .*

"Would you like to dance?"

She turned to Waring. He had a sardonic half-smile on his face. "Yes, anything."

He led her to the dance floor, guiding her into a slow waltz. But the movement didn't help her. She wanted to go faster, be whirled about, become dizzy.

"What you need, my dear, is a drink, a real drink. Whisky or brandy, I think. Not champagne."

"I do, do I?"

"Yes, if I were your doctor I would prescribe it."

"And where do I get it? At your place, I suppose?" How easily this banter came to her. How she despised herself.

He smiled. "If you wish."

She looked at him, so handsome, so sure of himself. "What I really need is some air."

At once, she broke away from him and walked as fast as she could in her narrow skirt across the ballroom, through the conservatory and, opening French doors, stepped onto the veranda that led down to the garden. The October air was chilly, but she didn't care. It felt so good to breathe in clean, fresh air. She looked up at the sky. There was a full moon speeding past tufts of gray-white clouds, creating deep shadows across the formal garden below. It was a beautiful night for England, but Sylvia could see only desolation. It was a world gone banal, futile, trivial, wanting to cry out in pain. *Milton, thou shouldst be living at this hour,* she remembered from her St. Regis days, *England hath need of thee; she is a fen of stagnant waters. . . .* But it was not Milton she was thinking of, no . . . it was Arthur Wicklow.

"I believe the Americans call it a harvest moon."

His voice surprised her. She hadn't realized Philip Waring had followed her.

"You might even call it heavenly." He laughed softly.

She turned to look at his smiling face. Confused, she couldn't think. She turned away from him, looking back at the moon, filling her lungs deeply with air, her chest expanding as she did so, shrinking as she exhaled.

"It's a magical night, Sylvia. Everything seems made of pearl."

She looked around, trying to see, but she could detect no beauty, not tonight. Then she felt something touch her shoulders. It startled her and she turned abruptly toward him, thinking he had put his arm around her. But he had not. He was in shirt sleeves. He had wrapped his uniform jacket around her and now held it fast under her chin. "You must be cold. You're trembling."

She was looking up at him, then he was bending and she felt his lips on hers, gentle, soft, tender, as though he were kissing a child. She wouldn't have expected this from Philip Waring. "I'm sorry," he said. "A saint could not resist you in the moonlight."

Still, she stared at him, blinking, once, twice. "You want *me*, Philip?" Perhaps he wasn't such a bad person, after all. His voice sounded kind, soothing.

"You know I do."

Still, she stared at him. She was numb, unable to think. Then he was kissing her again, more ardently now, moving, demanding, as though forcing passion into her. Yes, he wanted her. This man, so attractive, so masculine, wanted her. Arthur didn't want her. . . .

"Sylvia, I—"

She put her fingertips to his lips to silence him, then on tiptoe reached up to brush her lips over his. Yes, it felt good. Consoling.

"Is there a way out of here to the street?"

She heard the urgency in his voice. "Yes." She pointed down through the garden.

He grabbed her hand and pulled her after him. So fast did he walk, she had to run to keep up, clutching his coat over her shoulders, taking the tiny, mincing steps that her skirt permitted, her heels clattering on the brick path. She was out of breath by the time they opened the gate and reached the street, where he hailed a waiting hansom. Unseen by her were a pair of dark, Italian eyes, watching from an upstairs window.

Chapter Twelve

He took her to his bachelor's digs, a small flat, very masculine, the sitting room decorated with trophies for horsemanship and sharpshooting, photographs of the regiment and fellow officers.

She stood near the door, watching as he turned up the lights. He still had gas, not the new electricity. Her mind was hardly functioning, but she was aware that this was the second time she had been alone with a man. However, this was no thatched cottage, and the man turning up the lights was not Arthur Wicklow, shy, uncertain, protesting his desires, but Captain Philip Waring, the city's most famous man-about-town. Still, out on the veranda, he had seemed so nice. . . .

Most of what happened was now familiar to her, the joining of mouths, the linking of tongues, the soft, sweet caresses to eyes and throat and shoulders, the letting down of hair, the undressing, the praising of her beauty, the expressions of desire and wonder.

But there was a significant difference. Sylvia knew at once she was in the hands of a master. Waring was adroit and there was no mistaking it. She could feel it in his hands. There was self-assurance in his every touch. And, oh, the things he knew. When he kissed her, his fingers surrounded their joined mouths, creating a dark tunnel for his passion. She could feel his lips moving, not just against her lips, but his fingers as well, and the kiss became much more private.

intimate, hot with mingled breaths. She felt buffeted with sensation even before his tongue, sweet and smooth, began to lick the corners of her mouth, the inner surfaces of her lips, making her quiver with passion as it finally, ultimately, plunged inward.

Philip Waring, captain of the Royal Horse Guards, seemed to take command of her and her body. No movement was wasted. Nor did he hurry. There was a pace to everything, deliberate, lingering to permit each sensation to be savored—but never quite enough. His timing was flawless. She was still enjoying the kiss, eager for more, when it ended, and she was left to tremble as his lips brushed her eyes, nose, temples, ears, the corners of her open, craving mouth, her throat, neck, shoulders, returning again and again, but never often or long enough to her mouth. She ached, but always he slipped away, leaving her tormented with desire. She had an overwhelming need to be filled, but for a long time he would not satisfy her. Once, she caught his tongue, feverishly sucking it inside her mouth, but he pulled away.

Oh, the things he knew. His hands were at her breasts, caressing, stroking, rubbing, kneading. He made twisting motions to the hardened nipples, and when he finally bent to her, he rolled the hard, risen tips between his teeth to make quick, tender, biting motions. He did not hurt her, unless unbearable pleasure could be construed as pain. Her whole body seemed to jerk and twitch, and she had to hold on to his shoulders just to stand. It was an onslaught of ecstasy, and she knew noises were escaping her, moans, gasps, a groan, even a small growl.

Again, it didn't last long enough—nothing ever did—and he was on his feet, carrying her folded over his shoulder, his free hand caressing her buttocks. Momentarily, she thought it an insensitive way to carry her, like she was so much baggage, but she didn't care. Nothing seemed to matter anymore. And when he laid her on the bed, crossways so her feet dangled toward the floor, she saw him leaning over her, smiling. "I've been with a lot of women, Sylvia, but none like you."

Then, leaning on his hands, he lowered his head and kissed her. It was the sort of deep, prolonged kiss she had been hungering for, and her lips and mouth yielded to the pleasure of it. But it was not enough. She wanted more . . . much more. He left her mouth and slowly came down her body, kissing her throat and shoulders, biting her nipples, sliding his face and mouth, gently, slowly, over the bowl of her stomach, down, down. Eagerly, she felt his touch at her inner thighs, spreading her yielding legs.

"Please, Philip, hurry. I . . . I can't stand . . . any more."

Then, for just the smallest instant, she knew what was going to happen. Some thought, disbelief, perhaps protest, tried to enter her mind, but it was lost as his tongue found her. She cried out. It was as though her whole body had been rent open. It left her hanging on the edge of the unbearable, seemed to dissolve her. She felt utterly devastated by the licking and sucking, the exquisite torment of his mustache against her most sensitive place. She lay on her back, her arms extended above her head, moaning in surrender to ecstasy. Then his hands were at her breasts, his fingers searching out her nipples, finding, rolling them gently.

Her climax was just about to overwhelm her when he was gone, and she cried out, "No." She opened her eyes. He was standing above her, smiling down at her. "You like that, don't you?"

She could hardly speak. "I—I . . . never . . . knew."

"You do now." He was bending over her, moving her lengthwise on the bed, then he was on his knees over her, spreading her, probing. His entry made her scream with pleasure, then scream again and again as he descended into her, and she felt expanded to her limits, plumbed to her depths. With his first movement she began to tremble, then shudder, ever more violently, until she was writhing under him. For a time, it would seem to let up, and some order would come to her senses and she would hear him above her, "God, you can't be . . . such a woman you are." Then it would begin again, the shaking, the numbing of her brain, the anarchy of her senses. It seemed to happen over and over, even as she heard him groan and felt his release within her.

She would have no clear memory of what happened after that, just fleeting impressions of his pulling her from the bed, leading her into the sitting room, making her drink vile-tasting whisky, coughing, gagging, but feeling heat coursing through her body. He had photographs, momentoes, he showed them to her, they meant nothing to her but seemed to excite him, and that was exciting to her. At the same time, something inside her cried out in protest, cried, *Arthur, Arthur,* and she didn't want to be there, but he kept touching her, her breasts, between her legs, expertly, like the master technician he was. *False, false,* she thought, then again, *Arthur, Arthur,* but the thought of Arthur, the cottage, her innocence and his . . . it was all too painful, and she surrendered to mere sensation . . . she was so tired . . . she couldn't . . . if only he'd leave her alone. . . .

She had no memory of its stopping, but of awakening. He was standing over her, offering her a glass. Whisky. She shook her head.

"I put some water in it. It'll taste better."

She lay there a moment, alert now, conscious of her utter weariness, the aches in her body. Slowly, she rolled to her side and managed to sit on the edge of the bed, taking the glass and drinking. It tasted awful, but her throat was dry, sore. She looked at him. "Did I faint or what?"

He laughed. "I don't know. Call it what."

"Was I out long?"

"Only a few minutes."

"Is that normal?"

He laughed. "There's nothing normal about you, Sylvia."

"What do you mean?" She was frightened.

Again, he laughed. "You really don't know, do you?"

"No. Tell me. You wanted to educate me, once."

"So I did—but it is you who have educated me. Many can't do once what you did over and over. You're something special—and I should know."

"I couldn't stop. I wanted to but . . . but you wouldn't let me."

His laughter cascaded over her. "That's what I mean. Darling, to look like you do and do what you do—Sylvia, you are going to conquer the world."

She looked at him. "I don't want the world."

"You will—and you'll have it." He lifted his glass and swallowed deeply from it. "I've always regretted being the fourth son of an impoverished viscount. An army career hardly makes one wealthy. But I've never regretted my modest means so much as now. I just wish I had enough money to afford you." He smiled. "Alas, I shall have to content myself with the memory of this fantastic night with you—and the hope for others."

Suddenly, she saw him, really saw him and herself. He was naked. So was she. This was the second man she had made love with—and she hardly knew either one, let alone loved them. One hated her for it. This one—She sighed. At least, he didn't hate her.

"I'd better go home."

"Yes, it's late. I'll take you."

Slowly, she arose from the bed, feeling the ache in her legs, the tiredness of her body, and began to wash herself and put on her immodest ball gown. As she wound her hair around her head, she heard him say, "You know how remarkable I think you are, don't you?"

"You told me."

"I've never known a woman like you, Sylvia." He hesitated. "But I wasn't the first, was I?"

She glanced at him, but said nothing.

"Wicklow?"

Still, she did not answer.

"Was I . . .?"

She put the last of her pins in her hair, mostly to get rid of them so she wouldn't have to carry them. "Yes, Philip. There is no comparison. You're a most expert lover. Only. . . ."

He waited for her to finish. "Only what?"

She looked at him levelly. "I don't know. I'm sorry, I just don't know."

"He was better?"

"No, just different." Ready at last, she went to him, stood on tiptoes and brushed his cheek with her lips. "Besides, it's not a competition."

He laughed, if only to hide his embarrassment at his sudden insecurity.

It was after four in the morning when she arrived back home, wearing a baggy sweater of his against the chill. There was a moment of panic when she realized she had returned without a purse and had no key. She would have to wake up the house. But the door opened as she walked up the steps.

"Clara! You're still up?"

"I knew you had no key, miss. I dozed in a chair till just now. I heard the carriage."

"Thank goodness for that." As she walked across the foyer and mounted the steps, sudden fear gripped her. If Clara knew she had gone off, everyone else did too. She was ruined.

In her room, getting out of her gown, she said, "Did anyone say anything, Clara?"

"About what, miss?"

"About my . . .?"

The question, never quite asked, was answered by the entry of Lady Constance, hair in braids, wearing a voluminous robe. She was angry and imperious. "You *will* tell me where you were tonight?"

Sylvia sighed. "Of course, mother. That's Captain Waring's sweater. That should give you a clue."

"I *thought* so. How could you *do* such a thing?"

Sylvia's anger flared. "That's what you wanted, isn't it? You and he planned for my—what's the word? Oh, yes, deflowering." She saw the surprise on her mother's face. "You ought to be most pleased with yourself."

It took a moment for Lady Constance's aplomb to return. "I have no objections to your seeing Captain Waring—if you are discreet about it. Did anyone see you?"

"I don't think so. I'm sure we'll find out if anyone did."

"How can you be so *stupid,* Sylvia—running off in the middle of our own party?"

Sliding into her nightgown, Sylvia shook her head. "Now, *that* I can agree with. It wasn't the smartest thing I've ever done."

"I should say not. The *excuses* I had to make for you."

"What did you tell people?"

"Everyone believed your story about that dreadful girl. Thank goodness for that. I simply said you were upset, had a headache, asked to be excused and were in bed. God, Sylvia, how could you do this to me?"

"Did they believe you?"

"I don't know. I hope so. I'm not sure about Lord Charles. He—he looked . . . very strange."

Sylvia had a sudden image of Charles. He'd be hurt. But she was too weary to cope with it now. "Mother, I'm exhausted. Can we talk tomorrow?"

Her question was ignored. "I have no objections to your

being . . . being *with* Captain Waring, Sylvia. He is . . . can be . . . most dashing."

Sylvia turned to her maid. "I'm going to let my hair, makeup, everything go, Clara. Goodnight."

"Goodnight, Miss Sylvia."

"But you must be discreet."

Sylvia sat on the edge of the bed, kicking off her slippers. "And what does that mean?"

"It means you may have a . . . a dalliance with him. He is . . . most—"

"Dashing, didn't you say?"

Sylvia's scorn was unnoticed or ignored. "You will not become *involved* with him, of course. You must marry the duke. You will do nothing to jeopardize that."

From under the covers, Sylvia said, "If I agree, will you then let me sleep?"

The countess glared at her. "You are incorrigible, Sylvia. That's all there is to it." But she did turn on her heel and leave.

The light out, Sylvia lay abed, but despite her fatigue, sleep would not come. Arthur. Poor Arthur. It seemed an eon ago that he had confronted her, discovered who she really was, her cruel deception of him. Then she had gone off with Waring. She shuddered, images flicking across her mind. Why Waring? Then she remembered. Unable to cry when Arthur left her, she had numbly gone out into the moonlight. Everything had been so desolate. Waring came. Why had she gone off with him? Suddenly, she sat up in bed, staring into the darkness in horror. Because he was *there*. It needn't have been Waring. It could have been *anyone.*

Self-knowledge stabbed at her. Two men. She had given herself to Arthur, a total stranger. And she had even gone back a second time. Tonight it was Waring, practically a stranger. Certainly, she didn't love *him*. There had been no love in what they did. It had just been . . . And there was the duke. God, Charles.

It happened without warning. She was staring off into the darkness, then she was crying. She covered her face with her hands and shook with sobs. She couldn't help it, nor could she stop. Some corner of her mind asked what she was crying about, and her answer was *everything,* the loss of Meg, her treatment of Arthur, the horrid night she had just spent, the certain knowledge of the kind of person she was, a future as bleak as a Scottish moor. She couldn't remember the last time she had cried so. Probably not since her father died.

Chapter Thirteen

Another who didn't go to sleep right away was Clara D'Angelo. She lay in bed, staring at the darkness, planning what must be done. Events had come quickly, faster than anticipated. She must make her move immediately.

Even as she'd watched Sylvia run down the garden path with Waring, Clara had sensed the girl's danger. Stupidity. Utter folly. A scandal could ruin everything. At once, Clara had moved to protect Sylvia. She went downstairs, and from the butler and others learned a young man had showed up at the ball and said something to Sylvia which upset her, something about Meg, her former maid. Clara didn't believe it. A terribly thin excuse, but it would have to do. She waited a few moments until the countess was with a knot of people, then went to her. She curtsied, then said, "Miss Sylvia is not feeling well, mum. She has gone to bed and asks you to convey her apologies to the guests." There were appropriate expressions, "Oh, the poor child," "The news really upset her," "Tell her just to rest." It had worked—unless someone else had seen her with Waring.

Clara had waited nervously for Sylvia's return, knowing she had no key. As the hours wound on, she had even dozed off in a chair. But she was awake to open the door and hustle her young charge inside.

Clara had no need to hear Sylvia's admission to her mother to know what had happened. Sylvia's dishevelment, her near exhaustion, the odors of her body, all spoke volumes.

Abed in the darkness, Clara could now feel relieved. Apparently, Waring, if not Sylvia, had been discreet. Chances were they had not been seen together. Waring's disappearance at the same time Sylvia had "gone to bed" had surely been noticed. Tongues would wag. But there would be no proof. And the gossip just might be to Sylvia's advantage. Everyone would wonder if she really had spent a night with Waring. Such speculation would not harm her.

Clara smiled. Yes, Sylvia Hartley had this night taken a major step toward a brilliant future. Her innocence had surely been lost with Waring. And the lateness of her return indicated she had captivated him. Yes, Sylvia was far better for this night.

Except for her mother. In the darkness, Clara cursed the Countess Linfield as a meddler—and far worse. *You must marry the duke.* Clara knew it would be over her dead body. The duke was only a starting point—Sylvia Hartley would be the greatest courtesan the world had ever known. In the morning, Clara would speak to Sylvia. It would take care, tact. The girl was bossed enough by her mother and resented it. The proper method was to suggest, lead, guide. The child certainly needed guidance.

It was midday when Clara entered Sylvia's room carrying her breakfast tray. She greeted her, then opened the drapes. Sylvia awoke hard, her body aching in several places. With difficulty, she sat up and pulled the tray over her lap. The food did not appeal to her. All she really wanted was to be left alone to think.

Clara remained blessedly remote, tidying up the room, laying out a gown, drawing a bath. When she returned to the bedside, it was to say, "You're not hungry this morning, Miss Sylvia?"

Sylvia looked at the tray. She had nibbled a corner of toast and swallowed half a cup of tea. She could not remember doing it. "No."

"Your bath is ready. A nice hot soak and a massage will make you feel better."

Sylvia glanced at her. Clara seemed a little strange, but there was nothing Sylvia could put her finger on. She got out of bed—Lord, but she was sore—and languished in the tub. A half-hour later, she was face down on her bed, submitting to a heavenly massage. As her maid kneaded her flesh, it almost seemed to lift the soreness and tension out of her. No doubt about it, Clara was a much better masseuse than Meg had ever been.

"May I have a few words with you, miss?"

"Of course."

Clara's hesitation was contrived. "I know it is not my place, miss, but I thought, perhaps, just this once, I—"

"For heaven's sake, say anything you wish, Clara. I don't know where anyone's place is, not yours, certainly not mine." Hands were at her thighs now, and Sylvia winced with pain.

"Miss Sylvia, I couldn't help but overhear your conversation with the Countess Linfield last night."

"Yes. What about it?" She heard deep sighs above her, the sounds of a woman in distress. She raised her head to try to look at her. Unable to see, she rolled over to her back. "Well, Clara?"

"It is a great liberty, miss, I—"

"In the name of God, speak, Clara. I won't bite."

Clara hesitated a moment more. Yes, this was going well. "I heard your mother, I mean the countess, say you are to marry the duke. I'm sorry, but I think it would be a mistake."

Sylvia laughed. "Is that what you've been trying to say? Of course, it would be a mistake. The duke is hardly—"

"I don't mean that, miss. The duke is extremely useful to you, and will continue to be. You should see him, and, well, cultivate him. But do not marry him."

Sylvia was genuinely surprised. "What are you saying?"

"I'm saying I don't believe marriage to the duke or anyone else would be wise now—or in the near future. It would be a . . . a waste of your . . . your talents."

Sylvia stared at her. She had hardly thought Clara interested in her at all.

Clara saw the expression, quickly averted her eyes and resumed the massage. "If I have offended you, miss, I'm—"

"You haven't offended me. I just don't understand."

"I'm just trying to say, Miss Sylvia, that now that you have captivated Captain Waring, you'll—"

"How do you know I captivated him?" Sylvia's surprise was clear in her voice.

A LASTING SPLENDOR

"I don't see how you could have failed to." She raised her head and spread her lips into a slight smile. "The lateness of your return would indicate that—"

"And my appearance too, I suppose."

"Oh, no, miss, you looked beautiful, as always."

Sylvia gave a deprecating laugh. "Go on."

"I—I'm just trying to point out that after last night, you will be the toast of London, miss."

"You mean the scandal?"

"No, I think not. You left and returned discreetly. I'm just saying that, as you see the captain from time to time, people will realize you have ensnared—" Her smile was broader this time. "His reptuation is well known, miss."

"And so will mine be, doubtlessly."

"You will receive only approbation, miss. Your status as the leading P.B. of London is now assured."

Sylvia sighed, dismissing such talk. "What has all this to do with the duke or my mother?" She saw Clara hesitate and distress rise on her face. "Go on, tell me."

Clara sighed. "The duke is obviously in love with you. When he learns of Captain Waring, I'm sure he will be . . . well, jealous. But that should not be too great a problem. I think you can continue to captivate him too. He may well become even more enflamed."

"Heavens, Clara, what are you saying?"

"I'm saying, miss, don't marry him as your mother wants. Encourage him, enflame him. I think he may be brought to the—" She feigned distress, as though the words were difficult to say. "What you want him to do is set you up in your own home."

Sylvia stared at her, then suddenly sat upright, pushing Clara's hands away. "What kind of woman do you think I am?"

The words came quickly. "The only kind of woman you can be. With your beauty, your body, you will rank with the greatest courtesans in history. With Aspasia, Cleopatra, Madame du Barry."

"Courtesan!"

"Yes. Once in every few generations, a woman comes along. She has no money or title, but with her beauty and brains she rises to the heights of wealth and power."

"You're not serious!"

"Oh, but I am, Sylvia." Sylvia did not notice the absence of "miss" or the subtle change from servant to advisor it connoted. "I could have taken a position with a thousand women in London or Paris or Rome. I chose you. No other has your opportunity."

Sylvia simply couldn't believe what she was hearing.

"I'm telling you to use the duke, but not marry him. If you do, you will become just another attractive woman of title. Your future will be wasted. What you must do is get him to set you up in your own house. Then you will be free of your mother. You will have the independence to do as you wish."

Sylvia stared at her. "I never. . . ."

"I know you've never thought in these terms. But you must. I will help you."

With firmness, Clara pushed Sylvia down on the bed, rolled her on her stomach and resumed the massage.

Sylvia lay there, her mind filled with confusion. She couldn't think, not with this woman's hands on her, stroking, rubbing, kneading. Part of her wanted to tell her to stop, but she could not. It was pleasant, relaxing. Once again, Sylvia surrendered her mind to her body.

The massage seemed to go on for a long time, leaving Sylvia weak, her mind numb and vacant. Fluids were poured on her skin, an astringent to close the pores, oils to soften, colognes to sweeten. Finally, Sylvia asked, "Why do you do all this?"

"To make you beautiful."

"Am I beautiful?"

"Oh, indeed. But nature sometimes needs a little help."

More minutes passed in silence, then Sylvia spoke again. "I heard all you said, Clara."

"If I offended you, if I took too much liberty—"

"No, It's not that. I—I just . . . don't know. I'm . . . confused. I—I need someone to talk to."

Sylvia was on her stomach and Clara knew she could afford the luxury of a triumphant smile. "Yes, miss." Her voice was as proper and aloof as always.

"I'm not sure I know what a courtesan is, Clara."

"A courtesan is a woman of great beauty, charm and intelligence. She is a companion to men who hold wealth and power. Often, because of her charms, she influences those men. History is full of women who wielded great power in this way."

"She is their mistress? The men's?"

"Sometimes."

"Then she is a harlot, a prostitute."

"No. A courtesan is not a harlot. The difference is as great as between the pathetic and the sublime."

Suddenly, Sylvia rolled over and sat on the edge of the bed, looking up at the dark-haired maid, seeing her severe, dignified countenance. "You want me to be a courtesan. Why?"

A slight smile came to Clara's face. "If you will come, miss, I will show you."

Clara walked across the bedroom and Sylvia followed, stopping as directed in front of her mirror. She turned to look at her image. She was in profile, naked, her body glistening from the skin treatments.

"Look at yourself, Miss Sylvia. Really look. There is no more glorious figure than yours."

Sylvia looked, saw, knew.

"Stand on tiptoes, pull your stomach in."

Sylvia obeyed, saw the slendering of her legs, the tightening of her stomach, the rise of her breasts. *You are going to conquer the world.* Waring had said that.

"You drive men wild with desire."

Sylvia turned from the image to look at Clara.

"Was it not so last night?"

The words stabbed at Sylvia. Images sped across her mind. She met the level gaze of her maid, but could not answer.

Clara smiled. "Sit. I'll brush your hair."

Obediently, Sylvia sat, still naked before the mirror, watching herself as Clara raised the brush and began to stroke her hair. "Because I am beautiful and have this body, I am to be a courtesan?" She looked up, saw Clara's reflected smile.

"Did you not enjoy yourself last night?"

Again the images. "I don't know. I'm not sure."

"By reputation, Captain Waring is most expert."

"Oh, yes, he's that, all right." Sylvia saw herself smiling, never having consciously willed it.

"Does he want to begin a liaison?"

"I—I don't know. I'm . . . not sure."

"Don't. See the captain, let everyone know he is at your feet. Use him for your own reputation—your own pleasure, perhaps. But be discreet, always."

"You sound like mother."

"I do not mean to. The countess wants you to have a title and wealth. I want much more than that for you."

Sylvia was suddenly annoyed. All this was too intimate. She wanted it ended. "I don't want what either of you want. I want happiness."

"And how do you achieve that?"

"I—I don't know. Does anyone? I had thought of love, marriage, children."

"And had you thought of boredom, fat, wrinkles—a life of humdrum, ordinary, of wasted opportunities? Oh, you could marry the duke quite easily. You would be a duchess, a very wealthy woman. But would you be happy, then?"

"No. He is not what I had in mind."

"Captain Waring?"

Sylvia smiled. "Hardly."

"Someone poor, a rose-covered cottage perhaps, romantic daydreams?"

The word *cottage* triggered a memory of Arthur Wicklow, a pang of loss, remorse. "I—I don't know."

"I understand, Sylvia, you—"

"You don't understand at all. What I want—this morning especially—is a sense of decency, some virtue, some . . . some self-esteem."

"Those are but attitudes of the mind, Sylvia. Decency, virtue are for those of little talent who delight in poverty or the ordinary. Would marriage bring you decency?"

Sylvia looked at the face in the mirror in some surprise. "Why, yes, of course." She saw a sly smile on Clara's face.

"I fear not. A wife, particularly the wife of a rich man, is purchased. She is a possession, as surely as a house, a car, a fine-gaited horse. In return, her husband makes demands upon her, as urgent as those of Waring last night. She must submit—and when he tires of her and seeks novelty with a courtesan, a mistress or worse—she must submit to that too. Who then, is, better off? The wife or the courtesan?"

Sylvia could only stare at her.

"Self-esteem? Last night you captivated Captain Waring, did you not?"

Sylvia saw the bright eyes of her maid. "I—I suppose so . . ."

"What a triumph, child! A man who can have any woman wanted you. Have you no sense of your own power? You should be filled with pride. How remarkable you are! And you enjoyed yourself. What was enjoyed the first time can be a second . . . a third. . . ."

Sylvia stood up, turned and stared at Clara, her eyes wide with fear. Then she went to her bed and put on her robe, clutching it around herself.

"I understand, Sylvia. What I propose is novel to you. It smacks of indecency. You perceive it as a threat to the *real* you." Her smile was a mingling of tenderness and condescension. "Perhaps you will be lucky and find a man who will give you everything you want. But until you do, you have no choice but to pursue the course which began last night."

Sylvia could only stare at her.

"I think you will come to enjoy life. You have captured the duke and Captain Waring, the two most eligible bachelors in London. And, of course, there is a third."

Sylvia gasped. "How do you know?"

"Anyone can see it, my dear. Your stepfather adores you. He gives you everything, far more than he needs to." She smiled. "You see, my dear, you can get men to give you things by your mere presence. Your smile, your personality is enough. You need not do more—unless you want to for your own pleasure. Such talent you have. How fortunate you are!"

Clara picked up the brush and went to her, brushing a little, then beginning to braid. "This would be easier if you sat again."

Sylvia obeyed, then heard Clara say, "But Lord Linfield is up in years. He may be generous with you when he dies, but he cannot provide enough. You must think of your future. You need a house of your own. Independence is a woman's most precious possession—and it doesn't matter how she gets it. Believe me, I know."

Chapter Fourteen

The rest of that day, a Sunday in early October, was the last free time Sylvia was to have for a long time, although she had no way of knowing that. She basked in leisure, taking a nap, walking in the garden, trying to think.

She was unsuccessful. Too much had happened too quickly, and she spent most of the time remembering and assimilating, rather than interpreting and deciding on a course of action. She remembered Arthur and the horrid, hurt look in his eyes, the dignity with which he had walked out of her life. She had not intended to hurt him, But she had. She had not meant a dalliance only, but—why else had she given her name as Meg? God, it was awful. She shoved it out of her mind.

Philip Waring. Remembering, she blushed, inwardly if not visibly. The things he had done, she had allowed . . . wanted? How could she have? Standing there in the garden, she shuddered with revulsion. Would everyone know? Was she ruined by a single night? What kind of a woman was she? Bitterly she answered, the kind of woman who enjoyed it. Or had she? Strangely, it had been unsatisfying. Her senses had been satiated, her body exhausted. But why had she felt so depressed afterwards? Why had she cried? It had been different with Arthur. . . .

Unable to cope with these thoughts, Sylvia's mind switched to the remarkable conversation with Clara. *Courtesan.* Sleeping with men in return for what they gave her. Living by her body. Again, she shuddered. She couldn't. It wasn't possible.

But what had Clara said? *You have no title and no money. There is no other choice for you. Get a house of your own. Independence is everything.*

"My dear, I'm so glad we can be alone."

Startled, Sylvia turned to see her mother descending on her.

"The fall flowers are lovely. Why don't we sit over there and enjoy them?"

Right then, her mother was the last person Sylvia wanted to see, but, sighing, she accompanied her to a wrought-iron settee, painted white.

"I hope you did not take offense at what I said last night, Sylvia?"

"Not at all, mother." Actually, Sylvia could remember little of what her mother had said.

"I really am pleased you have . . . have made the . . . *acquaintance* of Captain Waring." She laughed nervously. "I—well, lately, you have been—well, preoccupied." Again, a nervous laugh. "I can understand why, now. Captain Waring *is* very attractive. And so . . . so. . . ." A third nervous laugh. "Well, now you know what I mean. Isn't it good to be able to talk about these things, dear, mother to daughter?"

Sylvia was unable to say a word.

"All I was trying to suggest last night—I mean, early today—" Another tittering laugh. "Oh, you *naughty* girl, Sylvia." She patted Sylvia's hand playfully. "I mean for you not to fall in love with Waring. He's—well, see him as often as you like, but—" She turned to look at her daughter. "You aren't in love with him, are you?"

The whole discussion disgusted Sylvia, yet she knew she must answer. "No, I'm not in love with Captain Waring." It was the truth.

"Good. Oh, mind you, I can understand that you might, a young girl with—he is very demanding, quite clever, really. But I'm glad you have good sense. The duke is the one for you."

Sylvia sighed. "Yes, mother."

"Now that you have . . . have tried your wings, so to speak, perhaps you will find the duke more attractive. At least, you will know how to entice him. I know for a fact, Sylvia, he is quite *mad* about you."

"Yes, mother."

The Countess Linfield stood up. "I'm glad we've had this little chat, Sylvia. I ask that you not waste your opportunity with the duke. He will make you a duchess. Think of it, a *duchess.*"

"Yes, mother."

The words signified not agreement but desperation to be rid of Lady Constance. It worked. A few minutes later, Sylvia went in and napped, missing tea. She had supper in her room and retired early. Her last thought before sleep was a wish that Meg were there to talk to. Meg would know what she ought to do.

It was with apprehension that Sylvia went to Lord Charles' the next day for her sitting. She would discover exactly how much damage her impetuousness with Waring had done. And she would have to face the duke. She cringed inwardly. Once before, she had seen hurt in a man's eyes. She couldn't bear it again.

He was not there when she arrived. Who could blame him? As she entered the salon and took her position before Wainwright, she sensed at once the change in her stature. The increased numbers of people in the room, the repartee, the teasing, the thinly-veiled references to her and Waring, all had meaning. She could take offense at nothing, but she knew there were no secrets in the British capital.

"My dear, I have never seen you look lovelier." It was Timothy Graves. "You're positively blooming. I wonder what might have caused it?"

"I was walking in the garden yesterday, Timothy. The mums were in bloom. Perhaps that is the cause."

Graves' laugh was luminous. "I'm sure that is the case, dear Sylvia. What else could it be?"

Lord Charles entered. She couldn't see him, but the sudden hush in the room told her he was there. She turned from her pose, looking for him. He was standing a little apart. There was no mistaking the hurt in his eyes, but it was carefully concealed behind a mask of dignity. Oh, God, she had done it again. Then she realized there was something else in his eyes. What was it?

She smiled at him. It was all she could do. She tried to make her smile say everything: a warm greeting, an apology, a request for forgiveness, an assurance of her regard for him. He looked at her a long moment. Silence seemed to stretch through the room. Then he smiled back at her, his wan, boyish grin. Silence continued.

Wainwright broke it. "Now that you have greeted our patron and benefactor, Sylvia, perhaps we can get on with our work."

The following laughter and hubbub told Sylvia all was well. Later, she went to Lord Charles, smiled at him again, touched his hand as they exchanged greetings. She felt his hand on her arm, leading her to a place of relative privacy. "M-My d-dear, it is s-so g-good to s-see you."

She smiled again. "Has it been so long, Charles? It *was* only night before last."

He laughed. "M-Much too long, my d-dear." He hesitated, but only briefly. "I-I was h-hoping you m-might ac-accompany m-me to the th-theater tonight."

Sylvia's mind raced. There was something on for tonight, but she couldn't remember. Nor could she conjure up an image of her calendar. But she knew that this night, of all nights, she should not refuse this man. "I'd love to, Charles."

"G-Good." Again, he hesitated. "I-I thought w-we m-might have a little s-s-supper afterw-wards."

Again, she smiled and touched his hand. "I'd like that, Charles."

"J-Just the t-two of us, I thought."

Now that was unusual. She had never had a late night tête-à-tête with him. But, again, she couldn't refuse. "Splendid."

She sensed the conversation was over, smiled and turned to go back to her place before the easel. He surprised her. "Sylvia, I-I would l-like to ask a f-favor."

She turned. "Anything, Charles, if I can."

A modicum of distress rose in his face. "W-Would you w-wear the dr-dr-dr—" He couldn't get the word "dress" out. "The g-gown you w-wore Sa-Sa-Saturday night?"

She looked at him sharply, puzzled. It was one thing to admire a woman's apparel, another to seek to control it. But her friendship with the duke was strange in several ways. She had learned never to interrupt or prompt him, no matter how difficult his speech. And she had learned, also, not to question him. She could only smile. "People will think it the only one I own. But, if you wish, Charles—of course, I'll wear it."

That afternoon, tea turned out to be a rather large affair, with several people dropping in. Most of the talk centered on Saturday's ball. Sylvia knew these people were really hoping to learn what else had happened that night. When would this gossip subside?

In the middle of tea, she was called to the telephone. It was Waring. "I thought about coming over, but reluctantly thought better of it."

"Thank you for that," she said.

His laughter came clear and distinct over the line. "You are quite the sensation of London, you know."

She said nothing, couldn't.

He went on. "Never fear. It's all talk, speculation. Nothing can be proved."

Still, she said nothing.

"Are you there?"

"Yes."

"I'm just trying to reassure you."

"Thanks. I need it."

"Can I see you tonight?"

"I'm going to the theater with the duke of—"

"Lord Charles. Good. That is the thing to do, I think. When can I see you?"

"I don't know. I must go now."

"All right. But soon."

Sylvia told Clara of her change in plans, asking her to phone and make some excuse for her not attending the dinner party marked on her calendar. Then she told her to press and lay out the green ball gown. She saw the questioning look in Clara's eyes. "Lord Charles especially asked me to wear it. I feel I must oblige."

"But—"

"I don't know why he wants it, Clara. I didn't ask. He didn't say."

But Sylvia really did know why. The second expression in his eyes, the one not understood at first, became clear when he asked for the daring dress. Clara knew why too. "Do you think it wise, miss?"

Sylvia sighed. "Clara, I haven't known what is wise or unwise for a long time."

"But, Sylvia, the duke—do you think it wise for you and he—"

"Clara, please, don't. I am uncertain of his intentions. And I have no idea how I'll react when I do know." She sighed. "There is no point in speculating now."

Clara smiled. "I'm sure, Miss Sylvia, you will do what must be done—and do it extremely well."

"Thank you for that, Clara."

The maid extended herself in preparing Sylvia for the evening, her mind made up that if the duke were going to press the issue this evening, it might be for the best. Doubtlessly, he knew about Sylvia and Waring. Clara smiled to herself. At least, he was not quitting the race. And his eagerness could be translated into something of value—a great deal, perhaps.

Clara struggled for a few minutes, trying to think of some subtle way to reinforce in Sylvia's mind the need for a house of her own. Then it came to her. "My," she said, "there were many people to see you at tea today."

"I doubt if it was me they—"

"You underestimate yourself, Sylvia. It was you they visited. And when you have your own establishment, there will be many more gentlemen callers."

Sylvia looked at her, but said nothing.

When she was nearly dressed, her mother came in for her nightly inspection of Sylvia's appearance. "Sylvia, you can't wear that again. You just—"

"I know, mother. The duke specifically asked me to wear it."

Lady Constance elevated her eyebrows. "Really? Why I never!"

"I couldn't refuse him."

Lady Constance smiled, her eyes suddenly bright with excitement. Obviously, the duke, now jealous of Waring, had in mind a seduction. "Of course, you couldn't refuse if that's what he wants. You should do *everything* Lord Charles wants."

Sylvia purposely avoided looking at her mother.

The duke of Glouston came for her in an immense Rolls limousine. The back where they sat was entirely private, partitioned off from the chauffeur and footman who sat in front. The privacy made her nervous, but nothing happened. Indeed, they rode to the theater mostly in silence. The duke disliked small talk and she was used to that. He didn't even take her hand. That too, was usual. Lord Charles was so shy, so inhibited and vulnerable, he had hardly touched her in all this time, except inadvertently. For this she was grateful. He held no physical attraction for her, none at all.

If he wanted what she feared, she would not, could not. She would refuse him, say or do anything to avoid what she could think of only as repugnant. Yet, she knew that would not be easy. If he knew about her and Waring, or even suspected. . . . Oh, he did know. She'd seen it in his eyes. *Oh, God!* He wanted as much. If she refused him, having given herself to Waring, he would. . . . Oh, why, why had she ever? Why hadn't she thought of the consequences?

With effort, she forced herself to control her inner panic. She would try to find some way to refuse the duke without hurting him. But if that failed, if he became hurt or angry, never speaking to her again, so be it. She had survived the hurt to another man. She would live with this one. No matter what, she would not give herself to the duke this night.

At the theater, it seemed to her there were signs to justify her apprehension, the frequency with which Lord Charles touched her arm or her bare back in guiding her to and from the box. None of this was unwarranted, but it was now more meaningful, somehow. Mostly, she could see his intentions in his eyes. She knew that look now. And she sensed that in the darkened box he was watching, not the stage, but her—and her half-exposed breasts. She purposely avoided turning to smile at him as she might previously have done.

She feared the ride to his home in the darkened Rolls. But nothing happened. He did not even hold her hand. Still, there was the chauffeur up front. That would inhibit him. They entered his home, she fearfully. Again, nothing happened. He had arranged no tête-à-tête. The usual complement of servants was present. Champagne was served. For a few minutes, he took her on a tour of his gallery. He was a serious collector of art and quite catholic in his tastes. Renoir, Cézanne, Toulouse-Lautrec and other impressionists hung beside a Titian, a Gainsborough, an El Greco and a small Rembrandt. All were mingled with portraits of preceding dukes of Glouston and their duchesses. Then they sat to supper in the dining room, he at the end of a long table, she to his right. Servants were everywhere. She refused to let down her guard, however.

"H-How did you like the p-play, m-my dear?"

It had been *Major Barbara,* by George Bernard Shaw. She hadn't seen it before. "I loved it, Charles. I was greatly moved."

"M-Moved? B-But it was a c-c-comedy."

"I know. But I thought the author had a serious intent."

The duke laughed. "Oh, yes, the satirist is usually most serious." How quickly his stutter went away; it did, sometimes, when he was speaking of books or the arts.

A full supper was served, including two wines. Not until the cognac was poured and the decanter placed on the table, did the butler ask if there would be anything else.

"Yes, W-Wuthering. Will you b-bring me that b-box from the b-b-buffet?"

The butler, moving with dignity, brought a wooden box, richly inlaid and decorated with mother-of-pearl, placing it at the duke's left. It was perhaps two feet long, a foot or so wide and about two inches high, with a hinged lid.

"Will there be anything else, milord?"

"No, Wuthering. And thank you for the excellent repast."

Despite her curiosity about the box, Sylvia could not fail to notice the clarity of the duke's speech. Strange, how his stammer came and went; but, then, since the ball everything seemed strange to Sylvia, somehow.

Chapter Fifteen

When they were alone, the duke, apparently ignoring the box, turned to Sylvia. "My d-dear. I-I kn-know—" He stopped and swallowed, struggling to gain some measure of control over his speech. "I-I asked you to w-w-wear this d-d-d—I mean, g-gown . . . I-I h-had n-no r-r-right, but—"

Sylvia broke her own rule against interrupting him. "I didn't mind, Charles. It's just—" She smiled wanly. "It is not my most modest, that's all."

"It b-becomes you, S-Sylvia." He said it looking at her face, not averting his eyes downward, for which she was grateful. "I m-m-meant to s-say, I a-a-asked you—" His affliction was now terrible, and he stopped in frustration. "P-Please, for-g-give m-me. I-I—" He reached for his snifter of cognac.

"You needn't hurry, Charles. Just try to relax."

He swallowed from the glass and set it down. "Thank you, Sylvia." He managed that much. "I-I am n-nervous."

"Don't be, please. We are friends now." Suddenly, she realized why he must be nervous. Good Lord, he would think she was encouraging him. She must be more careful.

"Yes." He breathed deeply a couple of times, then managed to speak with more success. "I saw you S-Saturday n-night. You w-were so lovely."

"Thank you."

"I-I have b-been w-wanting to g-give you s-something for

145

s-some time. S-Saturday night, I th-thought of wh-what it m-might be."

He stood up and opened the box, extracting an item of jewelry from it. Sylvia could only stare at what he held in his hands. "M-May I?" He came around behind her chair and draped a necklace around her throat, deftly fastening it behind her neck. She looked down, speechless, and brought her left hand up to feel the gems, for she could not see them clearly.

"May I use the mirror?"

"B-By all m-means."

He held her chair for her and accompanied her to a gilt-framed mirror which was on the wall across the table from her. She gasped, for she wore the finest necklace she had ever seen. It consisted of chains of tiny diamonds, pure and sparkling, linked into a series of three circles. In the center of each shimmering circle was a round, faceted emerald, each more than a half-inch in diameter. Hanging below, into the valley between her breasts, was a massive emerald on a pendant, also round, measuring perhaps an inch and a half in diameter.

Sylvia could not believe it. "Charles, I've never—"

"I w-want you to have it, S-Sylvia."

She stared at it, wide-eyed. "But I can't possibly, Charles, I—"

"Is it t-too old-f-fashioned?"

"Oh, no, it's beautiful, but, Charles, such a gift! It must have cost a fortune."

His laugh sounded nervous. "Not to m-me. It was a g-gift to my g-g-great-grandm-mother, the th-third duchess, I b-believe—or the f-fourth. I f-forget which."

"A family heirloom? I can't possibly."

"I b-believe the duchess re-received it as a g-gift from—" His laugh was again nervous, "—some a-a-amorous p-prince—French, I think, m-maybe Italian. It d-doesn't m-matter. W-We have b-boxes of these th-things. I w-want you to h-have it."

She looked at him in the mirror behind her. "Oh, Charles, I. . . ."

He smiled. "Wh-What g-good are they in b-boxes? They sh-should be w-worn—by a b-beautiful w-w-woman."

She looked at the necklace in the mirror. Her chest was

shimmering with diamonds, glowing with cool, green emerald fire. Never had she seen such a necklace. Then she looked at his reflection, seeing the pride, happiness and benevolence in his face. Impulsively, she turned and kissed him warmly, her arms around his head, her lips pressed against his. She had surprised him. He was stiff, wooden, his mouth hard. Then she felt him tremble, his hands clasped at her back, and she realized what she had done. She hadn't meant . . . hadn't intended.

Quickly, she broke away from him. He smiled nervously, obviously embarrassed, then turned away from her, back to the box on the table behind him. "There's m-m-more, I b-believe. This is p-part of a s-s-set."

To her consternation, he turned to dangle a pair of earrings before her. They matched the necklace, a two-inch string of diamonds with others clustered around an emerald at the bottom. Again, she could only gasp.

"T-try th-these."

She took them, an act of wonder rather than possession, turning back to the mirror. She removed her mother's baubles and fastened the precious gems to her lobes. As she finished, he was holding out a matching bracelet, perhaps an inch wide, all of diamonds and studded with a row of emeralds in the center. He took her left wrist and fastened it to her. She was still looking at it wide-eyed, feeling she couldn't breathe when, in the mirror, she saw a tiara, again in diamonds and emeralds, in his hand. She took it, wordlessly.

"I d-didn't know h-how to t-tell you to w-wear your h-h-hair." He gently lifted her arm. "P-Please t-try it."

She raised her arms and, with minimal difficulty, attached the tiara to her hair, seeing the bracelet sparkle against her wrist as she did so. She lowered her arms, looking at herself in the mirror in awe, scintillating with the most beautiful array of jewels she had ever seen.

Behind her, she heard, "I th-thought they w-would g-go with . . . your d-d-d—gown. I s-see n-now the e-e-emeralds m-match your eyes."

She looked at him in the mirror. His eyes were almost as bright as the gems. "I've seen these before, haven't I?"

"No, I-I—"

"Yes, in the painting." She turned and, nearly running, unmindful of her jiggling, went back to the gallery. It took only a moment to find the painting—a large, formal portrait of a regal-looking woman. She was wearing these same jewels. The artist had not done them half justice.

Lord Charles came up behind her. His voice distinct he said, "She was very beautiful, wasn't she?"

Sylvia looked at the painting. The woman was blonde, wearing an antique gown of white satin, very décolleté. "Yes, she was."

"H-Half of Europe w-was at her f-feet. K-Kings, p-princes wanted her. Wh-When she chose the duke, m-my f-forebear, the m-man who g-gave her these j-j-jewels was h-heartbroken."

She turned to him. "I can't accept these, Charles."

"Why? D-Don't you like th-them?"

"You know I do. I've never seen anything so beautiful. But I just can't, Charles."

"But you m-must. Th-There is no one m-more b-beautiful to w-wear them. The d-duchess would w-want it."

She felt a choking in her throat. "I can't, Charles, I can't." Abruptly, she turned and, again half-running, went back to the dining room.

She was over the box, her head turned, removing an earring, when she heard behind her; "Please, Sylvia. I-I a-ask for n-nothing—only that you a-a-accept these as a t-token of my f-f-friendship."

The motions of her fingers stopped and she turned to look at him. "You mean that, don't you?"

"Yes."

She bit her lips, searching for the right words to say. "But, Charles, these jewels are worth a *fortune*. You can't just *give* them away."

"T-They are m-mine to do w-with as I p-please."

"But, Charles, it's too *much*. Such a gift is—"

"I w-want you to have them, S-Sylvia."

She felt consumed with emotion. "Oh, Charles. . . ."

"That French c-count or wh-whatever—" He laughed. "I-I kn-know h-how he f-f-felt."

She surrendered then, running the few steps which separated them and embracing him. But she did not repeat her earlier mistake of kissing him. She just hugged him, her arms around his neck, her cheek against his. For the first time, she realized how short he was. In her heels, she could almost see over the top of his head and her breasts were not crushed against his chest, but against his shoulders. Again, she felt him tremble, then something else, his head turning, lifting toward her, seeking her mouth. He found her, his lips parted now, soft, moving hungrily. She stiffened, but did not pull away. Somehow, she couldn't. But she gave only her lips. She felt nothing.

It lasted too long. Then he was away, eyes bright, saying, "Y-You m-must know, S-Sylvia, h-how m-m-much I've l-longed to d-do that."

"Yes, Charles." She felt him raising his lips to hers again. Once more, she felt she could not refuse. It was only a kiss, after all. He was even more passionate this time. She felt only strangeness in kissing down rather than up to a taller man, the unusual location of her breasts against his body. Then his tongue came into her mouth, smooth, tasting strongly of cognac. She shuddered, but he only mistook it as passion and intensified his movement.

She broke away, her cheek against his, trying desperately to find a graceful way to check his passion.

Against her shoulder, his chin pressing into the soft flesh of her breast as he spoke, she heard, "Y-You m-must know I-I c-c-c—what I f-feel for you."

"But, Charles, you said—" Immediately, she felt him stiffen. He had read her mind. Instantly, the whole nasty sequence of words was known to her. If she finished that sentence, he would be hurt, angry. Waring would be thrown up to her. Names would be hurled, hateful words said.

She pulled back to look at him, seeing the hurt already beginning in his eyes. She bit her lip, waiting, hoping something, anything would happen to prevent this. Nothing did. She sensed his pain growing, his turning away from her. *Oh, what was the use?* She leaned down and brought her lips back to his, mouth open, accepting the inevitable. Instantly, he responded.

Depression came to her like a physical blow. What was the use? His response to her night with Waring was to want her himself. He knew what kind of woman she was. To insure having her, he made the gift of emeralds. That was more than Waring had done; but, then, Waring was more confident of his personal attractions.

When he began to lead her upstairs to his bedchamber, she

thought of making a protest about the servants. Then she thought better of it. What did it matter? Everyone would know of this night too. On the way up the ornate staircase, she passed several mirrors, in each glimpsing a girl shimmering with gems. Well, she was paying for them.

The bedroom was huge and lavish, warmed by a fire. All had been made ready. Even the bed was turned down, the lights low.

She discovered something she had never wanted to know. All men did it much the same. This was now her third man—*God, the third*—and his caresses, his movements were similar, the kisses, the hot breath, the eager exposure of her breasts, the wondering admiration, the hands, the mouth, the undressing, more admiration, caresses now familiar, his undressing, flesh against flesh. There was one difference. When she raised her arms to remove the jewelry, he asked her to leave it on. Thus, in her bejeweled nakedness she submitted to him, aware of his feverish, wild passion to touch all of her. But as a lover, he was clumsy. She felt nothing but boredom, and longed for it all to end. Wooden, unaroused, dead inside, she remembered she owed him something for the jewelry she now wore. And so, remembering her mother's hated advice of long ago, she tried to moan, move her hips, touch him. Over and over, she told herself she had done it with two others. What did a third matter?

When at last she was on her back on the bed, knees bent, the necklace of diamonds and emeralds fallen off to the side, she clasped him to guide him inside her, eager to get it over with. He went rigid, raised himself to his knees, cried out and splattered against her thigh. An expression of agony came to his face, then he plunged face-down on the bed beside her, burying his face in the pillow.

She lay there, mystified, wiping her thigh with the sheet. She realized then that he was sobbing, his whole body shaking violently. Suddenly filled with compassion for him, she touched his back with her hand, feeling its convulsive movement. "It's all right, Charles. It doesn't matter." His sobbing only intensified. "Please, Charles, don't. I can't stand for you to. . . ." The idea of a man crying like this was unbelievable to her. Long moments went by. She stroked his back gently, trying to calm him.

Finally, she heard, "I'm so . . . s-sorry. I . . . was . . . t-too excited. I've w-wanted you . . . for such a . . . long t-time."

She lay down beside him, propped up on one elbow, gently stroking his back, wanting to comfort him. She remained sympathetic, understanding how this little man, scrawny, thick of speech, yet so sensitive to the feelings of others, must be suffering. Here he was in bed at last with a woman he had long wanted, a woman he had given a priceless gift, and he had muffed it.

She sat up again, then kneeled beside him, bending. The tiara fell from her head, surprising her. She had forgotten she still wore it. She laid it aside, then began to drag her breasts along his back, over his bony shoulders, his buttocks, the back of his head, the huge emerald on the pendant sliding over his skin, obedient to her movements. Oddly, that glowing emerald, the scintillating necklace hanging down, excited her. She felt him stiffen, heard his breath, calmer at first, then more rapid. When she told him to roll over, he obeyed. It did not take too long.

The duke of Glouston was enraptured by her, telling her over and over how beautiful and wonderful it had been, how he had known it would be like that, asking her if she enjoyed it.

"Yes, Charles." That happened several times.

"I'm sorry, I—the f-first t-time. . . ."

She smiled. "It's quite a compliment to a woman . . . to excite a man too much."

"Oh, you did—you d-do."

She got up then, not able to bear any more, and began to dress. Then, as she was sliding her garter up her left leg to hold her stocking, she heard from the bed, "Sylvia, I l-love you. I want to m-marry you."

Unwilled, her hands stopped their movement. Her entire body seemed to halt for an instant.

"Oh, I don't m-mean now—or even s-soon. But, wh-when you're r-ready."

She raised her head to look at him. He sat, still naked, on the edge of the bed, looking at her. She quickly adjusted the garter, then stood up to face him. "Charles, I—"

"I know, you d-don't love me. You are young, b-beautiful,

you w-want to live your l-life. By all means, d-do. I want you to. I'll m-make no c-claim upon you. I just w-want you to kn-know I'll wait for you. Wh-When you're ready. . . ."

Her mouth came open, but somehow she couldn't speak.

"You n-needn't say anything, S-Sylvia. I q-quite understand."

For a moment, she could only gape at him. Then, conscious of how she must look, half-naked, bejeweled, mouth open, she managed to say, "Charles . . . I—" Suddenly, she smiled. "It's a good thing I don't have to speak. I don't know what to say. I'm honored, Charles. I'm only a commoner, after all, I'm—"

"Sh-h." He arose then, and began getting dressed.

Later, in the darkness of the limousine, he said, "I w-want to g-give you a g-gift, Sylvia."

She found and patted his hand. "Stop it, Charles. These emeralds are enough for a lifetime—and I shouldn't really accept them."

"I m-mean for your b-birthday. Isn't it c-coming soon?"

"Yes, but I won't hear of your giving me another thing, Charles. There is nothing I want or need from you—" Hurriedly, so it would not sound like an afterthought, she added, "—but your friendship."

She meant it. She honestly could think of nothing she wanted. As they stopped before her home, she brushed her lips against his. It was the least she could do.

Chapter Sixteen

The Countess Linfield burst into Sylvia's room the next morning as she was having breakfast. She was bubbling with excitement. "I hardly slept a *wink*, Sylvia. I knew I'd read about your jewels somewhere. I was just *certain* of it. I *burst* out of bed this morning and went to Winnie's library. I *found* it, right in this book. You'll never *believe* what it says."

Swallowing a corner of unwanted toast, Sylvia glanced up from the bed where she was sitting. Her mother, attired in her dressing gown, hair still down, carried a leather-bound book. She was rapidly turning pages looking for a passage to read.

Sylvia didn't want to hear it. Last night's fuss had been enough. She had arrived home, apparently not nearly late enough, to be greeted by her mother. Lady Constance had squealed with delight over the jewels, hugged and kissed her ecstatically, and asked myriad questions which Sylvia answered tersely or not at all. She was tired, emotionally drained. All she wanted to do was go to bed where she could be alone. But her mother followed her to the bedroom. "How did he happen to give them to you?" "He just did, mother." "But why? They're worth a fortune." "He just wanted to, mother. I tried to refuse." "Did you sleep with him?" An icy stare, laden with disgust. "Did he give them to you before or after you went to bed with him?" A deep sigh and the words, "Goodnight, mother."

Sylvia didn't want to hear another word about the jewels.

They were already loathsome to her, purchased by her body. She never wanted to see them again, let alone wear them.

"Here it is." She began to read, rather slowly, for the countess was not the most literate of women. "The Lombardy emeralds. Thought to have been collected by Lorenzo, the seventh duke of Milan, in the early sixteenth century. After his death, the emeralds became the property of the House of Lombardy, part of the royal collection of jewels."

"Please, mother, I don't want to hear."

"Of course you do. Now listen to this. 'In the early nineteenth century, Crown Prince Paulo of Lombardy had the emeralds set into a necklace, bracelet, tiara and earrings, emblazoned with many small diamonds. These were given to Elizabeth Byrne, Countess Medhurst, who later became the duchess of Glouston, in whose family the jewels remain'."

Sylvia sighed deeply, setting the breakfast tray off her lap. "Mother, please, no more."

Lady Constance apparently did not hear her, for she read on excitedly. "As a result of the gift, Crown Prince Paulo was stripped of his titles and forced into exile by his father, never succeeding to the throne." She looked up. "Imagine! That poor lovestruck man." She bent again to the book. "The centerpiece of the necklace is a large emerald, the fourth largest cut-emerald known to exist, round in shape and weighing—"

Sylvia, having got out of bed, tore the book from her mother's grasp and threw it across the room, fortunately not hitting anything. "I said to stop it!"

"What on earth for? You are being terribly silly. He gave you the Lombardy emeralds. Think of it, Sylvia. He gave you some of the most famous jewels in the *world.*"

"I don't care what they are, and I certainly didn't want him to give them to me. I have a notion to return them."

Lady Constance was horrified. "You will do no such thing! I *forbid* it." She wrestled with her poise a moment, quickly finding it. She smiled and patted Sylvia's cheek. "You're just tired, dear. When you have your bath and think about it, you'll come to your senses. The Lombardy emeralds. Imagine! Sylvia, I'm so proud of you I could burst."

Sylvia was already recovering from her petulance. Throwing objects was not like her. She sighed. "Perhaps you're right—about the bath, at least." She turned to Clara, who was standing in the bathroom doorway, a bemused expression on her face. "Is my bath ready, Clara?"

"Yes, miss."

Sylvia got into the tub but it brought her no solitude, for her mother kept coming in and out of the bathroom. She was in a high state of excitement, again and again exclaiming over the jewels, her pride in Sylvia, the likely consequences of the gift. She even put on the necklace over her dressing gown and wore it in to show Sylvia. "Breathtaking, child, simply *breathtaking.*"

Sunk into the sudsy water up to her neck, as though trying to hide, Sylvia replied, "If you like them so much, mother, why don't you take them? I'll give them to you."

Lady Constance was aghast. "You'll do no such thing. What's the matter with you? Don't you *know* what you've done?"

Sylvia sighed through pursed lips, rippling the water in front of her. "Oh, I know, all right, mother."

Her sarcasm was lost on the older woman. "Sylvia, you'll be the sensation of London. First Captain Waring, then the duke responds with such a gift. All England will be at your feet now." She reached up and began to unfasten the necklace. "Oh, there'll be so many things to do. There'll be so many parties now, invitations in a flood. I'll have to—"

"Yes, mother. Why don't you start right away?" Anything to be rid of her.

"Yes, yes, I'd better go. I'll need new gowns and I'd best write to Monsieur Poiret about you and—" She was gone from the bathroom, leaving Sylvia to sigh with relief. But not for long. Lady Constance returned to the doorway. "You didn't answer me last night, Sylvia. Did Lord Charles propose to you? He must have—to have given such a gift."

Sylvia ignored her, busying herself with the sponge.

"I demand an answer, Sylvia. Did he propose to you?"

Sylvia sighed. "Sort of."

"What d'you mean, sort of?"

Sylvia could see no way out of the trap. "He said he wanted to marry me."

The countess squealed with delight. "He proposed! Why on earth didn't you tell me? You accepted, of course."

"No."

"You *refused* him!"

"No, I just said nothing."

Lady Constance stared at her in utter dismay. When she spoke, there was a hint of the coal-miner's daughter in her voice. "Honest to God, Sylvia, sometimes I—what do you mean, you said nothing?"

"It wasn't that kind of a proposal, mother. He said he loved me and wanted to marry me, but he knew I was too young and not ready for marriage." A deep sigh escaped her. "He said he'd wait for me to decide."

Lady Constance clasped her hands under her ample chin, an expression of her joy. "Oh, how *perfect*. He'll wait for you. Oh, how *lovely!*"

In the tub Sylvia shook her head above the waterline, slowly, sadly, exasperated.

"He loves you and will wait. Wonderful! Of course, he'll wait. You'll drive him insane with desire. Then—oh, Sylvia, I could *burst* with happiness. My daughter, the duchess of Glouston."

"Mother, I—"

"Oh, I know you don't love him. You're young and foolishly romantic. But you'll come to your senses. We won't wait too long to accept him, will we?"

Mercifully for Sylvia, she then turned and strode from the bathroom and bedroom.

Lady Constance was right about one thing. Overnight, Sylvia Hartley became the sensation of London, the leading P.B., the most talked about, sought after and photographed woman in the British capital.

Every day, the post brought a stack of invitations, so many she could not cope, and let Clara or her mother decide which to accept. Her calendar was filled for weeks ahead with invitations to teas, dinners, balls, concerts, soirées, salons, bazaars, garden shows, exhibitions. Her appearance at a charity made it a success. In truth, Sylvia Hartley, P.B., was most useful in London in the autumn of 1910.

None of this was lost on the city's entrepreneurs, who begged her to visit their restaurants or theaters, or pleaded with her to wear a gown, hat or jewelry from their shop—no charge, of course. Photographers hoped that a single snap of the shutter would cement their reputations. Advertisers beseeched her to say she used their products. This she refused to do.

Sylvia tried desperately to keep some sense of herself through it all, but it was hopeless. She was adrift on a social sea, beckoned here, commanded there, her life a continuum of being beautiful or preparing to be beautiful, dressing for this event or changing to dress for the next. She had almost no time alone. Clara awakened her in the morning, then began, after a quick breakfast, the regimen of exercises, bath, massage, facials, hairdressing, all in the name of beauty. Sylvia had a few minutes, seldom as long as an hour, to tend to her mail. In the early afternoon, she went for her sitting. The painting had been set back. Lord Charles, who had commissioned it and had every right to his choice, wanted her painted in her sensational Poiret gown and wearing the Lombardy emeralds. Much of the painting had to be done over. The pose remained the same, but Sylvia's hair had to be changed to wear the tiara. And, each day, she had to change into the green satin gown at Lord Charles', which meant Clara had to accompany her, helping her into her gown, then back into her street attire. Sylvia came to hate the dress, for she was forced to stand day after day half-naked before throngs who came to see her. Again and again, she asked Lord Charles to make the sitting more private. He promised, but it never seemed to happen. And, as the painting took shape, it became the most talked-about portrait in London. Joshua Wainwright was ecstatic.

After the sitting, there was shopping or an exhibition or some charity function. Then came a quick change for tea. When it was at someone else's home, she was the center of attention. When it was at Lord Linfield's home, she was likewise the center of attention. It amazed her how many people just "dropped by" at tea time, many of them gentlemen she hardly knew. As was the custom in Edwardian England, they would take a seat, hat, coat and stick on the floor beside them, as if they had just happened by and were staying only a minute. A proper lady could not entertain gentlemen callers, but they could "drop by" as though in the neighborhood, bringing a friend or two.

Then came the elaborate dressing for the evening, with a new hairstyle, and always a different gown. Sylvia's public reputation, well-known to her mother and Clara, as well as the couturiers of England and France, lay not just in her beauty but in her costuming. Thus, she was nightly attired in a new gown, each of them novel and elaborate, both in fabric and design, and often daring in the display of her figure and skin tone. M. Poiret, who made a quick trip from Paris to see her, sensed her uncanny knack for rendering the impression of nakedness and sensuality when fully clothed. He did his very best to enhance that quality in the gowns he made for her.

Outwardly, Sylvia was the perfect P.B., utterly poised, seemingly self-contained, unaware how beautiful she was, unmindful of the attention showered upon her. Among strangers or in large groups, she said little, smiling when appropriate, appearing to be interested in others, even when she wasn't listening. In smaller groups, or among the rapidly-swelling body of friends and close admirers, she displayed a gift for wit and repartee. Perhaps her greatest talent lay in fending off the ardent, while keeping them still her admirers. She received each day at least one, sometimes several, invitations and proposals which a few weeks previously would have shocked her. All were thinly-veiled with etiquette, but the intent was clear. The gentlemen of London, indeed a few foreign nobility, knew or believed they knew what she did with Waring and the duke, and it maddened them that she would not with them. They showered her with gifts, some quite expensive. How she managed to accept these yet maintain her reputation gave Londoners something else to talk about. The effete Timothy Graves, with his usual clever turn of phrase, perhaps said it best: "My dear Sylvia, you have led the men of London to the true meaning of Alexander Pope's immortal words, 'Hope springs eternal for the human breast'."

Sylvia did not even blink as she replied, "I believe the poet said 'in the human breast,' Timothy."

Graves' smile was suave. "Did he? My unfortunate error."

If ever appearances were deceiving, they were in Sylvia's case. Her outward calm and poise masked a grinding inner tension, her smiles and repartee a consuming desperation. She was grossly unhappy, and knew it. She was perpetually tired. She ate almost nothing, used wine and, increasingly, spirits to enable her to get through the evening, then was too exhausted to sleep without a powder from the apothecary. She was stretched like fine piano wire, and more alone than she had ever dreamed it possible for a human being to be. Oh, there were always people present, her mother badgering her to accept the duke's proposal, Clara now unsubtly urging her to ask the duke for a house of her own so all this could lead to something of permanent value. Sylvia fended off both demands, sensing, even when she was too tired to articulate a thought, that if she did either, she would be lost forever.

In her desperation, Sylvia turned to her only friend, Meg. Late at night, propped against the pillows in her bed, she would often scrawl long letters to Meg as she waited for the sleeping powder to take effect, pouring out her fears and despair. In the morning, she would invariably find these pages incoherent, nonsensical and increasingly illegible, and tear them up. A couple times a week, she would dash off a short note to Meg in the morning, endeavoring to make it cheerful and chatty. Then, assuaging her guilt about Meg's poverty in comparison with her own luxuries, she would order Clara to send her discarded gowns to the shack in Hornby. They would be useless to Meg, but perhaps she could sell them for something. Once, Sylvia smiled. There would be enough for Meg to open a dress shop. She must remember to tell her that in her next letter. What Sylvia didn't know was that the garments never reached Meg. Clara sold them herself.

Sylvia was not promiscuous, though she could easily have been and to her great profit, but neither was she chaste. Lord Charles, having tasted honey and cream, became addicted. She fended him off frequently, pleading the lateness of the hour, weariness, a headache, the risk of scandal, but such methods were not foolproof. He showered her with jewelry, and reciprocation became inevitable for her. She endured, feeling nothing, hating every second of it, but she learned the value of pretense in bringing it to a quick and merciful completion.

It was Waring she gave herself to. After their first encounter she put him off for more than a week, hoping it would somehow not come to pass ever again. Then, after a trying session with the duke, she called him, ran down the back stairs and out through the servant's entrance to his carriage. She began after that to see him twice a week, once three times. Invariably, these were torrid, exhausting bouts.

She gave herself to him with what she conceived of as abandon, stunning him with her capacities, and all of it was for her a futile attempt to forget for a time just how unhappy she was. None of it worked very well, or for very long. Always, no matter how satiated her senses, she felt depressed afterwards. Something was missing. There were cascades of pleasure, flights of ecstasy, but not—what? She often stayed very late with him, almost till dawn, hardly able to make her way back to her own room. She knew why. Each time, when she was home in bed, she would inexplicably burst into tears which never relieved anything. She had learned to put that off as long as possible.

Chapter Seventeen

It was on the morning after such a night that she sat at her desk, bone-weary, reading her mail. Nothing from Meg. How long since she'd written! She picked up a packet of rolled newspapers. She opened the wrapper and read the masthead. VOTES FOR WOMEN. The publication of the suffragettes. There was a handwritten note.

Dearest Sylvia,

I still expect a visit from you. I have no phone at home, but you can often reach me at Clement's Inn, our headquarters. Meanwhile, I thought you might like to read our publication. I've enclosed a few of our more interesting back issues. And I've put you on our mailing list. Please do try to visit us.

> *Yours in the Cause,*
> *Kitty*

Sighing, Sylvia lay the letter aside—more demands on her time—and reached for another letter, obviously an invitation. But something made her look back at Kitty's note. A single word seemed to rise from the page: *Dearest.* She had rebuffed Kitty's overture at renewing their friendship, had shown almost no interest in the cause Kitty championed. Yet, here was Kitty calling her "dearest." Why would she do that? Why would she reach out to her in affection? And how long had it been since anyone, save Meg, had called her dearest? She found herself rereading Kitty's note, then picking up a copy of the suffragette newspaper.

It was the issue from January, 1910. On the first page was a photograph of Lady Constance Lytton. Sylvia knew her—she had visited St. Regis once, addressing a convocation—but read the appended biographical note anyway. Lady Lytton was the daughter of Robert, the earl of Lytton, a celebrated diplomat who had served as viceroy of India and ambassador to France. Lady Lytton had accompanied her parents to those posts. After her father's death, the Countess Lytton had been lady-in-waiting to both Queen Victoria and Queen Alexandra.

Sylvia continued to read. "Lady Constance has been an invalid since infancy, suffering from a weak heart and rheumatism. Her interests have been primarily in the fields of music and folk arts. Lady Constance became interested in the women's suffrage movement through her friendship with Mrs. Pethic-Lawrence who, with Annie Kenney, recruited her to the Cause. In January, 1909, she became a member of the Women's Social and Political Union, shortly afterwards joining a deputation which forced its way into the House of Commons. She was arrested on this occasion and sent to Holloway Gaol. This was the first of many arrests and imprisonments for Lady Lytton. In January, 1910, Lady Lytton took part in a demonstration outside Walton Gaol in Liverpool, where W.S.P.U. members were receiving barbarous treatment. She was arrested and sentenced to a fortnight in Walton Gaol. The following is Lady Lytton's personal account of her treatment there."

Sylvia began to read Lady Lytton's own words. She described in detail all that had happened to her, but Sylvia, her mind dulled by fatigue, registered only the pertinent facts. Lady Lytton, not wanting to receive special treatment as the daughter of a celebrated peer, had disguised herself and entered prison under the name of Jane Warton.

"I lay in my bed most of the day, for they did not disturb me, and I tried to keep warm, as I felt the cold fearfully. They brought me all my meals the same as usual, porridge in the morning at seven, meat and potatoes midday at twelve, porridge at four-thirty. When they were hot, I fed on the smell of them, which seemed quite delicious. I said, 'I don't want any, thank you,' to each meal, as they brought it in. I had made up my mind that this time I would not drink any water, and would rinse out my mouth morning and evening without swallowing any. I wrote on the walls of my cell with my slate pencil and soap mixed with dirt of the floor for ink, VOTES FOR WOMEN and the saying from Thoreau's *Duty of Civil Disobedience*—'Under a government which imprisons any unjustly, the true place for a just man [or woman] is also a prison'; on the wall opposite my bed I wrote the text from Joshua, 'Only be thou strong and very courageous.' That night I dreamt of fruits, melons, peaches and nectarines, and of a moonlit balcony that was hung with the sweetest-smelling flowers, honeysuckle and messamine, apple blossoms and sweet-scented verbena."

The words of this gentle woman stabbed at Sylvia. Such courage. No food, no water. She read on rapidly, wanting to learn what had happened to this valiant creature. On the fourth day of her hunger strike, a medical officer, joined by four wardresses, came in to force-feed her.

"The doctor leant on my knees as he stooped over my chest to get at my mouth. I shut my mouth and clenched my teeth. I had looked forward to this moment with so much anxiety lest my identity should be discovered before, and I felt positively glad when the time had come. The sense of being overpowered by more force than I could possibly resist was complete, but I resisted nothing except with my mouth.

"The doctor offered me the choice of a wooden or steel gag; he explained elaborately, as he did on most subsequent occasions, that the steel gag would hurt and the wooden one not, and he urged me not to force him to use the steel gag. But I did not speak nor open my mouth, so that after playing about for a moment or two with the wooden one, he finally had recourse to the steel. He seemed annoyed at my resistance and he broke into a temper as he pried my teeth with the steel implement. He found that on either side at the back I had false teeth mounted on a bridge which did not take out. The superintending wardress asked if I had any false teeth, if so, they must be taken out; I made no answer and the process went on. He dug his instrument down into the sham tooth. It pressed fearfully on the gum. He said if I resisted so much with my teeth, he would have to feed me through the nose. The pain of it was intense and at last I must have given way, for he got the gag between my teeth, which he proceeded to turn much more than necessary until my jaws were fastened wide apart, far more than they could go naturally."

Sylvia could feel her eyes smarting, tears beginning to come. But she read on.

"Then he put down my throat a tube which seemed to me much too wide and was something like four feet in length. The irritation of the tube was excessive. I choked the moment it touched my throat until it had got down. Then the food was poured in quickly. It made me sick a few seconds after it was down and the action of the sickness made my body and legs double up, but the wardresses instantly pressed back my head and the doctor leant on my knees. The horror of it was more than I can describe. I was sick over the doctor and the wardresses, and it seemed a long time before they took the tube out. As the doctor left, he gave me a slap on the cheek, not violently, but, as it were, to express his contemptuous disapproval, and he seemed to take for granted that my distress was assumed. At first, it seemed such an utterly contemptible thing to have done that I could only laugh in my mind. Then, suddenly, I saw Jane Warton lying before me, and it seemed as if I were outside of her. She was the most despised, ignorant and helpless prisoner that I had ever seen. When she had served her time and was out of prison, no one would believe anything she said, and the doctor, when he had fed her by force and tortured her body, struck her on the cheek to show how he despised her! That was Jane Warton, and I had come to help her."

Tears flowed down Sylvia's cheeks, dropping to the page below her. But she made no effort to stop them or wipe them away. She could only read the swimming words.

"When the doctor had gone out of the cell, I lay quite helpless. The wardresses were kind and knelt round to comfort me, but there was nothing to be done. I could not move and remained there in what, under different conditions, would have been an intolerable mess. I had been sick over my hair, which, though short, hung on either side of my face, all over the wall near my bed, and my clothes were saturated with it, but the wardresses told me they could not get me a change that night as it was too late, the office was shut. I lay quite motionless. It seemed paradise to be without the suffocating tube, without the liquid food going in and out of my body and without the gag between my teeth."

Sobbing now, Sylvia read the remaining words.

"Presently the wardresses all left me. They had orders to go, which were carried out with the usual promptness. Before long, I heard the sounds of the forced feeding in the next cell to mine. It was almost more than I could bear. It was Elsie Howey, I was sure. When the ghastly process was over and all quiet, I tapped on the wall and called out at the top of my voice, which wasn't much just then, 'No Surrender,' and there came the answer past any doubt in Elsie's voice, 'No Surrender'."

The editor appended a footnote, which Sylvia just managed to read: "Lady Constance Lytton as Jane Warton was forcibly fed a further seven times before her identity was discovered and she was released on 'medical grounds' on Sunday, January 23."

Slowly, tears streaming down her face, so choked she could scarcely breathe, Sylvia lowered her forehead to the desk. Her hands were in her lap and her body shook with convulsive sobs. All her anguish, sorrow, frustration, bitterness and fatigue seemed to be wrenched from her in spasms.

Clara, who had been ironing her dress, came in and found her. "Miss Sylvia, what's the matter?" She threw the dress on the bed and came to her, placing both hands on her shoulders. "What's wrong? What happened? Why are you crying?" There was no answer, except for Sylvia's persistent sobbing. Clara saw the *Votes for Women* newspaper on the desk, but it offered no explanation to her. "Did you get bad news from Meg?" That led to a response, a slow shaking of Sylvia's head against the desk.

Clara held her a moment, unsure what to do. Then, rather forcibly, she helped her, still sobbing, to her feet. "Just lie down, Sylvia. You'll feel better in a moment." Through streaming eyes, Sylvia saw the bed, stumbled to it and buried her face in her pillow. She lay there, crying uncontrollably, unmindful that her tears stained the satin spread. Clara sat next to her. "Do you want your mother? Shall I call a doctor?" Both queries received negative shakes of the head.

In time, Clara was able to turn her over onto her back.

Sylvia's crying had diminished a little, although her face remained screwed up and her breath came in savage, irregular gasps.

"What's the matter, Sylvia? Why are you crying so?"

Sylvia looked at her a long moment, eyes flooding, an expression of fright and horror in them. Finally, she could speak a little. "They . . . they . . . did that . . . to . . . to Kitty." As the last words were wrenched from her, she brought her clenched fists to her mouth, pressing them hard against her teeth, biting them, as a new burst of crying overwhelmed her.

Clara tried to smile. "I don't know who Kitty is or who they are, but nothing has happened to you, child. You're here, safe with me." It was the tenderest Clara had ever spoken to her.

She took one of Sylvia's hands from her mouth, holding it, patting it, trying to say soothing words. Finally, nearly spent, Sylvia managed to say. "Kitty . . . called me . . . dearest." This led to another fit of sobbing.

Ultimately, Sylvia cried herself out. The tears stopped, although the irregular gasping remained a while longer. Finally, she lay on her bed, looking up at the ceiling. She was emotionally drained.

"Shall I call Lord Charles and say you won't come for the sitting today?"

Sylvia turned to look at Clara standing above her. There was almost a benevolent look in her eyes. She stared at her for a long moment. It was almost as though she were seeing a stranger.

She shook her head. "No, I'll go."

Slowly, as though very old and tired, she forced herself to a sitting position on the bed. She held her head in her hands for a time, then got up, went to the vanity and sat down to begin the process of being made beautiful.

By the time Sylvia reached the studio, there was little evidence of her tears, although she remained weary and numb. She changed into the green satin and assumed her pose. At the last moment, she drained a generous snifter of brandy. This stimulated her, and she managed a word or two of repartee with Timothy Graves.

"Did you have a hard night last night, Sylvia?"

She smiled. "How could I have? I don't believe I saw you, Timothy."

He laughed. "Touché, my sweet. And it was my loss, I assure you."

Slowly, her mind, influenced by the brandy, began to function. She thought of Kitty and what she'd read, reacting now without the emotion of before. Such women. Such courage. How could they do it? At her break from the pose, she left the room and phoned the number of Clement's Inn, asking for Kitty Shaw. In a moment, she heard her voice and said, "Kitty, this is Sylvia Hartley. I got your note this morning."

"Did you? I'm so glad."

Sylvia hesitated, then said, "Kitty, I'd like to see you."

"Wonderful. When can you come over?"

"I don't know." Her mind raced. Charles was taking her to an art exhibition this afternoon. She could make some excuse. "I have time this afternoon, Kitty."

"I'd love to see you, Sylvia. Just come over here to Clement's Inn. You know where it is, don't you?"

"Kitty, I—I don't want to come there."

"But why?"

"I just can't, Kitty. Can't we meet somewhere else—your place maybe?"

Sylvia heard the hesitation on the line, then the words, "All right, my flat if you wish." She gave the address and, after appropriate goodbyes, the conversation ended.

Sylvia shortened the remainder of the sitting, changed, told a puzzled Clara to go on home, then went off alone in a cab.

Once again, Sylvia was shocked by the housing accommodations of a friend. The address she gave the cabman turned out to be on the East End, not far from the docks, the worst section of London. Kitty's flat was a walk-up on the fourth floor, small, sparsely-furnished and with no visible means of heat. Even as they hugged each other in greeting, Sylvia was aghast. Kitty Shaw came from a wealthy family. She was always pretty and well-dressed. To see her in tacky clothes in a place like this was not to be believed.

Kitty read her mind and smiled. "You're surprised to see me living in a place like this?"

There was nothing for Sylvia to say but, "Frankly, yes."

Kitty's laugh was bubbly. "I am too. But I told you father had cut me off. This is all I can afford. Besides, Sylvia Pankhurst and I are about to launch a campaign to organize the women of the East End. We should live among them, don't you think?"

"That's Mrs. Pankhurst's daughter?"

"Yes, the younger one."

There was a moment of awkwardness, broken when Kitty suggested tea, insisting over Sylvia's protests.

While the pot brewed, Sylvia sat in a simple wooden chair, Kitty on the edge of the bed. After a little hesitation, Sylvia said, "I received the newspapers you sent me."

"*Votes for Women?* Isn't it good? Christabel Pankhurst does it mostly."

"Yes." Again, Sylvia hesitated. She felt nervous. "I read the article by Lady Lytton."

"What did you think of it?"

Sylvia paused, uncertain of her ability to speak of it. "I—I burst into tears while reading it. . . . I—I was inconsolable . . . for a long time."

"It is terribly moving, isn't it? That's why I sent it to you especially."

"I can hardly bring myself to speak of it. I—I'm afraid I'll—" She smiled. "—cry another bucket of tears." In truth, she could feel emotion rising in her again.

"Why did you cry, Sylvia?"

"I—I don't know." She sighed. "I remember Lady Lytton from school. She was such a lovely, gentle person. To have . . . have such . . . such horrid things happen to her. I. . . ."

"I know. I remember her too. And she is still just as lovely, if not more so."

Sylvia looked at Kitty, her eyes already filling again. "And I cried for you, Kitty. You told me you were a hunger striker. They force-fed you. But I never knew, I never dreamed. . . ."

"I know. That's why we publish articles like that, so people will know what happens."

"But it's so *terrible*, Kitty. How could you bear it?"

The suffragette smiled. "Oh, it's not so bad—afterwards."

"But how could you, Kitty? Oh, maybe the first time, when you didn't know. But the second—how many times did it happen to you?"

"Oh, I don't know, a dozen at least."

Sylvia was truly shocked now. "A dozen times? When you

knew what was going to happen, how you would suffer?" She stared at her. "Such courage you have, Kitty."

"Oh, I don't think it took courage. I wanted it to happen."

"You *wanted* it!"

"Yes. Oh, there was pain all right, terrible indignity, but all through it I felt such happiness and peace. I felt a kinship with all the women in the world, the men too, who have suffered for a cause they believe in. My body might be tormented, but my spirit soared."

Sylvia saw an expression of joy on her face.

"It was the most beautiful experience of my life, Sylvia. I'd do it again tomorrow. I may well."

For a long moment, Sylvia stared at her friend in disbelief. Finally, she said, "I couldn't do it, Kitty, not knowing. I don't have the courage."

Kitty smiled. "Oh, I think you could. Everyone is brave when she believes in a cause."

"Not me, Kitty."

"I said the same thing." She laughed. "But then I went and did what I said I could never do."

Tea was made and served and slowly consumed, the two women chatting about their lives and activities.

"How is your portrait coming?"

"Oh, that. I don't think it will ever be finished."

"I hear it's very beautiful." She smiled. "A true likeness."

Sylvia had had many compliments, but this one unnerved her, somehow. She didn't want to be just beautiful when this girl across from her was so much more. "Kitty, if I am honest, I will have to say there was another reason for my tears this morning." She saw Kitty's expression of expectant interest and looked away, down at her hands. "I—I think I was crying for myself."

Kitty wanted to wait her out, but Sylvia was so long in speaking again, she prompted her. "Why would you do that?"

"Oh, Kitty, my life is so . . . I don't know, *empty*. I'm on the go all the time, teas, parties and such. But there is no *purpose* to it. I feel like I'm on a merry-go-round, a very beautiful one, very gay, full of lights and music, but it never goes anywhere. I'm just along for the ride." She looked up at Kitty. Her mouth was open to speak, but Sylvia gave her no chance. "And I'm so lonely, Kitty. How can that be? I know hundreds of people. I'm surrounded by them, hardly ever by myself. Yet, I feel so terribly alone. These people call me 'dear' and 'darling.' They seem to love me. Yet, I feel unloved, excruciatingly so."

"You are very unhappy, aren't you?"

"Yes." The word came out as a long, deep sigh.

Kitty got up from her place at the bed and poured more tea into Sylvia's cup. "I sensed that. It's why I wrote you, sent you *Votes for Women.* It's why I'm so glad to see you today." She hesitated briefly. "Sylvia, I was headed for the course you're on. Believe me, I do understand. Then, quite by accident, I met Christabel Pankhurst. She saved my life, Sylvia."

"You seem to be very dedicated, Kitty. But are you happy?"

"Oh, yes, yes. I never knew it was possible to be so happy."

"But marriage, a family. Have you given that up?"

Kitty laughed. "Not hardly. I've a fellow I like. Anything's possible."

For the first time, Sylvia was able to look upon Kitty as a confidante, smiling, sharing her happiness. "I'm glad for you—and him, whoever he is."

The new cup of tea was swallowed, then Kitty said, "Let me do something for you, Sylvia. Let me take you to Clement's Inn."

Sylvia shook her head. "No, I don't want to go there."

"But why?"

"I—I don't know. Really, I don't." She smiled. "I'm hardly dressed for it, for one thing." She wore an afternoon dress of the latest fashion, a form-fitting brown wool hobble skirt with a slit. She carried a fox muff which matched her fur piece, and her wide-brimmed hat was decorated with ostrich feathers.

"Don't be silly. You look lovely."

Thus, against her better judgment, Sylvia was taken to Clement's Inn, a large, squarish brick building which, through the largesse of Emmeline and Frederick Pethic-Lawrence, had become the headquarters of the Women's Social and Political Union. The place was a hubbub of activity. Outside in the garden, the W.S.P.U. fife band was being led through its paces by a drum major resplendent in her uniform. "That's Mary Leigh," Kitty said. "Nothing like a little music to attract a crowd."

Inside Clement's Inn, Sylvia at once felt out of place and in the way. Her stylish gown and corseted figure were in sharp contrast to the utilitarian and vastly more comfortable shirtwaist blouses and skirts or the sensible suits of the women there. And they were all so busy, making placards, writing letters or articles for the newspaper, holding meetings.

"Well, what do you think?" Kitty asked.

"I think I don't belong here."

"Yes, you do." At once she began to introduce her to people, so many her head reeled under the names. Kitty gave a running commentary, "Doctor Garrett Anderson, the first woman physician . . . Mrs. Alfred Lyttelton, the dramatist . . . Mrs. Hertha Ayrton, electrical engineer . . . The Reverend Doctor Anna Shaw . . . Beatrice Harraden, a leading writer. . . ."

"I didn't know women were in these occupations."

"Oh, yes, Sylvia, and many others. The talents of half the population have been wasted much too long. Our movement is helping women discover their abilities, giving them courage to enter fields long closed to them." Kitty took her arm and led her quickly into an adjoining room. "Here is someone you must meet."

In a moment, Sylvia stood before a rail-thin, severe-faced woman in her seventies, wearing quite old-fashioned attire. "Sylvia Hartley, I want you to meet Mrs. Charlotte Despard. She's secretary of the union and also head of the Women's Freedom League."

Smiles and handshakes were exchanged, and Sylvia heard herself say, "I'm surprised, Mrs. Despard. I thought suffragettes were mostly younger women." With dismay, Sylvia realized how tactless she sounded. "I'm sorry, I didn't mean—"

"It's quite all right, my dear. I am well aware of my years. Actually, we have women of all ages. Elizàbeth Wolstenholme-Elmy is senior to me, I believe. She once said, 'When you have enthusiasm for a great cause, you know you have discovered eternal youth.' I believe that is so. I just wish we'd had this movement forty years ago."

A LASTING SPLENDOR

Kitty broke in. "Actually, we did, Mrs. Despard. But it was broken by government indifference and police oppression."

"That's true." The old woman smiled. "We will not give up this time." To Sylvia, she said, "That's the reason for our slogan, 'No Surrender.' We will not give up our fight, no matter what is done to us, until all women, rich and poor, take their rightful place in English society—all over the world, for that matter."

"Yes." Sylvia's assent was more courtesy than commitment, however.

"Emmeline—Mrs. Pankhurst—has already carried our cause to America and been well-received there."

"Yes, I know." Sylvia remembered reading about Mrs. Pankhurst's visit to New York.

When the older woman excused herself, Sylvia asked if she would get to meet Mrs. Pankhurst. She was told there was a strategy meeting of the leaders. It would be breaking up soon, and Mrs. Pankhurst might have a moment.

The tour of Clement's Inn continued and so did the introductions. Sylvia was lost in a sea of names, but she was impressed that all strata of English society were represented. She met a couple of women bearing the title "Lady." They worked beside poorly-dressed girls who might have been their servants. And she was impressed too, with the faces: all bright, eager, their eyes shining with an inner light. She mentioned it to Kitty.

"You noticed that, did you?"

"Yes. But why?"

"Happiness, I suppose, believing in something larger than yourself, being committed to achieving it." She turned in response to voices from an adjoining room. "The meeting must be breaking up."

Sylvia turned in time to see a slender woman, perhaps in her thirties. She had a wide shawl wrapped around her head, nearly concealing light brown hair, parted in the middle. She was not a particularly pretty woman, with a nose too prominent, a mouth too wide. But she had, Sylvia felt, the brightest eyes she had ever seen.

"I won't try to introduce you now. She seems in a hurry. But that's Annie Kenney. What an inspiration she is to us all! She came from the humblest circumstances. She worked in a factory and came to see Mrs. Pankhurst when our movement

172

was in its infancy. If she hadn't, she'd still be in a factory, headed for an early death. She is living proof of what women can do with their lives."

"Oh."

"We'll wait a minute, then go on in. I know Mrs. Pankhurst wants to meet you, if she has time. Christabel and Sylvia too. How fortunate we are to have them, and from the same family. Sylvia is the fighter, so dedicated, so militant, not just for women's rights but against all injustice. I think I identify with her the most. Christabel is the pretty one. It's strange, really. She was popular at school, very active in art and dramatics. She doesn't have emotional scars, like Sylvia. Yet, Christabel is very much with us. She is the brains, the strategist. The whole approach to our campaign originates with her. We would be nowhere without her."

"I thought Mrs. Pankhurst . . . ?"

"Oh, yes, she's the leader, the inspiration." Kitty touched Sylvia's arm. "There's Sylvia Pankhurst now."

Sylvia saw a slender young woman, dark hair parted in the middle, arranged into a severe bun in back. Her face was oval and too fleshy to be pretty. But the full mouth and glowing, dark eyes made it an extremely passionate face.

"And there is someone you know. Come."

To her consternation, Sylvia was standing before a tall, extremely slender woman and stammering, "Lady Lytton . . . I'm sure . . . you don't r-remember me. St. Regis Academy. . . ."

"Oh, yes, St. Regis. A classmate of Kitty's, no doubt." She smiled. "Yes, I remember you—well, not you, exactly. But I do remember those eyes. How remarkable they are—and how beautiful you've become."

"I—I read of your—your imprisonment in . . . Walton Gaol."

"Oh, that." She laughed. "All my life I've tried to write poetry, even a story or two. I fear I'll be best remembered, if I'm remembered at all, for something I had no control over."

"I was terribly moved."

Lady Lytton merely smiled her acknowledgement. "Are you joining us, my dear?"

"I—I don't know."

"I hope you do. We need you."

In a moment, Sylvia was ushered into Mrs. Pankhurst's

office. She first met Mrs. Pethic-Lawrence, who was leaving, then was amazed by the beauty of Christabel Pankhurst. She was tall, taller than Sylvia herself, with a round face, framed by soft, brunette hair, dark eyes set extremely wide apart, and a very full and sensuous mouth. It was a most unusual face in its roundness, revealing at once openness, sensitivity and high intelligence.

These two women merely greeted her and left, then Sylvia turned to meet Emmeline Pankhurst. Nothing, certainly not her daughters, had prepared Sylvia for the mother. Although in her early fifties, her face mirroring her years of struggle for suffrage, the pain of widowhood, imprisonment and hunger strikes, Emmeline Pankhurst was nonetheless the loveliest woman Sylvia had ever seen. Her face was aristocratic, extreme in its delicacy, almond-shaped, less sensuous than Christabel's, less passionate than Sylvia's. Her whole person was thinner, her chin more prominent, the mouth wider, the eyes less commanding than either daughter's. Only the wide set of the eyes indicated a family resemblance.

"My dear, your photographs do not do you justice. You are simply lovely. Such eyes you have!"

As the older woman came around her desk to greet her, Sylvia found herself saying, "Not nearly as lovely as you, Mrs. Pankhurst."

"I'm sorry to have kept you waiting, but our meeting ran on. It seems we face a crisis. Since May and the assession of King George to the throne, we have observed a truce, hoping that in a spirit of goodwill the government would give priority to a bill for women's suffrage. We have just learned that it is not to be. The Right Honorable Herbert Henry Asquith—" she made the name drip with sarcasm, "—our esteemed prime minister, not to forget his chancellor of the exchequer, David Lloyd-George and his new home secretary, Winston Churchill, have determined women's suffrage has no place in British life. Therefore, the truce is now ended. We are stepping up our activities."

Excitedly, Kitty asked, "We are becoming more militant, Emmeline?"

The suffragette leader sighed. "I fear so. The government is apparently going to hear us only when we fill the streets with protest."

Sylvia saw Kitty almost applaud. Then Mrs. Pankhurst took her arm. "Come. Let's have some tea." They entered a small sitting room. "Well, Miss Hartley, what do you think of us?"

"I—I don't know, Mrs. Pankhurst. It is all new, strange to me."

"Come now, you must have some impressions?"

Sylvia did not want to appear stupid in front of this woman. "I saw women of all ages, all stations, working side by side."

"Yes. That is our aim—to break down the social barriers by which women have been enslaved."

"And everyone was very nice to me. I felt welcome."

"And indeed you are, my dear. Not because you have achieved some . . . some notoriety, but because you are a *woman*. It is nothing more, nothing less than that. Do you understand?"

"Yes." *They* don't want to go to bed with me, she thought. They like me for myself—like Meg.

"We are a comradeship of women, women working together for the benefit of women." Emmeline Pankhurst smiled. "Which is not to say we exclude the support of men. We have many male supporters. The Men's Political Union, the Daily Herald League, the Fabian Society, all support our cause. We have been asked to amalgamate with these groups. But we will not. Theirs tend to be class movements, mainly Labour and socialist. Ours is not a class movement. We take in everybody, the highest and lowest, the richest and poorest. Our bond is womanhood! The men must paddle their own canoe, and we must paddle ours."

"But, Mrs. Pankhurst, if women cannot vote and be elected to Parliament, how can men be made to give us the vote?"

She smiled. "Apparently, with great difficulty. But we have many who support our cause in Parliament. Only the leadership of the Liberal Party stands in our way. It's so exasperating! I can understand the older men like Mr. Asquith—understand, a little—but it is the younger men like Winston Churchill who confound me. He seems to feel that if women get the vote it will in some fashion threaten his little sins and excesses, his cigars, his addiction to brandy, his off-color jokes. Mr. Churchill is addicted to the double standard—for men only, of course." She smiled at Kitty. "But a new day is coming. What is the name of your young man, Kitty?"

"Wicklow, Arthur Wicklow."

"Yes, a fine young man, an MP with a future. I hope we'll hear wedding bells there one day." She looked from Kitty to Sylvia. "Chances are he would support us even without Kitty's being in love with him." She smiled. "But, then, love can't hurt, can it?"

The mention of Arthur's name, hearing him linked to Kitty, was like a stab in her heart. She tried to keep her face expressionless, and was reasonably successful. "I'm sure it won't, Mrs. Pankhurst."

"Nor would it hurt us to have you, Miss Hartley, a celebrated P.B.—" She saw Sylvia wince at the term. "Don't be ashamed. You *are* beautiful. Your status is deserved." She smiled. "I was saying, having you join our movement would influence many people. We have the Actresses' League, many writers, others of prominence. Your joining us would show we are not just a group of Plain Janes." She laughed. "We do have our comely members." Her laughter faded quickly. "Don't misunderstand. We don't want you just for your appearance. You have a good mind, obviously. There is much for you to contribute to the world—to the Cause."

"I don't know, Mrs. Pankhurst. It is all so new, so strange."

"Of course, you don't know, my dear. And I don't want you to let me, your friendship for Kitty, or anyone else influence you. You think about it. Make up your own mind. We want you to come of your own free will. Indeed, we will have it no other way."

Touched, Sylvia could only say, "Thank you."

"Good."

The suffrage leader stood up, and Sylvia sensed the interview was over. On the way downstairs and out of the building, Sylvia said to Kitty, "So, you're seeing Arthur Wicklow?"

"Yes. Do you know him?"

"I've met him. He seems . . . nice. Are you in love with him?"

Kitty smiled. "I am, yes, but. . . ."

When the sentence was not finished, Sylvia asked, "But what?"

"He seems devoted, yet—oh, I don't know. Sometimes, I think he carries a torch for another."

"Do you know who?"

"No, and that's the trouble." She smiled. "It's awfully hard to fight a phantom."

Chapter Eighteen

Arthur and Kitty . . . As she rode home, that knowledge seemed to blot out all other information she had gained this day. Arthur and Kitty. It couldn't be, yet it was. Her mind leaped to the only place she could visualize them together, the cottage in Hampshire, Kitty wet from the rain, standing before the fire in Arthur's robe, he brushing her hair, embracing her, the robe falling away, she being carried into the bedroom. . . .

Then Sylvia brought her fingers to her face, feeling the heat of it. Heavens, was she jealous? Arthur and Kitty. No, she wasn't jealous. She wouldn't allow herself to be. Arthur Wicklow meant nothing to her. It had just been a . . . a fantastic escapade, now over, finished, a pleasant memory. Only it wasn't pleasant. Arthur hated her. *I think he carries a torch for another.* She smiled. He didn't hate her. He still loved her. Her smile faded. No, he didn't love her. He loved Meg Gwynne, the girl who had come to the cottage. That girl, if she ever existed, was gone forever.

Arthur and Kitty. Yes. Kitty was her friend. She deserved happiness with Arthur. And they were right for each other. They held the same interests. Yes, Arthur and Kitty. If she ever saw Arthur she would tell him so, wish him well.

As the hansom made its way toward Regent's Park, Sylvia forced herself to think of her visit to Clement's Inn. Images crowded her mind; Emmeline Pankhurst, so lovely, so serene, the beautiful Christabel, the intense Sylvia, the

179

haunting Annie Kenney, the regal Lady Lytton. Such beautiful faces, so full of happiness and purpose. She envied them. She really did. And they all welcomed her, wanted her. A camaraderie of women. Yes, she could give herself to that.

Then other images entered her mind: Kitty in her East End flat, Kitty marching down the street, wearing chains, scuffling with police, being dragged away to the mariah. Then came the worst image of all, Lady Lytton, on her back, held down, teeth pried apart, food poured down a tube. It was too horrible, and she shoved the image aside. She couldn't do any of it. She knew she couldn't. It wasn't her. Kitty did it and found happiness. That was Kitty. But she was Sylvia Hartley. She could not, would not. As the image of the forced feeding crept into her mind, Sylvia shuddered.

She rode along, looking out the window, thinking of the Pankhursts, the other women she'd met, trying to have more pleasant thoughts. Then she remembered Kitty's flat. The squalor! Yet Kitty seemed happy there. Sylvia remembered her confession to Kitty, that her life was empty, purposeless, that she was alone, unloved, unhappy. Yes, it was all true. Kitty had offered her an alternative. *I was headed for the course you're on. I met Christabel Pankhurst. She saved my life.* Kitty and Christabel. Yes, they went together. They were fellow believers, united in purpose. Aloud, Sylvia whispered, "What purpose do you have, Sylvia Hartley?" Then, bitterly, she thought of Lord Charles and Philip Waring. "Some purpose."

She was nearly home, already late for tea, and she sensed these few minutes alone might be the last for a long time. She had to make use of them. She had to reach some decision. Clasping her hands together, as if in prayer, she articulated the promise to bring more purpose to her life. She would read *Votes for Women*, read about the women's movement in the newspapers. She would defend them whenever she could. Mrs. Pankhurst was right. Perhaps she would come to it in her own time. Meanwhile, she would keep an open mind. She would try to do better.

Sylvia was right about one thing. Her minutes alone in the hansom were to be the last she would have for days. As she arrived home, she saw several vehicles and carriages in front of Lord Winnie's home. With dismay, she recognized Lord Charles' Rolls with the crest on the door. Heavens, she had run off from the sitting without speaking to him. She had forgotten her engagement with him. Discarding her hat, muff and fur piece, she went immediately to the duke. "Charles, I feel dreadful. How could I have been so thoughtless?"

He did not seem upset. "It-It's all right, Sylvia. I j-just wondered wh-wh-what h-happened to you?"

"An old friend from school got in touch with me. I quite forgot my appointment with you. I'm so sorry."

He smiled. "It is of n-no importance. There was j-just someone wh-who w-wanted to m-meet you. He is h-here now, so it is all r-right."

Such a large throng had come to tea that it was being held in the drawing room. As Lord Charles led her across the room toward a group of people gathered there, she saw Waring standing off by himself. He smiled at her knowingly and nodded decorously. She looked back levelly.

The group she was led to included Lord Winnie and her mother. "Where on *earth* have you *been,* Sylvia? We've been waiting *ages* for you."

Sylvia looked at her mother. She seemed especially well-gowned and coiffed and more than a little twittery. Obviously, she was trying to impress someone. "I was held up in traffic, mother." It was almost the truth.

The reason for Lady Constance's agitation stood next to her, a man perhaps fifty, resplendent in an elaborate military uniform. He was short, heavy-bodied, with a paunch no amount of tailoring could hide. He had a square, obviously Germanic head, mostly bald, and a wide, carefully-waxed handlebar mustache over full, puffy lips. Sylvia saw a florid face, a rather bulbous nose marred by red veins and eyes that completely repulsed her—large, milky-blue and, as he looked at her, full of undisguised lust.

"Your Highness, m-may I p-present Miss Sylvia Hartley. S-Sylvia, His Royal H-Highness, the G-Grand Duke R-Rudolph Francis of A-Austria-Hungary."

He clicked his heels in the fashion of the Prussian military and bowed. Sylvia, remembering her manners, rendered a deep curtsy, from which the stranger lifted her. He did not release her hand, even after he had again bowed and kissed it. In a thick German accent, he said, "I read of your beautiful, Miss Hartley. De vords are not justice." Clearly, his English was not too fluent.

"Thank you, Your Highness."

"Your eyes, dey are most—how you say in Anglish? Un . . . un—" He turned to Lord Charles.

The duke took a guess. "Unusual, Prince Rudolph?"

The Austrian smiled. "Yah, dat is de vord—unusual."

Sylvia could only murmur her thanks while managing to free his grip on her hand. As she did so, she saw him looking boldly at her figure, all the way down to her exposed calf. He might have been undressing her. And when his eyes again met hers, she once again saw undisguised lust.

Lord Winnie made some query about Vienna, which led to a more lively conversation in which Sylvia did not participate. All she had to endure was the expression in the grand duke's eyes and the approving smiles he lavished upon her. From this conversation and questions she was later able to ask Lord Charles, she learned the visitor was the younger brother of Franz Joseph I, the Austro-Hungarian Emperor and, as such, a prominent member of the House of Hapsburg. He was not on an official State visit, but had come informally to open his country's exhibit at an international trade fair. Smiling, Lord Charles said he believed the real reason for the grand duke's visit was to have a good time.

"I have no doubt he will," Sylvia whispered. "I just hope this tea fulfills my obligation."

"I f-fear not, S-Sylvia. He p-particularly asked to m-meet you. That's wh-why King George especially a-asked me to be his h-host."

Sylvia looked at him sharply. "You're not serious?"

"I am, S-Sylvia. Very m-much so." Lord Charles then went on to explain the international situation to her. The British government had hopes of undermining the alliance between Prussia and the House of Hapsburg. At the very least, the government wanted nothing to happen during the grand duke's visit to drive the two enemies of England closer together. "Thus, Sylvia, the K-King has given me a h-heavy r-r-responsibility. I n-need your help, m-my dear."

"*My* help. What can I do?"

"I kn-know you c-cannot act as my h-hostess. But your p-presence will be of g-great a-assistance. I a-ask you to be n-n-n—pleasant to His H-Highness."

She sighed. "Charles, you must see how he looks at me."

"Oh, that, p-pay no a-attention." He laughed. "He has a

w-wife and ch-ch-children in V-Vienna. I think g-grandchildren too."

With more apprehension than mirth, Sylvia said, "I just wish they were here with him."

There began for Sylvia a most difficult period. As Grand Duke Rudolph was fêted by the leading peers of Britain, so was she. There were nightly dinners, balls and soirées honoring the Hapsburgs, many of them lasting till the wee hours of the morning. Sylvia had to be her most beautiful and charming, as well as lavishly gowned. Then, the grand duke wanted to take her horseback riding a few mornings or see her at lunch. Her attendance at tea or evening receptions was mandatory.

Sylvia had endured such spates of partygoing, but this one was particularly exhausting for her, for Grand Duke Rudolph was the most boorish, rude and forward individual she had ever encountered. The very first night, at a dinner at Lord Charles', he felt her knee under the table. When he danced with her, which was often, he held her indecently close, rubbing himself against her. He took the most outrageous advantage of his royal prerogatives, making risqué, even obscene remarks to her, and conniving constantly to be alone with her. Sylvia was driven to the limits of guile to keep him at bay.

At that, she was only partially successful. He tricked her into showing him Lord Charles' library. Once there, he closed the door behind her and immediately grabbed her, smothering her with kisses. Upset and repulsed, Sylvia struggled with him, finally pushing him away.

"But vhy? Never haf I seen anyone so beauty. Never haf I dis passionate." As proof—not that any was needed—he darted a hand out and squeezed her breast.

She jumped back. "Your Highness, please!"

He waved his hand to silence her. "Forgif me, but you haf great beautiful, *sehr*—how you say? Oh, yes, luffly. You are *sehr* luffly."

"Your Highness, I—"

"I luff you. I must haf you. I am . . . on fire mit passion. I gif you anything, anything in whole volrd. Vat you vant? Just tell me. I get it. Tonight I get it."

"Your Highness, there is nothing I—" She never got to finish, as he lunged at her, again sweeping her into his arms, pressing his mouth on hers, his hand groping inside the bodice of her gown. Mercifully, the butler Wuthering came into the library, forcing the grand duke to observe his royal manners. However, he whispered to her, "Tonight, my room. You come."

In her anger, she just managed to remember he was the brother of an Emperor. "Your Highness, you are such a tease," she said, as she bolted past him and out of the room.

As soon as she could, she told Lord Charles what had happened, protesting that she could not endure the man. "He's repulsive, Charles—I don't care where he's grand duke of."

"I-I know, S-Sylvia. That's wh-why I sent W-Wuthering to find you."

"Thank God you did. I will not be alone with him—and I will not go to his room as he wants."

"I underst-st-stand, S-Sylvia. You will n-not have to be a-a-alone with him again."

Lord Charles tried, but he was not entirely successful. Even in her own home, when Lord and Lady Linfield held a ball for the visiting royalty, she never knew when Prince Rudolph was going to pop out from behind a curtain or from around a corner to seize her. Waring was present that night. She begged him to help her. Vastly amused by her predicament, he tried nonetheless to stay at her side.

Later on in the evening, as he danced with her, Waring said, "Tonight?"

She glanced at him. "Lord, Philip, I'm too tired. All I want to do is fall into bed."

"Nonsense. You're just tense. You need some relaxation."

She laughed. "You're hardly relaxing, Philip."

"But I'm good for you. We're good for each other. And it has been over a week."

She shook her head, then heard him say, "Besides, I've a new acquisition I want to show you."

Sylvia heard his gentle, even breathing and knew he was asleep. It wouldn't last long. Philip always dozed off a few minutes afterwards. As quietly as possible, she rolled away from him and sat on the edge of the bed before she stood up. Almost at once, she felt her knees start to give way, and she steadied herself by leaning a hand on the nightstand. In a moment, she was able to make her way, lurching slightly, to his chiffonier and get out a black negligée he had bought her for these occasions.

Donning it, cinching the belt tightly, she made her way to his sitting room. She went directly to the whisky bottle on the table. No, she didn't want that. A few weary steps later, she had opened his liquor cabinet and found a bottle of Courvoisier. Yes, cognac would pick her up. She poured a generous amount in a snifter and, neglecting the ceremonial sloshing of it, raised it to her lips and swallowed deeply.

In a moment, she was sitting in a chair, legs crossed, unmindful that the skirt of the negligée had fallen away from her hip. She was bent nearly double, an elbow resting on her thigh, holding the cognac and smoking a cigarette. He had gotten her to try one before. It was hot, choking, unpleasant, but bold and daring. He had said, "You know, Sylvia, if you did that in public, you'd have half the women in London smoking cigarettes tomorrow." She looked at the burning cylinder. Why was she smoking when she didn't enjoy it? She shrugged. There was no answer.

She was relaxed, but exhausted to the core. She raised the brandy and swallowed again, returning to her former hunched position. The things they had done. Her throat was sore and neither the brandy nor cigarette was helping. She sighed. What did anything matter?

"So you liked my new car."

His voice came from behind her. She watched him stride past her in his bare feet. Naked under his maroon robe, he picked up the whisky bottle, poured. "Yes," she said.

"I thought you would."

When she had come out the servants' entrance, he was waiting in a new BMW two-seater roadster, his vaunted new acquisition. "But I'm surprised you've given up on horses."

"I haven't, but you have to keep up with the times."

"I suppose. It's a beautiful car. Must have cost a fortune."

"I suspect it did."

He was standing over her, sipping his whisky. "What are you drinking?"

"Cognac."

"More?"

"Might as well." She drained her glass and gave it to him. When he handed it back to her half-full, he said, "You all right, Sylvia? Anything wrong?"

She sighed, exhaling the last of the smoke. "No, I'm fine."

"I think not. You're not very happy, are you?"

She looked at him coldly. "That doesn't take much discernment from you, Philip."

"You want to talk about it?"

"No."

"Oh, come on, Sylvia. I'm trying to help. What's bothering you?"

She sighed again. Then, a little to her surprise, the words came tumbling out of her. "Everything. That's what's bothering me. You, me, you and me, everything. For over a week, I've done nothing but fend off the amorous advances of some gross Austrian duke. Believe me, he's not very grand, whatever his title says." She heard Waring laugh. "Then what do I do? I come here. . . . God, Philip, what am I doing here? Why do I go to bed with you when it's all going nowhere? Why am I sitting here in the middle of the night drinking cognac and smoking a cigarette I don't want? Why do I do it? Why do I waste my life this way? It's so stupid. So . . . false."

He smiled. "Why? Because you like it. Because we're good together." He saw her glare at him, shake her head in despair. "But you're right. You certainly are wasting your time with me."

That surprised her. "At least you admit it."

"I do. You should be with Lord Charles right now or—" He laughed. "—that crazy Hungarian or whatever he is. They can do something for you. I can't. I've no money."

"You do all right." She made a gesture to encompass the room. "This flat is nice. You dress well. You've money for the best places."

He laughed. "That doesn't take money—not real money. I can beg and borrow enough for all this. It isn't real money, though."

"What about your new car?"

"A gift, Sylvia. An admirer gave it to me." He saw her eyebrows rise in surprise. "She was a bit old for my tastes, but she was grateful. It's all that matters."

She stared at him, shaking her head. "Really, Philip?"

He laughed. "Be shocked if you want, but when you have

no money, it's the only way. I can't live on my pittance of an inheritance or my paltry army salary. I must do what I can. I have this face, this body. They are my only talents." He saw her shaking her head and was unable to tell whether it was in disgust or disbelief. "You could do much better than I, Sylvia. For starters, women don't have the money men do. Just by saying yes and doing what you did for free tonight, you could have anything you want. You want a motor car? You'll have a far bigger one than I do. Look at those emeralds our friend the duke gave you. You can have all the jewelry in the world. You want clothes, furs? It's easy. You want land, buildings, shares in some company, a nice nest egg somewhere? It's all yours for the taking."

"Stop it, Philip. I don't want to hear it."

"All right, I'll stop. But just tell me, what is it you want?"

"Nothing. I want nothing," she said dully.

"That's nonsense. Everybody wants something. If you could have anything in the world, what would it be?"

She looked at him; then, suddenly, inexplicably, she burst into tears, covering her face with her hands, her body shaking.

He let her cry, making no move to comfort her. Finally, he heard, "Meg. I want Meg."

"Who's Meg?"

He waited her out. The name sent her into another spasm of sobs, but finally, gradually, she came out of it, wiping her face with her palms, then using the hem of her negligée. He went to the bedroom for a handkerchief and gave it to her. While she wiped and dabbed and blew, he repeated his question. "Who's Meg?"

Finally, her voice breaking a little, she could answer. "Meg was . . . is my . . . dearest friend." She stopped, breathing deeply, trying to control herself. "We grew up together. She became my maid, but a special one. She got pregnant, had to get married. My mother sacked her. She never liked Meg."

"So?" He didn't understand; she could hear it in his voice. Arthur would have understood, she thought. But why think of Arthur, now? She went on:

"Meg lives out in Hornby, near Downhaven. She's . . . she's terribly poor. I—I want to help her. I—I want . . . her with me."

"Then have her."

187

She stared at him. "What do you mean?"

"I mean what I said. She was your maid. Hire her again."

"But I can't. I told you, my mother—she won't let her set foot in the house."

"That's her house—or Lord Winnie's. Get a place of your own. Hire whomever you please. You want Meg. Let it be Meg."

She stared at him again. He sounded so detached, so pragmatic. "I—I don't . . . think I . . . understand."

He laughed. "Sometimes, Sylvia, you're really obtuse. Look, it's simple. In a few days, no more than a fortnight, you're going to be twenty-one. Right?"

"Yes."

"You'll be of age. You can operate your own establishment."

"But I don't have—"

"Of course, you don't, but you can get it." He laughed. "That beserk Hapsburg. He wants you so badly, he'd give you half his empire just to have ten minutes in bed with you. He'd give you the finest house in London, if you'd just say yes."

Sylvia was horrified. "I couldn't. I never could."

Again, he laughed. "Oh, yes, you could. You'd be surprised whom you can sleep with if you want something badly enough. That lady with the motor car was—"

"No, never. I couldn't."

"All right, then forget the grand duke. How about the plain duke, your friend Lord Charles? He gave you a fortune in jewels. Surely, he's good for a house."

She seemed only to be able to stare at him in disbelief. "Charles? I couldn't."

"What d'you mean, you couldn't? You have already, haven't you? What's another tumble or two, if its the way to be with your friend. What's her name? Oh, yes, Meg. You want Meg. Have her. You really are silly, Sylvia."

She didn't reply. She half-envied his detachment—no, callousness. Half-feared it too. She could all too easily become a female Philip Waring—it was that she saw at the bottom of the abyss, and it terrified her. But what was the alternative? She was no longer the girl at the cottage, no longer the Sylvia who had existed before that—Meg's friend. Oh, Meg, Meg, if only she could be with Meg. . . .

Chapter Nineteen

"Clara, if I were to get my own establishment, would you like to come with me?"

Sylvia sat before her mirror having her hair done. She had hardly slept last night, yet she felt more exhilarated than in a long time. Her mind was alive with plans, as it had been ever since Waring had planted the idea in her brain. Meg would be her maid. There was no doubt of that. She wanted Meg close to her, always. But what would she do with Clara? She had no need for two maids, and she sensed that Meg and Clara would not get along. But Clara was a better hairdresser than Meg; indeed, better at a number of things. It was a problem for a time, then Sylvia came to a decision. Meg would learn from Clara, and Clara would become her secretary, maybe the housekeeper. But she would not be in charge of Meg. She would not give her orders. Brian would become chauffeur and gardener. Then she would need a cook, someone older, sweet and motherly. Yes, motherly. It would be a small staff, but it would do. She intended to ask the duke for only a small house, little more than a cottage, actually.

"Of course, miss. You needn't have asked."

Sylvia smiled at the reflection in the mirror. "I know, but I thought perhaps—well, your position here with Lord Winnie offers more permanency . . . other advantages."

Clara hesitated. "Has something happened, miss? Are you . . . ?"

With effort, Sylvia restrained her impulse to turn to Clara, hug her and let her wonderful plan for Meg bubble out of her. She wanted to share her happiness. But she must wait, tell Meg first. Oh, how thrilled she would be! Sylvia could hardly wait to rush to Hornby with the news.

Now, however, Sylvia restrained herself. "Nothing has happened, Clara. But I have been thinking of what you said. It occurred to me—well, Lord Charles has been asking me what I want for my birthday. I thought . . . perhaps . . . I might. . . ."

"Ask him for your own home?"

Sylvia smiled. "I would not expect him to actually *give* it to me. But, perhaps, if I were in my own place . . . it might offer . . . conveniences . . . to him, to both of us." She looked at Clara in the mirror. "What do you think?"

Slowly at first, then quite rapidly, Clara's face spread into the broadest smile Sylvia had ever seen on her. She noticed that Clara had a gold tooth at the far side of her mouth which Sylvia had never seen before. "Miss Sylvia, I think it's a simply marvelous idea."

Sylvia's smile mirrored her maid's. "I thought you might."

"Oh, yes! When do you plan to ask him?"

"I don't know. Whenever the opportunity arises. Lord Charles is very busy just now with the grand duke."

Sylvia was prophetic in that. Grand Duke Rudolph, the houseguest of Lord Charles, was omnipresent and apparently tireless in both his partygoing and his pursuit of her. Sylvia was in a quandary. She wanted to attract and enflame Lord Charles, and so she dressed provocatively. But the more décolleté her gowns, the more she had to fend off the visiting Hapsburg. Still, she managed. In her moments with Lord Charles, however fleeting, she strove for greater intimacy with him through smiles, a touch of her hand, once a seemingly impetuous brushing of his cheek with her lips and verbal expressions of how much she wished they could have some time alone. None of this was wasted. Lord Charles was delighted with her, but she was no nearer a house of her own than a few days previously.

Finally, the opportunity came. "I have wh-what I think is g-good news, Sylvia. The grand d-duke is g-going away for the w-weekend."

Sylvia's smile was radiant. "Forgive me. I know he is your guest, but this is the best news I've heard in my life. How on earth did you manage it?"

"It took some d-doing." His smile matched hers. "I c-convinced P-Palmerston to take him sh-shooting in the c-country."

Sylvia glanced around quickly to see who was there. They were alone, and she bent and gave the duke a quick kiss on the lips. "You are a miracle-worker, Charles, a wonder of wonders."

He beamed. "Yes, I th-thought so m-myself. Wh-What would you l-like to do t-t-tonight?"

"Ab-so-lute-ly nothing. I just want to collapse." She saw a hurt look coming to his eyes and smiled. "I want to spend a quiet evening with you, Charles. I don't want to go anywhere. Above all, I don't want to see anyone but you. Could we be alone? Just we two? A quiet dinner—here perhaps?"

The delight in his face told her the opportunity had at last arisen for her.

If Sylvia had ever taken greater pains in preparing for an evening, she could not remember it. All she said to Clara was that she was dining alone with Lord Charles, but it was enough; the maid took extra pains with bath and hair. Clara did something novel with her coiffure, arranging it so it seemed elaborate atop her head, but with a fall of rather girlish curls down the back of her neck. Ingeniously, it was so arranged as to be easily let down. There were a minimum of braids and pins.

The gown Sylvia selected was one she had never had the courage to wear in public before—certainly not with the amorous Austrian around. It was all of fine Flemish lace, quite elegant and seemingly demure, with fitted sleeves and bodice. The skirt was narrow, although draped at her hips to give the effect of greater fullness, and slit to reveal a white satin slipper. It might have been at least the beginning of a bridal gown, except that its modesty was only an illusion. The gown had no back almost to her waist, thus preventing any possibility of wearing a chemise. And the front of the empire-style bodice was just lace, nothing else, no slip, no hidden stays, no support of any kind. For practical purposes, she was naked to the waist, her breasts barely concealed behind a thin barrier of lace. In her mirror, Sylvia believed she could actually see the pink of her nipples. Worse—or, hopefully, for this evening, better—each turning of her shoulders, each step she took was reflected in the movement of her breasts. There was nothing to be done about it—nor did she want to this night. When she arrived at Lord Charles' and her wrap was removed, she knew from his face she had selected the right garment for the evening.

"A-A-Another new g-gown, Sylvia? I d-don't believe I've s-seen it."

"It's new. I hoped you might like it."

"I d-do, v-very m-much."

She smiled. "I'm glad. Needless to say, I wasn't going to wear it around you-know-who."

He laughed. "I should j-judge not."

She took his arm, being careful to press her breast against his elbow, and accompanied him to a small parlor, cozy with a fire, where he poured drinks, brandy for himself, sherry for her. Her taste for spirits was not something she shared with him.

"Oh, Charles, I feel blessed to have this evening with you." Her voice sounded false to her ears, but she must think of Meg.

"Why, my d-dear?"

"I'm so tired of people, Charles, the parties, the idle chatter, the emptiness. I feel sometimes I'm losing sight of myself." This, at least, was true.

"I'm sure y-you're not, Sylvia."

"Are you, Charles? I sometimes feel the only time I can really be myself is when I'm with you."

He was touched, firming his lips, blinking his eyes. "I b-believe, Sylvia, that is the n-nicest thing you have ever s-said to me."

"I mean it, Charles. I really do." She smiled intimately at him, then raised the sherry to wet her lips. "I wish we could always find the time and place to be alone, just talking like this." Strangely, she meant it. Charles, whatever his shortcomings, was real. For that, she was grateful.

He came to her then, embracing and kissing her. Her lips moved hungrily against his, and she was surprised by her own arousal. The gown, her feeling of nakedness, her kindliness toward him and her hopes for the evening must have conspired to make her so. Certainly, she had never before responded to him like this.

He pulled back, his hands on her shoulders. "My dear. . . ."

"Oh, Charles. . . ." She leaned toward him and the kiss renewed, now deeper, more probing. She did not resist, but felt his quickened breath, heard his tiny moans of pleasure. Then she felt his fingers searching over her breast, pressed high against his chest. She contrived to move away, giving him access, letting him squeeze her risen nipple.

Again, he broke away, panting a little. "I f-fear I'm as im-impetuous as the g-grand duke."

She smiled, her lips still wet. "I was wondering when Wuthering was coming to rescue me."

"He'd b-better not."

She leaned forward again, but bending more, allowing their mouths to join, both his hands to find her breasts. It was heavenly, what he was doing with his hands, and she felt the sharp rise of desire, heard her sounds of arousal echoing his.

"M-My d-dear, hadn't we b-best w-wait?"

She smiled. "I fear so."

He held her, his hands now on her upper arms, looking at her soulfully, tenderly, happiness reigning on his face. "My d-dear, I do love you s-so."

"Oh, Charles, I—"

"You n-needn't sp-sp-speak, Sylvia. J-Just having you h-here is enough."

"You know I wanted this, Charles." She didn't know what she wanted, just now. But he was a kind person—she felt that strongly at this moment.

"Yes. I have b-been so h-happy the last few d-days, Sylvia. You s-seem so . . . m-more—" He paused, grappling for control of his tongue. "D-Dare I th-think you . . . are b-b-beginning to c-care for m-me?"

She smiled. "Charles, you must know I do. Am I not here now?"

"Oh, yes, and so l-lovely, it w-wounds me." He started to pull her to him again, then stopped, smiling. "W-We'd best b-behave, h-hadn't we?"

She laughed. "Again, I fear so."

He led her back to where the liquor was and refreshed both their glasses. They stood near each other, talking and laughing, mostly about the grand duke and his very unregal antics.

"I f-fear P-P-Palmerston will not sp-speak to me after th-this weekend."

"It will be worth it, I assure you."

Never had she been so conscious of her breasts, their size, their movement in response to her every gesture, even her laughter. But seeing his eyes on her frequently, she made no effort to hold herself still. On the contrary. . . .

His gaze rose to meet hers, and he smiled shyly. "I love your g-gown, S-Sylvia. I c-cannot take my e-eyes off it."

She laughed. "I think it is not the gown, Charles." She saw him start to redden and her laugh deepened. "Oh, come, Charles, you and I can't possibly have any secrets anymore." She saw a flicker of distress in his face. She almost loved him for it—thank God, all men weren't Philip Warings. Then he smiled with good humor.

Their supper in the dining room was as private as Wuthering could make it, and quite lengthy. Sylvia was animated, chattering amiably, laughing a great deal. As they were having dessert, she said, "I'm starting to get excited about my birthday. I guess being twenty-one is special, isn't it?"

"Indeed, my d-dear. And you m-must tell me wh-what I am to g-give you."

She laughed. "I told you, Charles, I want nothing from you." She hated the role she was playing, but then it was for Meg.

"That's s-silly. I m-must give you s-something, and I w-will. But I so w-want it to be s-something you r-really want. Something sp-special from me."

She reached out and patted his hand. "That's very sweet, Charles."

"I in-insist. T-There must be something. P-Please tell me wh-what it is."

She smiled. "I tell you, Charles, there is nothing." She laughed, seemingly shyly. "Of course, there is always *something* a girl wants, but this is—"

"Tell me, p-please."

"No, it's ridiculous, truly so." But it wasn't ridiculous—it was for Meg. She had to think of Meg to get through this.

"I insist, Sylvia."

"Oh, all right, if you insist." The smile and glance she gave

A LASTING SPLENDOR

him were pure coquetry. "But later, when we are . . . alone."

"Oh, t-tell me now, p-please."

She duplicated her smile, the movement of her eyes, and whispered, "It's better in *private*, Charles. Just be patient."

After dinner, he led her into the drawing room and asked her to play for him. She sat at the piano and sang "Rose of Tralee." He stood behind her, hands on her shoulders and joined in "Galway Bay." His tenor voice was more than adequate, and his words were clear of any stutter. She felt sincere tenderness for him—she only wished she could feel more.

They sat at cards then, playing two-handed rummy, laughing and squealing over their various fortunes. It was all, she knew, killing time, waiting for the servants to retire. Frequently, he clasped her hand and looked at her soulfully. He was doing so when Wuthering entered, clearing his throat, and asked if there would be anything else. Lord Charles thanked and dismissed him.

They played out their hands, both feeling mounting nervousness, then Charles came around the table, pulled her to her feet and embraced her. Sylvia could feel her passion flow from her mouth into his, for she was exultant, knowing the evening was going well, that he would give her anything she wanted.

As they made their way upstairs to his bedroom, arm in arm, stopping frequently on the stairs to embrace, she tried to rein in her sensuality. He was naturally shy, reserved. She should not be too bold with him.

As he kissed her and kissed her in the bedchamber, he said, "I have never seen you s-so a-a-aroused, Sylvia."

Mouth open, lips bruised, she replied, "I don't think I have ever been this way before, Charles."

There was no faking of her passion this time. She felt filled with desire, and her breasts, her thighs, her whole body became instruments of it. She stunned him with her passion, but she was careful to show some restraint, asking him if he wanted her to do what she was doing and hearing his moaned affirmative before going on. And she was careful to do nothing too bold, avoiding anything he might consider wanton.

At last, they lay beside each other, she in the crook of his

195

arm, her knee curled over his hips. "I'm sorry, Charles. I—I don't know what . . . came over me. Was I, you know, too . . . too—"

"You w-weren't t-too anything, Sylvia. You were perfect."

"You mean I wasn't . . . ?"

"D-Don't be silly. I l-loved it. I-I love you. You en-enjoyed it, d-didn't you?"

"Oh, yes, yes, Charles." She moved her arm across his chest, squeezing him. "I didn't know it could possibly be so heavenly." Suddenly, she remembered Arthur then, and winced.

"N-Nor I." He smiled. "I c-certainly d-didn't know I could d-do it so often."

They lay together for a time filled with caresses and intimate words. Sylvia was pondering whether it was wise to arouse him again; or would that seem too forward?

"Oh, I almost f-forgot. Your b-birthday. You were g-going to t-tell me what p-present I am to give you."

She felt a burst of excitement. The time had come. "Don't be silly, Charles."

"You m-must. You p-promised."

She laughed lightly. "I've quite forgotten what it was, Charles."

"Don't t-tease, Sylvia."

"All right. I know you must give me something, Charles. But just make it some trinket. Surprise me. I love surprises."

"No, Sylvia. Wh-What is it you w-want."

She sighed. "There is something, Charles, but I don't think—"

"I'm g-going to be a-angry with you. What is it you w-want?"

"Oh, Charles, I—it is just too much to ask."

"W-What is? Tell me. I'll g-give you a-anything."

At last, he had said it. She turned, more to her side, leaning on her right elbow, holding her head, her breast resting against his chest. Looking down at him she said, "You can't be serious, Charles."

"I assure you, I have n-never been m-more s-s-serious in my life."

She smiled. "Anything, Charles?" God, how she hated this.

"Yes, j-just tell me wh-what."

With the fingers of her left hand she began to trace around his lips, over his chin. Then she stopped. Her expression serious, she said softly, "I want my independence."

He was surprised. "Your in-in-in . . . ?" He could not get the word out.

"My independence, that's what I want."

"But how? I d-don't un-understand."

"Lord Winnie is most generous with me, but it is still his home—and my mother's. I must do as they wish. Oh, it is not a heavy burden. I don't really mind—most of the time. I—I am grateful. But, after all, it is *their* home." She hesitated, pursing her lips a little. "More than anything in this world, Charles, I want a place of my own, a home of my own, a place for my things, my servants, a place where I can be myself."

He was looking at her, mirroring her seriousness. "That's what you w-want? A h-home?"

"Yes." She smiled. "A place where you can come and we can be alone as often as we wish—for just such lovely evenings as this one."

She saw his seriousness. He was surprised by her request, no doubt of that. But she'd won. Inwardly, she exulted.

He looked at her, unblinking, for a long moment, then he looked away to his right, obviously thinking. She waited, knowing that when he again looked at her it would be to give her a house. She thought of something else. "I don't have in mind anything grand, Charles. Just a small house, a servant or two." She waited for him to speak, jubilant, knowing what he would say. Idly, she again began to trace his lips with her forefinger.

He took her wrist and moved her hand, then slowly, still not looking at her, he moved her away from him, pushing her shoulder gently. He rolled and sat on the edge of the bed. She too, sat up, touching his shoulder. "What's wrong, Charles?"

He stood up, turning, looking down at her. "I'm sorry, Sylvia. I couldn't possibly give you that, a house." His stammer had suddenly left him.

It began inside her like a wound, an ulcer. "But you said—"

"I know what I said."

"—anything." No Meg? She thought. No Meg? All this . . . for nothing?

Distress came to his face. "But I had no idea. I thought you m-meant some j-jewelry, some b-bauble. I had no i-idea you w-wanted. . . ." He sighed deeply. "I can't, Sylvia, I just c-can't."

"But why?"

"If you are u-unhappy at Lord Winnie's, I have o-offered you my h-hand in m-marriage. I will m-marry you, Sylvia, t-tomorrow if you wish. I will g-give you a home, this h-home, but . . . but I c-cannot g-give you a house."

She could feel her stomach knotting. "At least tell me why, Charles." She saw him look away, not wanting to answer. "Charles, if I have in some way offended you—please, Charles, you must speak. I—I don't understand what you are saying."

He stared at her a long moment; then, when he spoke, his stammer had worsened. "I l-love you, S-Sylvia. I r-r-respect you. I-If I g-give you a h-h-house, I w-will be m-making you my m-m-mistress. I c-can't d-do that to y-you."

Her inner wound split open, pouring out her shame and humiliation. She got to her knees on the bed, looking at him. Then her reaction came as anger, boiling, seething inside her. She opened her mouth, wanting to scream at him, *What do you think we've just been doing?*

She did not speak, but rather got off the bed and strode to where her clothes were.

"A-Are you a-angry with m-me, Sylvia?"

She pulled up her abbreviated pantaloons, buttoning them, then sat on the chair and bent to slip on her stockings. "You have not made me feel exactly happy, Charles."

Now he was really distressed. "But w-why?"

"I hadn't wanted to tell you. You insisted. I certainly am sorry I ever did." She looked up, saw the pain on his face and didn't care. "You gave me the Lombardy emeralds. I will send them back in the morning."

"God, S-Sylvia, you c-can't."

"Why can't I? What's the difference, jewels or a house? I'm sure the jewels are worth far more."

"B-B-B—" In his distress he could not get a word out. Repeatedly, he tried, wringing his hands. Finally, he managed. "J-J-Jewels are a g-g-gift of love. A h-h-house is a . . . a. . . ." Again he lost his speech. When he recovered, it was to say, "S-S-Sylvia, y-you are y-y-young. You d-d-don't kn-know. I must l-l-look after y-your r-reput-t-tation."

By the time he finished, she was already into her dress, buttoning the waist in back. With all her heart she wanted to scream at him, *Were you looking after my reputation just now, in bed?* But she did not. In a voice not too sarcastic, all things considered, she said, "I'm sure you know what's best, Charles."

Chapter Twenty

As soon as she saw Sylvia's seething anger, an expectant Clara knew something had gone wrong. When they were alone and Clara was taking Sylvia's wrap, she said, "Things did not go well, miss?"

Sylvia turned to look at her and said, her voice flat and icy, "I have learned one thing, Clara. One must ask for what one wants *before*—not *after*."

Clara smiled inwardly. She had thought this girl already knew that. "The duke refused?"

"Did he ever! God, what an *impossible* man. Ab-so-lutely *unbelievable.*"

Clara watched as Sylvia angrily stalked to her dressing table and began to pull pins out of her hair, throwing them on the vanity. "I'll do that, Sylvia. Just be seated."

"No, I'm too angry to sit. I'll do it."

"Whatever you wish, miss." She watched as Sylvia angrily pulled and tugged at her hair until it had fallen down her back. The movement of her breasts as she raised and lowered her arms jolted even the placid Clara. Surely, the duke had been enflamed by that. "Did he give a reason, miss?"

Sylvia, reaching behind her back to unbutton her dress, turned to her maid. "A reason? Oh, yes, he had a reason all right. He *loves* me. He *respects* me. If he gives me a house, everyone will think I am his mistress. He *can't* do that. He must look after my *welfare*, my *reputation.*"

A LASTING SPLENDOR

"I see."

"No you don't see, Clara. There I am, naked in his bed, having just . . . and he's worried about my *reputation*." In her anger, she actually stamped her foot. "The gall of the man. What a *hypocrite* he is. I've never *known* such a hypocrite."

"I quite agree, miss."

"Oh, how I wanted to *tell* him."

Alarm pricked at Clara. "You didn't, did you?"

Sylvia's anger now flared at her. "What kind of fool do you think I am, Clara?"

The servant knew the wisest course was to say nothing.

"I just *wanted* to say it. Oh, how I wish I could have!"

"I quite understand, miss. No one could have blamed you if you had." She went to her, assuming the task of getting her out of the gown. "I mean no offense, Miss Sylvia. I was just—"

"Oh, I'm sorry, Clara." The words came out with a long sigh. "You've done nothing. I've no right to take my anger out on you."

"I didn't think you were, Miss Sylvia."

The task of unfastening and stepping out of the gown took only moments, but it was long enough for Sylvia's anger, now vented, to leave her. Suddenly, she felt tired. Slipping into the robe Clara held out for her seemed to take all her strength. While Clara put away the gown, Sylvia slid onto the bench before her vanity. When Clara turned back to her, Sylvia was bent over, elbows on her thighs, both hands pressed against her face.

Clara observed her a moment. She was not crying. The maid felt a twinge of compassion as she crossed the room toward Sylvia. This girl was young. She had much to learn. Right now she needed her confidence restored. Picking up the hairbrush, Clara asked, "Are you all right, miss?"

Sylvia felt the brush against her hair and, rousing herself, sat up. "I'm just tired, Clara and—oh, it was awful. I felt like. . . ." She sighed, unable to express her feelings.

Without altering the rhythm of her brushing, Clara said, "Don't despair. When the duke has had a chance to think about it, he will change his mind. I'm sure of it."

"No, he won't."

Clara smiled. "Well, I have seen it happen. When his

... shall we say, desires? ... return, his lofty ideals may ... not seem so vital to him."

Sylvia said nothing, but she was able to think more clearly now. Yes, perhaps Charles would change his mind.

She heard Clara speak. "Meanwhile, you should get some rest."

"Yes. I'm not going to set foot out of bed all day tomorrow."

"I believe you are to see Lord Charles tomorrow?"

"No, I'm not going to. I'm going to be—" She smiled. "—indisposed. A headache, I think. You will send a note to him tomorrow."

"Is that wise?"

Sylvia's smile broadened. "Yes, most wise."

Behind her mask of servitude, Clara smiled inwardly. The girl was learning. She would do all right.

The hair-brushing continued a few moments, then Sylvia spoke with surprising vehemence. "Clara, I will have that house. One way or another, I will have it. Make no mistake."

"As I say, I believe the duke will relent."

"I hope you're right. But if he doesn't, I will still have it."

Behind her back, making downward strokes against her hair, Clara asked, "The Austrian?"

Sylvia shuddered. "If need be. I will do anything." To herself she added the words *for Meg*. Beginning then and for long after she was in bed, Sylvia held to her resolve. All this was for Meg. It was the only way to be reunited with her and to help her. She visualized the shack in Hornby. October was ending and it was cold already. Meg must be freezing.

Sylvia's hope that Lord Charles would change his mind ended Monday morning, as she read his note.

My Dear Sylvia,

Please forgive my writing to you this way, but it is far easier for me to express myself, and if, as I fear, you never wish to see me again, I will at least have the satisfaction of knowing I have made known my high regard for you.

I spent a most lonely and disconsolate evening last night. A hundred times, I wanted to telephone you, begging your forgiveness. My love for you cries out for me to grant your every wish, to fall at your feet, asking only for the opportunity to grant your heart's desire.

But, my darling, reason must sometimes rule the heart. If I grant you your wish for independence and provide you with a domicile, I will have set you on a course which defies wisdom. I know your motives are of the purest, but, unfortunately, we must live in this world. The cynical, the jaded and the wicked will misinterpret my motives for giving, yours for accepting, what you asked of me. However painful it may be for me, however great my risk of losing you forever, I must in my love do what I think is best.

Yours in Despair,
Charles

She read it again, then shrugged as she handed it to Clara. "That," she said, "is that."

At once, Sylvia's mind was filled with what she must do next to obtain the house she was determined to have. But first, she forced her mind and hand to construct a suitable reply to the duke of Glouston.

My Dear Charles,

I was as lonely as you last evening, but I rested and my headache has quite disappeared today.

Please do not despair, for my affection for you has only grown in the knowledge that I have such a devoted friend who gives me such wise counsel. I had not, of course, realized the implications of my request. I am eternally grateful to have such a wise and true friend.

Yours in Affection,
Sylvia

She did not mean a word of it. Quite unfeelingly, she addressed the envelope and sealed it, then asked Clara to see that his lordship received it at once.

Sylvia abandoned any other correspondence that morning, although she had promised herself to write to Meg without fail. But she could bring herself to think of nothing but Grand Duke Rudolph and what she must do to get him to give her a house. The task was made far easier when, just as Sylvia was dressed to leave for her sitting, her mother burst into her room. She was very excited. Count Hohenbaum, aide and secretary to the grand duke, was downstairs requesting an interview.

"With whom?"

"You, my dear. Isn't it *exciting?* What can he want?"

"I can't imagine, mother. We'll just have to see—and don't you try to eavesdrop."

She had met the count, of course. He was tall, military in his bearing, with pomaded blond hair, a great, hooked nose and the most astonishing mustache she had ever seen. It was waxed to a fine point, spread a good three inches on either side of his face, like bat's wings.

His greeting to her was heel-clicks and a formal bow. She led him to a small, sunny parlor, where the chances of their being overheard were small.

"I thank you for receiving me, Miss Hartley." His English was formally correct, although uttered slowly. His accent was minimal.

"I am honored that you have come, Count Hohenbaum."

He sat stiffly in his chair, his uniform helmet in his lap. After clearing his throat, he began. "I come at the request of His Royal Highness, the grand duke."

"Yes."

"His Highness feels his English is inadequate to express what he wishes to say. Since you do not speak German, he has asked me to come in his behalf."

"I see."

"His Highness also feels that because of his deficiencies in the English language, you do not understand his intentions."

Fortunately, Sylvia's inner amusement was not revealed on her face. "That may be so, Count Hohenbaum."

The throat-clearing was longer and louder this time. "His Highness has asked me to say that he considers you the most beautiful woman in London—no, His Highness said the most beautiful woman he has ever seen."

Her smile was slight. "Please thank His Highness. His flattery is most generous."

"During the remainder of his stay in London, he would like the honor of your company."

"Again, thank His Highness. I have seen the grand duke often during his visit. I expect I will continue to do so."

The count was a little flustered by this reply, but quickly masked it. "I believe His Highness wishes to invite you to dinner."

"May I ask who else has been invited? The duke of Glouston, perhaps?"

A massive throat-clearing now ensued. "I believe His Highness has in mind a private dinner, Miss Hartley."

"I see." She paused, perhaps a shade too long. "Count Hohenbaum, I must speak frankly. His Highness is married, is he not?"

"Yes, to the grand duchess, Maria Wilhemina."

Again, she gave a slight smile. "Then you understand my position, Count Hohenbaum."

"You may be assured of His Highness' discretion."

"I'm certain of that, but—I can only hope His Highness will understand and forgive me for declining his invitation."

The Austrian count seemed totally unaffected by her reply. "His Highness has asked me to relay another message to you."

"Yes?"

A more modest throat-clearing now. "His Highness is most desirous of presenting you with a gift."

"A gift?"

"He wishes to express his appreciation for your beauty and his gratitude for the time you have spent with him."

"I see."

The count hesitated, bowing slightly to her. "Miss Hartley, as you perhaps recognize, His Highness has a rather . . . passionate nature. He has asked me to tell you he is prepared to give you anything within his power to give."

She paused, trying desperately to think. Never had she anticipated such an interview. It was like a business negotiation. She got up then and went to the doorway, making certain neither her mother nor anyone else was listening. When she again sat, it was in a chair closer to the count, so she could lower her voice.

"My dear count, I am most flattered by the grand duke's offer. There is one thing I want, a gift which will assure my high regard and continued affection."

"And what might that be, Miss Hartley?"

Forcing all other thoughts from her mind, she said, "I want a residence of my own. I want a clear title in my name and a sufficient annuity to operate it as I see fit." There, it was said.

She saw him smile. She could not have been more surprised by his answer. "Is that all, Miss Hartley?"

She realized she was visibly shaken, and quickly endeavored to hide it. "You may assure the grand duke that would be most generous."

"I shall happily do so, Miss Hartley. And I can personally assure you that His Highness will provide you with the finest dwelling in all Vienna."

"*Vienna!* I don't want it in Vienna. I want it here, in London."

She might be dismayed, but he was not. "I see. Then His Highness will want to give you two homes, I'm sure."

"Two!"

"Yes. One here, a second in Vienna. His Highness is unable to come to London as often as he might want. I'm sure he will want you to spend part of the year in Vienna."

She sat back, too amazed to think.

Count Hohenbaum was not at all nonplussed. He stood up. "If you will let me know the dwelling you desire here in London, Miss Hartley, I will see that the proper papers are drawn up."

She could only stare at him. It couldn't have happened so easily.

"Meanwhile, about His Highness' invitation to dinner. You will accept, of course?"

A house. Just like that, she was to have a house—no, two houses—one in London, another in Vienna. Wait till she told Meg. Her dreams were coming true. She and Meg could be together again.

"I repeat, you will accept the grand duke's invitation to dinner?"

She heard him this time. "Of course. When is it?"

"Tonight. His Highness is most . . . eager to see you."

Suddenly, she shuddered. Grand Duke Rudolph. She couldn't. "Tonight? So soon?"

"I said His Highness is most eager to . . . to see you."

Tonight? She stared at the count, his outlandish mustache

seeming to grow before her eyes. Tonight? She shrugged. Why not? Might as well get it over with. "Do you have the time?"

He pulled a large pocket watch out of his uniform, snapped it open. "Ten before one, Miss Hartley."

There was time. If she hurried, she could get to Hornby, tell Meg the good news and still get back to . . . to. . . . "Count Hohenbaum, I have a busy schedule as you must know. Tonight is most sudden, most difficult for me." She saw him opening his mouth to protest. "I fear it will have to be later this evening."

He smiled. "Of course. A late supper perhaps. Ten? Eleven?"

She sighed. "Eleven."

He stood up. "Eleven o'clock then. His Highness has engaged a suite at the Royal Albert Hotel."

"Yes, I'll remember."

He reached inside his uniform, extracted an envelope, handed it to her. "His Highness asked me to give you this as a . . . token of his esteem."

After he had gone, she opened the envelope. It contained a significant stack of twenty-pound sterling notes.

Chapter Twenty-one

Sylvia boarded the train for Hornby determined to feel only happiness. Laden with gifts for Meg, Brian, even the unborn baby, she was on her way to tell Meg the glorious news. They were to be reunited. No more shack, no more cold, no more loneliness. They were to be together, now and forever.

Riding along, looking out at the countryside, Sylvia was mesmerized by the clickety-clack of the wheels on the rails. Why couldn't she feel happy? It was everything she wanted, everything she'd worked for. Why did she have this sinking feeling? It must be the weather, rainy, cold, damp to the bone. Yes, if the sun were shining, she would feel better. She tried to visualize the scene with Meg, her squeals of joy, hugging Sylvia with happiness over the great news she had brought. She could imagine it, but somehow it did nothing to elevate her spirits.

She thought of the house. It shouldn't be too large nor too small. It ought to be on a quiet street with a circular drive and hidden behind a wall to ensure privacy for those who came and went. Yes, it would be exciting, mistress of her own home. Mentally, she selected her rooms, planned the furnishings. Yes, her own home, her own things, doing as she wanted. Independence. A woman's most precious possession. Yes, it was what she wanted.

Try as she would to prevent it, other thoughts forced their way into her mind. There would be scandal, terrible scandal.

There would be pain in Lord Charles' eyes, mocking laughter in Waring's. And Timothy Graves. Oh, what he'd say, what everyone would say. She would have to tell her mother and Lord Winnie. Oh, God, what a scene. How angry they would be. Over and over, she told herself she didn't care what anyone thought. It had to be done. Anything . . . to have Meg at her side again.

Then came the worst thought of all. The grand duke, his horrible body, the wet lips, the bulging eyes, his hands on her, his. . . . Suddenly, she sat up in her seat, looking around the railway car, fearful everyone must be looking at her, reading her thoughts. Tonight. Oh, God, eleven o'clock tonight. She would have to steel herself, be ready. She must do it. Anything for Meg. It might not be too bad. . . . She could close her eyes, pretend she was back at Arthur's cottage. Hadn't she done that already with Charles . . . and even with Waring?

She took a taxi from the railway station to Meg's place, carrying her parcels in the suddenly heavier rain up the muddy ravine to the shack. No one was home, but the door was unlocked, so Sylvia entered.

She laid her parcels on the table, then called out both their names. No answer. She looked around, saw signs of recent occupancy. They must have stepped out. She would wait.

Once again, the shack appalled her, earthen floor, cracks between the slats in the siding through which the chill entered, the paucity of furnishings, the cold stove. Lord in heaven, had they no heat? She looked at the woodbox. Just a few slats of an old crate, some limbs fallen from trees, all obviously hoarded to cook the evening meal. She glanced back at her parcels. Instead of these silly gifts, she should have brought coal. And she would. Before she left, she would have a bag of coal delivered, two bags.

She continued her inspection, seeing everywhere signs of Meg the homemaker. She had made curtains for the window. Sylvia smiled as she recognized the fabric as one of her old dresses. How clever of Meg. The bed was neatly made, a quilt on top. Again, Sylvia recognized swatches of her old gowns in it. She lifted a corner and inspected the bedding. A single horseblanket. Not enough to keep them warm, not nearly enough. She shivered, both from the chill and from fear. She had to get Meg out of here. This was no way to live. At that moment, Sylvia knew she was doing the right thing. Anything to get Meg out of this place."

She went to stand in the open doorway, looking for Meg to return. The rain was pelting down hard now. Oh, the infernal rain. Why didn't it stop? Why didn't the sun shine? Then she saw Meg, down below, turning up the ravine. She wore a simple black skirt, a brown sweater with a dark-colored shawl around her shoulders. In one hand she carried a parcel, groceries most likely, in the other an umbrella. Tattered. Sylvia could see a rip in it. What good was an umbrella like that?

Meg didn't see her. She was looking down, avoiding puddles, the torrent of water running down the ravine. Why didn't she have boots? Everyone should have boots in weather like this. Meg was closer now. Sylvia could see her thickened middle, the bulge in her skirt, the slow, careful way she walked. Meg looked up, sensing her presence. In that instant of Meg's recognition of her, she saw tiny lines around her eyes. Was that from pain? And she was so pale!

Then the face was lit by the happiest of smiles. "Oh, Sylvie."

She ran the remaining steps to the cottage. There was an awkward, wasted moment getting rid of her parcel and the umbrella, then they were in each other's arms, embracing, kissing, salty tears mingling with drops of fresh rainwater on Meg's face, and many repetitions of names, "Meg, oh, Meg," "Sylvie, dear Sylvie."

In a moment, Meg stood away. "What am I doing? I'm drenched. I'll ruin your dress."

"Who cares about an old dress?" They embraced again. Against her hair, Sylvia said, "Oh, Meg, it's so good to see you. I wanted to come sooner, but—"

"I know. I read all about you in the papers, every word. A woman in the village saves them for me." She pulled away, her hands still on Sylvia's shoulders, and smiled. "Emeralds from the duke of Glouston. Imagine!"

Sylvia could think of nothing to reply.

Moments were used up in the business of removing hats, shaking out the umbrella and Meg's shawl, putting away the foodstuffs Meg had bought. "It's freezing in here. Let me build up the fire."

Sylvia wanted to stop her, inwardly wanting to scream at

her friend to save the wood for later. Then she remembered her promise to send coal and vowed again to do so.

As Meg laid the fire, Sylvia asked, "Are you well, Meg?"

"Oh, I'm fine, Sylvie, just fine." It wasn't true. Beneath her skirt, her legs were swollen and painful, and she suffered from bouts of dizziness and weakness. Sometimes, she couldn't seem to catch her breath. But she didn't complain to her husband. She was not about to say anything to her friend.

"Are you sure? You were sick before."

Meg looked at her and smiled. "Oh, that. It was just a cold."

"Meg, let's not lie to each other. You look—oh, I don't know . . . tired."

Again, Meg smiled reassuringly. "Of course, I get tired. I'm walking for two now."

Sylvia laughed. "I imagine that's true. Can you feel the baby?"

"Oh, yes. The way he kicks I know he'll be a boy."

Their mutual laughter hid what might have been an awkward moment. "Have you been to the doctor, Meg?"

"I've been to see Mrs. Collins, the midwife. She says the baby's fine."

The awkwardness came then. Sylvia sensed something was wrong. Meg was not telling the whole truth. But she could not pin her down. "How's Brian?" She endeavored to make her voice brighter.

Meg picked up the tone. "He's fine, wonderful as always. He went to repair a lorry this morning. Thank goodness he's in out of the rain."

"You've found no garage for him?"

"Not yet, but we're still hoping."

Behind Meg's back, Sylvia bit her lip, feeling depressed about the way Meg lived, the awkwardness of her visit. Why couldn't she get close to Meg? She was determined to keep trying. "Is Brian finding work?"

"Some. Times are hard just now. But we're getting by. We're happy still. That's what counts."

Again, Sylvia bit her lip. "Yes, I can see you're happy. But Meg, what of the gowns I sent you? I was hoping you could sell some . . . make a little money that way."

Meg turned, having laid the fire, and smiled. "You can see what I did. Recognize the curtains?"

"Yes, the quilt-pieces, too. But I sent so many more, quite a lot recently." She saw the confused look in Meg's face. "Haven't you gotten them?"

"No. Must have been lost in the post. Often happens, I'm told."

Sylvia shook her head in despair. She'd wanted Meg to have the dresses.

"But no matter, Sylvie. You do so much for me. Just look at all these things you've brought. As soon as I get the water on for tea, we'll open them."

Time passed more happily then, with Meg squealing and hugging her as she opened the gifts. Sylvia decided her choices were not entirely impractical, a heavy woolen shawl for Meg, a nice warm jacket for Brian. But, Sylvia thought, they needed so much. She was pleased when Meg declared the jacket would fit Brian and how much he needed it. For the baby she had brought two outfits, a little dress in pink, a suit in blue. "Since no one knows which it'll be, I bought both. If it's a boy, he's going to look awfully silly in a dress."

"Brian will never let him wear it, I can tell you that."

Happy laughter led to Meg's bringing out the baby clothes she had knitted. With a pang, Sylvia realized yarn, simple yarn, would have been a far more practical gift. Soon, she told herself, there would be no more need for gifts. Meg would have everything she needed.

Tea was made and served and the two friends sat at the table, Meg at the end, Sylvia at the side. "Here I am prattling on about myself when I'm dying to know all about you, Sylvie. You look ab-so-lute-ly fabulous."

Sylvia smiled, remembering her own use of the word had come from Meg.

"What an exciting life you must lead. Why, the papers are *filled* with you. Miss Sylvia Hartley today attended. . . .' 'Accompanying the duke of Glouston was Miss Sylvia Hartley.' 'Wearing her Lombardy emeralds was. . . .' Oh, it must be so exciting, Sylvie."

Sylvia did not enjoy the litany, but she didn't know how to stop it.

"And your photograph. I can't tell you what it means to me to see your picture in the paper. I cut them all out, save them."

"Please, Meg. . . ."

Friend looked at friend, then reached out to squeeze hands. "But you're not happy, are you?"

Sylvia's smile was wan. "I am now. I'm going to be happy from now on."

Meg misunderstood. "You're marrying the duke!" It was more exclamation than question.

"I don't know."

"Has he asked you?"

Sylvia sighed. "Yes, sort of."

"He must love you. After all, he gave you the emeralds."

"Yes."

Meg hesitated. "But you don't love him."

"No . . . I can't, somehow—not yet, anyway."

Meg's laugh was as bright as a brook. "He is sort of short for you, isn't he? I can tell by the photographs. Is it true he stutters?"

Sylvia nodded, unable to prevent a smile. "Quite badly, actually."

"I had a feeling he wasn't exactly a Casanova." Meg squeezed her fingers, holding her smile. Then, gradually, it faded, and she busied her hands pouring more tea. Rather nervously, she got up, went to a cupboard and, from a tin, served some tea biscuits. As she placed the food in front of her friend, she asked, "Have you and the duke . . . ?" There was no immediate answer, and Meg sat down so she could look at Sylvia. "Tell me it's none of my affair, but is that why he gave you the emeralds?"

Sylvia bit her lip as though there was something to hold in. "I suppose. I'm not sure." Her voice was husky, little above a whisper.

"And Captain Waring. You and he are . . . ?"

"Yes. . . ." The word barely escaped her lips.

Unthinking, Meg blurted out, "God, Sylvie, so *many!*" At once, she wished she could bite off her tongue, as she watched the beautiful face of her friend slowly screw up and crumple into tears. "Oh, God, Sylvie, what have I done?" She reached out, but not in time. Sylvia's hands covered her face and she sat there sobbing into them. "Oh, Sylvie . . . darling Sylvie." She leaned forward, both her arms around her. "I'm so sorry. I didn't mean it. Oh, God, my tongue. How you must hate me."

Meg heard words, greatly distorted by sobs and by Sylvia's

hands, which were over her face. At first she didn't understand, then she did. "How can I hate you? You're the only one I have to love."

The tears flowed a while longer, then Sylvia began to control them. A handkerchief was produced and, amid the dabbing and wiping, Sylvia said, "What a mess I am. I've cried more lately . . . than in my . . . whole life. I'm . . . practically . . . a sponge." She tried to smile, but her lips trembled. "And I don't even . . . know why."

The new outpouring was brief, and Meg, taking the handkerchief, began to dab at her friend's eyes. "It's because you're unhappy, Sylvie. That's why you're crying."

"No, no, I'm not." She sat up straight, determined to stop crying. She resumed control of the hankie, blew into it and forced some order into her breathing. "I'm not unhappy. I'm just a mess, that's all. I came here to tell you happy news, the happiest in the world. And I'm spoiling it by being—" She smiled. "What's that place in America? Oh, yes, Niagara Falls. That's me, Niagara Falls."

Meg laughed, delighted to see Sylvia stop crying. "What's your happy news, for heaven's sake?"

Suddenly excited to be telling it at last, Sylvia said, "You'll never believe it. So just sit back in your chair and get ready for the surprise of your life." Meg did as she was told, smiling happily to be part of the game. Pausing for dramatic effect, Sylvia said, "We're going to be together."

Meg was puzzled. She wanted to react properly to Sylvia's excitement, but she didn't understand. "What do you mean?"

"You and I. We're going to be together. At last. Oh, Meg, it'll be just like it used to be." She saw the confused expression on Meg's face. "Aren't you just *thrilled*, Meg?"

"But how? Has your mother . . . ?"

"No, no, not that. I'm getting a house of my own. You'll come live with me. Brian too. He can be chauffeur and I don't know what-all. Whatever he wants to do. And you—well, we'll call you my maid, but you know that's not all you'll be. Isn't it wonderful, Meg?"

Meg forced a smile. She knew it was expected. She wanted to please her friend. But she felt a sense of trepidation. "You're getting a house of your own? Your own place? To run?"

"Yes, isn't it wonderful?"

"But how? Did Lord Winnie . . . ?"

"No, no." She waved her hand in a gesture of dismissal. "It doesn't matter who or how. I've just got it, or soon will. We can all be together, you and Brian and me." She smiled. "And the baby too, when he comes."

Meg tried to smile again, but it was futile. Slowly, she stood up, moving away from Sylvia to the other side of the table. "I'm sorry, but it does matter." She swallowed. "How did you get the house?" She saw a tormented look in Sylvia's eyes.

"Don't ask me, please."

"Did the duke give it to you?"

"I asked you not to ask."

"I must, Sylvie. Did he?"

"No." Sylvia looked down at her hands. "I asked him. He wouldn't."

"Then who did? Captain Waring?"

"No, he has no money." She was suddenly aware that her hands were wringing themselves. "There's . . . someone else." The words could hardly be heard against the rain on the roof.

"Who?"

"Don't ask."

"Who, Sylvia? Who gave you the house?"

"He hasn't yet. He's going to."

"Who, Sylvia?"

She raised her head to look at Meg, anguish in her eyes. "The grand duke . . . Rudolph . . . of—"

There was no need to identify him further. Meg knew him. Her eyes widened and she gasped. "Him? That funny little man with that awful mustache?" She shook her head in disbelief. "I saw his picture. Why, he's awful. So *old!*"

Panic rose in Sylvia. "What does it matter? I'll get the house—for you, for us."

"Oh, it *does* matter." She shuddered. "I could never live in a house—not knowing how it . . . what you. . . . I just couldn't."

"But I'm doing it for you. I can't bear—" With her head, her arms, she made an expansive gesture. "—your living here, in this cold, this dampness, this . . . this hovel."

Meg's voice rose in anger. "Hovel it may be, but it's mine. I can live here in pride. I didn't get it by. . . ." She saw hurt, a great deal of it, rise in Sylvia's eyes. But in her anger, she didn't care. "Have you slept with that awful man?"

"Not yet . . . tonight." The words could hardly be heard.

Meg's anger was flaring now. "And how many men will that make, Sylvia? The duke and Waring, this awful old man. And there was one before. That's at least four. Oh, Sylvia, how could you?"

For a moment, Sylvia hung on the edge of pride and anger. But she and Meg had never fought, not once. She couldn't now. The pain of denunciation and humiliation won out. She crumpled into her seat, head down, shoulders slumped. She did not cry. There were no more tears in her.

Meg saw it all. She came around the table and put her hands on Sylvia's shoulders. "I'm sorry. How could I have hurt you so?" She dug her fingers into her friend's shoulders as though trying to push some strength and resolve into her. "Would you really do that for me? Sleep with that old man to get a house?"

"Yes."

"Lord, you must love me, Sylvie."

"Yes."

Meg shook her head. "Oh, God, Sylvie. I can't let you do it. I just can't. Do you understand? I couldn't live there . . . knowing. . . . Promise me you won't?"

Sylvia slowly nodded her head.

"Say it. Swear by all that's holy."

Sylvia, still looking down, nodded. "I swear."

Meg sighed. "It wouldn't have worked, Sylvie. I miss you too. I want to be with you. But Brian and I are beginning our own life here. It's not much, but it's ours. Can you understand?"

"Yes."

Meg smiled, then laughed a little. "Besides, Brian would be the world's worst servant. He's never done it. I can't see him doing it." Meg didn't know what to do to comfort her friend. Then, since her hands were on her shoulders, she began a gentle massage. In a few moments, she said, "Don't take the house, Sylvie."

"I said I wouldn't."

"It's no life for you."

Slowly, as though it took great effort, Sylvia raised her head, straightened her back and turned to look at Meg. "What kind of life is for me?"

Meg smiled. "Oh, I don't know. There are lots of them, I suppose." She laughed. "I guess a shack in Hornby wouldn't do, would it?"

Despite her depression, Sylvia smiled, then felt Meg turn her around and begin a more serious massage. She surrendered it to as she heard Meg say from behind her, "I guess a married woman always thinks of marriage first. Isn't there someone?" Sylvia shook her head. "How about the duke?"

Sylvia sighed. "Mother wants it."

"But you don't. All right, that's out. How about Captain Waring?"

"Not hardly."

Meg, trying her best to be cheerful, carried on. "Well, there must be someone who would want to marry an old hag like you. I know. Who was that first fellow—last summer? You never told me who he was."

Sylvia sighed. "Do I have to?"

"No."

"His name was Arthur Wicklow."

Meg gasped. "Really? Arthur Wicklow?"

"You know him?"

"Oh, yes. He's very nice. But I would never have— imagine! You and Arthur Wicklow."

"How do you know him?"

"He lives here. Bought a cottage on the far side of town, nice little place, thatched roof and all. You must know the place."

"He *lives* here?"

"Oh, yes. He's away a lot, of course, being in Parliament and all." She felt Sylvia trying to turn to look at her, but held her firmly with the massage. "Quite a future in Parliament, I hear. He's very popular among the workers, people in the village. He's on their side, everyone says. Why, I hear talk he may even be in the cabinet one day, maybe even prime minister. Never can tell."

"You *know* him?"

"Oh, yes. He came to the door one day. 'Course I didn't know who he was then. He just stared at me like he'd seen a ghost, mumbled something and left. Then, a few days later, he sent me flowers, a lovely little bouquet. Had his card with it and the words, 'To Meg' written on it. I figured it was an apology or something for coming to the door—although he needn't have. It seems so—I don't know, romantic, somehow. Oh, I know he didn't mean anything. But I never did tell Brian who the flowers came from. I wouldn't want to make him jealous."

Chapter Twenty-two

Sylvia remained with Meg another hour or so. She told herself she was waiting for the rain to subside. In truth, she was too despondent to decide anything for herself and simply gave in to Meg's entreaties that she stay.

For her part, Meg did her very best to cheer up Sylvia, prattling away about this and that, relating incidents about Brian, laughing often, hoping it would be contagious. Always, she had been able to make Sylvia laugh. This time, she was rewarded with no more than a wan smile. She had hoped her chatter about Arthur Wicklow might affect her more. It did not. Perhaps there wasn't as much between those two as she had hoped.

The effort was draining for Meg. More than once, she had to hold onto a chair as the room reeled around her. Finally Sylvia saw it. She went to her, put her arm around her and sat her in a chair. "Are you all right, Meg? Should I get the doctor?"

"No, I'm . . . fine."

"I should say you're not."

The wave of nausea was passing. "I'm all right, Sylvia, really. I'm just tired . . . need a little rest."

Sylvia looked at her, so pale, the pain lines etched so sharply. "Then it's rest you shall have. I'm putting you to bed."

"No . . . I want to visit."

Sylvia smiled, a real smile this time. Meg's vertigo had

221

brought her out of herself. "No, you need to rest—and I really must go, anyway. I'll miss my train."

Sylvia turned down the bed, then led Meg to it. "Do you want to undress?"

"No, I'll just take a short nap."

"All right." She sat Meg on the bed and, bending, removed her shoes. Such pathetic shoes, still damp from the rain. When she had her under the horseblanket and quilt, she said, "You have a nice rest now. I'll visit again soon."

As she was putting on her coat, attaching her hat with a long pin, she heard, "I wouldn't hurt you for the world, Sylvie. You know I love you."

Sylvia finished inserting the pin, then went to sit on the edge of the bed. "You needn't say it."

"I could cut out my tongue for what I said. It was just—"

"I know." With her hand, she brushed a hair from Meg's brow. Her skin felt so cold. "The truth hurts sometimes. I'm . . . not . . . very proud of myself."

"Oh, Sylvie, please. I didn't mean—"

"I know, darling, I know. The words just came out. You didn't want them to." Again she stroked Meg's forehead, her temple, cheeks. "I've lost myself somewhere, Meg."

"No."

"Yes, I have. Look at you. You live here. Not much, really." She smiled wanly. "Terrible, in fact. But I'm envious. You're married to a man you love. You're a mother, or about to be. You have hope." She pursed her lips. Her eyes suddenly smarted. "You have something else . . . something I can never hope to regain. You have your . . . decency."

"Oh, Sylvie. . . ." Meg's hand came from under the cover, clasping Sylvia's hand, which was against her cheek, squeezing it.

"Oh, Meg, tell me what to do! I miss you so. I'm lost without you."

Then it was Sylvia's cheek touched by the hand of friendship. "I can't, Sylvia. How do I know? I only know I love you. No matter what, I love you."

Sylvia left abruptly then, making her way down the ravine through what was now a light English drizzle, and hailed a cab, to take her to the station. As soon as she was inside, she slumped back, closing her eyes. She was so tired, so enervated. Feelings, impressions, half-formed thoughts whirled through her brain: Meg, her horrible living conditions, her illness, Meg's shocked refusal to move into a house obtained by. . . . It was all too much. Sylvia could sort out none of it.

At the station, Sylvia suddenly remembered. Coal. She ordered the cabby to take her back to the village, the coalmonger's. There she paid for two bags of coal, ordering it delivered that day to Meg's house. House? It wasn't a house. On impulse, she opened her purse and made it three bags of coal. Outside, standing before the waiting hansom, she tried to think of what else to do for Meg while she was still there. She couldn't seem to think. Her mind wouldn't function. Later, she would wish fervently that she had commissioned the doctor to look after Meg.

"Where to, miss?"

Seated in the hansom, Sylvia opened her mouth to say the railway station. Different words came out. "There is a cottage at the west edge of town. I'll tell you which one." Why had she said that? Why did she want to go there?

She looked at the cottage. It seemed unchanged. Sighing, she opened the door of the cab, alighted, went up the walk and knocked. The door opened abruptly, as though he had been watching. He was in shirt sleeves. He looked no different.

He was amazed and overjoyed to see her, but everything went wrong at first. His greeting was sardonic. "Well, well, Miss Hartley, I believe. What brings you here?"

She stared at him, finally able to say, "I . . . don't know. . . ."

"Perhaps to get in out of the rain?"

She completely misunderstood. His smile seemed a smirk to her, his words a taunt. She stared at him in dismay and abruptly turned to go.

He grabbed her arm. "I didn't mean that! I swear I didn't. Forgive me." He held her arm firmly. "Come in. You're here. You might as well stay." With his hand, he waved the cabby away.

She allowed herself to be led inside. It was all so familiar, cozy, warmed by a fire. He seemed unchanged—tall, gaunt, a trifle awkward.

"Let me take your hat and coat."

She saw his smile. There was warmth in it now. "No, I can't stay."

His smile broadened. "I sent away your cab. You might as well stay a bit. Would you like tea? Maybe a spirit against the cold?"

She sighed. "All right, yes." He assumed she meant brandy. After he had taken her outer garments, he went and poured two small brandies. But a proper woman does not drink spirits. If she took it, he would know—no! Don't think it. God, he was glad to see her.

He returned, carrying two glasses. He handed one to her. "You look very well, Sylvia." It was the truth. Lord, she was beautiful!

She glanced at him. Her expression signified nothing. Her words of thanks might have been for the glass she accepted, not his compliment.

He raised his glass, made a slight toasting gesture, and sipped, watching her do the same. "Well, Sylvia, what brings you to Hornby?"

"I came to see Meg."

"The real Meg, that is." At once, he saw her expression change. "I'm sorry. I didn't mean to say that."

"But you did."

"Please, Sylvia, I don't want to quarrel. I *am* glad to see you." He had softened her a little, but she was still on guard. "How is Meg?"

"I don't know. I'm not sure. I—I don't think she's well."

"Anything serious?"

"I don't know. She seems to tire easily."

He smiled, hoping to reassure her. "I wouldn't worry. A certain amount of fatigue is normal in pregnancy, I should imagine."

"I hope so."

He looked at her sharply, then remembered his manners. "You must be chilled from the rain. Come over by the fire." He led the way, standing, a hand on the mantel. She followed and sat on the sofa. With a pang, he realized she had sat in that spot once before. He watched her raise her glass and sip the brandy again, and he felt guilty for his earlier thoughts. Brandy was appropriate on such a day. And he had given her brandy. She would have taken sherry, had he offered it. "You care about Meg, don't you?" He asked softly.

She looked up at him. "She's my oldest and dearest friend."

"I'm surprised." At once, he saw her bristle. "Look, Sylvia, I'm apparently saying all the wrong things, and I don't mean to. I don't want to quarrel. It's just—" He sighed. "I'm trying to say it is unusual, that's all, for a girl like you to have a friend like her." Again, he saw her expression and again he sighed, shaking his head in frustration. "Oh, I know how that sounds. And I don't mean it. I'm trying to say, here you are, a . . . celebrity from London, best friends with a young wife of an impoverished . . . I don't know what her husband does."

"He repairs motor cars."

"There you have it. You have to admit it's unusual." He smiled. "Really, that's all I meant."

She let her pique subside. "I suppose it is."

He sipped his brandy, not knowing what else to do. This woman aroused such bittersweet feelings, such anguish.

"You are fortunate, Sylvia—to have such a friend."

"Yes, I know," she said lamely.

"I'm not sure you do." He smiled. "I'm probably just talking myself into trouble again but—well, people of the upper classes, with all their privileges, seldom get the opportunity to. . . ." He sighed. "What I'm trying to say is that people like, well, your stepfather, for example, visit Hornby, see how people live, but it means nothing to them. You are fortunate in that, caring about Meg—Sylvia, doesn't it affect you, how she lives, I mean?"

"Yes. I'm appalled."

"That's what I mean. You don't just notice the conditions, perhaps regretting a little. You really feel for your friend— even suffer a little with her." He felt himself warming toward her, his mistrust subsiding.

"Yes."

"And can you realize there are millions of people like Meg and what's his name—Brian, many of them far worse off than those two young people?"

"I hadn't thought." Oh, God, was he going to get political again?

"Perhaps you'll be able to now." She said nothing more and he stood there, towering over her, feeling a little awkward. He sipped his brandy, but the action filled only a moment. "I still don't know what brings you here." He laughed. "I mean *here*, here."

She glanced up at him, then down at her hands holding the brandy. "I don't know either, Arthur. I shouldn't have come. Meg said you had acquired this cottage. I—I . . . Meg said you'd sent her flowers. I—I suppose I wanted to thank you."

He smiled. "Oh, yes, the flowers."

She raised her head. "Why did you send them?"

"Oh, I don't know." His mouth suddenly turned somber. "I suppose it was an act of . . . of affection for Meg Gwynne. She was a nice girl. I—I cared about her."

There was a moment of silence, filled by eyes, one pair brown, the other green, searching out each other. "And Sylvia Hartley?"

"I hardly know her. I met her only once. She—she was very beautiful."

Again, silence, broken by Sylvia. "And who is here now?"

Finally, he replied, "I'm not sure. Not at all sure."

They looked away from each other then, tinkering with their brandies.

"I hear you're seeing Kitty Shaw, Arthur."

He was surprised. "You know her?"

"Yes, we went to school together. St. Regis."

"But how . . . ?"

She saw his discomfort and smiled at it. "We've been in touch lately. She visited me and I—"

"Did you . . . ?"

Her smile broadened, but it was benign. "No, Arthur. She does not know about Meg Gwynne? Nor will she ever—from me." Again, she smiled. "She's a fine girl, Arthur. She's right for you."

"You know of . . . her activities?"

"Yes. I started to say, she took me to Clement's Inn, showed me around. I met—"

"What did you think of it—the movement, I mean?"

"I was impressed. They seem so . . . so dedicated, so busy, so full of purpose. They are all happy women, I think."

"Yes. Did they ask you to join?"

"Yes."

"And?"

"I don't know." She laughed. "You know me, Arthur. I can never make up my mind about anything. I may. I don't know. We'll see."

"I wish you would. Do you a lot of good."

"Would it, Arthur?" It was an honest question, sincerely asked.

"Yes, Meg—I mean Sylvia, yes." Perhaps he was upset by misnaming her. Suddenly, he became agitated. "Oh, I know you're Sylvia Hartley, that great London beauty in her elegant gowns, friend of this and that duke, seen with the most dashing and fashionable men. But inside there, somewhere—" His voice had risen. "—is the girl who came to this cottage—came twice, a real, live, honest girl, a girl I fell in love with."

"No, Arthur. It wasn't real. You mustn't."

As quickly as his agitation began, it stopped. He let the air out of his lungs slowly. "I know, you're right."

"Kitty's the one for you, Arthur. I can never be."

He looked at her a long moment, an agonized expression on his face. It gradually faded. "As I started to say, I think joining the suffrage movement would be good for you." As he went on, his tone of voice became more normal. "If I were a woman, I know I would join. Mrs. Pankhurst and the others ask for a simple thing, the simplest—the right to vote, the right to participate in the affairs of the nation as free, responsible adults. It should be theirs by birthright. That they have to fight for it in the streets, suffer the pain and humiliation of arrest, incarceration as common criminals, forced feeding and the rest—well, that's criminal. The treatment of these women will forever be a black mark on the lives of the Liberal leaders. Asquith, Lloyd-George, Churchill, the others, will never live it down. I, for one, think it will ultimately destroy the Liberal party. In a few years, Labour will rule this nation."

"Very eloquent, Arthur." She meant it as a compliment.

He smiled. "And, no doubt, boring. I should save it for the Commons. They are used to it." He hesitated, looking at her, as if trying to drill his earnestness into her. "I mean it, Sylvia. I think you should give the W.S.P.U. a chance."

"I know you mean it." She smiled. "Perhaps I will." She shook her head. "Or perhaps not. Arthur, I'm trapped into a certain type of life. I don't know how to escape."

"You can—anytime you want. We all have free will."

"I only hope you're right." She held his gaze a moment, then rose, "And now I must go."

It was all said silently with eyes and mouths and movements

of the head. He said: Don't go. I want you to stay. I need you.
I want to make love to you. Images of hardly-forgotten events
flooded her mind. But she shook her head, saying: I want to
too, Arthur, but we should not. It's better if we don't. He
nodded. She was right, of course.

He went to fetch the gig to take her to the station. On the
way, she said, "At least one good thing has come of this. We
are friends. You don't hate me?"

"I never did, Sylvia. I never could, really." He waited for
her train with her, longing for her, hoping he would have the
courage to take her in his arms and kiss her goodbye. He did
not. All he could do was take her hand and say, "Good luck."

Chapter Twenty-three

As the train sped her back toward London, Sylvia remained lost in thought, unmindful of fellow passengers, the flight of scenery outside her compartment window. She thought of all that had happened—Meg, Arthur—but mostly she tried to decipher what she realized were changes in herself. She had a sense of new beginnings. But of what?

At some point, perhaps near High Wycomb in Buckinghamshire—later, she would decide it must have been near there—she realized she probably loved Arthur Wicklow. It was a surprising thought, a quiet awareness, a self-deprecating amusement that she, Sylvia Hartley, was in love—and with Arthur Wicklow, no less. Sitting there, rocking on the train, hearing the steam whistle ahead, she smiled. Meg had known. All that talk about Arthur living in Hornby, sending flowers—such a romantic thing to do, but she couldn't make Brain jealous. Oh, yes, the people were fond of Arthur. He had a great future in government. Meg knew. Meg always knew everything before she did.

Arthur Wicklow was an impossibility, of course. Again, Sylvia surprised herself. From her daydreams, Sylvia would have expected to be plunged into the pits of despair to be in love with a man she couldn't have. She felt no despair. Rather, she felt a sort of satisfaction, almost a happiness at knowing she would never have the man she loved. She would always love him, always think of him as the man who loved her—flowers for Meg Gwynne—the great unfulfilled love of her life. She would always think of what might have been, a simple cottage, the good life, virtue, cooking and sewing. Impossible—but true.

Yes, she loved Arthur Wicklow. He *was* a good man. Not the handsomest, far from dashing. He was not rich, nor was he the most expert lover. All that she now knew. But integrity, that's what he had. He cared about things . . . and people. He wanted to help others. Oh, he was no preacher, no goody-goody. He was just *good*. And he loved her. No, not really her. He loved the best in her. For the first time, Sylvia felt her eyes begin to smart. Yes, she had been loved by a good man. And she loved the goodness in him. That was a lot. Better to have loved and lost. . . . Suddenly, she wished the train were heading the other way. He had wanted to make love to her. She had seen it in his eyes. And she had wanted it too. She should have—one last time. No, it was better this way. No sense in making it any harder than it already was.

Sylvia thought about more than Arthur. Indeed, that train ride back to London was the first time she felt able to think clearly about herself and her life. She made several decisions. She was going to begin at once to live a more virtuous life. She would break off immediately with Grand Duke Rudolph. She would refuse to see him. She would turn down the house; and his money, still in her purse, would be returned. Those decisions alone elevated her spirits. And she would pay no more late night visits to Waring. Or Lord Charles, for that matter. Meg was right. She had given herself to three men, almost a fourth. Lord, how could she have? A new-found self-awareness filled her. All right, she had done it. She hadn't acted like a nice girl. But people change. It wasn't too late for her.

With the decision to change came a flood of resolutions. She was going to stop being a P.B. She was going to dress more conservatively, be less singular and provocative. She would refuse invitations, stay home, read, study, improve her mind. She should practice the piano more. She should learn needlework. She might even try her hand at painting. Ever since school, she had felt she could paint if she tried. Yes, she could do something with her life. She smiled. Twenty-one was hardly too late to start over.

Kitty Shaw entered her mind. Kitty was doing something with her life. And it was important. Sylvia felt she could do no less. Perhaps she ought to join the suffrage movement. Then the image of women in the streets, scuffling with police, prison and forced feeding came to her, driving away her positive thoughts. But Kitty had said she didn't have to do that. There were many other activities. As the train pulled into Paddington Station, Sylvia promised herself to think seriously about joining the W.S.P.U.

It was early evening when Sylvia returned home. She had been gone all afternoon, missing tea and dinner, facts her mother quickly listed.

"Where have you been?"

"I went to Hornby, mother—to see Meg."

"That awful girl. Why do you persist in seeing her?"

"Because she is my friend."

Lady Constance dismissed such a reason with a wave of her hand. "A great many *important* people came to see you at tea. I did my *best* to make excuses for you, Sylvia, but it wasn't easy. The least you could have done was tell me where you were going."

"I suppose, mother. Sorry."

"I'm trying to treat you as an adult, Sylvia, but you must show more consideration for others."

"Yes, mother."

The countess was not placated, but she dropped the scolding. "The grand duke and Count Hohenbaum were here. They seemed most disappointed not to see you. And there's this." She handed a letter to Sylvia. "Lord Charles asked me to give this to you personally. He said it was urgent."

In her bedroom, Sylvia opened the letter.

My Dear Sylvia,

I am miserable.

I cannot abide the consequences of my own actions.

I should have realized how important independence is to a young woman of spirit such as yourself.

I am prepared to give you a home of your own and

whatever else you may need, and to do so immediately.

Please telephone me at your first opportunity.

Yours Despondently,
Charles

Sylvia re-read the note, dropped it on her desk, then asked Clara to draw her a bath.

"As you wish, Miss Sylvia. Have you eaten?"

"No, but I'm not hungry."

As Sylvia languished in the bath, Clara seized the opportunity to read the note from Lord Charles, reacting with elation. The duke had come around. There was no need for the Hapsburg, but perhaps he had served a purpose. Sylvia now had two houses to choose from. It would not be difficult to make a selection.

In the tub, Sylvia thought about Charles and his note, in light of her new resolves. She could feel no triumph in winning over the duke. On the contrary. . . . Quickly, she finished her bath and dried herself. Still in her robe, she phoned Lord Charles and arranged to see him that evening. She would come to his home. When she stripped off her robe, she told Clara she wished to hurry. She had things to attend to at once. Clara was consumed with curiosity, but she could not pry, for she was not supposed to have read the duke's note. She could only assume Sylvia was going to accept his offer.

When she was dressed, Sylvia sat at her desk and penned a short note to Count Hohenbaum. She had changed her mind and would not be able to accept the grand duke's invitation to dinner. She offered no explanation. Then she addressed a large envelope, put the money the count had given her inside, along with the note. Not trusting Clara to deliver it, Sylvia dropped it off at the Royal Albert Hotel on her way to Lord Charles'.

Wuthering opened the door for her, but Charles was waiting in the foyer, an eager, expectant expression on his face.

"M-My dear. Thank you for c-coming."

"It is I who must thank you, Charles. Your note has helped me come to my senses."

He led her to the small parlor where they had talked on her last visit. A fire made the room comfortable. He stood before it, looking at her tenderly, lovingly. "You are l-lovely, as a-always, my d-dear."

Clara had urged a décolleté evening gown on her, but Sylvia had insisted on a simple black skirt and a white ruffled blouse over a chemise. She looked both demure and childlike. "Thank you, Charles." He offered sherry and she accepted. While he poured, she said, "I'm sorry I missed you at tea, Charles. I went to Hornby to see my friend, Meg Trout."

"Oh, yes, your f-former m-maid. Has she r-recovered from her i-i-illness?"

"I'm not sure, but she seems all right. She tired easily." Suddenly, Sylvia knew he didn't really care anything about Meg. All this was just empty courtesy. She wanted to get right to what she had come for. "Charles, I—"

He turned, handing her a glass of sherry. "My d-dear." Then came the inevitable raising of glasses in salute, the ceremonial tasting. "M-My note was h-hastily w-written, but much th-thought about. I m-meant every w-word."

"Charles, I—"

"I was a f-fool. Y-You were right all a-along. I sh-should have l-listened to you." She opened her mouth to speak, but again he gave her no chance. "I w-want to provide wh-whatever h-house you want—for your b-b-birthday."

Finally, he gave her a chance to speak. "Charles, I have changed my mind. I no longer want the house. You were right all along. I'm just glad I had your wise counsel."

He was surprised. "B-But . . . ?"

She hesitated, but only fleetingly, then plunged ahead with what she had rehearsed in her mind. "You asked me once to marry you, Charles. You said you would wait until I was ready. I am ready now." She saw his surprise deepening. "I will be your wife, Charles, if you still want me."

He stared at her in disbelief.

"I know I am unworthy of your love. If you have changed your mind and no longer want me as your wife, I will understand."

"O-Of c-course I w-want you, but. . . ."

She had expected him to be ecstatic with joy, sweep her into his arms. His stuttering disbelief, his standing there staring at her was not at all how she thought it would be.

"But wh-why, Sylvia? Y-You don't l-love m-me."

"Perhaps I do, Charles, more than you think. I know I am fond of you. I know you are a very *good* man, who will be good to me. I know you and I will have a happy life together." She smiled. "I am certain I will soon come to love you in the way you want me to."

He continued to stare at her.

"I thought you would be happy, Charles. Don't you want me?"

A moment longer, he gaped at her. "Oh, God, Sylvia, I do w-want you. N-Never have I w-wanted a-anything so m-much. I j-just can't b-b-believe it."

She smiled radiantly. "Believe, Charles. I meant every word."

There was a brief awkward moment as he set his sherry on the mantel, then he swept her into his arms, kissing her passionately. She did her best to respond.

Against her ear, he said, "I'm s-so h-happy. I c-can't b-believe it."

"Yes, darling, I am too."

He stood away from her, hands on her shoulders, happiness on his face. "Oh, S-Sylvia, Sylvia. I w-want to t-tell the whole w-world. I want to sh-shout it from the r-rooftops."

She laughed. "But not tonight. If you wish, I thought we could announce it at my birthday party."

Again, he swept her into his arms, smothering her mouth. When it was ended, he stammered, "Oh, my d-darling. I-I m-must tell s-someone." He almost leaped to pull the bellcord. When the butler appeared, he said with strange formality, "Wuthering, y-you have b-been with m-me all my life, and w-with m-my f-father b-before me."

"Yes, milord."

"I am p-pleased to inform you that M-Miss Hartley has a-a-accepted m-my p-p-proposal of m-marriage. We are to b-be wed."

Wuthering did not bat an eye. His master might have just suggested the silver needed polishing. "My congratulations, milord." He turned to Sylvia and bowed. "And my best wishes to you, Miss Hartley. It will be a pleasure to serve you."

"Thank you, Wuthering."

"Champagne, W-Wuthering. I think we n-need w-wine."

"As you wish, milord."

It never did become much of a party, even though the housekeeper, Lord Charles' valet, a couple of maids and even the cook came in to bow and curtsy and extend congratulations and best wishes. There was considerable movement in the room, yet Sylvia noticed Lord Charles whisper to Wuthering, who left briefly, then returned to hand something to his employer. It was all strangely formal; Charles ordered wine for the staff, and Sylvia figured the real festivities went on downstairs. But she was affected. This big house. All these servants. For the first time, she realized the responsibilities, the greatly altered lifestyle that would result from her marriage.

Carrying stemmed glasses, they went to the gallery, Charles leading the way. He stood before first one portrait, then another, until he stood below the one of his great-grandmother wearing the Lombardy emeralds. "My d-dear, the d-dukes of Glouston have always ch-chosen b-beautiful women as their d-duchesses. The first m-moment I s-saw you, I kn-knew you belonged h-here, in this room—the f-fairest, most b-beautiful of all the duchesses of G-Glouston."

It was the first time she thought of herself as becoming a duchess. It was difficult for her to contemplate. She had to say something. "Thank you, Charles, but . . . but I am unworthy."

"Not h-hardly, my dear." He took a small box from his pocket and opened it, extracting the largest diamond Sylvia had ever seen. She gasped. Her mother would declare it forty, even fifty karats. "For g-generations, this r-ring has been w-worn by the d-duchesses of Glouston as the s-symbol of their b-b-betrothal." He smiled. "I cannot t-tell you the p-pride with which I g-give it to you."

It was a flawless blue-white diamond, set as a solitaire, and seemed to burn with a light from within itself. "Oh, Charles. I—I don't know . . . what to say."

He smiled. "You've already s-said it—that you w-would m-marry me." He took her right hand, to slip it on her finger, then laughing, corrected himself to take her left hand. She extended her hand in front of her, turning it, seeing the facets catch the light.

"Oh, Charles. . . ."

Again, he embraced her, and she responded. In a moment,

his arm around her waist, he walked along, pointing to the portraits of the duchesses. "See, they all w-wear that d-d-d—that ring. I will ask W-Wainwright to add it to your p-portrait. It will h-hang here, my d-dear. I kn-knew it w-would when I c-commissioned it."

"Yes, Charles. Perhaps I knew too."

Again, still holding her, he circled the gallery. Suddenly, he laughed. "The dukes all l-look a little d-dour, don't you th-think? They are e-envious of me. W-Well they m-might be."

"You'll make me blush, Charles."

"It will b-become you, my d-darling. Everything d-does." Again, he embraced her, and she accepted his ardor. "J-Just wait until I t-tell my cousins."

"Your cousins?"

"Yes, the K-King and Queen M-May."

The words made her gasp. She was about to become related by marriage to King George V.

"H-He'll be as p-pleased as I am."

She shook her head. "I can only hope so, Charles. I—I feel . . . so unworthy."

"D-Don't be silly. You will m-make a s-s-splendid duchess."

"But, Charles, I don't know what to do—how to act, what is expected of me."

He laughed. "Nothing is e-expected of you, b-but what you a-are, b-beautiful, k-kind, generous, th-thoughtful."

"But, Charles—"

"Stop w-worrying, Sylvia. You'll be f-fine. We'll live a p-perfectly ordinary life. Oh, th-there are a f-few S-State occasions wh-which can be s-stuffy. And, of c-course, being c-close to the C-Crown, we must set an ex-example."

"What sort of example, Charles?"

"Of p-propriety, of c-circumspection. There can be no sc-scandal, no involvement in c-c-controversial a-affairs." He laughed. "D-Don't worry your p-pretty head, my d-darling."

As though dismissing her sudden worries as groundless, he led her back to the parlor and refilled their glasses, toasting her and their happiness. He embraced her several times, but mostly they talked.

"May I a-ask, Sylvia, wh-why you d-decided to . . . to a-accept my p-proposal?"

The query was not unanticipated by Sylvia. She had previously decided to tell the truth as she saw it. "I told you I went to visit my dear friend in Hornby. She was my maid, but we grew up together. However unusual our relationship, she is my dearest friend. She has married now and is going to be a mother. She and her husband live quite simply—in considerable poverty, actually. But Meg is so very happy. I found myself envying her happiness." She paused, seeing the serious expression on the duke's face. "I realized I would find happiness in marriage to you."

He cleared his throat. "And that is wh-why you a-accepted me? To f-find h-happiness?"

"Yes. I have been . . . unhappy . . . for weeks, Charles. I do not like the life I'm leading. A P.B. That's what I'm called." Great earnestness entered her voice. "I don't like it. I don't want to be that. It is not my true nature, Charles. I realized just today . . . you and I are much alike. We are both serious by nature. We have common interests—the arts, books, music. There is where my happiness lies—with you."

She saw him looking at her, a serious expression on his face. She saw the beginnings of hurt in his eyes.

"Please, Charles. I sense you want me to be . . . oh, I don't know, madly, head over heels in love . . . to have some sort of schoolgirl crush. But, really Charles, isn't it better that I come to you with my eyes open . . . with intelligence and forethought?"

He softened at once. "Yes, of course it is, my d-dear."

After that, he embraced her again. Then, sipping wine, they made plans. She wanted an early wedding. He agreed. He wanted to honeymoon on the Continent. She agreed. They would live in the house where they were now, unless she preferred another place. She did not.

He surprised her. "If Lord Winnie does not see fit to provide you a proper trousseau, I will, of course—"

"I'm sure he will, Charles."

Her surprise became even greater. "You will want, of course, your friend from Hornby and her family to come live with you. I will find places on my staff."

She nearly cried. "Oh, Charles. . . ." Her gratitude that he had offered without her having to ask made her very responsive to the kisses he lavished upon her.

"My d-dear, m-may I . . . may w-we—"

She put her fingers to his lips to silence him. "Oh, Charles, I know what you want. I do too. But—do you mind? I would like—oh, I know we have, but . . . I would like to wait until we are married."

He smiled. "I kn-know. You're r-right, of c-course. I r-respect you f-for it."

"Thank you, Charles." She smiled her best. "And now, I really should go. I must tell mother, Lord Winnie."

His smile matched hers. "M-May I c-come too?"

"Of course. We'll do it together."

The earl of Linfield beamed with pleasure when told, proffering his congratulations to the duke of Glouston. The Countess Linfield was beside herself with joy and triumph. The specter of an impoverished old age fled her mind, like a thief stealing away in the night, and she wept with relief. Only Clara D'Angelo, when the servants were told, was less than enthusiastic. But she did not show it.

That night, Sylvia said to her, "I fear you are disappointed in me, Clara."

Her face a mask, the maid replied, "No, miss. I wish only your happiness."

Sylvia did not believe a word of it, but replied, "Thank you, Clara."

Shortly thereafter, the soon-to-be duchess of Glouston lay in her bed consumed with fear and misgivings. Hers had been an impulsive act, she knew. She had thought of marriage to Charles only as an escape from her dilemma and the conflicting demands of Clara and her mother. It was an escape from the temptations of Philip Waring, Arthur Wicklow and—she shivered—how many others in the future? She wanted virtue. Not virtue in a cottage, but in a mansion, and Charles offered it. She leaped at the opportunity while she still had it—and she was lucky he would still accept her.

But she had not thought of being the duchess of Glouston. She shuddered at the memory of those sedate portraits, the dignity of Wuthering. She was to be a cousin of the King. Impossible to believe. She could not do it.

She lay awake for a long time. Such a day. It had begun with her bargaining to become mistress to a Hapsburg grand duke—and ended with her a future duchess, related to the Crown. Again and again, she thought of all that had happened, and, with her new-found decisiveness, came to a

conclusion. She had done the right thing. She was better off
to be a duchess—by far—better off financially, in reputation
and in virtue. She did not love Charles, probably never
would. But she could abide him and she could respect and
look up to him. *Propriety, circumspection. No scandal or
controversy.* It was not much to ask. She would make a good
duchess. She would find a way to be happy too.

Chapter Twenty-four

She felt better the next morning. Indeed, the next several days brought her the first real happiness she had known in a long time. Surely, virtue was bringing its own rewards.

It began almost at once. Lord Winnie paid a visit to her room, embracing her, telling of the happiness she had brought him through the years, the joy he felt at her forthcoming marriage. A splendid match. He wished her every happiness.

"Thank you, father." The word came strangely easily to her. "I know you mean it."

"I do. And I hope you will allow me to give you the finest possible wedding and to escort you to the altar as my daughter."

She was touched. "I would have no one else, father."

Her mother entered then, obviously by prearrangement, and the three of them embraced. It was the first genuine affection Sylvia had felt for her mother in quite some time. She wasn't even offended when her mother again raved over the engagement ring and said several times, "To think! My daughter, the duchess of Glouston, a cousin to the King!"

Sylvia's engagement to Charles set London society agog. It would be the marriage of the decade, even the century. Imagine, a commoner marrying so close to the Crown. But wasn't it a symbol of the changing times? Wasn't everything becoming more egalitarian? Liberals and Labour tended to

241

think the match a good thing. And even the most hidebound Tory could not blame the duke. She was a beautiful girl, no doubt about it.

Sylvia gave more time to her sitting, for there was now a great urgency to finish the painting. Nor did she mind, now that she knew where it was to hang. She enjoyed the fuss made over her, the initial burst of applause when she entered the room the day after her betrothal, the myriad congratulations and expressions of best wishes. Timothy Graves called "duchess" and said, "You always were one to me, Sylvia."

Touched, she had nonetheless smiled and maintained their usual banter. "Then see that you speak to me like one, or I'll have your head, Timothy."

Everyone was very nice to her, and she basked in the attention, surrendering to growing excitement, knowing she had at last made a wise decision in her life. The duchess of Glouston. Lady Sylvia. Yes, it had a nice ring to it. She was going to be happy.

She was determined to carry out her vow of virtue. She wrote to Waring, trying to make it light as she explained her engagement. She said she had enjoyed the pleasure of his company, but no more. As a personal bit of humor, she underlined the word *pleasure*.

She wrote a long letter to Meg, explaining in the most honest and intimate terms why she had decided to marry Lord Charles. "Seeing your happiness with Brian was the main reason I decided to accept Charles." Sylvia truly believed that was so. As an addendum, she mentioned Lord Charles' invitation to her and Brian to become part of his household. "He simply knew of my affection for you, Meg. He is a sensitive and generous man, and he sensed how much having you live with us would mean to me. I urge you with all my heart to accept, Meg. Please, please, *please*. Don't think for a minute that uniting us is my reason for marrying Lord Charles. I gave my reasons above. They are the truth." She sealed the letter and gave it to Clara to be mailed. But she remained unhappy with it. She could not be sure Meg would accept Charles' offer.

When she gave the letter to Clara, she said, "Oh, yes, I've intended to ask. Meg did not receive those dresses I asked you to send her. Did you?"

"Yes, miss."

"I wonder why she didn't get them?"

"I don't know. The post is not always reliable, though."

"Yes, I suppose that must be it."

Sylvia did not believe her, but she did not pursue the matter. Clara would be leaving soon, searching for a more willing—or pliable—courtesan.

Unforseen consequences resulted from Sylvia's decision to write to Kitty Shaw. It was just a note, telling of her engagement, inviting her to the party Saturday, thanking her again for the tour of Clement's Inn and assuring her she was still thinking of her. On impulse, Sylvia included a ten-pound note—a generous gift, really—as proof of her interest. After all, she was receiving *Votes for Women*. She ought to pay for it. "I hope you can make use of this." She intended it for Kitty's personal use.

To her surprise, Sylvia received by return mail a card signifying her membership in the Women's Social and Political Union, along with a note of personal thanks from both Kitty and Emmeline Pankhurst. She had not intended to join. But why not? What was wrong with supporting women's suffrage?

The next day, the newspapers reported both Sylvia's forthcoming engagement and her membership in the W.S.P.U. One columnist in particular had a bit of fun, noting the disparity of the two actions. That evening, Lord Charles asked her about the membership. He did not do so angrily. He was merely puzzled. He hadn't known of her interest in women's suffrage.

She told him the truth. "I intended only a donation, Charles. I did not plan to become a member. I hardly think I can rescind it now."

"I u-understand, S-Sylvia. I th-thought it m-must be something l-like that."

"Are you upset with me, Charles?"

He smiled. "N-No, n-not at all. I w-want my w-wife to be a-a-active in ch-charity."

Charity?

"Y-You will not, of c-course . . .?" He looked at her questioningly. "Y-You are not p-planning to be . . . active . . . in s-street d-demonstrations . . . that s-sort of thing?"

To her surprise, Sylvia felt herself bristling inwardly, but she replied, "No, of course not, Charles."

The newspaper reports of Sylvia's forthcoming betrothal brought her a visitor. She received Arthur Wicklow in the small, sunny parlor which afforded the most privacy. She saw that he was serious, very tense, and sensed why he had come. Despite her fears of what might be an unpleasant scene, she was glad to see him. She loved him, yes, but she was not made for love in a cottage. He would marry Kitty, she Charles, that was their destiny. . . .

"Is it true? You are to marry the duke of Glouston?"

"Yes. It will be announced Saturday night." She held her ring finger out toward him.

"Well, I cannot compete with that." He looked at her a moment, shaking his head. When he spoke it was with some vehemence. "You can't, Sylvia! It's a terrible mistake."

She smiled. "I have accepted Lord Charles, Arthur. There is no going back now."

In his agitation, he rose from his seat, pacing back and forth in front of it for a moment, then looking out a front window, his back to her. "When . . . when I read of your forthcoming engagement in the paper. . . ." He sighed. "I cannot tell you how it made me feel. I was . . . disappointed. I had . . . a feeling of . . . irretrievable loss. I knew then. . . ."

He paused so long, she had to prompt him. "Yes, Arthur?"

Slowly, he turned to face her. "I knew then . . . that I loved you, truly loved you. And I hated myself. My monstrous pride, my colossal stubbornness, had caused me to lose the one woman I would ever love in my life."

His words thrilled her. She could feel her heart pounding. But, her voice composed, she said, "You don't love me, Arthur. You love—"

"Meg Gwynne? Oh, yes, I know all about that. Indeed, that's what I've thought for all these last months—that I loved a chimera, a fantasy. I not only didn't love Sylvia Hartley, I didn't even know her. What little I knew, I detested."

"You were only right to do that, Arthur," she replied in a low voice.

"No, I was wrong, completely wrong. You *are* Meg, Sylvia." He saw her shake her head vigorously. "Yes, you are. I don't mean the real Meg, the girl in Hornby, your ex-maid. I mean you are the girl who came to my cottage. That was the *real* you. This other person, this glamorous

P.B., the toast of London, the one who is to marry a duke, is not the real you. You can't marry him, Sylvia, you just can't."

"I'm afraid I am, Arthur."

He brightened immediately. "There, you said it yourself. You're *afraid* you are."

"It was just a figure of speech, Arthur. It meant nothing."

"Do you love him, Sylvia?"

She hesitated. He had no right to ask. "I'm very fond of him, Arthur."

"Fond? What is that?" An edge of ridicule crept into his voice. "How can you marry someone you don't love?"

She bristled just a little. "Really, Arthur, none of this is any of your business."

"I'm sorry, but it's no one's business more than mine. When I realized that I truly loved you, I knew my own terrible mistake. My pride, my selfishness in thinking only of my own hurt feelings, had caused me to forsake you. I should have been helping you come to your senses. I should have been fighting for the woman I love—not wallowing in self-pity. But, starting now, I intend to fight for you, Sylvia. I intend, somehow, to keep you from your own folly."

She sighed. "Arthur, please. It's too late for that—for us."

"Oh, God, Sylvia, why are you marrying a man you don't love?"

"Please don't raise your voice, Arthur. I'd like this to be private."

"I'm sorry." Visibly, he controlled himself. "Why? Just tell me, why?"

"Oh, Arthur. . . ." She gave a deep sigh. "You are correct when you say the girl who was—and I emphasize *was*—a P.B. is not the true me. I was dreadfully unhappy. When I visited Meg and you a few days ago, I realized why I was unhappy. The frantic, empty life I'd been leading was a factor, to be sure. More—" Again, she sighed. "Arthur, marriage to Lord Charles enables me to recapture my sense of propriety, of decency, of virtue." She hesitated, looking at him earnestly. "Can you understand?"

It seemed to her a long time until he answered. "Sylvia, I can offer you virtue—and more, much more—a life of purpose, of social conscience, of activity toward some worthwhile goal. He cannot do that."

"Oh, Arthur, please."

"I can make you so much happier. I can give you everything—except his money and his title. The duchess of Glouston. Is that what you want, a title?"

"You can't think that of me."

"No, that's just it, I can't. I can't believe you're going to become a duchess, marry that man."

"He's a good man, Arthur. You don't know him."

"I'm sure he is, but that has nothing to do with it. You can't marry a man just because he's *good*."

"I'll come to love him. I will." She saw him shake his head, denying her. "Arthur, listen to me. If I had been Meg—if I had been a servant girl who came to your cottage, I think . . . I know . . . you and I. . . . It would have worked out for us. I'm not made of stone, Arthur." She could feel her eyes beginning to smart, her voice choking. "I have . . . feelings for . . . for you, Arthur." She swallowed, hard, forcing back her emotion. "But I am not that girl who came to you, never was. I'm Sylvia Hartley, daughter of a countess, stepdaughter of an earl. Very common blood may course in my veins, but I have been afforded a certain type of life. I had no control over that. Certain things are expected of me. Truly, Arthur, I have no choice in what I'm doing."

"Nonsense." He hurled the word. "Everyone has choices. All life is choices. Your trouble is, Sylvia, you're too passive. You just want to float along with the tide, drifting here and there, making easy choices, then lamenting that you have no choice."

"Please, Arthur, I don't want to quarrel."

Abruptly, he sighed. "I'm sorry." He gave a small, deprecating laugh. "What a mess I am. I came to tell you I love you and intend to fight to the last to have you—and what do I do? Scold and lecture you."

"It's all right, Arthur." She smiled a little. "I think I'm coming to expect it from you."

They looked at each other. He was despondent, yet sensed there was no more to say. "I'd best go."

She stood up to show him out. "Yes—my friend. Are you still that?"

"Much more, Sylvia."

She nodded. "Will you come to my birthday party Saturday night? And bring Kitty. *She* is the one for you, you know."

"No, she's not. I'm going to break off with her. I'm hardly being fair, loving someone else and seeing her."

"Give it a chance, Arthur. You may come to—"

"No." He smiled. "Now who's running whose life?"

She nodded and smiled. "Will you come Saturday?"

"If you want me, yes. And I'll bring Kitty, she cares for you—I'll bring her—" He laughed. "—if she's not throwing rocks through windows or plotting a bombing."

Sylvia's resolve to dress more modestly did not extend to her gown for her birthday-engagement ball on November 5, 1910. She surrendered to her mother's choice—"Charles wants to see what he's getting"—and wore a gown of brilliant white satin, extremely low cut and, at her fiancé's request, the Lombardy emeralds. Thus, Sylvia made a dazzling, glittering sight at the ball given for her by Lord Winnie. She looked and felt ravishing, and when the formal announcement of her engagement to Lord Charles was made, she beamed at the applause and surrendered to happiness as everyone crowded around to congratulate her.

The King and Queen came—Charles' little surprise for her. King George wore a red Guards uniform, and with his full, dark beard, erect posture and reserved demeanor, he made a handsome sight. Despite the tightness of her skirt—and being awed at the presence of the King at her party—Sylvia managed a deep curtsy. He bowed. "My dear, when Lord Charles told me I was to have a new cousin, I had no idea it would be such a charming one."

"Thank you, Your Highness."

Again, she curtsied before Queen Mary, beloved as Queen May, so elegantly gowned, so statuesque, her hair encased in a toque which she had made the fashion. "My dear Sylvia, you are so very lovely. I hope we will see you often."

Sylvia smiled. "Thank you, Your Majesty."

Captain Philip Waring was there. She really had to invite him—and dance with him. It was important that she relegate him to the role of a friend. He was entirely helpful in that, warmly congratulating Lord Charles, chivalrously expressing his disappointment in losing out to a better man. It was all extremely proper, except that when dancing with her, he said, "I *will* see you again—and sooner than you think."

She smiled, mostly for public consumption. "No, you won't—and don't be naughty."

He also smiled. They might have been discussing her choice of silver pattern. "How about tonight—later?"

"Stop it, Philip. The answer is no, never."

"Then after you're married? You know I prefer married women."

"You *are* a rogue."

But she realized that her no's and never's had a hollow ring to them.

Arthur came with Kitty and that pleased her. He looked more appealing than ever in his evening suit, and although Kitty's gown was a bit out of style, she looked nice. Sylvia hugged them both, then asked Kitty if she could steal Arthur away to dance with her.

He was, she realized, a surprisingly good dancer. And she felt a special thrill at being in his arms again. "Do you know this is the first time . . . we have ever danced together?"

"I am quite aware, I assure you."

She felt her heart thumping. She loved him. She knew she did. She could only hope the duke and others didn't see it.

"You look stunning, Sylvia." He smiled. "Almost as good as Meg Gwynne."

"Oh, Arthur, thank you for coming. Thank you for . . . everything." She felt she might cry and forced a smile to prevent it. "It's better this way, Arthur. Believe me it is. It's you and Kitty, not you and I."

He did not exactly frown, but his lips were pressed together in a thin line. "We'll see. I should warn you, I have not given up the fight for you."

"Do, Arthur, please. All this is for the best."

When they returned to Kitty after the dance, Sylvia heard, "Emmeline is giving an important speech Thursday. Would you like to go?"

"What it that, the tenth?"

"Yes. Why don't you come?"

Sylvia laughed. "My, but you work at women's suffrage constantly, don't you?"

Kitty smiled. "Of course. Now, if I can just talk to the Queen. . . ."

"Don't you dare. Not at my party."

"Then you'll come to the lecture?"

"I'll see, Kitty. I'll think about it."

Kitty's smile was mischievous. "I wonder whom I can get to introduce me to the Queen?"

Sylvia laughed. "All right, all right, you blackmailer. I'll come—if I can."

Chapter Twenty-five

Sylvia attended the "women's parliament" largely because there was nothing else to do. She would not have gone if Charles had not made plans for the evening. He had—a fête honoring his engagement at his club—and she was not invited to the all-male event. It seemed appropriate to her to go on such a night to a women's event. When Charles asked her what she was doing that evening, she said she was attending a lecture at Prince Albert Hall. It was a half-truth.

"That's f-fine, dear. I'm g-glad you're i-interested in things e-educational."

Sylvia could see no empty seats in the hall, which was packed with thousands of cheering women, but also a surprising number of men. There were several speakers, including Christabel and Sylvia Pankhurst, Annie Kenney, Mrs. Pethic-Lawrence. Several men took the podium to make brief remarks, Keir Hardy and Viscount Castlereagh from Parliament—and Arthur Wicklow. Sylvia felt a special thrill as he spoke. My, but he was a good orator, his voice ringing throughout the hall. And he seemed to lose his instinctive shyness when standing before an audience.

His words were stirring too. "The Labour party stands foursquare behind the oppressed of this great nation, all the oppressed, men *and* women!" Cheers greeted that. "The Labour party supports—with its dying breath, if need be—*votes for women!*" More and louder cheering. "The Liberal party, led by the bigotry of Asquith, Lloyd-George and

251

Winston Churchill, shall not be permitted to bring their personal shame to *all* members of Parliament. Labour, its strength growing daily, will not long permit half our population to be denied their birthright!"

Arthur received a standing ovation from the audience. Kitty Shaw, sitting next to Sylvia, was on her feet cheering madly, and Sylvia found herself calling out and applauding vigorously.

During a brief lull before Mrs. Pankhurst's address, Kitty explained, "Arthur is smart. An election is coming up and the Liberals are in danger of losing control of Parliament. If they do remain in power, it will be only through a coalition with Labour—and Arthur is doing all he can to increase Labour's strength."

"But women don't have the vote."

"True, but women have a lot to say about how their husbands vote. Nobody knows that more than the Liberal leadership. They don't want to give us the vote—but they don't want to make us too angry, either. A big demonstration, violence, mass arrests—these are the last things Asquith wants right now."

"I gather that's what he's going to get, however."

"You couldn't be more right, Sylvia."

Emmeline Pankhurst strode to the podium and, after a burst of applause and cheers, a hush fell over the audience. Sylvia thought she made an extraordinary figure, slender, fragile, utterly feminine in her tailored suit and ornate hat. But it was her voice and manner of speaking that deeply impressed Sylvia. She did not shout or scream, yet her voice was heard in the furthest reaches of the hall. She did not engage in histrionics or hyperbole, but explained what had happened, what must be done, in a simple, logical manner.

Even Sylvia, who had not followed the parliamentary maneuvers for women's suffrage, could understand Mrs. Pankhurst's summary. Because the Liberal government would not introduce a suffrage bill, the issue had been brought to a vote as a private member's bill called the Conciliation Act. This had come up for a vote on its second reading in the last session. "Thirty-nine speeches were made, the prime minister showing plainly that he intended to use all his power to prevent the bill from becoming law."

Mrs. Pankhurst continued. "The Conciliation Act passed

its second reading by a majority of a hundred and nine, a larger majority than the government's far-famed budget had received. In fact, no measure during that Parliament received so great a majority—299 members for it as against 190 opposed.

"We all had faith the Conciliation Bill would receive its third reading and final passage in the autumn session of Parliament, which opens November eighteenth. Resolutions urging the government to enact the bill during the autumn were sent, not only by the suffrage associations, but from many organizations of men. The corporations of thirty-eight cities, including Liverpool, Manchester, Glasgow, Dublin and Cork, sent resolutions to this effect. Cabinet ministers were beseiged with requests to receive deputations of women. Yet, early in October, Mr. Asquith told a deputation of women from his own constituency of East Fife that the bill could not be advanced this year. 'What about next year?' they asked. He replied: 'Wait and see'."

A groan came as one from the audience, and Sylvia too, felt indignation at the prime minister.

"The Women's Social and Political Union has offered a truce to the government since enactment of the second reading—and to honor the new reign of His Majesty King George V. This has not been an easy time for us. Many members of our organization believed the truce to be an error, that we should have maintained our pressure on the government. I must now agree that I should have listened to those voices."

A spontaneous cheer arose from the audience.

"We will make one last constitutional effort to secure passage of the bill into law. If the bill, in spite of our efforts, is killed by the government, then, first of all, I have to say there is an end to the truce. If the Conciliation Bill does not come up for a vote, then our first step is to say, 'We take it out of your hands, since you fail to help us, and we resume the direction of the campaign ourselves'."

Another deafening cheer, as though from a single throat, filled the hall.

"When the autumn session of Parliament convenes on November eighteen, another deputation of the W.S.P.U. will carry a petition to the prime minister. I myself will lead it—and if no one cares to follow me, I will go alone."

The last words were all but drowned out in a spontaneous roar from the crowd. Sylvia saw dozens, scores, hundreds of women, Kitty Shaw among them, on their feet shouting, "I will go! I will go!"

Sylvia was extraordinarily moved by the speech, so much so that when Kitty asked her, as they were leaving the hall, what she thought, she replied, "What is so terrible to men about letting women vote? Why do they oppose it so?"

Kitty smiled. "Truly, I have no idea."

They walked down the street for a while, Sylvia finally catching a cab. Kitty said she would take an omnibus. "Are you sure I can't take you home?"

"No, it's better this way." They looked at each other. "Are you glad you came, Sylvia?"

"Yes, very glad."

"Will you come on the eighteenth? We need all the support we can muster."

Sylvia knew there was no possibility of her joining the demonstration. But she didn't want to say no to Kitty. "I'll see. Will that do for now?"

Sylvia did not intend to participate in the November 18th demonstration. But events conspired against her. For one, Lord Charles' comments annoyed her.

"My d-dear, wh-when you said you were g-going to a l-lecture, I did not r-realize you were g-going to hear that w-woman."

"*That* woman? Mrs. Pankhurst is a very fine lady."

His smile was patronizing. "My dear, y-you are y-young and i-i-impressionable. I cannot p-permit you to p-participate in such th-things."

"Really, Charles, all I did was listen to a discussion of matters of public interest. I should think you would want me to."

"O-Ordinarily, my d-dear, but not this m-matter."

"What is so wrong about women voting, Charles?"

His smile now turned condescending. "These are m-matters b-best left to g-government, Sylvia."

"I should not think about them?"

"It is not pr-proper for you to i-involve yourself in such m-matters. Now that I th-think of it, I-I w-want you to r-r-rescind your m-membership in that o-organization." He saw the hostility in her eyes. "B-Believe me, S-Sylvia, I kn-know wh-what is b-best. Do you u-understand?"

She nodded, but what she understood was not necessarily what he wished her to understand.

She received a note from Arthur urging her to join the demonstration. "This is going to be an historic protest for human rights. One day you will be sorry if you do not participate." And she received two phonecalls from Kitty asking her to march beside her. "We will meet at Caxton Hall, then march to the Strangers' Entrance at the House of Commons. Mrs. Pankhurst will lead us. All we want to do is state our case to the prime minister. It is a simple exercise in the rights of every British citizen—or ought to be."

Sylvia could not bring herself to accompany Kitty. Nor could she stay away. In the end, she decided on a compromise. She would go to Parliamentary Square. Perhaps her presence in the crowd would be to some purpose.

She arrived a little late, her cabby unable or unwilling to get close to Westminster because of the crush of people. Pushing and shoving, she made her way to a point where she could see the courtyard outside the Strangers' Entrance. The crowd was immense, at some points perhaps a dozen people deep, and very noisy, cheering, calling out, some for the police who clustered inside the courtyard, others for the women who were already approaching. She saw Mrs. Pankhurst in the lead, so tiny, her step quick and firm. She persisted in her stride, approaching the line of policemen who barred the way. Surely, she would stop. But she did not. With what seemed only a small shove, the linked arms of the bobbies separated, and Mrs. Pankhurst and three others gained the steps of Parliament. Sylvia felt a sense of triumph as she saw how easily it had been accomplished.

But the victory was short-lived. The women did not march in defile. It might have been better if they had. Rather, they came in small groups of four, five or six. All this, Sylvia learned later, was in accordance with a court order limiting the number of demonstrators. They carried signs and banners reading: ASQUITH HAS VETOED OUR BILL, WHERE THERE'S A BILL THERE'S A WAY, WOMEN'S WILL BEATS ASQUITH'S WON'T. They seemed determined to Sylvia, firm of step, enduring the catcalls, confronting the police. She suddenly had a great sense of pride in these women who, after all, wanted such a little thing, the right to vote.

As the second knot of women approached the police cordon, the resistance of the uniformed men stiffened. A struggle began, the women determined to break through to reach the steps where Mrs. Pankhurst stood, the police determined to keep them away. As pushing and shoving ensued, the third group of women entered the fray, threatening to overwhelm the police. Sylvia heard whistles; then, from the courtyard of the Foreign Ministry, rushed a coterie of police reinforcements. They lunged at the women, grabbing them from behind, hitting them in the face, throwing them to the pavement. In horror, Sylvia saw a woman—she had to be in her seventies—being kicked in the shins. When she fell to her knees, she was kicked in the midriff, then kicked again as she lay on the ground. Sylvia heard herself screaming protests at the top of her lungs.

Still the women marched forward in their little groups, resolutely exercising their constitutional right of petition—marching forward into certain danger. Halfway to their goal they were assaulted, wrestled to the ground, their signs broken and the pieces used to strike them. Sylvia saw women pummeled with fists, others knocked to the ground several times, still others thrown from man to man to be hit and shoved aside. Several women were simply thrown into the crowd. Some were helped or pushed back into the fray. Others were swallowed into the crowd. Just ahead of her, Sylvia saw a woman grabbed by the mob, hands reaching for her breasts, under her skirts. Sylvia screamed, but she knew that would not help.

Then, to her horror, Sylvia saw Kitty approaching, tiny, but resolute, marching, carrying her sign. Sylvia was screaming and screaming for Kitty to stop, to turn back, not to come forward. Then, as the first rough hands tore the sign from Kitty's grasp and seized her, Sylvia was sobbing. Kitty was thrown to the ground, only to get up and attack a policeman who had grabbed another woman. He swung an arm to knock her away. She took the blow but staggered forward, climbing on the back of the uniformed man. Even over the noise of the crowd, Sylvia could hear the man bellow. Other officers rushed to his aid. Two men grabbed Kitty, lifting her off the man's back, each pulling at an arm, as though unwilling to let go of a prize, then each wheeled and drove a free arm into her midriff. It seemed to Sylvia she could hear Kitty's cry of pain as she lurched backwards into another officer, who pushed her to still another, as if she were a rag doll, until an officer drove her to the pavement with a blow from his truncheon; then, for good measure, drove his boot into her.

Crying, screaming, Sylvia clawed and fought her way forward into the crowd ahead of her, pushing past people, scratching and grasping for space until, at last, she was free of the crowd. Stumbling, falling once, she ran to where Kitty lay on the pavement and knelt over her, calling her name. Suddenly, she felt excruciating pain in her ribs. Someone had kicked her. Then another blow sent her sprawling. She tried to get up and go to Kitty, but another blow sent her reeling. Then she realized she was being tossed about, hands were grabbing at her, pinching. They didn't seem to be policemen. Who were they? Later, she would read that "gangs of well-organized, well-dressed toughs entered the fray." Repeatedly, Sylvia was knocked down, finally blacking out as her head hit the pavement.

When she awoke, dazed, confused, the mêlée was still going on. Women were still marching into the hopeless battle—in all, more than three hundred of them—and the police, aided by the toughs, still battled them. It would go on for more than five hours and the press would label it "Black Friday."

Crouching on the pavement, Sylvia remembered Kitty and began to look for her. Some distance to her left, Kitty had been dragged out of the courtyard into the crowd. Crawling, crouching, Sylvia stumbled to her and, kneeling over her, cradled her head in her arms. She seemed lifeless. "Help!" Sylvia screamed. "Somebody do something! Get a doctor, an ambulance!"

"Ain't gonna get no ambulance in here, lady."

"Please. Somebody help me get her out of here."

Hands did, helping to lift Kitty and carry her down an alley to a doorway.

Sobbing, filled with panic, Sylvia again knelt beside her friend, cradling her head in her arms. "Kitty, oh, Kitty, please, please." She seemed so still, so lifeless. Indeed, Sylvia had no idea if she were alive or dead. Then Kitty's eyes blinked and opened. "Thank God, thank God, you're alive."

A sort of smile lit Kitty's face. "Sylvia. You marched."

"Yes, yes." She didn't know what else to say.

Then, in horror, she realized life was leaving Kitty, ebbing slowly away from her. "No, no, don't die." The words were wrenched from her. "You can't die." Then, as though trying to hold life in her, Sylvia lifted Kitty in her arms, squeezing her as tightly as she could, begging her not to die. She began to kiss her face, over and over, tasting the salt from her own tears as they bathed Kitty's face.

Against her ear she heard words, knowing they would be the last Kitty would ever say: "Be good to Arthur."

She held her for a long time, weeping quietly. Then, when there were no more tears, she lowered Kitty's head and shoulders to the steps of the doorway and stood looking down at her. Numb with her own inner pain, Sylvia bent over, picked up the dead weight of Kitty Shaw and began walking slowly. She had no idea where she was going. She just carried Kitty away from the place where she had lost her life.

Chapter Twenty-six

Sylvia awoke in her own bed. That came as no surprise, but the nurse who came to hover over her was.

"You're awake, miss?"

"Yes."

"How do you feel?"

Sylvia looked at her hard. She was a severe-looking woman, perhaps in her late forties, with hair pulled back into a bun. She wore steel-rimmed glasses, a white cap and a heavily-starched uniform. "I'm all right, I guess. Have I been ill?"

"Oh, very, miss. You've been unconscious for two days."

"I have?"

A sort of smile, a widening of the lips, came to the nurse's face. "We have all worried about you. I'll go at once and tell the countess you are awake."

Sylvia watched the nurse turn and leave the bedroom. Sick? For two days? Then it came back to her, the riot outside Parliament, women being assaulted, Kitty coming, being beaten, knocked down, and herself running to Kitty's aid. Yes, she remembered all, being knocked out, seeing Kitty so lifeless, then . . . yes, Kitty dying in her arms. Kitty dead? Kitty, who had called her "dearest"? *Oh, Kitty. . . .*

These memories came to Sylvia in a strange way. She felt grief at Kitty's death, but none of the horror she had felt at witnessing the attacks on women. And, while she could remember her own participation, she did so without feeling.

It was almost as though her mind was a detached observer of her own actions. She had acted most uncharacteristically. She knew that, but was unable to remember anything that happened after Kitty died. How had she gotten home?

"My dear, my dear, thank God you're all right." Sylvia saw her mother rush into the room, elegant as usual, the nurse trailing behind. "We thought you were *dead.*" She sat on the bed beside her daughter. "Oh, Sylvia, my child, say *something,* let me know you're all *right.*"

Sylvia tried to smile. "I'm fine, mother."

"Are you *sure,* darling?"

"Yes, mother, I'm all right."

"Thank goodness. I've done *nothing* but pray. Heavens, the way you *looked* when you were brought home, all bruises and filth. The doctor said nothing was broken. Just a slight concussion and shock. But when you didn't *wake up.* Oh, God, Sylvia, I've never been so worried in my *life.*"

Sylvia stared at her. "How did I get home?"

"Why, the police, of course. Oh, I know, they probably should have taken you directly to the hospital, but they recognized you, brought you home. Thank the Lord for that. You received better care here than you *ever* would have in a hospital. Doctor Edwards came at once and. . . ."

Sylvia tuned out her mother's prattle. She was still puzzled about what had happened to her. "The police brought me home?"

"Of course, dear. Don't you remember?"

Sylvia shook her head against the pillow, hoping to clear away the fog over her memory. "No, I don't seem to. I remember—"

"Oh, yes, Doctor Edwards said you might have a little— what was that word, Nurse Croggins?"

"Amnesia, milady."

"Yes, amnesia. He said you might not remember. And it's *just* as well, I can *tell* you that."

"Mother, I remember everything, the riot, Kitty—"

"That *dreadful* girl."

"She died in my arms, but I don't know what happened after that."

"You *carried* that awful girl to the police station. Sylvia. How you *managed* it, I'll never know. But it was fortunate you did. When you collapsed in the station, the police knew what to do—bring you *home* where you belong."

"I see." Actually, she still couldn't remember, but it was an explanation of what must have happened.

"Oh, Sylvia, child, *child*, how could you get involved with those *nasty* women—fighting with the police, acting like a *madwoman*. I swear, Sylvia, I don't *understand* you sometimes."

"Kitty was my friend."

"Oh, yes, from school. But look at what she *became*. You can't have a friend like *that*."

"Milady, forgive me, but I think the patient needs to rest now."

Lady Constance immediately ceased her scolding. "Of course." She patted Sylvia's cheek affectionately. "The main thing is that you're going to get well. Everything will be all right."

Sylvia watched her mother stand up. "What could be wrong?"

"Oh, my dear, a great deal, but fortunately the police are not bringing charges against you. And the duke—well, I'll tell you, he's being very noble about the whole thing. He's prepared to forgive you." She smiled. "Now you just rest, dear. I'll phone Lord Charles at once to tell him you're all right. He's been so *dreadfully* worried about you, the poor man. He's *dying* to see you, but I'll *insist* he wait till later. You just rest." Imperiously, she turned to Nurse Croggins. "Shouldn't she have something to eat? Broth, at least?"

"It's coming, milady."

Sylvia did swallow a little warm beef broth; then, to her surprise, fell asleep again. When she awoke some hours later, she consumed all the broth hungrily, then asked for and ate solid food, feeling a quick return of her strength. When her mother came in to report Lord Charles was downstairs hoping to see her, Sylvia summoned Clara to comb and braid her hair, apply a little makeup and help her into a wool robe of soft green. Thus, while still in bed, she was sitting up and looking reasonably well to receive her fiancé.

"Thank G-God, Sylvia, you're all r-right."

"I'm fine, Charles." She smiled. "All this fussing over me will make me quite spoiled."

"N-No, my d-dear. You were v-very i-ill. I was t-terribly worried."

"You needn't have been. We Hartleys are hardy stock."

"When I th-think of what m-might have h-h-happened to you, I. . . ."

He never finished expressing his fears. Sylvia looked at him a moment, waiting; then, suddenly, she felt awkward. She looked down at her hands, toying nervously with the edge of a knitted coverlet. "I imagine you disapprove of my actions, Charles."

He cleared his throat. "W-We will sp-speak of it later, my d-dear. You m-must—"

"But, Charles, can't you understand that . . . that Kitty Shaw was my friend?"

Again, he attacked the phlegm in his throat. "I do, of c-course. I q-quite understand. You saw wh-what was h-happening to your friend, b-became upset. You r-r-rushed to her a-aid." He looked at her unhappily. "But. . . ."

She waited in vain for him to continue. "But what, Charles?"

A moment longer, he hesitated. "It m-must be o-obvious to you n-now, my d-dear, y-you should not have been th-there."

"Many were there, thousands, actually."

"I know, b-but—" He broke off to smile at her. "We'll d-discuss this another t-time, when you are—"

"I'm fine, Charles." She hesitated. "You realize, of course, I was not—I did not *participate* in the march. I—I merely went to . . . to observe it."

"Yes, I kn-know."

"I don't understand. What did I do that was so . . . so wrong?"

Now he looked away from her, a distressed expression on his face. "You have b-been un-un-un—" He could not say *unconscious*. "—ill until today. P-Perhaps you don't know."

"Know what?"

"The s-suffragettes are m-making y-you a hero—I mean, h-heroine. Th-That is not s-something I—b-being so c-close to the C-Crown—can have h-happen."

"I see." She studied his face. "As your fiancée, I brought disgrace to you." The deepening distress she saw provided her an answer. "Then I am truly sorry for that, Charles. If you wish to break our engagement, I'll—of course, I'll understand."

She might have pricked him with a pin. "You're not s-serious, S-Sylvia?"

" I am, Charles, very much so. If I have embarrassed you and—"

"M-My dear, p-please. I w-won't hear of it. The whole e-episode has been un-un-unfortunate. P-please, don't m-make it w-w-worse." She waited him out, saying nothing to ease his difficulties. "It is j-just that—My d-dear, you were t-tricked into j-joining that o-o-organiz-zation—the suffrag-ettes. Y-You m-must b-break all t-ties to them. You m-must not b-become in-involved in c-controv-versy."

She stared at him. "Anything else I must do, Charles?"

Again, he cleared his throat. "Yes. The p-press has been c-clamoring to t-talk to you. Y-You must make a s-s-statement exp-pressing your r-regrets at your—"

"But I don't regret anything, Charles." The words just came out. "Kitty was my friend. She was there. The police were hitting her, knocking her down . . . kicking her." Memories, now filled with horror, came to her. "I couldn't allow—"

"Sylvia, the p-police were only d-doing their j-job."

"Kicking women is their job?"

His voice took on a sharper tone. "We are a n-nation of laws, Sylvia. Without l-laws, we w-will have a-anarchy, B-Bolshevism. You c-can't want th-that?"

She realized the futility of arguing further with him. And, suddenly tiring, she had no arguments to make. She did not know enough about law, politics, or anything, to stand up to him. Sighing deeply, she said, "If I express my regrets, is that all you want me to do?"

"Th-that and b-breaking all ties to those wo-wo-wo—people."

"Then you'll forgive me?"

He smiled. "It is not a c-case of f-f-forgiveness, Sylvia. You are y-young. It is my t-task to g-guide you."

"I see." She closed her eyes and sagged against the pillows.

"My d-dear. I kn-knew I sh-shouldn't have g-gone into this now. How th-thoughtless of m-me."

"It's all right, Charles. But I am tired."

She opened her eyes to see him bending over to kiss her. She turned her cheek to him.

"I'd b-best be g-going."

"Yes, Charles."

"I'll s-see you t-tomorrow. We'll t-talk m-more then."

"Yes."

Sylvia recovered her strength quickly, and her bruises from her scuffle with the law faded away. Her emotional state remained something else, however. Her mother, Clara, Lord Charles, others who came in contact with her, only thought her quiet and withdrawn, ascribing it to her illness.

The truth was that Sylvia could not get Kitty Shaw off her mind. Repeatedly, she relived "Black Friday" and Kitty's death. She faced her own horror at what had transpired and she understood her compulsion to run to Kitty's aid. She remembered trying to hold the life in Kitty, her friend's look of happiness when she thought Sylvia had marched, her last, strange words: "Be good to Arthur." When she was alone, Sylvia wept for Kitty. She had been so brave, marching forward into the ranks of police, knowing what was going to happen. All those women had been brave. And Sylvia knew she was not, could never be . . . she had come as a bystander.

Sylvia asked for back papers and read every word she could find, including *Votes for Women*. The versions varied widely, the *Times* and other papers presenting the official view, downplaying the size and significance of the riot, playing up the role of the police as preservers of the peace, simply doing their duty to maintain law and order. The suffragette publication ran several photographs of women being beaten with truncheons, roughed up, carried off. *Votes for Women* declared that it was a black day when women were treated like common criminals for only trying to exercise their constitutional right of petition.

In a separate article, Christabel Pankhurst exposed the police actions. The Liberal leadership, facing an election, did not want to lose votes by arresting a great many women, then face the public spectacle of hunger strikes and forced feedings. Home Secretary Winston Churchill devised the scheme of simply having the police keep the women away from Parliament without arresting them. In the end, this failed. Over a hundred women were taken away by the police, but at the station all charges were dismissed—save for those women who had thrown rocks. The new tactic may have led to wholesale assaults upon women, but it avoided the political "problem" of mass arrests.

The death of Kitty Shaw also received conflicting coverage in the press. The *Times* printed the official police version that Miss Shaw had been attacked by unknown, unspecified "ruffians" at the scene, despite the valiant efforts of police to rescue her. The suffragette publication described the assault on Kitty much more accurately.

As for her own role, the *Times* wrote, "Miss Sylvia Hartley, stepdaughter of the earl of Linfield, was slightly injured while attempting to come to the aid of Miss Shaw, a friend from their days at St. Regis Academy. Miss Hartley, who is engaged to marry the duke of Glouston, in a valiant action carried Miss Shaw to the nearest police station, but was too late to save her friend's life. Miss Hartley then collapsed from her exertions."

Votes for Women trumpeted Sylvia as a "heroine of the struggle for freedom." The article went on, "Unmindful of her personal safety, Miss Hartley rushed to the aid of Kitty Shaw, struggling with police until she was herself knocked unconscious. Dazed, bruised, Miss Hartley then carried the lifeless body of Kitty Shaw to the police station, depositing the martyred Kitty on the desk of the police sergeant. Clearly, Miss Hartley was offering the body of Kitty Shaw as a sacrifice to police brutality. This gesture of defiance will forever inspire the women of the world."

Sylvia read and reread the words in disbelief. She still couldn't remember carrying Kitty's body away. Surely, she had never intended a "sacrifice," a "gesture of defiance."

Among her mail was a letter from Emmeline Pankhurst.

Dearest Sylvia,

I have tried to visit you, but have been turned away at the door. Therefore, until I can see you to express my thanks personally, I want to take this means to express my personal admiration, as well as that of the entire membership of the W.S.P.U., for your courageous efforts to save the life of our sister and friend, Kitty Shaw. Your act of defiance to the police, laying our dead sister on the altar of police savagery, inspired us all.

*You have our sincerest wishes for a speedy recovery.
And do visit me at Clement's Inn shortly.*

> *Yours in the Struggle,*
> *Emmeline Pankhurst*

When she finished reading, Sylvia realized her eyes were moist. None of what was said was true. She had never intended anything. But she was touched, nonetheless. Like Kitty, Emmeline had called her *dearest*.

She also received a note from Arthur Wicklow—attached to a dozen roses. It said simply, "I'm proud of you." That made her smile.

These two messages were the only exceptions to the general disapproval of her "unfortunate" actions. Lord Winnie joined the doctor, the vicar and all her other visitors in deploring her "misguided" conduct. They did not actually scold her as her mother and Lord Charles had. Mostly, she was treated as a wayward child who had done an "unwise" thing, having been "led astray" into "mistaken" actions. Of course, she would never do anything like it again. This was said as though the speaker took that for granted, yet the need to say it indicated a measure of doubt.

Actually, a good bit of effort went into seeing that Sylvia returned to the "normal" course of her life. Any untoward influences were kept away. When Lady Constance saw that Sylvia received *Votes for Women*, she left strict orders it was never again to be let into the house. Sylvia's visitors were carefully screened, especially at tea. Captain Waring was urged to tease her mildly, which he did, suggesting that, if she wished, he would impart to her some instructions in the "manly art of self-defense." Joshua Wainwright came to plead with her to resume the sittings. Timothy Graves said he had learned that three police officers had gone on sick leave as a result of her efforts. "You may be assured, dear Sylvia, I shall watch what I say to you most carefully from now on."

Sylvia was not unmindful of what was going on, but she hadn't the energy to oppose it. Her grief for Kitty and her horror at her death, while real, inevitably began to recede. And still she felt no sense of commitment to women's suffrage. At one point, she argued mildly with Lord Charles. "What's wrong with women having the vote?"

"Nothing, my d-dear. I b-believe women, such as y-yourself, sh-should vote. And they w-will—but in g-good t-time. There is n-nothing you, nor I, nor a-anyone else can d-do to s-speed it up."

Sylvia had no answer to that. She couldn't escape the feeling that her actions on Black Friday were atypical of herself. She had never done such a thing before. Something must have come over her. A sort of temporary madness, perhaps. Nor could she visualize herself doing it again. She sensed she was somehow changed by all that had happened, but exactly how she didn't know. Thus, she began to drift back into the life she knew, resuming the sittings, seeing Charles, going to the opera or parties with him. But she remained aloof, diffident, uncommitted and, she knew, vaguely unhappy.

On December 2nd, Sylvia received a letter from Meg. The content was not terribly surprising. Meg had read of her "exploits" in the paper. "How courageous you are, Sylvia. I hope you are as proud of yourself as I am." There were a couple of sentences about how well Brian was doing, then a final line that all was well and she would write more later. Sylvia was alarmed. The brevity of the letter, Meg's shaky scrawl instead of her usual fine hand, told Sylvia that Meg was not well. This was a letter written by a sick person. Meg was ill. She knew it. As quickly as she could, Sylvia rose from her desk, dressed and headed for the train station and Hornby.

Chapter Twenty-seven

The normally short train trip to Hornby seemed to Sylvia to take forever. She spent it consumed with worry, reading and rereading Meg's note, seeing not the reassuring words but the hideous scribbling of her friend. If anything happened to Meg it would all be her fault for neglecting her. She had spent these last weeks worrying about herself and her problems when it was Meg who really needed help.

At last, the train arrived, and Sylvia took the taxi to the edge of the ravine. Once again, it had begun to rain, a cold, incessant December rain, as Sylvia began the trek up the ravine toward the shack. She didn't know what she expected, but it was not having the door opened by a smiling Meg delighted to see her. There were the usual hugs of greeting, followed by the question, "What brings you to Hornby, Sylvie?"

She looked at her friend, making a careful appraisal. Meg seemed all right, but she was very thin in the face and shoulders, her complexion sallow, her blue Welsh eyes a little shrunken. On impulse, Sylvia answered as casually as she could, "Oh, I just came up to see how you are—and maybe have a gab. How are you, Meg?"

'Meg's smile was lavish. "Oh, I'm fine, just fine."

"Really?"

A laugh joined the smile. "Yes, really. Oh, I get a little tired—but that's normal. I'm fine, truly—healthy as a horse." She patted her belly. "And almost as big."

"I have a feeling you wouldn't tell me if you weren't."

"Of course, I would, Sylvie. You didn't come all the way out here in the rain because you were worried about me, did you?"

Sylvia had the sense to let it go. "No. I just wanted to see you—to talk."

"Then let's. I'll make some tea."

While that business was begun, Sylvia looked around the cabin. It seemed no better, maybe worse than before. The coal she had sent the last time had dwindled to a small hoard, and the cabin was damp and very chilly. She would have to get some more.

"Where's Brian?"

"Oh, he's out back working on a motor car."

"In the rain?"

Meg laughed. "That's what I asked him. But he said he was working underneath, and that would keep the rain off him. He'll be in soon to get warm, no doubt."

Sylvia watched as Meg carried the tea kettle to the stove, then bent to build up the fire. She seemed to move slowly and unsteadily, as though in pain. Meg's movements were like those of a very old woman. And, when Meg straightened up, she involuntarily raised the back of her wrist to her forehead. It seemed to Sylvia she swayed a little before steadying herself.

"Meg, are you all right?"

"I'm fine, Sylvie. I told you."

"I know what you told me. But I don't believe it."

"Really, I'm fine. I just have a little headache, and I get dizzy when I bend over. It'll go away in a moment."

Sylvia went to her and took her arm. "At least, sit down."

Meg smiled. "That I will do. A watched pot never boils." She sagged heavily into a chair at the kitchen table. "Yes, that does feel better." She smiled. "Did you get my letter?"

"Yes, today."

"I meant every word, Sylvie. How brave you were!"

"Not really, Meg, not at all. I just saw what was happening to Kitty and ran to try to help her."

"That's brave."

"No. Kitty was the brave one. She, all those women, knew what was going to happen to them—and they just kept marching forward. That's courage—to know and still do it."

Meg smiled. "Well, I still think *you're* brave. No one else came to the aid of those women. I'm proud of you. Aren't you proud of yourself?"

Sylvia sighed. "I don't know what I am—" She gave a wan smile. "—other than confused."

"About what?"

"Oh, everything—myself, my life, what's happening to me."

The two friends looked at each other a long moment, mostly in sadness. "Sylvie, why did you get engaged to that duke? You know you don't love him."

"No."

"You can't marry someone you don't love. You'll never be happy."

Another long sigh escaped Sylvia. "Oh, maybe I will. He's a good and decent man. He loves me. He gives me anything I want. He's—"

"He's not the man to make you happy—however rich he is."

Despite herself, Sylvia nodded her head sadly.

"Then you can't marry him. You just can't." Meg reached both hands over the table top and gripped Sylvia's fingers, squeezing tightly as though to enforce the conviction of her voice. "Isn't there anyone you love?"

"Yes. You know who."

"Arthur Wicklow?" When there was no answer, Meg's words burst out of her. "Then for God's sake, marry *him*."

"I can't," she replied forlornly.

"Why not? Is there something wrong with him?"

"Yes." She forced a small, rather bitter smile. "Can't you just hear the Countess Linfield if I said I was going to marry Arthur Wicklow?"

"Who cares what she says? It's your life—not hers."

Sylvia smiled. "Meg, you make everything sound so easy—but it isn't. I couldn't marry Arthur."

"Why couldn't you?"

"Oh, Meg, you know how I've been brought up—a rich man's daughter, even if I'm not really his daughter—big house, squads of servants, looked after, pampered, told what to do constantly. Meg, I can't even boil water for tea—" She smiled. "—like you're doing right now."

Meg smiled too. "See what I said. Don't watch it and it'll

boil every time." Slowly, pushing down with her arms much more than her legs, Meg rose, turned to the stove and carried the steaming pot to the sink, filling the teapot. "You're talking nonsense, Sylvie. You can boil water, you can make tea. You can do anything you want to, or need to."

"Including cook a man's supper, I suppose—and wash and iron his shirts, scrub floors. Oh, Meg, don't you see? It would never work. I'm a hot-house plant. I've never had to rough it. I'd make a terrible wife for Arthur. I'd only make him miserable—myself too. It would never work."

Meg came back to the table carrying the steeping pot of tea. "You're ridiculous, Sylvie. I was an upstairs maid. What did I know about all this? But I learned." She smiled. "Took five minutes—and it was fun. Oh, Sylvie, love enables you to do anything."

Sylvia's answer was to shake her head, as Meg, with labored steps, went to bring the cups for tea. Halfway back, she stopped. Horrified, Sylvia saw her stand there a moment, her eyes glazed, weaving on her feet. The tea cups fell from her hands and she slowly began to crumble, knees first. Screaming, Sylvia reached her in time to keep her from falling, grabbing her around the arms and shoulders, then dragging her to the bed, laying her head on the pillow, then lifting her feet and legs onto the quilt. At once, she patted her cheeks and called out her name. There was no response. She opened Meg's blouse at the throat, then moved to take off her shoes. When Sylvia raised her friend's skirts, she shrieked at what she saw. Meg's legs were swollen to almost twice their normal size. "Oh, God, Meg, what's wrong with you?"

Then she remembered Brian. She ran to the back door and screamed for him. Finally, he heard her against the steady drone of the rain. He slid out from under the car, looked at her and understood her frantic motions. Covered with mud and grease, he ran inside to Meg.

"Did she pass out again? Oh, Lord!"

"What's wrong with her, Brian?"

"I don't know." Quickly, he stepped to the sink, returning with a damp cloth, which he put on Meg's forehead. "This happened two other times. She came out of it all right."

Sylvia watched him wipe Meg's face with the cloth, then gently pat her cheeks as she had done. "Have you had the doctor, Brian?"

"No. She's all right. Just fainted."

Gently, he moved Meg to a sitting position on the edge of the bed, then lowered her head between her legs. "This will do it."

"Brian, we've got to get a doctor."

"Ain't no doctor. He's sick."

"There has to be a doctor somewhere, Brian. Have you seen her legs?"

"The midwife says not to worry about it."

"The midwife must be mistaken, Brian. There's something seriously wrong with Meg. I know it. That's why I came here today."

"She comin' round now."

And she was, sitting up now, although she looked extremely pale. She glanced at Brian, then at Sylvia. "Goodness, what a ninny I am!"

"You all right, Meg?"

She gave her husband a little smile. "I'm fine, Brian, really." She touched her cheek. "Except you got my face greasy."

"I'm sorry, honey, really I am." Gently, he laid her back on the bed. "You just lie there and rest now."

When he moved to take off Meg's shoes, Sylvia said, "Here, I'll do that." As she bent to the task, she watched Brian out of the corner of her eye. He loved his wife, but he was so stubborn, so proud. Meg needed medical attention— right now.

When the shoes were removed from the swollen feet, Sylvia said, "Brian, will you let me—"

"We don't need nothing, Miss Sylvia."

"But you do, Brian. Can't you see she's not well?"

"I'm fine, Sylvie. Really, I am."

Sylvia looked at Meg in exasperation as Brian picked up his wife's words. "See? She says she's fine. And she is. Lots o' women have fainting spells."

"No, she's not fine, Brian. She won't tell you the truth, she won't tell me. She needs a doctor."

"Got no money for doctors."

Sylvia fought against her fury at Brian's pigheadedness. "I know she's your wife. But I'm her friend. We both love her. Why won't you let me help?"

"We don't need help. We're getting along fine."

From the bed came Meg's voice. "Listen to him, Sylvie. I'm fine, really I am."

Sylvia sighed. There was no point in arguing with them. She would simply do what had to be done—get proper medical attention for Meg—then let them protest later, if they wanted to.

As soon as she could leave, Sylvia went into the village to search out Dr. Crowley. He was a terribly old man, but he might at least know what made Meg's legs swell like that and what caused her to faint. Brian was right. Dr. Crowley was sick with typhoid fever, barely alive himself. His wife said the doctor in Pudlington would come over, but only if it were an emergency. Pudlington was eleven miles away.

"Is it an emergency, Miss Sylvia?"

"I don't know, Mrs. Crowley. I guess not."

Sylvia climbed into the cab to get out of the rain, trying to decide what to do. Meg was sick. There was no doubt of that in her mind. But how sick? What ought she to do? Then she thought of Arthur. Yes. He would know what to do.

Minutes later, she stood in the rain rapping on the door of Arthur's cottage. There was no answer. Timorously, she tried the latch and felt it give. Opening the door, she called out Arthur's name, then stepped inside. The fire was cold, the desk clean. He wasn't there. Then she remembered. Parliament was in session. He was probably in London.

London. The best thing to do was return there. She would find a doctor and bring him back to Hornby. Better yet, she could arrange to have an ambulance take Meg to a hospital where she would get proper care. Yes, that was what she must do. But she would need money. The few pounds in her purse would not be nearly enough. Winnie. She would ask Winnie for money.

Sylvia arrived in London late in the afternoon, her spirits buoyed that she at last had a plan to help Meg. From the station, she went home and asked for Lord Winnie. The butler told her he was at his club. She left the house immediately, hailed a hansom and went to the Regency Club, the poshest in the city, gaining entry by saying she was Lord Linfield's daughter and it was important that she see him. For five minutes or so, she sat in the reception room, a large,

A LASTING SPLENDOR

ornate and richly-paneled room, drenched in dignity and privilege.

He came down an open staircase toward her, accompanied by Lord Charles. "My dear child, what is the matter?" She stood up to greet them. "You look a fright. Has something happened at home?"

For the first time that day, she was aware of her appearance. She had been rained on several times. She looked down, saw mud on her skirt. Her hair must be a fright and her makeup long gone. "Everything is fine at home, Winnie. My problem is something else." She looked at her fiancé, seeing a concerned expression on his face. "I didn't expect to see you here, Charles."

"W-We were having t-tea, Sylvia. Is s-something w-wrong?"

She managed a wan smile. "I'm afraid there is."

"Well, do sit down." Lord Linfield motioned for her to sit, while he and the duke pulled up chairs to sit opposite her. "Now, my dear, tell us what brings you here."

Once again, Sylvia felt her stepfather's regard for her and knew she had done the right thing to come to him. "I was hoping, father, I might borrow some money from you—against my allowance, of course."

He smiled. "You may, indeed—and you need not disturb your allowance." He reached for his wallet. "How much do you need?"

"A hundred pounds."

"A hundred?" He laughed. "Of course, I can let you have it, but why so much? And why do you need it in such a hurry? If some dress or hat has caught your fancy, you can just have them bill me as usual."

"No, father, it's nothing like that." She hesitated, saw the expectant looks on the faces of the men and knew she had to explain. "Do you remember my former maid Meg Gwynne, now Meg Trout?"

"Oh, yes," Lord Winnie said, "the one who got herself in the family way and had to marry the poor chap."

It seemed to Sylvia her stepfather was almost snickering as he spoke. "Yes, that's her. I've just come from Hornby, father. Meg is very ill. I know she is. She needs medical attention—and they have no money."

275

"And you want the money for a doctor or whatever?"

"Yes, exactly, father." She smiled, grateful that he understood.

He said nothing right away, but glanced at Lord Charles. Then he put his wallet back into his inside coat pocket in a rather elaborate fashion. "I'm sorry," he said finally, clearing his throat. "I'm sorry Meg whatever-her-name-is-now is ill, but that can be no concern of ours."

Sylvia couldn't believe her ears. "But—but, you can't *mean* that."

"I'm afraid I do, my dear Sylvia—I mean it very much."

"But—but she's my dearest friend."

"A mere childhood attachment. It's time you got over it."

Sylvia could only stare at him, unable to believe his callousness. "But she's *ill*, father—maybe *dying.*"

His smile was pure condescension. "I'm sure she's not, Sylvia. But in any event, there are institutions to look after her—various charities, which I support generously, I might say. And the Church of England has facilities for the poor. Isn't that right, Charles?" He glanced at the duke, who was nodding, then he looked back at Sylvia. "You should not permit yourself to become so upset. These matters are best left to others." He patted her hand. "I suggest you go home, have a nice hot bath, a pot of tea, then make yourself as beautiful as you always are."

She continued to stare at him, her eyes wide. "God, father, have you no heart?"

Lord Winnie bristled. "You're upset, Sylvia, therefore I'll ignore your impertinence. May I remind you, I took that girl into my household as an orphan, gave her an opportunity for a lifelong position. She chose to throw it away on—" His smile became a sneer. "—shall we say, on a fling? She is now paying the piper for her folly. Paying the wages of sin. So be it."

Sylvia bolted out of her chair, angered at what she was hearing. Lord Linfield arose more slowly, facing her wrath. "Your mother has forbidden you to see that girl. I wish to enforce the countess' action. You will go home this instant and await my arrival."

She opened her mouth, ready to sling barbed words at him, but did not. She turned to her fiancé, who was also standing now. "Charles, will you help me?" She saw him hesitate, his mouth open in a half-formed stammer. "Or are you going to sit here too, barricaded behind your luxury and privilege, smoking your cigars, drinking your brandy and just let Meg die—to teach her a *lesson*." She had raised her voice, each word bitten off, hurled.

"Sylvia, I demand that you control yourself."

She ignored her stepfather, fastening her anger on Lord Charles. "Are you going to help me or not?"

Finally, he could speak. "M-My d-dear, I'm a-a-a—I fear Lord W-W-W—your stepfather is r-right. There are in-in-institutions for—"

"Oh, sure, there are people to look after her—the under-takers, the gravediggers in potters' fields. God, Charles, how can you *be* like this—so stupid?"

She had provoked his anger. "It is j-just this sort of a-attitude you m-must get o-over if—"

"If what, Charles? Am I on trial? Have you taken me home to your bed on approval—the merchandise to be returned later if unsatisfactory?" She saw the shock in the faces of Charles, her stepfather, to whom she turned. "And now where are your wages of sin? When are you going to give Charles one of your pious little lectures?"

She wheeled then and stalked out of the Regency Club. In the cab she fumed a few moments, then deliberately forced her anger aside. None of it was helping Meg. She must get some money. Where? She thought of her mother, then instantly discarded that idea as preposterous. Her mother would never help her. And if she returned home, she might be forcibly prevented from leaving. Winnie had ordered her to go home and stay there. Whom could she turn to? Arthur. He was probably at Parliament right now. Quickly, she told the cabby to take her there.

She alighted from the hansom at the Strangers' Entrance, briefly remembering that this was the place Kitty had lost her life. To the doorman, she said, "My name is Sylvia Hartley. I must see Arthur Wicklow, the member from Liverpool, on a matter of the utmost urgency."

The doorman bowed, spoke to a page, who left with the message. In a few minutes, a rotund man in his fifties appeared. He gave his name as Jarvis. Sylvia assumed he must be some sort of Parliamentary aide.

"I'm sorry, Miss Hartley, but Mr. Wicklow is not in the chamber."

"He's not? Where is he?"

"I believe he's gone to Liverpool, miss."

"Liverpool? But why?"

"He intended to campaign for the forthcoming elections, miss."

She could feel her panic rising. "But I must see him. Can he be reached in Liverpool?"

"Not immediately, I'm afraid. I imagine he is attending meetings, that sort of thing."

"Oh, Lord. . . ."

"He may return in a day or so, or he may contact us. I could give him a message, miss."

"Oh, could you?" She let herself be escorted to a small desk, sat and tried to compose herself to write something sensible.

Arthur,

   Meg is ill—very ill, I think. I'm going to Hornby to look after her. Will you come as soon as you can?

                                                                    Sylvia

She handed the note to Jarvis. "Will you see that he receives this?"

"You have my word, Miss Hartley."

Somewhat dazed, frustration and depression oppressing her, she returned to the waiting cab, sat in it, trying to decide what to do next. Quickly, she inventoried all others who might help her. Then, realizing she had no other choice, she gave the cabby an address.

Perhaps a quarter hour later, she was knocking on the door of Philip Waring's apartment. To her relief, he opened the door. He wore his dress uniform, obviously planning to go out.

"My dear Sylvia." Obviously, he was surprised to see her.

"May I come in, Philip?"

He opened the door wider and stood back. "Of course. There is no one I like to see more than you, you know that."

She read his meaning. When she was inside and the door

closed, she said, "That's not why I came, Philip. I need a friend. I need help."

He smiled broadly. "I didn't really think that was what you had in mind—at this hour. And—" He laughed. "—forgive me, my darling, but what have you been doing? You look a fright."

"I know. Let me tell you what happened."

"I'm really pressed for time—but you need a cognac first."

While he poured and delivered the beverage, she told him of her day, her visit to the Regency Club, the attitude of her stepfather and Lord Charles. "I came to you, Philip, because I need help. I need some place to stay tonight. It's too late to go back to Hornby. May I stay here?"

"Of course. You know you're welcome here."

"Oh, Philip, I don't mean that. I couldn't—not tonight."

Again, his laughter swept over her. "Nor do I mean that, either—although there is no woman on earth like you." Once more, he laughed. "I'll tell you what. I was just preparing to meet a . . . a charming lady for a . . . shall we say a rendezvous? Chances are I may be spending the night elsewhere—if not, I can always enjoy the hospitality of the barracks. You stay here. Have the run of the place. There's some cold mutton in the kitchen, I believe. And there's wine and brandy. You know where the bed is."

His laughter made her smile. "Thank you, Philip. You *are* a friend."

He nodded, his smile fading. "Unfortunately for me, that is the case." He studied her a moment. "You asked Lord Winnie for a hundred. That's way beyond my means, but I'm good for a fiver. Would that be of assistance?"

"Yes, Philip, anything."

He dug out his wallet and opened it, handing her a note. "Here's a tener. Best I can do, I'm afraid." As she took it, he said, "May I give you a word of advice—for old times' sake?"

"Yes."

"You're being awfully silly, you know. First this suffragette business—now a wild goose chase to help a pregnant girl. It won't look good, Sylvia. You're wasting your opportunity." He saw her purse her lips, watched her eyes grow solemn. Then he smiled. "But who am I to give advice? A person does what he or she has to do, right?"

"Yes, I must help Meg. I can't let anything happen to her."

He stood up. "As much as I'd rather be with you, I can't keep my lady waiting. You make yourself at home here. Just lock the door when you leave in the morning."

She arose from her chair and accompanied him to the door. "Philip, you are a dear friend. Just don't tell anyone I stayed here."

"Of course not." He smiled. "Bad for my reputation."

Impulsively, she stood on tiptoe and brushed his lips with hers, a gesture of thanks. Instantly, he grabbed her and kissed her passionately. But only briefly. He broke away, shaking his head sadly, then went out the door, leaving her alone.

She found the cold mutton and some brandy and ate hungrily, drinking a little wine. He had no bathtub, but she washed thoroughly and climbed into his bed. To her surprise, she fell asleep instantly, rising in the morning to take the earliest possible train to Hornby. Again, it was raining.

Chapter Twenty-eight

Sylvia knew at once that Meg was worse. She vomited shortly after Sylvia arrived, and thereafter was unable to get out of bed. Meg's pretense of being "fine" gave way to obvious distress, nausea, a second bout of vomiting, headache and acute dizziness each time she tried to rise.

Sylvia did what she could, cleaning up after Meg, wiping her brow, trying to keep her warm—she even put her own coat over her—building up the fire from the small hoard of coal. She discovered she could make tea, which she tried to get Meg to drink. Although filled with panic, she did her best to remain cheerful with Meg, chattering about how soon she would get well, how beautiful the baby would be.

"If she's a girl . . . I want . . . to name her . . . Sylvia." Meg had forgotten she had already told her that.

Sylvia hugged her. "I could have no greater honor."

Still, there were times that morning when Meg seemed to drift away. She would seem asleep, yet she would talk nonsense about fixing Sylvia's hair, getting her ready for the ball. Then she would laugh at some mental image. Sylvia knew enough about sickness to realize Meg was delirious at such moments.

At first, Brian Trout seemed to resent her coming, saying he didn't need any help, insisting he could look after Meg. But, soon, he softened. "Miss Sylvia, I do need you. Thank you for coming."

"I'm just so worried about her, Brian. We need a doctor."

"Yes. If I can get this car finished outside, then I'll have some money. I'll go to Pudlington for the doctor."

"Yes, hurry. You work on the motor car. I'll look after Meg."

Thus, the arrangement was made. He worked outside in the rain and mud, appearing frequently to check on Meg, while Sylvia did all she could to make her friend comfortable. There was so little she could do, however.

At midday, Sylvia cooked the first meal of her life—boiled potatoes, cabbage, carrots and onion, all she could find in the house. She was fearful at first. She didn't even know how to begin. But in the end she wielded a knife valiantly and, with the addition of some salt at the table, made a palatable meal for Brian and herself. Sylvia hoped to feed some of it to Meg, but she shook her head and fell back asleep.

While they ate, Sylvia said, "Brian, there's a cottage at the end of the village. A man named Arthur Wicklow owns it, but he's not there now. I want to take Meg there."

"No. She stays here—with me."

"Brian, listen to me—*please*. She'll be warmer there and dryer. I can care for her better there."

"No, I won't have it."

Sylvia could feel tears welling up. "God, Brian, we both love her. We can't let anything happen to her. We've got to do what is best for her."

He hesitated, looking at her sharply. "You love her, don't you?"

"Yes, yes, more than life itself."

Once more, he hesitated. "How you going to get her there?"

Sylvia stood up at once. "I'm going to Downhaven to borrow a horse and rig. You stay here with her. I'll be back as soon as I can."

"The car. I gotta finish it. It's important."

Frantically, Sylvia glanced at Meg. She seemed to be sleeping. "All right, but look in on her often. I shouldn't be long."

Coatless, hatless, unmindful of the cold and the heavy rain, Sylvia ran down the ravine into the main street of the village. Frantically, she searched for Hornby's only cab, but it was nowhere to be found. Then she ran toward Downhaven. The main house was perhaps a half-mile across the fields. Sylvia ran it all, pushing herself for all possible speed, picking herself up when she fell. She was soaked to the skin and her long skirt weighed heavily on her. But, at last, barely able to breathe, she arrived at the stables. She slumped over, hands on her knees, laboring to catch her breath.

When she raised herself, Tom Stone was standing there, looking as though he was seeing an apparition. "Oh, Tom . . . thank God, it's you." She panted a moment, then gulped in air. "Get me a horse and rig, a covered one, as soon as you can." These words used up all her breath and she again bent over, hands on knees.

"Miss Sylvia, I can't, unless—"

She raised herself, her anger flaring. "Tom! Don't argue, for once. Do as I say." She saw him wavering. "Please, Tom." Suddenly she was crying. "It's a matter of life and death."

"Whatever you say, Miss Sylvia."

As he turned to get the horse, she said, "In God's name, please hurry, Tom."

She raced the horse and carriage back to the ravine as fast as she could make the animal run, stopping only to buy some meat and vegetables. They had to have something to eat.

As she entered the shack, she knew at once something was wrong. Brian was not there, nor did he answer when she called his name. Then, from the bed where Meg lay, she heard gutteral, animal sounds. Sylvia ran to her, dropping the groceries on the table.

"Oh, God, no!"

Meg was rigid, shaking all over. From the side of her mouth ran a rivulet of blood.

"Oh, God, Meg, don't. Please, don't."

She was biting her tongue. With all the strength in her hands, Sylvia pried open the rigid jaw, pushing down, pulling up to hold it open. Desperately, she looked for something to put in it. But nothing was within reach. Deliberately, she slid the side of her own hand into the mouth and at once felt the pain of the clenching jaws cut into her skin. Sylvia screamed: "Brian, Brian, come help." Over and over she called. There was no answer. Where was he?

It seemed an eternity until Meg's seizure ran its course. She lay on the pillow now, seemingly lifeless. Sylvia called her name, patted her cheeks, even shook her. "Meg, Meg, answer me. Don't die. You can't die." Sylvia bent her ear to her friend's mouth. She was breathing, but barely. "Oh, Meg, Meg, I won't let you die."

She leaped from the bed and ran to the back door, screaming for Brian. "Why don't you answer me? Don't you care what happens—" Then she saw his feet sticking out from under the car. She bent and shook his feet, but there was no response.

"Oh, no!"

She stretched out in the mud on her stomach to peer under his car. She could see his torso and head. She shook his leg again, but he didn't move. "Brian, Brian." She scampered to her feet and in the mud and pouring rain went to the back of the car. At once, she understood what had happened. He had jacked up the rear of the car to work under it, and the jack had slid in the mud. The car had fallen on Brian.

"Brian, Brian." Once again, she pleaded for life. "Don't die! You can't die!"

Sliding in the mud, she went to the opposite side of the car and prostrated herself in the mud to see beneath it. She could now see Brian's head. It was pressed into the mud. A long cylindrical object—Sylvia knew absolutely nothing about motor cars—was against his forehead, which was bleeding profusely. It seemed to her that this object pressing against his head was holding him.

She slid herself forward in the mud under the car until she could reach his head. She felt the warmth of it. Thank God, he wasn't dead. She tried to move his head, but couldn't. She had to get him out of there. She had to.

Quickly, she pushed herself out from under the car and scampered to the rear of it. For a minute, she tried to pull the jack out. Finally, she managed that, but when she tried to work the jack to raise the car, she didn't know how. Filled with panic, sobbing, Sylvia again lay under the car, and with her fingers began to scoop and pull the mud from beneath Brian's head. She worked as hard and as fast as she could, and it seemed to her his head was dropping from the cylinder. A moment more she worked at the mud, then she tried to move his head. It seemed to move, a little. She scooped some more, reaching as far under his head as she could. Then, finally, she was able to turn his head sideways. It never occurred to her that the car might drop onto herself as she crawled further under the chassis until, hands against his shoulders, she was able to slide his head free of the crankshaft. Once more, she crawled from the mud and, sliding on the incline, falling to her knees once, she went around the car, grabbing Brian's ankles and pulling as hard as she could. He didn't move at first. Then, when she dug in her heels and jerked backwards, his body slid out. She fell down backwards from her exertion, but he was free before the car collapsed further into the mud.

She got to her knees and looked at him. He had a nasty cut on his forehead from which a great deal of blood oozed. He was unconscious, but he was alive. Getting to her feet, she started to drag him feet first into the shack. But when she saw his head bobbing in the mud. she dropped his feet and picked him up by the shoulders. It was much heavier and harder for her, but she sensed that his head should be protected.

Panting, more weary than she had ever been in her life, she dragged his feet over the threshold and into the shack, laying him carefully on the floor. She stood over him a moment, catching her breath, then raised her hand to brush what she thought was hair from her forehead, soon realizing it was mud. She was covered with mud; hands, arms, face, the whole front and back of her dress. Her impulse was to clean herself, then she remembered that she had to get a doctor. Brian was badly hurt. A car had fallen on him. And Meg. She seemed lifeless, lying there on her back. She wasn't just asleep. Something else had happened to her. Yes, she had to get a doctor, somehow.

Sylvia had made a half-dozen strides toward the front door, when she stopped and turned around. She couldn't let Brian lie there on the wet floor. She returned to him, looking frantically for blankets. But the only ones in the place were over Meg. Oh, Lord, why hadn't she bought blankets instead of such silly gifts? He had to be kept warm. Quickly, she grabbed anything she could find, clothes, curtains from the window, and spread them over Brian. Struggling with his weight, she even shoved apparel underneath him to protect him from the damp earth. Then she built up the fire, using all but a little of the coal. Now she could go for help.

She again stopped near the door, however, turning, looking, sensing something was wrong, not knowing what. Then she looked at Meg. She was moving—not Meg herself.

but the mound of her pregnancy was moving. She could see motion under the blankets. Quickly, she went to her, pulled back the covers and raised Meg's nightgown. She gasped at the sight, the great stain on the bedding, the contractions. Oh, God, the baby was coming.

Sylvia reacted with panic, running out of the shack, slipping and stumbling through the rain and mud toward the horse and rig. The midwife. She had to find the midwife. She had climbed to the seat and picked up the reins. when she suddenly stopped. She didn't know the midwife. She didn't know where to look for her. By the time she found her, it might be too late. She knew time was important.

Sylvia climbed down from the rig and ran back to the shack, falling twice on the slippery incline. Inside, she uncovered Meg and looked at her. The baby was coming. *Oh, Lord!* Bending low to look, she could see black hair on the baby's head.

At age twenty-one, the pampered stepdaughter of an earl, Sylvia knew virtually nothing about babies and the process by which they enter the world. Indeed, despite living much of her life in rural Hampshire, she had never seen any kind of a birth—not a horse, dog, cat, nothing. Post-Victorian England dictated that girls of quality be protected from such sights. But now, faced with the prospect of Meg's baby, she knew she must do something, help her friend.

She bent over to reach for Meg and saw her muddy hands. God, that would never do. She turned back to the washstand, ladled water into a basin and began to wash her hands and arms, finally cleaning the mud from under her broken nails with the point of a knife. While she did so, she talked out loud. "Oh, Meg, I'm so scared. I don't know what to do." She turned to look at the form on the bed and smiled. "But whatever has to be done, we'll do it together, won't we? You and I, we can do anything." She knew Meg was unconscious, unable to hear her, but it bolstered her own courage to say these things.

At last, she stood over Meg. She moved her legs, spreading them apart. Then she just stood there, as though paralyzed. She didn't know what to do. She began to cry, her tears streaking the mud on her face. "Oh, Meg, I love you so. If anything happens to you, your baby. . . . Oh, Meg, what am I supposed to do? Tell me what to do, Meg." But there was no one to tell her. Suddenly, she felt excruciatingly alone, more alone than she had ever been in her life. She screamed, "Doesn't anybody *care*? Do they just want to let them *die*?"

For a minute she stood there, weeping in helplessness and frustration. She couldn't. It wasn't possible. Then, from deep inside her mind came words. *You're a woman.* Yes, she was a woman. Women have babies. She ought to know what to do. A little calmer, trying to act, not think, she bent over Meg. It seemed to her she could see more of the baby's head. It was coming. Timorously, fearful of even touching Meg, she nonetheless pushed gently against Meg's abdomen. It seemed to help and she did it again, harder. Soon, enough of the baby's head was out for Sylvia to take hold. Pushing, pulling, turning, the baby began to be delivered. A sense of wonder filled her. "Oh, Meg, Meg, it's so *tiny*. I didn't know babies were so small. Oh, Meg, it's coming, just a little more. It's got black hair." Then, "Oh, darling, it's a boy, a boy, just like you said it would be."

In a moment, the baby lay on the bed with Sylvia staring at it in wonder, but also with a little revulsion at the way he looked. From behind her she grabbed the towel, a far from clean one, and began to wipe the baby's face and body. "Wake up, baby, wake up." She saw the cord linking the child to Meg. It should be cut, she knew. She picked up the knife, but hesitated, unable to use it. But in a moment, she forced herself. Maybe the baby would wake up then.

A moment later, she held the baby in her arms, wrapped in the towel. She cradled it, rocking it back and forth. "Oh, baby, baby, please wake up." Then she remembered. Of course. She unwound the towel from the infant and swatted its bottom. No cry. Nothing. Again, she did it. A third time, harder. Then she knew. Words were wrenched from her throat like a scream of agony. "It's dead. I killed Meg's baby!"

Slowly, she collapsed to the edge of the bed, holding the stillbirth, rocking it, weeping bitterly, more desolate than she had ever been in her life, moaning over and over, "I killed it, I killed it. Oh, Meg, Meg, I killed your baby!"

Ultimately, she got up and lay the dead child beside the unconscious Meg, then did what she felt had to be done for Meg, disposing of the afterbirth, cleaning and washing her with whatever she could find. When she could think of nothing more to do, she covered her, then sat on the bed beside her. She kissed her cheek, her hair, unmindful of the muddy stains her own face left, and repeatedly beseeched her unhearing friend to forgive her. "I didn't mean to, Meg. I didn't mean to kill your baby."

Then a new thought came to her. Was Meg alive? She snatched back the cover and saw her shallow breathing. She was alive, but barely. "Oh, Meg, don't die. If I've killed you, too, I'll—I'll kill myself. Oh, Meg, you've got to live!"

That became the refrain for the longest afternoon and night of Sylvia's life. There were three bodies in that little shack, but two of them were still alive. She had no idea what to do—and she was afraid to leave them to seek help. So she just did what she could think of. She raised each head in turn and forced what water she could down their throats. Using the meat she had brought, she made some broth and time after time, throughout the night, spooned a few drops into their mouths until she saw them swallow it. At one point, she cleaned the deep cut on Brian's head as best she could and bandaged it with a piece of her petticoat. At least it had stopped bleeding. She could think of nothing else to do for them, except to make frequent determinations that both were still alive.

Chapter Twenty-nine

Sylvia had no awareness of dozing off, yet when she heard the knock at the door it was daylight. She was sitting at the kitchen table, her head on her arms. The rapping made her bolt awake. Arthur. He had come, at last.

She opened the door to Tom, the stableboy. He was standing in the rain, which had let up to a drizzle, staring at her in shock. "Miss Sylvia, is that really you?"

In her weariness, she had a sense of how she must look to him. "Yes, it's me, Tom. What do you want?"

He stood there, fidgeting on one foot, then the other. "Miss Sylvia, I got to get Luke back."

"Luke? Who's Luke?"

"The horse, Miss Sylvia. I got to take the horse and rig back, or I'll catch the dickens."

"Oh, yes." She peered past him to the tethered animal. It had been there all night. "I understand. Go ahead. Do what you have to do." He turned away and she began to close the door, when, suddenly, she thought. "Tom, come back, please." When he was again at the door, she said, "Help me move Meg and Brian. Then you can have the rig."

"Miss Sylvia, I—"

"God, Tom, stop arguing and help me." She reached out, grabbed his arm and pulled him inside. "I can't move them myself. You have to help me."

He ceased his protests and began to help her, bringing the wagon to the door and helping her carry them out to the carriage—Meg first, wrapped in bedding, then Brian, swaddled in the motley collection of garments she had thrown on him. Before leaving, she took a last look around the shack to see if she would need anything. The dead baby. The baby she had killed. Hurriedly, she scooped it into her arms and started out. Then she remembered. Quickly, she scrawled a note: "Arthur, I've taken them to your cottage. Sylvia." On the way to the cottage, she thought of one other thing, making Tom stop while she hurriedly purchased some meat and other foodstuffs. They would all have to eat.

There was no doubt in Sylvia's mind that she'd done the right thing in moving Meg and Brian to the cottage. It was larger and far dryer, and after she had built a roaring fire, much warmer. The pump provided plenty of water. And the woodbox was well-filled. The cupboards offered a hoard of tins, flour, beans and other food. They would eat—if only she could cook.

With Tom's help, she laid Meg and Brian side by side in Arthur's bed, the bed where she had. . . . Through that whole day and night, she maintained her vigil, giving them water frequently, making broth over the fireplace, feeding them, eating a little of the meat herself. She also bathed them both, even stripping away Brian's wet garments and wrapping him in Arthur's robe, the robe she had worn that first day. There were plenty of blankets to cover them. At least they were warm.

. Sylvia drove herself throughout the vigil, hardly aware in her concern for Meg and Brian of her own numb weariness. She had stopped begging them aloud to live, yet the thought was constantly in her mind. She had killed Meg's baby—which she had laid in a corner, out of sight, not knowing what to do with it—but, somehow, Meg, Brian too, had to survive. She could detect no change in him. But it seemed to her Meg was taking on more color, her breathing becoming a little deeper. Or was she only imagining it?

There was no doubt in her mind that Arthur would come. She had such a sense of his presence there in the cottage. Everything she touched reminded her of him. He would come. It was only a matter of time.

When there was a knock at the door the next morning, she again leaped to open it, sure it was Arthur. Again, she was disappointed. George, chauffeur to Lord Winnie, was there. Beyond him, she saw the black Rolls, the Linfield crest on the side, her mother alighting from the rear, then striding purposefully toward her, eyes glinting with fury.

"My God, Sylvia, what *are* you doing? You look a *fright.*"

Involuntarily, Sylvia stared down at herself. Her dress was caked with dried mud and liberally sprinkled with blood, also dried. She suddenly realized she hadn't done anything with her hair in days.

"Sylvia, I *demand* an answer."

She sighed. "I'm taking care of Meg and Brian. Both are ill."

"Well, I don't care what you're doing. You're coming home this instant."

Sylvia had hoped to block the entrance simply by standing in the doorway. But Lady Constance marched forward like a corseted tank, and Sylvia had no choice but to give way backwards, allowing her mother to enter.

"What is this place? What are you doing here?"

"I told you, I—" Again, she sighed, suddenly too weary to face this unexpected scene. "How did you find me?"

"I figured you were with that dreadful girl. I went there. I mean I drove there. I wasn't about to walk through that mud to that horrid shack. George went and found this." She waved Sylvia's note to Arthur. In dismay, Sylvia realized Arthur wouldn't know where to find her. "A few inquiries in the village led us here. Who is this Arthur, Sylvia?"

Sylvia saw the demanding, imperious look in her mother's eye. "He's a friend."

"You will *tell* me who he is?"

"He's a member of Parliament, mother. Quite a distinguished man, really."

"Is he, indeed?" The countess' words dripped sarcasm. "I don't care if he's the Christ himself. You won't be alone in his cottage. He's not here, is he?"

Sylvia smiled. "No, mother, he's not here."

"Thank God for that. We'll just have to see to it Lord Charles does not learn of this. Can you imagine what he'd *think* if he could see you now?"

"It is difficult to imagine, isn't it?"

"Well, never mind. Get your things and come at once."

"I'm not going, mother. I'm staying with Meg and Brian."

"You will do no such thing." Servants, shopkeepers, even Sylvia herself had often wilted before that tone of voice. Sylvia did not wilt this time.

"What do you want me to do, mother? Just let them die?"

"I don't care what happens to them. Nobody does. What matters is that you are engaged to a duke, and you're coming home this instant."

Suddenly, Sylvia was screaming. "No! I care a whole lot more about Meg than I do you, the duke, Winnie, anybody I know. She's better than all of you!"

"I'm tired of your stupidity, Sylvia. You're coming with me."

Lady Constance reached out to grab her arm, but Sylvia jerked away in time and began to retreat through the cottage, her mother coming toward her.

"I'm taking you home where you belong. You're going to stop all this foolishness. You're going to marry the duke. You're going to *behave* yourself.

Sylvia's screamed "No's" did not halt her mother. She backed up until she was against the mantel, the fire hot against the back of her legs. That keyed a thought, and she bent and picked up a wrought-iron poker, raising it above her head, brandishing it at her mother. "You come one step closer, mother, and I'll use this."

Lady Constance took one step more, then stopped, staring at her daughter wide-eyed. "You would threaten your own mother?"

"I'm not threatening, mother. I intend to use it. Now you just get out of here."

"Why, I *never!*"

Sylvia did not take her eyes off her mother as she said, "George, if you want to see your mistress in one piece, you'd better take her out of here."

The chauffeur hesitated, then stepped forward to touch the countess' arm. "Milady, perhaps we had better go."

She wavered a moment, glaring at Sylvia. "All right, George, I'll go." To her daughter she said, "But I'm not through with you, young lady."

"Oh, yes, you are, mother. You just don't know it yet!"

Slowly lowering the poker, she watched her mother leave the cottage, muttering as she went about "ungrateful" children and all she had done for her daughter.

The scene with her mother seemed to drain the last of Sylvia's strength. She stood there, gripping the mantel, fighting back a wave of nausea and vertigo. But it passed in a moment, and she pushed herself to her nursing chores, repeating the nourishment, changing Brian's dressing. It was all she could think of to do. At one point, she became aware of the huge diamond still on her finger. Charles. She couldn't marry him, not now. Somehow, she couldn't think ill of him, but she couldn't live the life he wanted her to live. Not anymore. She was too tired to think clearly, but she knew she was changed. She couldn't go back to her old life, not after all this. Oh, where was Arthur? He'd know what she should do.

He came shortly after four in the afternoon. She opened the door. He stood there with another man. She noticed that the stranger carried a black bag—he was a doctor. Then she passed out into Arthur's arms.

She awoke, momentarily mystified as to where she was. She realized she was in Arthur's bed in the cottage at almost the exact moment she turned her head and saw him sitting in the chair beside her, smiling.

"Good morning, sleepyhead."

She glanced at the window, saw daylight. "How long have I . . . ?"

"You've had a good, much-deserved night's rest. It is the next morning. It has stopped raining. The sun is shining. It's beautiful. Want to get up?"

"Yes." She sat on the edge of the bed facing him, saw her bare legs, then inspected her garment. She wore one of his shirts as a nightgown. "Did you?"

"I figured the presence of Doctor Hotchkiss made it all right."

The doctor. Memory flooded back and she turned to look at the bed behind her. "Meg and Brian, are they. . . ?"

"They're fine, Sylvia. Both are in the hospital. They're going to get well."

"But—"

"Brian has a cracked skull and a concussion, but he'll come around in a few days. You saved his life. I saw the car and figured what happened. Actually, the rain and mud did the trick. The mud gave way beneath his head. If it hadn't, his skull would have been crushed. But you got him out of there, then you did absolutely the right thing. You kept him warm, gave him plenty of liquids. That prevented shock. He's going to be all right."

"Meg?" She was almost afraid to ask.

He smiled. "You should be a nurse, Sylvia. You saved her life too. She had a very serious condition known as—let me think, oh, yes, uremia. As I understand it, in some pregnancies the mother can't dispose of her body wastes properly. They build up, actually poisoning her. It can be fatal, if not caught in time. And if she goes into a coma, as the doctor said Meg had, it's usually certain death."

"She had a seizure too, Arthur."

"The doctor didn't know that. But he says she's going to be fine. Actually, she came to just as we were loading her in the ambulance. Asked about you. She knows you saved her life."

"But how?"

"The doctor said that if she'd been in a hospital, where she should have been, the doctors would have taken the child to save the mother. It's standard procedure. You saved her life when you delivered the baby."

"But I didn't, Arthur. It's dead. I killed it."

He came out of his chair to sit beside her, his arm around her. "No, you didn't, darling. The baby was already dead—a stillbirth. Dr. Hotchkiss said Meg's body used a natural defense mechanism to save her life by ridding itself of the baby—which was the whole cause of her illness."

Suddenly, she couldn't stop her tears. "Oh, Arthur, it was so awful. I didn't know what to do. I wanted to get the midwife, but I didn't know. . . . I was so afraid."

He squeezed her shoulder. "That's the point, darling. If you'd gone for the midwife, it would have been too late. You saved Meg's life."

Once started, she couldn't stop crying. "Oh, God, Arthur. The baby was dead and. . . ."

"She'll have other children, Sylvia. The doctor told her so."

It took a moment for Sylvia to register that, but finally she brightened. "She will?"

He had his handkerchief out, wiping her tears. "Yes, and Hotchkiss is a good doctor. The best in London. He came without hesitation. I only wish it had been sooner."

She turned to him, her arms around him, her face buried in his shoulder. "You came. That's all that matters."

He was patting her back. "Yes, dearest, yes."

"No one else would help. Only you."

"I'm sorry I wasn't here when you needed me. But I am now. Everything is all right." He pulled her away. "And how about some breakfast? I'll do the cooking."

"How did you know I was here?"

He smiled. "It wasn't hard to figure out. Come, let's eat."

She padded after him on bare feet into the main room of the cottage, unmindful of the shortness of her garment. She saw her dress and chemise drying before the fire. He had washed them. "You did my dress. Thank you. What would I ever do without you?"

"It looks to me like you do quite fine by yourself."

She saw him smiling and she had to join him. "Yes, I did well, didn't I? I saved two lives, delivered a child." She laughed. "I even cooked. I never thought I could do that."

He was looking at her then, intently, seriously, his familiar social unease returning. Earnestly, he said, "Sylvia, I love you."

"And I love you, Arthur."

He seemed not to have heard her, launching into what was obviously a well-rehearsed speech.

"You can't marry the duke."

"No, Arthur, I don't want to."

"Oh, I know, I can't give you jewels and big houses and a title. I can't make you a duchess."

"I don't want that, Arthur."

"But I can make you happy. And mind you, I'm not without means. One day, I'll inherit my father's place in Dorset. It's lovely. You'll adore it."

"I'm sure I will, Arthur."

"But just because I'm landed doesn't mean I'm going to surrender my principles. Not for a minute. I'm going to work for the common man, for a sharing of wealth. There's no need for sickness and poverty in this land."

"I want you to, Arthur."

"And I'm going to be reelected. The party has assigned me a safe district. I'll be in Parliament for many years. I've got a future."

"Oh, yes, Arthur, yes."

"And members of Parliament are to start being paid. I'll be able to take care of you, Sylvia—and go on with my work."

"I want to help you, Arthur."

Suddenly, he stopped. "What did you say?"

"I said I want to help you, Arthur. What you want is what I now know I want. Meg almost died—Brian too, because no one would help them. How many people are like that? I want to work for them. If women get the vote, it will come to pass. It is women who have the babies. It is women who know of pain and poverty, trying to feed a family on potatoes and cabbage. I want to see everyone—"

"I don't mean that. What did you say before?"

"I don't know."

"Did you say you loved me?"

She smiled. "Oh, that. Of course, I love you. But what I want to say is that Britain is as strong as its weakest citizen. We must pull up the bottom without weakening the top. We—"

He was laughing then. "You sound like the best Labour MP I ever heard."

She was laughing too. "When women get the vote, I just might run."

He came to her, sweeping her into his arms. It felt so good, so right to her. "Do I have to wait till you get the vote to marry you?"

"Oh, Arthur, I hope not." She was leaning her mouth toward his when she stopped. "Maybe some day we'll be the first man and wife members of Parliament."

"Not a bad idea." And as his lips came to hers, she knew that was the best idea of all.

ROMANCE LOVERS DELIGHT

Purchase any book for $2.95 plus $1.50 shipping & handling for each book.

_____ **LOVE'S SECRET JOURNEY** by Margaret Hunter. She found a man of mystery in an ancient land.

_____ **DISTANT THUNDER** by Karen A. Bale. While sheltering a burning love she fights for her honor.

_____ **DESTINY'S THUNDER** by Elizabeth Bright. She risks her life for her passionate captain.

_____ **DIAMOND OF DESIRE** by Candice Adams. On the eve of a fateful war she meets her true love.

_____ **A HERITAGE OF PASSION** by Elizabeth Bright. A wild beauty matches desires with a dangerous man.

_____ **SHINING NIGHTS** by Linda Trent. A handsome stranger, mystery & intrigue at Queen's table.

_____ **DESIRE'S LEGACY** by Elizabeth Bright. An unforgotten love amidst a war torn land.

_____ **THE BRAVE & THE LONELY** by R. Vaughn. Five families, their loves and passion against a war.

_____ **SHADOW OF LOVE** by Ivy St. David. Wealthy mine owner lost her love.

_____ **A LASTING SPLENDOR** by Elizabeth Bright. Imperial Beauty struggles to forget her amorous affairs.

_____ **ISLAND PROMISE** by W. Ware Lynch. Heiress escapes life of prostitution to find her island lover.

_____ **A BREATH OF PARADISE** by Carol Norris. Bronzed Fiji Island lover creates turbulent sea of love.

_____ **RUM COLONY** by Terry Nelson Bonner. Wild untamed woman bent on a passion for destructive love.

_____ **A SOUTHERN WIND** by Gene Lancour. Secret family passions bent on destruction.

_____ **CHINA CLIPPER** by John Van Zwienen. Story of sailing ships beautiful woman tantalizing love.

_____ **A DESTINY OF LOVE** by Ivy St. David. A coal miners daughter's desires and romantic dreams.